"A fun, fast-paced, and fiery romance."   —*Road to Romance*

"Ortolon's protagonists must overcome some tough emotional issues before they can set their sights on the future, but their journey is laced with humor and even a little history (provided by the inn's ghosts). Earnest and endearing, Ortolon's newest is a heartwarming and at times heartrending read."   —*Publishers Weekly*

"Readers will root for Allison and Scott to overcome the obstacles keeping them apart in this entertaining and touching story."
—*Booklist*

"[Ortolon] has finally come into her own with this funny romance."
—*Columbus Dispatch*

Falling for You

"I hadn't realized what a wonderful knack she has for building her characters and putting them into knotty real-life situations. Nor what depths and emotions I'd find in *Falling For You*. If the sexual tension alone is not enough to keep you reading, there is excitement in watching the plans for the Pearl Island B&B go forth, and suspense in the social repercussions of Chance and Rory's mingling."
—*Romance Reviews Today*

"I had a blast reading *Falling for You*, and enjoyed it so much that I'm really looking forward to her next book. As long as Julie Ortolon is writing books like this one, romantic comedy is in good hands."
—*All About Romance*

TURN THE PAGE FOR MORE ACCLAIM . . .

Dear Cupid

Drive Me Wild

"A smart and funny story that I found very enjoyable to read."
—*Rendezvous*

"A romantic, funny, and sexy story that will bring many accolades to its author. Julie Ortolon has done an outstanding job of creating a cast of characters that bring this story to life. This is a fast-paced book that can be read in one sitting. . . . [Ortolon] is sure to be one of the shining stars of the future." —*Writers Club Romance Group*

"Julie Ortolon's . . . *Drive Me Wild* will drive readers to ecstasy in this superb romance about a handsome TV anchor, who returns to his Texas hometown for a 'Dating Game' fundraiser and ends up winning a wild ride to finding true love when he chooses his childhood best friend. Ms. Ortolon is a gem of a new author and readers will certainly want to watch for her future books!" —*Romantic Times*

"*Drive Me Wild* is a fun and completely captivating story from this bright new author. Ms. Ortolon has given us believable characters with a wonderful range of personalities . . . Many of the scenes really sizzle! I thoroughly enjoyed *Drive Me Wild* and recommend you not miss this first offering from a promising new author."
—*Romance Communications* (romcom.com)

"Debut author Julie Ortolon offers up a small-town story about two people who have problems and need each other to work through them. Will they confide in each other and share their hurtful pasts in order to heal them? This new author will gather many fans if her first title, *Drive Me Wild,* is any indication of the way she tells a story. She delivers her first novel with quick wit, snappy dialogue, sensuality that smokes, and a good story line. This is one worth your time and will give you a pleasurable read."
—*Under the Covers* (Carol Carter, Reviewer)

Don't Tempt Me

Julie Ortolon

St. Martin's Paperbacks

DON'T TEMPT ME

Copyright © 2004 by Julie Ortolon.

ISBN: 0-312-98349-2

Printed in the United States of America

St. Martin's Paperbacks edition / February 2004

St. Martin's Paperbacks are published by St. Martin's Press, 175 Fifth Avenue, New York, NY 10010.

10 9 8 7 6 5 4 3 2 1

For all the women who asked for Adrian

A special thanks to marine archeologist Steven Hoyt with the Texas Historical Commission for answering my numerous questions. I'll cross my fingers and hope I got everything right, and take full blame if I didn't.

Thanks also to the crews of the *Elissa* and the *Star Clipper* for sharing their love of sailing, and to fellow passengers Bob and Sandy, James and Mary, Peter and Georgia, for making our trip to the Caribbean so much fun.

Chapter 1

Jackie Taylor had little use for fairy tales and even less for charming princes, which was why it really irritated her when *he* came striding back into her life. One minute she was straddling a workbench as she repaired a sail for her charter ship, the next she looked up to find Adrian St. Claire filling the doorway of her dockside shed. The brilliant sun of the Texas coast silhouetted his six-foot-plus frame as he came toward her with cocksure grace.

"Dammit," she muttered under her breath. Didn't she have enough problems on her mind without Mr. Gorgeous coming around to scramble her brain cells?

"What's that?" Tiberius, her first mate, glanced up from his end of the workbench. A wide smile split his face, his teeth a startling white against his mocha-colored skin. "Weeell, A-drian," he said in his distinctive Caribbean accent. "What you doin' in Corpus Christi, mon?"

Jackie knew exactly why the man had come, but refrained from kicking him out . . . yet.

"It was a nice day for a motorcycle ride," Adrian said. "So I thought I'd head down the coast from Galveston and see what's shaking on your stretch of beach."

As he moved out of the glare of the light, she couldn't stop her gaze from sliding over his lean body. She might have little patience for men who collected female admirers just by walking down the street, but that didn't keep her from enjoying the view. And he did provide a nice one dressed in a red T-shirt and faded blue jeans. He'd pulled his long black hair into a ponytail, and a small gold hoop earring glinted in the shed's dim light. As the two men shook hands, she marveled at the contrast between them. Ti, with his shaved head and hard body, reminded her of a massive, steady frigate while Adrian made her think of a clipper, sleek and beautiful and rigged for racing.

Adrian nodded toward the slice of bustling dock visible through the door. "From all the tourists snapping pictures of the *Pirate's Pleasure,* I trust business is going well."

"It would if da harbor stop chargin' a fortune for our slip," Ti said with good humor, touching on the source of her current woes.

Adrian turned toward her and his smile softened with lazy sensuality. "Jackie. Long time no see."

For a moment, she lost herself in clear blue eyes surrounded by sinfully long black lashes. His features were so flawless, they'd be "pretty" if he weren't so . . . breathtakingly *male*. That level of masculinity should have made her feel more feminine in contrast. Instead, he made her more aware of her callused hands, wiry build, and the fact that she'd cut her hair boyishly short since the last time she'd seen him.

She raised her chin, irritated with her uncommon flare of insecurity. "I gave your family my answer on the phone. And the answer was no."

His brows shot up in surprise. "Well, now, that's cutting right to the chase, isn't it?"

Ti flashed her a questioning look, since she hadn't confided in him about the St. Claires' request.

"I find a direct approach saves time." Securing the large needle in the canvas, she thrust the sail aside and rose. "Now, unless there's something else you want"—*besides my great-grandfather's letter*—"I'll let you be on your way."

His gaze moved over her face with obvious interest, making her stomach flutter. "What if the 'something else' I wanted was to take you to dinner?"

"Right." She snorted. Conscious of her first mate hanging on every word, she crossed to a water cooler by the door. Beyond the shadows of the shed, tourists wandered the pier, buying fresh shrimp off the backs of boats. Their voices mingled with the rhythmic rush of waves underfoot and the incessant cries of seagulls. Unseasonable heat for early November hung heavy in the air, and the denim shirt she'd tied at the waist over a sports bra and shorts stuck to her skin.

After filling a paper cup with chilled water, she glanced at Adrian as he came up behind her. "I have no desire to waste an evening listening to you try to talk me out of something I have no intention of giving you."

He said nothing at first, but she could feel him watching her. "I think the question here is, what am I prepared to give you?"

She turned and found him leaning against a worktable, his scuffed motorcycle boots crossed at the ankle. "Oh?"

He wiggled his brows playfully. "I'm here to make you a proposition."

Her heart pounded even as she laughed in his face. "Don't even try to sweet-talk me. We both know I'm not your type."

His warm chuckle strummed her senses. "And what would 'my type' be?"

"Tall blond beach bunnies with Barbie doll figures," she tossed back.

"That's just packaging, sugar. But if it comes with a personality and some brains, absolutely."

The man was impossible to rile. But then, she should have remembered that from their brief association a year ago. He and his two sisters had hired her ship, a two-hundred-year-old Baltimore schooner, as part of the entertainment for the annual Buccaneer's Ball. The event had been held at the Pearl Island Inn, a bed-and-breakfast owned by Adrian and his sisters, located on its own private island near Galveston. During the few days the *Pirate's Pleasure* had been anchored in their cove, Adrian had flirted with her shamelessly. Not that she took any of it seriously. The man quite simply enjoyed flirting.

"Now, about dinner . . ." he said.

"In case you misunderstood, that was a no." She downed the cold water and crumpled the paper cup.

"I was thinking somewhere quiet—"

"I'm not going out with you."

"—where we can discuss what my sisters and I are willing to offer in exchange for your help."

"No."

"Or . . . I can proposition you right here." He leaned closer and she caught a whiff of him. Oh, God, he even smelled good: like soap and sunshine and a fresh sea breeze. His gaze dropped to her mouth, then lifted back to her eyes. "Although I think we'd both be more comfortable talking over seafood and a nice bottle of wine."

She shook her head in exasperation. "Do you ever take no for an answer?"

"Honestly?" He cocked a brow. "I'm not sure. It's not a word I hear too often."

"I just bet you don't." Narrowing her eyes, she contemplated hefting him over her shoulder, walking out onto the pier, and tossing him into Corpus Christi Bay. Considering his size, she didn't think she'd get too far with that plan. "Okay, what the heck. I'll have dinner with you. It's your money and your time, if you want to waste them, that's your business."

"Great." His eyes lit with pleasure. "How about the Wharf? Early enough to enjoy the sunset. Unless you'd rather go somewhere else."

"No, the Wharf is fine." Perfect, in fact, since it was right at the end of her pier. She'd be close enough to home to ditch him if he became too annoying.

"I'll pick you up around six, then," he said. "I assume you still live on board your ship."

"I do."

"Then I'll see you this evening." With a wave to her first mate, he strode past her, back into the sunshine. She watched as he wound his way past tourists and fishermen to the black Harley he'd left parked at the end of the pier. He donned a black leather jacket but left it unzipped in deference to the warm weather. With a move that made her pulse hum, he swung a leg over the seat, kicked the engine to life, and had it roaring with a few twists of his wrist. Then he zoomed off down the busy four-lane road that skirted the beach.

She couldn't help but shake her head in amusement. He was persistent, she'd give him that. And more gorgeous than any man had a right to be. The gene fairies must have been in a wicked mood the day they made Adrian St. Claire or they never would have unleashed all that sex appeal on womankind.

"Care to tell me what dat about?" Ti asked from the workbench.

She glanced at him. "Adrian and his sisters have been bitten by the treasure-hunting bug."

"Ah . . ." Ti stretched the word out. "De allure of Lafitte's missing treasure. I guess we lucky you not cursed with more requests to help find it, since it supposedly go down with your great-great-granddaddy's ship."

"Well, at least this is a new spin on an old tale." She crossed back to the bench and swung a leg to straddle it. Taking up her needle, she resumed mending the sail. "The St. Claires want to go after the real 'treasure' rather than chase some fool's dream of sunken chests of gold."

"Dat hardly a fool's dream." Ti swept the air dramatically with his big, callused hand. "Many riches litter da sea floor. Spanish doubloons, precious jewels, and artifacts worth a king's ransom to the right collector. Or do you forget da thrill of findin' lost booty?"

She sent him a mutinous glare. "Are you forgetting the pact we made? No more treasure-hunting. Ever."

"Just rememberin' past glory." His dark eyes twinkled. "And a little girl who love to dive for old coins and gold rings."

Bittersweet memories stirred at his words. How exciting the world had seemed back then, with one adventure after another. "I'm not a little girl anymore."

"No. But when it come to findin' lost treasure, you better dan your father—and many people think he da best."

"For all the good it did us, since he always spent

every dime we made on those dives going after bigger prizes." She stabbed the needle through the canvas. "I'm through chasing legends and dreams."

"Chasing legends, yes. But it never hurt to dream."

"Reality works just fine for me."

"If you say so." He resumed sewing, but under his breath, he started singing an old sailing ditty about the treasures of the deep blue sea.

Jackie rolled her eyes, but joined him on the chorus, the song building in volume as their needles kept time to the music.

At six that evening, Adrian rang the old-fashioned bell that was mounted on a wooden sign with the name of Jackie's ship emblazoned in gold script. He assumed the bell was the appropriate way to announce his presence since a tall, chain-link gate prevented people from walking up the gangway.

As the clanging sound faded, he let his gaze glide over the wooden vessel. Even at rest, the Baltimore schooner whispered of adventure on the high seas with her three masts rising high overhead. A beautifully detailed mermaid arched beneath the jib boom while red and gold railing trimmed the forecastle and quarterdeck.

Jackie appeared on the main deck, bringing his body to attention. Something about the woman stirred him up every time he saw her. Too bad the proposal he'd come to make was strictly business. If she accepted, she'd be a partner of sorts and off-limits for the kind of things he'd like to propose.

She stopped at the top of the gangway and glanced at her black diving watch. "You're punctual."

"And you're ready." He smiled.

"You sound surprised."

"I have two sisters. I'm astounded."

She came down the ramp wearing a yellow chambray shirt and khaki trousers. The soft, buttery color brought out the gold tones of her tanned skin and hazel eyes. He studied her hair as she came through the gate and turned to lock it. A year ago, her hair had hung in a thick, mahogany-colored braid down her back. Since then, she'd cut it short—very short—except for a few wispy fringes around the face and nape.

"Nice hair," he said.

Reaching up in a self-conscious gesture, she finger-combed the fringes by her ear. "Yeah, well, this is what you get when you tell some scissor-happy hairdresser you're sick of messing with long hair. *Whack!* All gone."

"I meant I like it." He cocked his head. "It sets off your eyes." And the rest of her exotic features. The word *"subtle"* would never describe Jackie Taylor, with her thick black brows over hazel cat's eyes, slender nose, high cheekbones, a square jaw, and a lush mouth he'd fanta-sized about for months. "You hungry?" he asked.

"Ravenous."

"Me, too. *Always*." He added the last in a playfully seductive tone, hoping for one of those saucy comebacks that cracked him up. Most men would probably call him crazy, but he liked the way she verbally sparred with him rather than fell at his feet, sighing in hopeful surrender. He'd never had a woman turn him down before. The experience was . . . intriguing. And liberating. It gave him the freedom to flirt as outrageously as he wanted without the fear of setting off wedding bells in her head.

As they started toward the restaurant at the end of the

pier, Jackie fidgeted, as if uncomfortable in his presence. "So, is that why you became a cook? Your appetite?"

"Chef," he corrected. "But yeah, my appetite may have had something to do with it. The aunt who raised us worked nights, so if we were going to eat something besides TV dinners, we had to fix it ourselves."

"Was she a waitress or something?"

"No . . ." He grinned, trying not to laugh at the image of his aunt waiting on anyone. "Actor. The Incomparable Vivian. She's been a star on Broadway for the past several years, but back then she limited her work to Houston—a sacrifice she made for us. In return, I helped take care of my elderly grandmother and two younger sisters by learning my way around the kitchen. And since I've always enjoyed indulging my senses, I figured if I was going to cook, I might as well go 'all the way.'" He put enough sexual connotation in the words to make that stubborn chin of hers go up. "What about you?"

"When I'm hungry, I usually grab whatever's cheap and easy."

"Cheap and easy? Mmm . . . I could be talked into that."

She stopped and faced him with the surf at her back and the wind playing in her short hair. "You know, as much as I'm enjoying this little double-entendre thing you have going here, let's get one thing straight. We are not on a date. We are going to dinner so I can get it through your head that I'm not going to help you."

"I thought we were going to dinner so I could proposition you."

She turned to stomp back to her ship but he slipped a hand around her elbow, stopping her.

"Sorry, you're right." He tried for a sheepish look.

"Since this really is a business dinner, I'll try to behave myself."

She studied him a moment before nodding. "All right."

"Although if it weren't a business dinner, I'd be compelled to ask . . . has anyone ever told you, you have a great mouth?"

Her head snapped back in surprise. "A smart mouth, you mean."

"No, I was being quite literal."

"Come off it." She laughed and blushed. Imagine that. Jackie Taylor could blush. "My mouth isn't anything but big."

Adrian stepped closer, just enough to invade her space. "Your mouth is a work of art. I can't imagine any man alive who could look at your lips and not want to taste them."

She glared up at him, but the color in her cheeks spoke more of pleasure than anger. "You call this behaving?"

"Behaving is a new concept for me. It may take me a while to get it right. You'll have to be patient." He tugged gently on her arm and smiled when she fell in step beside him. "Let's see, what were we discussing? Ah yes, I remember. Food." He glanced at her sideways. "My *second* favorite subject in life."

Jackie rolled her eyes but didn't take the bait. He was a man, so she knew his first favorite subject without even asking.

When they reached the restaurant, Adrian held the door and she stepped into an atmosphere where fishing nets and life preservers hung on weathered wood paneling.

An impossibly perky hostess glanced up from the

bamboo podium. "Hi," she greeted them cheerfully until she saw Adrian. Then her jaw actually dropped.

"Two for dinner," Adrian said, seeming unaware that the girl was about to drool on his boots. Not that Jackie blamed her. The man looked particularly droolworthy in a pale blue shirt open at the collar, unbuttoned gray vest, and dark blue trousers.

"Two. Yes, of course." Perky Girl grabbed menus. "If you'll just . . . follow me."

Jackie trailed behind as the hostess led the way. A few locals had gathered around the bar in the middle of the room, swapping fish stories, but the tables and booths were empty.

"I guess you get your pick of tables." The hostess smiled up at Adrian.

"How about the one in the corner with the killer view?"

"Oh, good choice." Perky Girl sighed in admiration as if he'd just announced the cure for cancer. As they took their seats, she handed them each a menu. "Sandy will be your server this evening, but can I get you anything while you're waiting? Water? Wine?"

My body, Jackie added silently, reading the invitation in the girl's eyes.

"Water would be nice. Thank you." Adrian smiled and the girl nearly melted before hurrying off.

Jackie turned to him. "Can I ask you a question?"

"Certainly." He casually opened his menu.

"Do you do that intentionally, or does it just come naturally? You know, like breathing?"

"Do what?" He frowned.

She resisted the temptation to whack him over the head. "Send women into a swoon."

He looked confused for a second, then amusement registered, crinkling the corners of his eyes and carving long dimples to either side of his mouth. "Jealous?" he asked.

"In your dreams." She snapped open her own menu. Any woman fool enough to fall for a man like Adrian deserved to have her heart broken. Unless that woman liked to share—which Jackie didn't.

Their server, Sandy, arrived—a no-nonsense woman who refrained from ogling, thank goodness—and they placed their order.

"Okay." Jackie folded her hands on the table. "Down to business."

"Naw-uh. Our food hasn't even come. First we eat, visit, watch the sunset, then we'll talk about the offer."

"Well, if you're planning to offer me part of the salvage rights, save your breath. I'm not stupid. Texas doesn't grant salvage rights, so the minute you and your sisters brought the Texas Historical Commission into this, you lost everything that was on that ship. If you wanted to go after Lafitte's treasure, you should have just done it."

"Are you kidding?" A scowl lined his face. "First of all, that would be illegal, and second, the bulk of the shipwreck is buried under mud from the nineteen hundred hurricane. Do you know how much excavating it will cost?"

"I have a pretty good idea, which is what confuses me. Why is everyone suddenly so hot to go after a worthless artifact? I explained to the writer guy—"

"Scott Lawrence." Adrian supplied the name of the famous suspense novelist who had called her a few months ago claiming to be researching a new book.

"Yes, him. I explained that the so-called treasure is

nothing but a powder horn. It's not gold. It's not some valuable jewel. It's a stupid powder horn my ancestors jokingly referred to as 'Lafitte's treasure.' So, what's the big deal?"

"Ah, and here's our first course." Adrian smiled as the server brought an appetizer of shrimp cocktail and a bottle of wine. Jackie drummed her fingers as he went through the ritual of tasting. When the woman was gone, Adrian turned back to her. "So, how do you like running a charter ship?"

She narrowed her eyes, wondering when he planned to answer her question. Of course, since Lafitte's treasure was her least favorite subject, she shrugged it off. "The work is never-ending, tourists can occasionally be a pain in the butt, and I barely make enough to cover my expenses."

"You hate it that much, eh?" He grinned knowingly, as if he could see through to the truth: that her ship meant the world to her, and she'd fight tooth and nail to keep her business going, a battle she was currently losing.

"How about you?" She dipped a chilled shrimp in cocktail sauce. "Do you like running a B and B?"

"Most of the time." He popped a sauce-drenched shrimp into his mouth and wrinkled his nose. "Too bland. Mind if I doctor this up a bit?" At her nod, he rummaged through the condiments on the table. "I could do without getting up before dawn to start breakfast every day of the week, but it beats the heck out of filling orders off a menu in someone else's kitchen." He tried another shrimp. "Mmm, better. Try it now." He dredged a shrimp through the sauce and held it to her mouth.

She pulled back with a wary frown.

"Come on . . ." he coaxed.

She narrowed her eyes slightly, then opened her

mouth and took the shrimp. His fingertips brushed her lips, sending a shot of tingling heat through her, followed by the spicy chill of the sauce.

"Delicious, huh?"

She nodded, trying to focus on food, not thoughts of what Adrian might taste like. "So, who's cooking while you're gone?"

"My sisters, Rory and Alli. They aren't exactly slouches in the kitchen, although they're no match for me."

"You should get that ego checked." She waved a shrimp at him. "I think it may be growing."

"No, it's always been this big."

She shook her head, thinking his charm would be so much easier to resist if he took himself more seriously. He clearly didn't, though, and his easy manner lulled her as effectively as the wine over the next hour. Their conversation flowed between bites of blackened redfish and creamy pasta. By the time they'd finished dinner, other patrons were scattered about the restaurant. Candles had been lit, lending a touch of romance to the rustic decor. Outside, dark had fallen so that only the white crests of the waves shone in the lights from the pier.

Jackie relaxed back in her chair as the server cleared away their plates and asked if they wanted dessert. When Jackie said no, Adrian ordered something for himself and two cappuccinos. Then, taking up his wine glass, he leaned back as well and turned slightly toward her. She had an odd sense of intimacy, as if they were lounging side by side somewhere private, rather than sitting at a table in a semicrowded restaurant.

He studied the wine in his glass. "How much do you actually know about the powder horn?"

The question jolted her. In the past hour, she'd almost forgotten why he'd taken her to dinner.

"Now, don't get all stiff on me," he said in a lazy drawl. "I just want to know if you're aware of the whole story."

She crossed her arms over her chest. "I know the powder horn once belonged to Jean Lafitte. He gave it to my ancestor, Jack Kingsley's grandfather, before sailing for South America. Several of the pirates who had followed Lafitte from New Orleans to Galveston decided to stay in Texas and start a new life. Jack's grandfather was one of them. In an impromptu ceremony, Lafitte presented the powder horn to Reginald Kingsley as a memento of their adventures together. Since Lafitte liked to refer to the horn as his 'most treasured possession,' my family called it 'Lafitte's treasure' as a joke. Unfortunately, the joke has gotten out of hand over the years."

"Do you know why Lafitte called it that?"

"No. I only know that every treasure hunter out there thinks there's a chest of gold somewhere, and that—as a Kingsley descendant—I should know where it is. Only, there is no chest of gold. It doesn't exist."

"What if"—Adrian looked directly into her eyes— "I told you the powder horn was worth more than gold?"

Chapter 2

The waitress picked that moment to arrive with the dessert and cappuccinos. Jackie waited impatiently for her to leave before turning to Adrian. "What do you mean, the powder horn is more valuable than gold?"

Rather than answer, Adrian picked up his fork and took a bite of pie made of coffee-flavored ice cream smothered in chocolate and whipped cream. "Mmm. This is good. Here, try some."

"I don't want dessert, I want you to answer my question."

"Come on . . ." He waved the folk, tempting her. "One bite."

Holding back frustration, she opened her mouth, then smothered a moan of pleasure as the frozen treat melted on her tongue.

"Let's go back to your conversation with Scott Lawrence a couple months ago," Adrian said as he swirled his fork through the whipped cream.

Jackie recalled the day clearly. The author had started out asking if she were, by any chance, descended from Jack Kingsley. She'd tried to deny it, knowing that the instant the truth came out, he'd start asking about the treasure, and he had.

In a moment of sheer frustration, she'd told him about the letter she'd inherited. It had been written by the first mate of the *Freedom,* Jack Kingsley's ship, to Kingsley's illegitimate son, describing the incident that had taken the captain's life. The letter, combined with stories handed down through the years, painted a fairly detailed picture of what had happened that stormy night during the Civil War. The stories had grown into the Legend of Pearl Island: a tale of ill-fated love between Captain Kingsley and Marguerite Bouchard LeRoche, the beautiful wife of a Galveston shipping baron.

Jackie sat forward, lacing her fingers. "Like I told Scott Lawrence, the crew members who overheard Jack Kingsley shouting that he wouldn't leave the ship without the treasure assumed it was something valuable. They didn't know its only value was sentimental."

"Because it reminded Jack of all the things he didn't want to be," Adrian said, surprising her. "All the reasons he wanted to be an honorable man rather than to follow in his father's and grandfather's footsteps."

She stared at him in shock. "How in the world do you know that?"

"Because my ancestor Marguerite wrote about it in her diaries." He shrugged as if his knowing her family secrets were nothing. "She asked him once if the rumors were true, that he'd inherited Lafitte's missing treasure from his grandfather. He laughed as if it were an inside joke—which I guess it was—and said that yes he had it and he kept it in his cabin as a reminder of his goal to give up smuggling. Unfortunately, he never told her what the treasure was, so there's no mention of the powder horn in her diaries. That's the link we're missing in our research, and the reason we need your letter. The Historical Commission won't grant the permits we need to hire an archeologist unless we have compelling evidence that the powder horn was on board when the ship went down."

"Marguerite wrote about Jack Kingsley?"

"Extensively."

Jackie's skin tingled at the thought that someone had written about her legendary ancestor. Her namesake. Not word-of-mouth stories that grew with every telling, but firsthand accounts. What was he like, really? Brave and valiant as his first mate claimed? Or another charming opportunist like so many men in her family, including her own father?

"I need to know one thing," Adrian said. "What exactly did the first mate say about the powder horn?"

She hesitated, too used to avoiding all talk of the letter to discuss it openly. But as Marguerite's descendants, Adrian and his family were a part of the tale. And they held the answers to questions she'd kept locked in her heart all her life. "He, uh, he said Jack had always wanted to pass the treasure on to Andrew, his son, to help him remember why a man should strive for honor rather than easy riches."

"We need specifics, though." Adrian leaned closer, his expression intent. "On the phone with Scott, you said the letter states very clearly that the 'treasure' was a powder horn that Lafitte gave Kingsley's grandfather."

"It does."

"Perfect." He relaxed visibly. "That's exactly what we need in order to plead our case to the Historical Commission."

She nearly pulled away at the mere mention of the government agency that so hated scavengers like her and her father, but the lure of Jack Kingsley held her in place.

"Okay, now it's your turn for show-and-tell. Why is the horn so valuable?"

"After Scott got off the phone with you, he did some research about the powder horn and found out it has quite a history. And I mean *quite* a history." His brows rose as if he had to struggle to take it all in. "Did you know it originally belonged to George Washington? And that he carved his initials into it?"

Her head dropped forward in surprise. "You're kidding."

"Finally caught your interest, eh?"

"No. Not at all."

"Liar." He held another forkful of dessert before her and she took it without thinking.

"So"—she held a hand in front of her mouth—"how did Lafitte wind up with it? Did he steal it from somebody?"

"Nope." Adrian sliced off another bite for himself. "During the Revolutionary War, a very young Andrew Jackson served as a messenger for the militia. On one occasion, Washington hid a message in his personal powder horn, and gave it to Jackson to carry behind British lines. Jackson kept the horn as a souvenir and had it with him in 1814 at the Battle of New Orleans. Since your ancestor sailed with Lafitte, I assume you know the Barataria pirates were instrumental in winning that battle."

"I know a lot about the cutthroats who hid out in the Louisiana swamps. They were a horrible, brutal band of thieves. Captain Reginald Kingsley may have been an exiled British noble, but he fit right in."

Adrian nodded in agreement. "From what I've read, I think 'cutthroat' sums them up accurately enough, but they did help defeat the British."

"One good deed does not a good man make."

"True. But when the battle was over, a celebration ball was held. At the ball, Jackson presented the powder horn to Lafitte. Lafitte made a lavish speech and claimed he would treasure it forever in remembrance of serving such a 'fine leader of men.'"

"Good ol' Jean." Jackie toasted him sarcastically with her cappuccino. "He knew how to make speeches . . . even if half the words that fell from his lips were pure lies. That one being a perfect example, since he didn't keep the horn forever. He gave it to my ancestor Ruthless Reggie."

"So we hope to prove . . . with your help."

"But what's in it for you?" Jackie asked. "Like I said, the state of Texas doesn't grant salvage rights. Anything you bring up will belong to them, so you have nothing to gain."

"Actually, we have a lot to gain." He smiled. "It's called tourism. The Legend of Pearl Island attracts a lot of guests to our inn, especially those who want to scuba dive around the wreck site. Try to guess how much our business will increase if the commission uncovers more of the ship with a partial excavation?"

"Then there's no talk of raising the ship?"

"No. They only care about the items that went down with the *Freedom,* not the ship itself. Plus we'll have had all that lovely media about the history surrounding the wreck." His smile broadened. "God, you can't buy better publicity than that!"

"True. And I can see how it will be good for you. However . . ." She rested her elbows on the table and laced her fingers together. "I fail to see what's in it for me."

"Ah. What's in it for you, indeed?" He pushed the

dessert plate away, and leaned forward on his forearms. With his face so near, she watched candlelight play in his blue eyes. "We'd like to work out a deal with you similar to what we have going with your friend Captain Bob."

She frowned at the mention of the casual friend they had in common. Bobby Johnson had lived in Corpus when she first started chartering her ship, but later he'd moved to Galveston to start his own tour boat business. He'd been the one to tell the St. Claires about her ship. "What does Bobby have to do with this?"

"In addition to his regular Galveston Bay boat tours, Captain Bob and his wife, Paige, do a Haunted House Lunch Run every Saturday that has been extremely profitable for all of us. They ferry tourists from Galveston's historic district out to Pearl Island, where we serve lunch on the veranda that looks out over the cove. We even wear costumes to give people the illusion of stepping back in time. Tourists love it, and pay a nice price for the meals we serve."

Jackie raised both brows, remembering the costume Adrian had worn at the Buccaneer's Ball. It was far more elaborate than the costumes she and her crew wore on occasion. Lord have mercy, if that's what he wore to serve lunch, no wonder the lunch run was so popular. Any woman with a pulse who saw him wearing that red jacket and those tall jackboots probably had pirate/captive sex fantasies for months. She'd certainly had a few.

Just thinking about it stirred heat low in her belly. "So . . . you, um"—she cleared her throat—"do this lunch run thing with Bobby . . ."

"And my sister Rory, the brainstorm kid, started thinking, wouldn't it be great to take it a step further?"

"Go on."

"I need you to fantasize for a moment here." His gaze held hers and her mind drifted back toward erotic images of him in that red jacket. "You already know how much people will pay for dinner and an evening of sailing on an authentic Baltimore schooner. Think how much more they'll pay to take a trip on that ship to Pearl Island, where the notorious Henri LeRoche once entertained smugglers in his mansion."

Longing tightened her chest, since running the *Pirate's Pleasure* as a fully functioning cruise ship had been a lifelong dream. "A lot. They'd pay a lot."

"Yeah." He smiled and candlelight danced over his features. "We'd do it as a joint venture, sharing the cost of promoting it, then each of us profiting from our end. You from the cruise, us from the dinner and the increased attention for our gift shop and inn. *If* you're interested."

For a moment, one tiny moment, she let herself dream. She pictured paying her slip rental without cringing, hiring more hands, replacing tattered sails.

"All you have to do," Adrian said in a low, intimate voice, "is help us convince the commission that the powder horn was on the *Freedom* when she went down."

Her fantasy of new sails and solvency burst like a bubble. He might as well have said: All you have to do is stand naked before a crowd, tell them all your sins, and wait to be stoned.

She closed her eyes as regret filled her. "I'm sorry. Really. It would be great, but . . . I can't." Before he could respond, she leaned back and flagged down the server. "Excuse me. We're ready for our check."

Adrian shook his head to clear it. "What do you mean, you can't?"

"Exactly that. I can't help you."

The server arrived with the bill. Adrian's wallet had barely cleared his pocket before Jackie stood, eager to leave. He left a hefty tip rather than wait for change.

The minute they were out the door, she turned and offered her hand. "Thank you for dinner, but if you'll excuse me, I have a huge catered dinner party on board tomorrow night, so I need to be up early to get ready."

He took her hand as if to shake it, but held on. "I'll walk you back to your ship."

"No need for that."

"We're going the same way," he pointed out. She looked ready to argue but voices drifted toward them. Glancing up, he saw another couple coming down the pier toward the restaurant. "Come on, walk with me. That was our deal, after all. I buy dinner. You hear me out."

"I did hear you out. My answer is no. I can't help you."

"Okay. Explain that to me." He turned and started down the pier, slowly, to give them time to talk. "I offer you a deal where you have everything to gain and nothing to lose, and you turn it down flat."

"It's not that simple. Taking my ship out for an evening cruise is one thing, but it took me two weeks to get her seaworthy enough to sail all the way to Galveston last time. And that was without passengers on board. To offer multi-day cruise packages, I'd need more sailors and galley hands, not to mention finishing out the cabins. I can't afford it."

"Sorry, I don't buy that. The point is to make money, and I think we'd make a bundle. All we're asking is for you to let us use your letter." He watched as she thought it over, her emotions hard to read in the faint light along the pier.

"Why do we have to go after the powder horn to do

the cruise packages?" she finally asked. "You're right, it's a solid business idea and could be profitable for all of us."

And if he agreed, she'd never share the letter, that much was blatantly clear. "Sorry. No letter, no deal."

"But *why*?"

"Jackie . . ." He stopped beneath a lamppost where pale light enclosed them in a small circle. "This project is important to us. Not just because it'll be good for business—that's the least of our priorities. It's . . . personal."

"How so?" She looked up at him with troubled eyes as moths swirled about them like fairies in the gilded light. He heard music in the distance, just over the sound of waves lapping at the pilings. The moment held a kind of magic that almost made him speak freely.

He quickly checked the impulse.

If he told her that he and his sisters wanted to do this for Jack and Marguerite, to help their spirits find peace, she'd think they were crazy. Hell, maybe they were. He could tell her part of it, though.

"Okay, truth." He exhaled. "Marguerite gave Captain Kingsley a necklace. It's a pearl pendant with a colorful history of its own. We think he kept it inside the powder horn."

"A necklace? Oh God, I should have known." She snorted in disgust. "For a while you had me going, but in the end, you're no different than all the other treasure hunters looking for lost gold and precious gems."

"Actually, we don't know if the necklace has any monetary value. That's not why we want it. Jackie, it's part of our family history. Surely you can understand that. We want to see it recovered."

"Enough to give it up to the Historical Commission the minute it's found?"

"What's our alternative?" he demanded. "Plunder the site like a bunch of thieving looters?"

She jerked back as if he'd struck her, then turned and walked off.

Damn it! He wanted to kick himself as he remembered her father had been a treasure hunter.

"Wait." He went after her. "I didn't mean that the way it sounded."

She glared at him. "Just drop it. Okay?"

"Okay. Although what I meant to say was that we want the necklace recovered, even if it means losing it. That probably makes no sense to outsiders, but it makes sense to us."

"You don't know what you're asking." She stopped at the end of the gangway to her ship and unlocked the gate. "I'm sorry. I can see this means a great deal to you, and I'd like to help, but I can't. The answer's no. Now, I have a busy day tomorrow, so thank you for dinner and good night."

"At least say you'll think about it. I'll stop by in the morning before I head back and we can talk more."

"No! I don't want to talk more, and I don't want you coming around bringing any of this up in front of my crew."

"Then come by my hotel in the morning, and we'll talk there." He gave her the hotel name and the room number.

"Oh yeah, right." She rolled her eyes. "Like *that's* gonna happen."

"Then call my room when you get there. I'll meet you in the lobby and take you to lunch."

"I told you, I have a private party on board tomorrow night. I'll be busy all day getting ready."

"Okay, breakfast."

"No, no, no. Feeding me another meal is not going to change my mind."

"Just sleep on it, will ya?" He cupped her head in his hands for emphasis. "Please."

She looked caught between laughter and exasperation. "Don't you ever take no for an answer?"

"No." On impulse, he leaned forward to give her cheek a friendly kiss. Her startled jump made his lips land closer to hers than he'd intended and their mouths brushed—just barely—as he pulled back. The tantalizing contact caught him off guard, and sent a bolt of arousal through him as he realized her lips were every bit as plush as they looked. Damn. Information like that did not bode well for a good night's sleep. Especially when she stared up at him with wide eyes but made no move to pull away. In fact, she looked like she might welcome a real kiss.

Resisting the urge, he stepped away. "Sweet dreams, Jackie. I'll see you in the morning."

Chapter 3

"Sweet dreams?" Jackie grumbled as she punched her pillow and wished it were Adrian's stomach. That's what she should have done when he kissed her—punched him. Not gaped at him like a lovesick moron, her whole body suddenly alive from that simple contact. Unfortunately, the man was even more tempting than the business offer he'd made, and that was saying a lot. The offer had been very tempting. Beyond tempting. It could have been the start of a whole new era in her life, one that didn't include acid reflux every time she balanced the books.

Flopping onto her back, she stared at the ceiling of her cabin and remembered all the years of work she and her father had put into the *Pirate's Pleasure*, all the plans they'd shared while working side by side. They'd traveled regularly to the Caribbean—her father more than her—but someday they dreamed of sailing the *Pirate's Pleasure* there and living like captains on the high seas.

"And we'll visit my cousins?" she'd always asked.

"Of course," her father would promise.

"And Grandma Merry?"

"Absolutely," he'd say.

"And Mother?" she'd ask more quietly.

"Watch that varnish, nutmeg, it's about to drip."

Yes, someday, they'd sail the *Pirate's Pleasure* to the islands she loved so much, and she wouldn't be the misfit relative. She'd be dashing, like her swashbuckling ancestors. And when her mother saw how beautiful the ship was, she'd want to sail away with them.

That fairy tale may have died with her childhood, but she still dreamed of sailing the ship to the Caribbean at least once in her life. If she took the St. Claires up on their offer, could she earn enough for such an endeavor?

Unfortunately, she couldn't accept their offer without resurrecting the scandal surrounding her father's death. Thinking of it now brought a horrible rush of memories that made her want to pull the covers over her head so she could hide forever. She could still remember the sick feeling in the pit of her stomach when people learned her father was a crook and then looked at her with accusation and distrust. She'd left the islands to escape all that. By working her butt off for the past eight years, she'd managed to build a business out of the only good thing he'd left her, a dilapidated ship. A legitimate business. No cons. No forging artifacts. And no illegal salvaging of shipwreck sites.

What was the term Adrian had used? "Thieving looters," that was it. And he'd said it with enough disdain to make her flinch. Well, if she brought attention to herself by making the letter public, a lot of people would call her that.

Or would they?

Eight years had passed since her father died, and all that mess had happened in the British West Indies. Could she possibly make the letter public and not have the past slap her in the face?

She shook the thought off. *Don't go there. You're*

only asking for trouble. Think about something else.

Turning over, she forced her mind away from Adrian and his offer only to have Jack Kingsley slip into her thoughts. Not a vast improvement, since Adrian looked just like the mental image she'd always carried of Captain Jack: tall, broad-shouldered, and charming to the hilt.

But what had Jack Kingsley really been like? she wondered, staring about the dark cabin. Moonlight slanted through the aft windows, casting mysterious shadows about the room as questions about her namesake played through her mind, along with the new knowledge that Marguerite, the great love of his life, had written about him in her diaries. If she helped the St. Claires, would they let her read the diaries?

She pushed the thought away and flipped onto her other side. *Think about work.*

Unfortunately, that brought on images of a dwindling bank account, a growing stack of bills, and a long list of repairs that needed to be made. Which brought her right back to the St. Claires' offer.

Dammit, dammit, dammit! She punched the pillow again, this time wishing it were her father.

Okay, think it through logically.

The media frenzy after her father's death had happened nearly a decade ago, and a long way from Texas. Her father's motto had always been: "Never piss in your own pond"—which was why he'd never conned anyone close to home. It was also why she'd felt safe returning to Corpus Christi. People here knew a few vague facts, but nowhere near the whole truth. Would involving herself in a ship excavation change that?

She turned the problem over in her mind throughout the night.

By the time the first light of dawn seeped through the windows, she knew she had two choices: go quietly bankrupt and lose the *Pirate's Pleasure,* or risk everything she'd built over the past eight years for the chance to win financial security. She didn't care about great wealth, but she did care passionately about making an honest living.

Now wouldn't her buccaneer ancestors have a great laugh at that? Either that or moan in shame. The question was, had she inherited enough of their courage and daring to take a risk this big?

Adrian lounged in the hotel chair, his bare feet propped on the unmade bed, a cup of coffee in one hand and the morning paper spread in his lap. The headlines barely registered, though, as he tried to figure out where he'd gone wrong last night. Normally he had a knack for reading women, but Jackie confused him at every turn.

She wasn't after him.

She didn't need rescuing.

She didn't even want to be friends.

In fact, she didn't seem to want anything to do with him. That was a first, and perhaps the reason she intrigued him more than any other woman ever had.

When women wanted him, he knew how to judge how much they expected and if they could part as friends. If the answer was no, he kept his hands to himself. If the answer was yes, he made sure they both had fun and that things stayed light.

When a woman needed him—for encouragement or outright rescuing—he knew when to give advice, when to shut up and offer a shoulder to cry on, and when to step in with action. In fact, he knew how to handle nearly every sticky situation a woman could throw at a man, situations that sent most men into states of pure panic.

But he didn't know how to handle Jackie.

The one thing he did know was that he'd blown it last night. And his failure was going to devastate his sisters. They'd all become single-minded about recovering the necklace. When initial attempts to work with Jackie had failed, they'd decided to send Adrian down to Corpus to charm her into helping. He'd arrogantly believed he could do it, no sweat . . . but instead he'd blown it.

Was it the flirting? he wondered.

No, Jackie didn't take that any more seriously than he meant it. Not that he wouldn't *like* to mean it. From the moment he'd met Jackie Taylor, he'd wanted to sleep with her. She'd slammed the door on that idea by making it clear she wasn't the least bit interested in him.

The question was, could he make her want him? Now that might prove a delicious challenge. And if he'd blown the business deal, nothing stood in the way of giving it his best shot. His body warmed eagerly to the idea. He could stay one more day and take her out again, but this time forget the teasing and go for all-out seduction. Then he'd bring her back here, taste those luscious-looking lips, peel away her clothes, and—

A sharp rap came at the door, jarring him from thoughts of Jackie naked beneath him. He waited for someone to call, "Housekeeping." When it didn't come, he set the paper and coffee cup aside and went to the door. A peek through the spy hole revealed Jackie standing in the hall with her hands thrust into the pockets of a foul-weather jacket.

His first thought was that she'd changed her mind about the business deal, which would thrill his sisters but put a halt to his newly hatched plan. Then he noticed the determined set of her jaw. The bill of a ball cap hid the rest of her face, but her stance said she'd come to do battle, which did not bode well on any front.

Braced for anything, he stepped back and opened the door. "Jackie, what a surprise. I didn't expect you so early."

Jackie's response stuck in her throat when she found herself eye level with Adrian's bare chest: his very nice, smooth-skinned, well-muscled bare chest. She tipped her head back to see his face with his black hair hanging loosely past his broad shoulders. *Ho, mama.* Heat flooded her whole body.

"Come on in and have a seat while I grab a shirt."

No need to get dressed on my account. "D-did I wake you?"

"No, I'm so used to rising with the roosters I don't even need an alarm anymore."

As he moved away, she noticed he wore a pair of wildly colorful chef's pants. Something that baggy shouldn't have been sexy, but with a body like that, he'd look good in anything. Even better in nothing.

"Can I get you some coffee?" He gestured toward a miniature coffeepot. "There's nearly a full cup left. It's yours if you want it."

"No, I'm fine."

"Okay, then give me a minute and I'll take you to that breakfast I promised." He headed for the main part of the room and the motorcycle saddlebags he'd left sitting on one of the beds. His back muscles flexed as he pulled on a dark blue T-shirt and reached for a pair of jeans.

She looked away only to have her gaze land on the other bed, the one he'd apparently slept in. Images flashed through her mind, making her blush. "Actually," she called as he disappeared into the bathroom, "I don't have time for breakfast. I need to get back to the ship. I just . . . I came by to tell you I've thought about your offer—"

"Before you tell me no," he said in a rush as he emerged tucking in his t-shirt, "why don't you at least come to Pearl Island and talk to the rest of the family? Rory's husband, Chance, can explain the money stuff and you can hear Rory's ideas on promotion—"

"That won't be necessary. After last night—"

"About that, let me just say, I realize now that I may have flirted with you just a little too much and given you the wrong idea. I assure you, if I were seriously hitting on you, that's not how I would go about it. I just like getting a rise out of you, because, well . . . you really are cute when you're flustered. But that's all there is to it. So if you're worried that I'll be chasing after you every time you come to the inn, I promise, you have nothing to worry about. Swear."

She stared at him, not quite believing her ears. He thought she was "cute"? And not worth hitting on? Well, now, didn't that just make her day? "Are you done?"

"I'm done." He let out a big breath.

"All right, then. I've made my decision." All the nerves from too little sleep and too much coffee burned in her stomach. She pulled a roll of antacids from her pocket and popped one into her mouth, praying it worked quickly. "I have a condition."

"Oh, Jesus, is it serious?"

"What?" She pressed a hand to her diaphragm in a vain attempt to squelch the fire.

"Your condition." Worry lined his face as he glanced at her hand. "Is that why you said no last night? You're sick?"

She choked. "Not that kind of condition, you idiot. A condition to my agreeing to do this deal."

"Oh." He placed a hand over his heart. "You scared me. I thought you had terminal cancer or something. So, what's your condition?"

She squared her stance. "If I do this, I want to read Marguerite's diaries."

He waited for her to go on. "That's it?"

"I may have other stipulations later, but that's the main one for now. So, yes or no?"

"Oh, gee." He pinched his bottom lip as if deep in thought. "I don't know . . . we don't normally let anyone outside the family read the diaries. They're very personal."

"You're asking me to let the whole world read my great-grandfather's letter, which is also very personal."

"I'll have to talk to Alli and Rory, though. Be sure they're cool with this."

"Fine." She headed toward the door. "Let me know what y'all decide."

"Whoa, wait." He grabbed her arm, laughing as he pulled her back. "I was joking."

"I wasn't."

"Yeah, I've noticed that about you. No sense of humor."

She narrowed her eyes, wondering if he was teasing her or insulting her.

He sighed at her lack of response. "The answer is yes. If you help us, we'll let you read the diaries. But I have a condition of my own."

"Terminal horniness?" She cocked a brow.

"Only when I'm around you." He winked.

"What happened to your promise to behave?"

"We're still negotiating, so we're not partners yet. Besides, flirting doesn't count with you."

"Why not?"

"Because we both know you're not the least bit interested or impressed. Which wounds me deeply. I'm not sure my ego will survive."

She rolled her eyes. "What's your condition?"

"You have to read the diaries at Pearl Island. I can tell you right now, neither of my sisters will agree to let them out of the inn. They're irreplaceable. Besides, we all need to sit down and work on our proposal to the Historical Commission and hammer out the details for the cruise packages. The easiest way to do that is for you to come stay at the inn for a while."

"Makes sense," she said, even though the thought of leaving the safe world she'd carved out in Corpus had her stomach burning again.

"So when can you come? We'll put you up in one of the rooms, as long as it's soon. Once Thanksgiving gets here, we're booked solid through New Year's."

"Actually, I can come next week."

"Sounds perfect. Let me give you our number. We can work out the details on the phone." He retrieved his wallet from the dresser, pulled out a business card, and held it out to her. "I suppose a kiss to seal the deal would be totally out of the question."

She shook her head. "You are a lost cause."

"Yeah, and it's really a shame. As a boy I had such potential."

She plucked the card from his hand and headed for the door. "See ya next week." When she reached the door, she turned and blew him a kiss.

"Hey, come over here and do that. I dare ya."

"Never dare a pirate." She smiled and breezed out of the room. The minute the door closed behind her, she fanned herself with his business card. He thought she wasn't interested? Lord, if he only knew. Although thank goodness he didn't. As long as he never found out how much she wished his flirting were real she could handle being around him. She hoped.

Chapter 4

When Jackie drove out of Corpus Christi a week later in her battered blue pickup truck, her first stop was a convenience store for Rolaids and Advil. She and Ti had fought that morning—again—even though they hardly ever fought. But boy, they'd had some doozies over the last few days. He'd been like an uncle to her for as long as she could remember, and when they'd left the islands, they'd promised each other: no more treasure-hunting ever again. And while he liked to reminisce, he was serious about that pledge.

She'd tried to explain that this wasn't like that. This would be a legitimate excavation done by marine archeologists. Instead of being appeased, he'd only become more incensed and called her reckless. Her jaw had dropped at that accusation, since he usually teased her about being too uptight and cautious.

What choice did she have, though? Go down without a fight? The problem was, Ti didn't know how bad things were, so she couldn't explain her reasoning. Yes, odds were fifty-fifty at best that she was making a mistake, but the gamble was worth it. Or so she assured herself repeatedly during the long drive up the coast.

When she reached the causeway that connected Pearl

Island to Galveston, though, she knew Ti was right. The small, private island lay before her, a lush green world unto itself, filled with the romance of old legends, but rather than lift her spirits with hope, the sight of it made her stomach churn with dread.

She was being reckless.

The world of marine archeology was a close-knit community that kept tabs on treasure hunters. Her only hope was that the archeologists on this project wouldn't make the connection between Jackie Taylor and Buddy Taylor. If they did, she was screwed and so were the St. Claires. No respectable organization would raise money for a project of this magnitude based on evidence she presented if they knew her history.

Well, she told herself as she followed the tree-lined drive across the island, whatever was going to happen, she couldn't back out now. Adrian and his sisters had arranged a meeting in the morning with the Galveston Historical Society, a private group that planned to back the project if the state agreed to put the artifacts recovered on display in the Texas Seaport Museum in Galveston.

That was her first hurdle. If she could get past tomorrow's meeting, she could breathe a tiny bit easier.

As she broke from the trees, the inn came into sight, a three-story, fanciful structure overlooking a deepwater cove. She found a parking place in the crowded oyster-shell lot to the side and sat for a moment, awed by the beauty of the old mansion. Built of pink granite, it had a turret at one corner topped with a tall spire. A large veranda stretched across the front while gargoyles snarled down at her from the third-floor balcony—the very balcony from which Henri LeRoche had fired the cannon that had killed Jack Kingsley.

Now there was a comforting thought.

Don't think about failure, she told herself. Wasn't that what her father had always said? *Picture everything working out exactly the way you want, and it'll happen.*

That philosophy may have gotten him killed in the end, but it had worked like a charm for years before that, years of living high and living fast. She only needed it to work once. Glancing sideways, she saw the document envelope that held the letter. She picked it up, closed her eyes, and tried to picture all new sails for the *Pirate's Pleasure.* When the image refused to form in her mind, she tried for something less ambitious: having enough money to make payroll without dipping into savings. That alone was lofty enough, considering how many new crew members she'd need to pull off the St. Claires' idea.

That concern waited way off in the future, though. Right now, she simply needed to get through tomorrow.

Don't think about failure, she reminded herself as she chomped down on another orange-flavored antacid and climbed out of the pickup. The sunny day held only a slight chill of autumn and the tangy scent of the Gulf. As she grabbed her duffel bag from the bed of the truck, the back of her neck prickled as if someone were watching her. She whirled around, scanning the parking lot, but saw no one. She looked toward the cove and the dazzling light on the water made her squint behind her sunglasses.

Was Jack Kingsley's ghost really out there, haunting the waters of the cove? The mere possibility raised goose bumps on her skin—not that she believed in ghosts, she reminded herself.

Swinging the duffel bag over one shoulder, she headed up the path to the inn. Confetti-colored chrysanthemums bloomed to either side of the stone steps, adding a cheerful touch. She barely noticed them, though, as she made her way to the ornate front door. Since the sign said WELCOME, COME ON IN, she opened the door and stepped inside. From somewhere in the distance came the muffled sound of a TV.

"Hello?" she called, taking off her shades to glance about the wide central hall. The place hadn't changed much since her first visit; Victorian sofas and chairs sat in a conversational grouping before a massive fireplace. Carved sea serpents supported the mantel while more nautical beasts had been carved into the crown molding. At the far end of the hall, a wide staircase curved upward, lit by three tall, stained-glass windows. "Anybody home?"

She was about to step back out and look for a doorbell to ring when Adrian's youngest sister appeared in the doorway to her right, a stunning young woman with reddish-gold curls tumbling about her supermodel figure.

"You made it!" the sister said, coming forward with a smile as bright as her hair. "I don't know if you remember me, but I'm Aurora Chancellor, or Rory, whichever you prefer."

"I remember." Jackie nodded, feeling dwarfed since the woman nearly reached six feet.

Rory's gaze dropped to the envelope. "Oh, goodness. Is that it? The letter?"

"Yeah." Jackie tucked it closer to her body.

"I can't wait to see it. But first let me grab the key to your room, then we'll go find Adrian. He'll want to know you're here." Rory ducked into the office, then led the way through the inn, walking backward half the time, chatting away. "We're so glad you agreed to come stay with us. Even Scott is excited, though with him it's hard to tell. You haven't met him yet, have you?"

"Scott?"

"Lawrence. My sister's fiancé. The guy who called you last summer."

"Scott Lawrence is engaged to your sister?" Oh great. On top of everything else, they had a celebrity involved in the project, which would bring that much more attention to it. Although publicity was the point, she supposed, as long as it didn't get out of control.

"You'll like Scott," Rory assured her as they reached the dining room. "He's really nice . . . once you get to know him."

Jackie nodded absently as she glanced at the fresco on the ceiling of King Neptune charging toward the doorway with his triton. Looking at it, she wondered what Jack Kingsley had thought of the ornate surroundings when he'd sat in this very room as a dinner guest. Probably that his host had too much ego and too much money. And in the early days before he'd reformed, he'd likely spent a good portion of the evening wondering how to lighten ol' Henri's pockets a bit. That was when he hadn't been plotting ways to sleep with the man's wife.

As they passed through the butler's pantry, she heard Adrian's voice ahead. He sounded as if he were teaching a cooking class. "You have to be really careful when you sprinkle on the nuts so you get just the right amount," he said slowly. "See, like this."

A squeal of delight split the air as she and Rory entered the vast kitchen where commercial-grade appliances contrasted with aged-wood rafters and red brick walls. Adrian stood at a center island sprinkling nuts over several trays of brownies, with an adorable little cupid perched on his hip.

"Ma-ma-ma-ma!" the baby chanted, her golden ringlets bouncing.

"Hey, peanut." Rory hurried forward, hands outstretched. "I didn't know you were awake. Adrian, you should have told me. I would have taken her off your hands."

"Like I mind having her to myself for a few minutes." He let his sister take the baby from him. Spotting Jackie, he smiled. "You made it."

"I made it." She shrugged.

"Great." Wiping his hands on a dish towel, he came toward her. He looked as fabulous as ever wearing a gray pullover with the sleeves pushed up to the elbows and black jeans. He'd traded his usual gold hoop earring for a dangling silver one. "Did Rory tell you about dinner?"

"Dinner?" Jackie asked.

"We thought we should all get together this evening," Adrian explained. "You know, celebrate your being here, read the letter, go over what to expect tomorrow, unless you have other plans."

"Nope. No plans." She smiled stiffly, wondering why they couldn't have waited until after she read the diaries to get the ball rolling.

Adrian turned back to his sister. "Hey, sis, could you slide the next batch of brownies in the oven for me while I show Jackie to her room?"

"Certainly. Here." Rory tossed a ring with two keys and he caught them one-handed, then reached for Jackie's duffel bag.

"I've got it," she insisted. "Just lead the way."

Rather than return through the dining room, he took her through a back hall and pointed toward a set of narrow stairs that led downward. "The family apartment is in the basement. Come on down around six so you can visit with everyone before we eat. We invited Bobby and Paige, but haven't heard if they're coming."

When they slipped through a small door into the main hall, she noticed a couple in the music room watching a TV that had been set into an antique armoire. Another couple was coming down the stairs as they started up. Adrian, the congenial innkeeper, greeted both pairs.

"You appear to have a full house," she observed as they reached the landing where the stained-glass windows bathed the area in colored light.

"We've survived our first year at least, and business has really picked up since we built a few bungalows along the jogging trail." He continued up the stairs, explaining the schedule and the amenities. The upper hall had another sitting area, this one cozier than the one downstairs. A vase of fresh flowers sat on a sideboard next to a wicker basket of individually wrapped tea bags. "We put coffee and hot water up here every morning so you don't have to come down for your first cup."

The small luxury brought back vague memories of life before her parents had divorced, when she'd lived in one island resort after another, her father preying on other guests, her mother ordering room service and lounging on white sand beaches while Jackie built sand castles.

Adrian moved toward a bank of tall windows opposite the stairs. Gauzy curtains obscured the view, but she could make out a balcony and the blue and white cove beyond.

"Here we are." Adrian opened a door to the left of the windows. "We call this room the Pearl, since it was Marguerite's. The best room in the house."

Jackie walked to the middle of the large, airy room

and let her duffel bag drop to her feet as she took it all in. The soft white walls, gilded furniture, and filtered light from the sitting room in the turret made her feel as if she'd stepped into a cloud. The headboard even had a painting of cupids flying against a gold background.

She turned back to him. "Don't you have something smaller? Because I really don't want to be obligated to quite this extent."

"Ah, I see you're on to me already."

"I usually am."

"True." He came toward her. "I might as well confess my dastardly scheme."

"I'm sure I'll be shocked."

"Actually, you will, since it doesn't involve anything more than your returning the favor. Whenever we get the cruises going, I'd like to be on the first half of the first trip. I'd do the whole thing, but hate to take off for that long."

"I suppose you'll want my best cabin."

"Unless you're short on space." His eyes twinkled, and she saw some suggestive remark coming.

"Don't," she warned. "You're on your best behavior, remember?"

"Darn it." He grinned, completely unrepentant. "But for now, come check this out." He led her through the elegant sitting room in the turret to one of the tall windows, which was actually a door.

Following him onto the balcony, she caught her breath at the view.

"Gorgeous, isn't it?" he said. A change came over him as he looked out to where palm trees guarded the mouth of the cove. Sunlight sparkled off the waters of the bay beyond but something brighter seemed to shimmer around him. "I've often wondered how many times Marguerite stood in this very spot, thinking about Captain Kingsley and wondering when she'd see him again." He glanced at her. "Maybe she's still here, waiting."

Jackie blinked at his shift in mood, this quiet side of him she'd never seen before. "Do you really believe in ghosts?"

A sudden breeze came off the cove, and he turned in that direction, his face in profile against the blue sky. "Let's just say that sometimes, when I stand here, looking out toward the bay, I feel . . . something. A sense of expectation mixed with grief and longing. As if the house is waiting."

"Waiting for what?"

A smile turned up the corners of his lips. "For Captain Jack to return, of course."

A shiver raced down her spine. "What about the diaries? You said I could read them."

"We'll hand them over at dinner tonight." He checked his watch and sighed. "Right now I have some catering orders to fill. Please make yourself at home. Feel free to borrow any of the books or magazines lying about, watch TV downstairs, or explore the island. I'll see you at six."

She watched him go, almost wishing he would stay. Impossible as it seemed, Serious Adrian was even harder to resist than Playful Adrian. What on earth did she do about that? Tell him to go back to teasing her?

Shaking her head, she stared across the cove and her thoughts shifted to Marguerite. How would it feel to have to wait like a prisoner in this house, day after day, year after year, for a few stolen moments with a secret lover? Knowing the penalty for getting caught would be brutal and swift. Jack Kingsley must have been one hell of a man for Marguerite to risk the wrath of her violent husband to be with him.

Chapter 5

Adrian looked up as Sadie, his sister's sable and white sheltie, came bounding down the apartment stairs, heralding the arrival of Allison and Scott. The dog raced into the living area where Rory was bottle-feeding Lauren. The baby squealed in delight and tried to wriggle free as Sadie took off to greet Rory's husband, Oliver Chancellor, who sat at the bar that divided the living and dining area from the kitchen. Chance laughed as the dog dashed around the bar to beg for treats.

"You are completely spoiled, you know that?" Adrian told the sheltie as he nudged a piece of toasted French bread onto the floor.

"So, where's our guest of honor?" Allison asked as she reached the bottom of the stairs with Scott right behind her. In complete contrast to his youngest sister, Alli had a petite build, hair as dark as his, and a shy manner that had caused men to overlook her for years—until Scott Lawrence had checked into the inn last spring.

"I told her six o'clock, so she should be down soon," he answered, then nodded to his future brother-in-law. "Hey, Scott. How goes the new book?"

"It goes," Scott sighed, looking like one of the villains in his own books in his all-black attire.

"Hey, Alli. Hey, Scott," Rory called as she gave up trying to feed Lauren and carried the baby to Chance.

Allison shrugged out of the cardigan sweater she wore over her long-sleeved T-shirt and jumper. "It's exciting, don't you think, to have Jackie here? Almost like a family reunion."

"Did she bring the letter?" Scott hung his jacket and Allison's sweater in the closet beneath the stairs. "After all the research I've done, I can't wait to read it. It's the last piece to the puzzle."

"She had it with her when she checked in." Rory went to wash her hands and help in the kitchen.

"Da-da-da-da." Lauren gave her father a slobbery, milky kiss on the cheek. Chance retaliated by lifting her frilly dress and giving her a raspberry on the tummy that sent the baby into peals of laughter.

As his sisters visited, Adrian realized how little nonworking time he spent with them these days. The inn hadn't even opened before Rory had moved into Chance's apartment. Chance had started out as their financial advisor and later became a partner, then part of the family when he married Rory. The two of them had built a small house just behind the inn, so they were nearby, but it wasn't the same as having Rory live under the same roof. And now Alli was marrying Scott, and they planned to live in the Bouchard Cottage in town.

The cottage had been built by Henri LeRoche as a way to banish his and Marguerite's daughter, Nicole, claiming she wasn't his daughter at all. And upon his death, Pearl Island and the LeRoche Shipping empire had gone to a nephew. Rather than fight him, Nicole had taken her mother's maiden name, then followed in Marguerite's footsteps to become a star of the stage in New York, London, and Paris, only to die divorced and destitute in the small Galveston cottage.

All of Nicole's descendants had lived in the cottage since, as those "scandalous Bouchards," whispered about by Galveston's "polite society." Adrian and his sisters had grown up in the cottage after their parents' death. But when Pearl Island had been foreclosed on by Chance's bank, they'd jumped on the opportunity to turn the old mansion into a bed-and-breakfast.

The cottage currently belonged to their aunt, Vivian Young, but since she lived in New York, she'd offered it to Scott and Allison. Which meant Adrian hardly saw either of his sisters in the evenings.

They all still worked together, with Rory and Chance handling the business end of things. Allison ran the gift shop, and Adrian handled the cooking. They served breakfast together each morning, and on Saturdays they served lunch on the veranda to the boatload of tourists Bobby and Paige brought for the Haunted House Lunch Run; but they never had time to sit and visit like a family anymore.

"You know, I've been thinking," he said as he set a plate of appetizers on the bar.

"Always a dangerous thing," Rory said.

"No." Adrian smirked playfully at her. "It's dangerous when *you* start thinking."

Chance choked, earning a sharp look from his wife.

"What I was about to say," Adrian continued, "is that we might want to reconsider the housing situation."

"What housing situation?" Rory asked, handing her daughter a piece of bread crust to gnaw on.

"The situation that has me living by myself in this four-bedroom apartment while you married people live in houses that are half the size. Doesn't this seem a little backward?"

"What do you suggest?" Allison asked. "That Scott and I move in here after the wedding and you move back to the cottage?"

"Wait a second." Scott held a hand up. "I like living in the cottage. And no offense, but I don't want to live here. I need privacy and quiet to write, not guests hounding me all day and night."

"Understandable," Adrian agreed. "But it seems ridiculous for me, the only single one left, to have the biggest place."

"Except you're the oldest," Rory said. "And you won't always be single."

"I plan to be for a while, at least. I mean, yeah, I'd like a wife and kids eventually, but not right away. I'm not even seeing anyone." Jackie sprang to mind, but he pushed the thought away. Even if she were interested, she didn't strike him as the kind of woman who was looking to get married—which would have made her perfect for his current interests if she weren't off limits.

Chance looked at him over the top of Lauren's head. "If Scott and Allison don't want to move, would you be interested in swapping with us?"

Adrian tried not to jump on the offer too fast, since he'd love nothing better than to swap living quarters with Chance and Rory. But he'd been hesitant to suggest it, because Chance had built the house behind the inn with his own money. He kept his voice nonchalant as he checked on dinner. "I might be persuaded."

Chance smiled sheepishly at his wife. "I have to admit, I've felt guilty for taking Aurora away from the inn. Part of her reason for buying the house and restoring it in the first place was because she's always dreamed of living here. Yet she's the one who never has, because of me."

"Like I regret marrying you." Rory smiled at him.

"No, but you do regret not getting to live here."

"True." She turned hopeful eyes to Adrian. "Would you really consider swapping with us?"

"It is a perfect solution," Adrian said. "You two will be on premise, which will make it easy for you to manage the inn, but I'll still be close enough to walk to work in the morning. That is, if Chance is willing to make me a good offer."

"We'll work something out on the money end," Chance said.

Rory looked at her brother. "Won't you be lonely, though, cut off from the inn?"

"Privacy? Quiet?" He sighed. "It'll be a burden, but I think I'll adjust."

A sound on the stairs drew his attention. He looked up to see Jackie standing on the bottom step—and did a double take when he noticed what she was wearing. It was a simple, long-sleeved T-shirt with horizontal stripes of red and white tucked into blue slacks. But it fit her more snugly than what she usually wore and had a scooped neck that showed a tantalizing hint of cleavage to a pair of incredible breasts.

The sight threw him, since he'd thought she was nearly flat-chested. Then he realized that every time he'd seen her, she'd been wearing one of those sports bras that squashed a woman flat, or a top so loose he couldn't tell what was beneath.

The fact that he'd found a flat-chested woman such a turn-on had mystified him, because he happened to like breasts. In fact, he considered them among God's finest creations. He'd reasoned that her spunky personality and sexy face had outweighed her lack of curves.

The realization that Jackie had a spunky personality, sexy face, *and* curves sent a rush of heat through him more intense than anything he'd felt since high school. *Oh, man,* he wanted to whimper, *why does she have to be off limits?*

"I, um . . ." She shifted nervously. "There wasn't a door, so I just came on down. I hope that's all right."

"Hmm?" Adrian shook himself. "Oh. Yes! Of course. Come in." He hurried over to usher her into the room. "We were all waiting for you. Let's see, it's been a while since you were here, so let me reintroduce everyone."

Jackie braced herself as he pulled her into the circle of his family. It wasn't that she disliked people; she liked them fine. She'd just never been good at idle chitchat. Give her a crew to command or passengers to welcome, and she did much better.

"You met my sister Aurora earlier—"

"Hi." Rory waved at her.

"—and this is her husband, Oliver Chancellor."

"It's good to see you again." Jackie offered her hand for a firm shake with the tall gangly blond man with wire-rimmed glasses and conservative haircut. She remembered Chance well enough to know he and Rory hadn't even been married the last time she'd been here, and now they were parents. She nodded to the baby in his arms. "You work fast."

"Apparently." Smiling, the man turned his daughter to show her off. "This is Lauren. Lauren, say hi to Captain Jackie." Lauren kicked her feet and let out an ear-piercing screech. Chance cringed at the sound. "We're, uh, still working on her social skills. Obviously."

"My other sister, Allison," Adrian continued.

"How do you do?" Allison greeted her with a soft smile and a friendly handshake. "We're delighted to have you stay with us."

"Thanks." Jackie returned the smile.

"Is that the letter?" Allison nodded at the envelope.

"Yes." Jackie's grip tightened.

"We can't wait to see it," Allison said.

"And this is Alli's fiancé, Scott Lawrence," Adrian finished.

"Ah yes, the writer." She shook his hand, taking in the dark hair, whiskey-colored eyes, and trimmed beard that accentuated, rather than softened, the sharp angles of his face. She searched for something appropriate to say. "I've read some of your books and always wondered, where do authors get their ideas?"

To her surprise, the man burst out laughing and turned to Allison. In unison, they said: "Online from Plots.com."

Heat climbed up Jackie's neck as she wondered what faux pas she'd committed.

"Sorry," Scott said, still smiling. "Inside joke. It's good to finally meet you in person."

She laughed self-consciously. "I wish I could say the same, but I haven't quite forgiven you for putting two and two together."

One of his black eyebrows arched upward. "You mean figuring out you're Jack Kingsley's descendant?"

"Exactly. Although I'm curious as to how you did figure it out."

"Your friend Bobby told me you were named after Jack Kingsley because your father was enamored of tales about Lafitte's missing treasure. So I started thinking,

'What if he named you after Jack for another reason?' Then I learned Jack Kingsley had had a child by a barmaid in Corpus Christi, and it clicked into place."

"That's all you had to go on when you got me to confess?" She shook her head in self-disgust.

"Sorry." He shrugged, clearly unrepentant. "But once I read the diaries, I couldn't let it go. I had to know what happened after they ended."

"Speaking of the diaries . . ." She glanced around. "When do I get to see them?"

"First we eat." Adrian plucked the envelope from her hand.

"Does food always take precedence over business for you?"

"Food is my business. And it's taught me that anticipation makes the dessert taste sweeter. Sort of like foreplay."

She started to complain as he carried the letter to the living area, but then he laid it on the coffee table next to a canvas book bag. Her interest was piqued as she realized the diaries must be in the bag.

"Bobby called to say they can't make it—Paige has the flu—so it'll just be us."

How in the world would she eat a bite, knowing the answers to so many questions sat there, waiting for her, mere feet away?

Chapter 6

A wonderful sort of chaos reigned throughout the evening as the family passed huge bowls of chicken pasta, tossed salad, and steamed vegetables around the table. Little Lauren, who truly was one of the cutest babies Jackie had ever seen, banged happily on the high-chair tray while a pretty sheltie cruised beneath the table for crumbs.

"So, tell us about your great-grandfather," Scott said as he passed Jackie a basket of bread. "What happened to him after Jack died?"

"Sweetheart, at least let her finish eating before you start interrogating her." Allison gave Jackie an apologetic look. "You'll have to forgive Scott. Ever since he read the diaries, he's been fascinated by Jack Kingsley."

"And frustrated by how little I've learned."

Jackie looked at Adrian. "I thought you said the diaries told all about Jack Kingsley."

"They reveal what manner of man he is, but very little about his past or his family history."

"Apparently, he didn't like to talk about himself." Allison gave her fiancé a meaningful look. "Sort of like someone else we know."

"Few men want to parade their past sins before a woman they're trying to impress," Scott said.

"Only because they underestimate a woman's ability to admire them even more for what they've overcome." Allison smiled at him.

Watching them, Jackie felt a pang of envy. What would it be like to have that sort of total acceptance?

Scott turned back to her. "Not to badger you, but can you tell us anything about your great-grandfather? Marguerite mentioned his name was Andrew Kingsley even though Jack never married the mother, but I can't find him in any of the census records after the Civil War."

"Actually, he's my great-*great*-grandfather, but that's such a mouthful, I usually shorten it."

"Same for us and Marguerite," Adrian said. " 'Great-great-great-grandmother' sounds like we're stuttering."

"Exactly." Jackie nodded. "Anyway, he was christened Andrew Taylor Kingsley. Andrew after his father, whose full name was Andrew Jackson Kingsley, and Taylor because it was his mother's last name."

"Jack's name was Andrew Jackson?" Rory asked, wiping a glob of orange baby food from her daughter's hair. "Well, there's something Marguerite never mentioned. No, no, peanut, let's *eat* the carrots, not *wear* them."

"Ca-ca!" Lauren shouted loudly, making Jackie blink with the force of her lungs while Adrian and Scott burst out laughing.

"Don't laugh," Rory pleaded. "You'll just encourage her."

"Ca-ca!"

Chance shook his head. "Every time she says that, it sounds like she's saying S-H-I-T in Spanish. And wouldn't you know, carrots are her favorite food."

Jackie hid a smile as the baby clapped her sticky hands. Lord, she was adorable.

"Ca-ca! Ca-ca!"

Chance turned to Jackie with a long-suffering sigh. "You were saying . . ."

Jackie pulled her attention away from Lauren. "I was just explaining why there's no Andrew Kingsley in the census records. He went by Andrew Taylor after his father died."

"Why?" Adrian asked from the opposite end of the table, where he sat as the head of the family.

"Well, you know . . ." Jackie looked around uneasily.

"Ah, let me guess." Adrian topped off his glass of wine. "Did it have anything to do with Henri's accusations that Jack Kingsley was a Yankee spy, so that he could literally get away with murder?"

"I don't think Andrew believed it." Jackie toyed with the pasta on her plate, wishing she had more of an appetite. The little bit she'd managed to eat tasted incredible. "He had the letter that claimed otherwise, but during and after the Civil War, being connected to an accused Yankee spy could be hazardous to one's health. The crew members of the *Freedom* who survived had to scatter and go into hiding for fear they'd be killed. Through the years, most of my family has preferred to deny the connection. The war may be over, but Southerners have long memories."

"True," Adrian said. "But in this case unfair, to Jack and to your family."

"Although," Allison said, as she passed the bread, "it's one more reason to excavate the *Freedom*. We'll all be working closely with the Galveston Historical Society on the museum display, and we want to be sure the right story is told. We want people to finally know the truth about Jack and Marguerite. Even if that means including excerpts from the diaries, something we've never shared before."

"And your letter," Rory said to Jackie, as the baby started to fidget. Now that the meal was winding down, Rory pulled Lauren from the high chair onto her lap.

Jackie looked at everyone around the table, frowning. "Won't it bother all of you that telling the truth means telling the world that Henri LeRoche was the leader of a smuggling ring and a murderer?"

"Not at all." Allison looked at her in surprise. "After what our family has put up with since he disowned his daughter, Nicole, having people know the truth about Henri will be long-awaited justice."

"But Henri is as much your ancestor as Nicole and Marguerite," Jackie pointed out. "Having people know about him won't bother you?"

"Well, it's not like his sins have anything to do with us personally," Rory said. "The important ones are Jack and Marguerite. After all these years of waiting, they deserve to be exonerated." She looked at her siblings. "Right?"

Jackie saw a flash in Adrian's eyes as he glanced her way, a moment's hesitation. And she knew in that instant that he and his sisters actually believed Jack and Marguerite were trapped between worlds. She looked at Scott and Chance for their reaction, but they were calmly finishing their dinners, showing no surprise at Rory's statement. So that was why they were doing this. These people believed in ghosts.

She looked back at Adrian. *You can't be serious.*

He lifted his wine glass. "To Jack and Marguerite . . . and the truth."

"May it help to set them free," Allison added, touching her glass to her brother's with a bell-like ring.

"To Jack and Marguerite," the others echoed, raising their glasses.

Jackie joined the toast even as her mind raced. Did they think clearing Jack's name of false charges would free his spirit? The thought of erasing that one blemish at least from her family name thrilled her on one level, but frightened her on another. Searching for truth held all the dangers of opening Pandora's box.

How did one control how much truth escaped?

As she lowered her glass, she found Adrian watching her. Worry showed in his eyes and she could almost read his mind: *You're not going to back out, are you?*

No, she sighed. He and his sisters might be nuts, but at this point she was committed.

"Okay, then," he said, standing. "If everyone's done, why don't we have dessert in the living room so we can take a look at the letter?"

Jackie's stomach churned as she realized the time had come. Allison and Scott started clearing the table while Adrian headed for the kitchen to serve dessert.

"I need to change Lauren's diaper," Rory said. "Don't y'all dare get started without me."

"Who wants coffee?" Chance asked, then glanced at Jackie. "That's my one culinary achievement—brewing the coffee. You want some?"

"I'll stick with wine, thanks," she said, deciding she might need it to settle her nerves. "Is there anything I can do to help, though?"

"Absolutely not," Adrian said. "You're the guest of honor. Just sit back and let us wait on you." She chafed a bit at being cut out of the tight circle, but when it came to families, she supposed she should be used to being the outsider.

Within minutes, she found herself seated in an armchair in the living area with a plate of Black Forest cake that looked delicious even though she knew she couldn't possibly eat a bite. Adrian sat in a straight-backed chair beside her, having no trouble devouring his dessert. Rory and Chance settled on the sofa as Lauren lay on her tummy between them, showing the first signs that her energy wasn't infinite.

"So, who's going to read the letter?" Rory asked.

"Me!" Scott said as he took the chair opposite Jackie. Allison perched on the arm, balancing her dessert plate as she ate.

"Why you?" Adrian challenged.

"Hey," Scott said, "if it weren't for me, y'all wouldn't even know it existed."

"True," Adrian conceded. "So I guess the honor goes to you, unless . . ." He turned to Jackie. "Do you want to read it?"

She shook her head, trying to relax.

"Okay, then." Scott wiped his fingers thoroughly on a napkin before opening the large envelope. For the first time that evening, the room fell quiet as he extracted the protective sleeves that held several aged and brittle pages.

Jackie kept her eyes fixed on her wine glass. If Adrian and his sisters believed in ghosts, they were going to love the very part of the letter she feared would make most people doubt its validity.

" 'Dear Andrew,' " Scott began, his voice relaxed yet resonant, as if accustomed to reading aloud. " 'It is with sincerest regret that I have not written sooner. By now, I know news of your father's death has reached you along with any number of rumors. First let me assure you that those who accuse your father of betraying the South are nothing but lying traitors themselves who seek to cover up their own treachery. Your father loved four things in this world: you, Texas, his ship, and a woman named Marguerite. He would never, nor did he ever, betray any of those loyalties.

"'Forgive me. I've hardly begun, and already I digress. I shall endeavor to speak simply, so as not to confuse you more, though I must confess, after these past months, my passions run high.'" Scott glanced up at Jackie. "I take it the man wasn't used to corresponding with children."

"I don't think so, no."

"How old was Andrew?" Rory asked.

"Nine or ten." She cleared her throat. "Old enough to understand he'd lost his father and that people were saying some horrible things about him."

"Tough age," Scott said before going back to the letter. He read on about the night of the tragedy, of how Jack had received word from Marguerite saying Henri had found out about them and she feared for her life and the life of her child. The letter relayed it all in chilling detail, the lightning and thunder, anger and fear, as if the man scribbling words across page after page were exorcising his own demons in an outpouring of emotion.

"'When the first blast from the cannon struck the ship, the captain took the wheel himself, looking as if he meant to run the ship right onto the beach in his effort to reach Marguerite. I argued with him to bring the ship about, but he shook me off. Then a second cannon blast caught us, igniting the gunpowder in the hold.

"'I saw in his eyes he knew we were sinking. At last, he gave the order to abandon ship. Yet rather than head for the lifeboats with the rest of us, he ran through the flames toward his quarters. I went after him, I swear upon my honor. You must believe me when I say I did not abandon him to his own insanity in that final hour. Still did he push me away, shouting that he would not leave the ship without the treasure.

"'I pray that you remember the treasure of which I speak, for I heard him tell you many times the tale of Jean Lafitte and his grandfather as he showed you the powder horn that hung in his cabin on the wall behind his desk—'" Scott glanced up, excitement lighting his eyes.

"Wow . . ." Chance sat forward, shoving his wire-rimmed glasses higher on his nose. "That couldn't be more perfect."

"No kidding." Adrian set his plate aside. "It's exactly what we need—confirmation that the powder horn was on board, plus an indication of where."

"Okay, great, but read the rest." Rory waved a hand at Scott.

He turned his attention back to the letter. "'As your father raced down the passageway ahead of me, a great blast came from beneath us. The heat and fire knocked me back toward the hatch. When I recovered enough to stand, I saw a sight I shall never forget.

"'At the end of the passageway, I saw your father trying to open the door to his cabin, yet he could not. His hand passed through the handle, unable to turn it. I heard him roar in frustration just as one of the masts crashed to the deck, and I stumbled to keep upright.

"'It was then I realized the figure at the end of the passageway couldn't be the captain, only my wild imaginings, for your father lay dead at my feet.

"'I carried him to a lifeboat, refusing to leave him to a watery grave, yet did that strange apparition of him remain behind, as if even in death, he could not leave the powder horn behind. The memory of it haunts me still, compelling me to write and tell you why Lafitte's treasure meant so much to him. He wanted to pass it on to you as a symbol of all his dreams for your future, all his hopes that he had passed on to you the best of his blood, not the worst.

" 'I sailed with your father for many years, Andrew, and I know what honor meant to him. I pray you now and always to remember that. To remember everything your father ever told you about facing life with true courage. If only he had realized that that was the treasure he had to leave you, not a mere object from your family's past.

" 'The powder horn is gone, sunk in the cove of Pearl Island. But your father's dream for you lives on, of that I am certain. Treasure that, and hold this letter close to help you remember. Live honorably as your father lived in his last years. Do not take the easy route to riches, but seek the path that will let you live in peace with yourself. And learn to value those things that have worth beyond monetary measure.

" 'Respectfully Yours, Bernard Kramer—' " Scott frowned, then cleared his throat. "He, um, started to sign it 'First Officer of the *Freedom*,' but crossed that out and signed it, 'Your Friend.' "

A moment of silence followed. "Well." Adrian released a pent-up breath. "That's some letter."

"Yes." Jackie cleared her throat. "That's why my family kept it."

"And we're glad they did." He smiled at her softly. Then, without warning, he took her hand and brought her to her feet as he stood. She found herself engulfed in a brotherly embrace, and too startled to return it. "Thank you," he said, releasing her. Before she could recover, Aurora and Allison were there, hugging her in turn, both of them crying.

"Yes, thank you," Allison said. "We know this isn't easy for you. We understand."

Looking into her eyes, Jackie realized they did understand. All of them. Suddenly, she wasn't outside the circle, but standing right in the middle. The show of acceptance made some unfamiliar emotion expand inside her chest as everyone resumed talking at once. Their voices and excitement swirled around her and the newness of solidarity filled her so completely, she feared she'd start crying, too.

Chapter 7

Jackie stood on the balcony outside her room gazing up at the night sky and listening to the wind rustle through the trees. The fist of anxiety that had gripped her stomach for the past week had finally relaxed; not completely, but enough for her to do something she hadn't done in years: dream about the future.

The St. Claires' excitement had proved infectious. Perhaps tomorrow everything would go well and this would be the start of an exciting and lucrative endeavor.

On the horizon, a falling star streaked across the sky.

She wanted to laugh as she remembered all those childhood wishes made on stars, wishes for a place to belong filled with security and love. How did the old rhyme go? *I wish I may, I wish I might . . .*

Odd, but she couldn't remember the rest. Even so, she squeezed her eyes tight and made a wish with all her heart: *Please, God, don't let me screw this up.*

As if in answer, a burst of night wind kissed her cheeks and ruffled her hair. She hugged the moment to her, committing it to memory: the scent of flowers blooming below her, the rustling of the palm trees, the chill in the air, all held a sense of magic.

A loud click sounded behind her. She whirled just as

one of the tall windows into the hall swung open and she realized it was a door, like the one that led into her room. Adrian stuck his head out.

"I thought I saw someone out here."

She slapped a hand over her racing heart. "You startled me."

"Sorry." He stepped onto the balcony. "I expected you to be sound asleep, or sitting in bed reading the diaries."

"I meant to do just that," she admitted. Her senses, already alive with the night, tingled at his nearness. "But I'm too anxious about tomorrow to read or sleep. What has you up prowling at this hour?"

"Same thing, I guess. Plus, I remembered I hadn't made my rounds to lock up." He came to stand beside her, leaning sideways against the rail, his expression playful. "If you're interested, I know the perfect cure for sleeplessness."

"I just bet you do." She chuckled.

"Good God, the woman laughs." He put a hand to his heart.

"You've heard me laugh before."

"But not often enough. A shame, too." His gaze held hers. "You have a really great laugh. Low and sexy with no girly giggling. A woman's laugh."

Her heart sped up at his words. Flustered, she looked up at the sky. "Do you know, I think you can see nearly as many stars from here as you can out in the Caribbean."

"Really?" He looked up. "Hey, I have an idea. Let's grab a blanket and go lie on the beach to count stars. You know, sort of like counting sheep."

"Yeah, right!" She laughed. "Adrian, tell me, honestly, do you ever think about anything but sex? And food, of course."

He cocked his head, studying her. "Actually, I was serious." Then a mischievous smile had his dimples flashing. "But if you'd rather have sex, I'm game."

She shook her head and resumed stargazing. "I like your family."

"Let's see, changing the subject means no to sex, right?" He gave a loud sigh. "Okay, but I've heard it's a great sleep aid."

"Are you saying sex with you would be so boring, it would put me to sleep?"

"Oh, you are a cruel woman, throwing out a challenge like that when you know I can't take you inside and prove you wrong."

She cocked her head, studying him. "This flirting really is just a game to you, isn't it? You have no real intention of seducing me."

It was his turn to scoff. "As if you'd let me."

If only he knew! "I'm glad to see you're smart enough to recognize an impossible feat."

"You *are* tempting fate, now, with two challenges in a row."

She leaned slightly toward him and pitched her voice low. "Maybe I like living dangerously."

His gaze dropped to the scooped neck of her top. "Must be all that pirate blood."

"Must be." Although he was right, she was tempting fate standing alone with him on a moonlit balcony.

"So, how about it?" He rested his weight on one elbow, bringing his face down to her eye level. "You wanna walk down to the cove and lie on the beach?"

"Do I look stupid? I know what happens when a man and a woman take a blanket down to a beach at night. Besides, don't you have to be up early to cook breakfast?"

"I'll manage." His gaze moved over her face. "And we already agreed I'm not going to seduce you, so you have nothing to fear." ·

"No. We agreed that I won't let you seduce me." She grinned at him, feeling reckless. "However, I'll tell you what I will let you do."

"Oh?" His eyes lit with interest.

She stepped before him, and he turned to face her, his back to the rail, his weight on both forearms. His expression turned wary when she straddled his feet and placed her hands on the rail to either side of him. She leaned so close, their bodies nearly touching but not quite. With her lips near his ear, she could feel the heat of his skin, smell his scent, almost hear his heart beat.

"In the morning . . ." she whispered in a husky voice, "I'll let you cook my eggs . . . hard and scrambled . . . and serve my bacon . . . crisp."

She saw him shudder and felt an echo of it flutter in her own stomach.

Pulling back, she found his eyes had gone dark and the teasing smile had finally vanished. He didn't move a single muscle, just watched her with a hungry gaze as she stepped away.

"Sweet dreams." Smiling, she turned and walked as sensuously as she knew how to the door to her room, then glanced over her shoulder.

He stared at her as if fighting the urge to pounce.

She slipped inside, and the second she had the door closed, she clamped a hand over her mouth to stifle her laughter. She couldn't believe it. She'd finally figured out the way to best Adrian at his own game: fight fire with fire. A very apt phrase, she thought, fanning herself.

Although how would she ever sleep with her pulse hopping like the beat of a steel-drum band? Her gaze fell on the diaries, which she'd left on the nightstand. A little reading might distract her from fantasies of rolling naked on a beach with Adrian.

After changing into an oversized T-shirt, she climbed in bed and searched through the stack of leather-bound volumes for the one she wanted. Allison had put them in chronological order but had bookmarked the first mention of Jack Kingsley. Stuffing a pillow behind her, she opened to the bookmarked page. She fully intended to read all the diaries, but couldn't resist reading this one entry out of order.

Her eyes scanned the first few sentences, and she scowled in disappointment. It was a description of what Marguerite planned to wear for dinner that night. As if Jackie cared about women's fashion in the 1800s. As she read more, though, she caught the bitterness behind the words and realized the newly arrived gown from Paris was something her husband had commanded her to wear.

Apparently, Henri was throwing a lavish dinner party for the captains who carried cargo for his shipping company. Marguerite described the expected guests as the "coarsest of seafaring men who will devour every delicacy put before them with all the manners of drunken sailors in a dockside tavern while Henri secretly laughs at their crudeness."

The low-cut gown would also have the all-male dinner guests salivating onto their plates, making Henri feel even more superior since she "belonged" to him.

What a jerk, Jackie thought, recoiling at the plight of women in a time when they were little more than property.

The exquisite sapphire bracelets Marguerite would wear
with the gown suddenly sounded more like a prisoner's
manacles than fine jewelry.

With a note of resignation, Marguerite ended the
diary entry in order to dress.

A second entry for the same day followed, though,
and Jackie's attention was piqued, since it had been written after the party.

> *Tonight at dinner there was a man, a man I've
> not seen before. He was a sea captain, like the
> others, and yet not like them at all. I still can pic-
> ture how he looked in that first moment I saw
> him. Seated near the head of the table next to
> Henri, he was leaning back in his chair, holding
> a goblet of wine. He watched the room with lazy
> eyes and a half-smile that said he found the other
> men amusing but beneath him. There was about
> him an unmistakable arrogance, as if he, not the
> painted Neptune over his head, commanded the
> very tides to do his bidding.*
>
> *Then his eyes lifted and he saw me. For the
> barest heartbeat, the detachment vanished and
> he looked . . . surprised. He rose with the kind of
> gallantry I once took for granted and now sorely
> miss. And as his gaze held mine I saw such admi-
> ration that some of the numbness in which I've
> cloaked myself these past years faded. I felt raw,
> exposed. Like a person again, rather than a
> porcelain possession with no purpose save that
> of being displayed. I cannot recall what he said
> to me by way of a greeting, but the respect in his
> voice nearly made me weep.*

*I could almost hate him for that, for making
me feel again. Yet, a part of me yearns to see him
once more. As painful as it was to be in his presence, for a moment this evening I remembered
that I am still a woman, I am still alive, and I am
still capable of longing for love.*

Jackie stared at the page, caught off guard by an
instant stab of kinship. Tonight, watching the St. Claires,
she too had longed for things she'd thought she'd forgotten: family, home, a sense of belonging. No wonder she'd
almost cried when Adrian and his sisters hugged her.
Hope could be both joyful and painful.

Marguerite's hope had ended in tragedy. A warning
Jackie decided to heed as she set the diaries aside and
turned out the light. And yet, she thought as she lay in the
dark, sometimes, surely, as long as one didn't dream too
big, dreams could come true. Couldn't they?

Chapter 8

The following morning, Adrian headed for Chance's BMW parked in the small lot behind the inn. He planned to ride with Rory and Chance and meet the others at the Visitors' Center. The throaty rumble of a big engine came up behind him and he turned to find Jackie sitting in a truly ugly pickup truck on which blue paint fought a losing battle with primer gray.

She rolled down the window and flashed him a playful grin. "Hey, mister, need a lift?"

"I don't know . . ." He made his expression intentionally leery, remembering last night on the balcony. "Will I be safe?"

She laughed. "What if I promise to be on *my* best behavior?"

"If your best behavior is like mine, that's not very reassuring."

"Do you really want it to be?"

The look of sensual challenge she gave him set off danger sirens in his head even as his body hummed with glee. He stepped over to Rory, who was buckling Lauren into the baby seat. "I'll meet y'all there, okay?"

"What?" Rory glanced from him to Jackie and back again. Her brow arched in speculation. "Oh, okay."

"Now, don't be getting any ideas," he told her. "We're just playing around. But *not* the way you're thinking."

Rory gave him a sure-you're-not look, which he ignored. Crossing to the truck, he opened the passenger door, then waited for Jackie to make room on the seat by moving a toolbox into the back of the cab.

"Just kick that stuff out of the way," she said, motioning to the rigging blocks that littered the floorboard.

He climbed in and rolled the window down to enjoy the crisp fall weather as they followed Chance's car along the winding, sun-dappled drive. Shifting to face Jackie, he soaked in the sight of her in a denim shirt, silver earrings, and sunglasses. "Did you like your breakfast?"

"I did." She laughed, and the rich sound turned the low hum in his belly to a steady purr. "Although I'd like to know what you told Rory, because she gave me a really funny look when she brought out the plate of bacon and eggs made to order just for me."

"Funny look?" Actually, he hadn't told Rory anything. He'd just handed her the plate and asked her to take it to Jackie. "Funny how?"

Jackie tipped her head to look at him over her shades. "Like she was trying to figure out if we had something going on and found the possibility hunky-dory with her."

"Rory finds a lot of things in life hunky-dory."

"I've noticed that." The breeze through the windows picked up as they reached the short causeway that connected Pearl Island to Galveston. "Maybe you should explain to your sister that we're not each other's type."

"As a matter of fact, I just told her something to that effect," he said, then scowled. "What do you mean, 'not each other's type'? What kind of man is your type?"

"For a serious relationship?" She mulled that over.

"Quiet, reliable, and not so gorgeous I'd spend all my time beating off the competition."

"I'm reliable."

"One out of three?" That really got her laughing. "Sorry, mister, not good enough."

So she did find him attractive, just not in a serious-relationship sort of way. Which was good, he assured himself. Having Jackie fall for him would complicate things. He'd been through that with too many co-workers back in his days as assistant chef at Chez Lafitte. Still, he was starting to chafe at her cracks about his looks and taste in women. "You overestimate my appeal, and underestimate your own."

"Oh yeah?" Her brows went up. "Are you saying you're ready to forsake your legions of admirers to pursue me and only me?"

He studied her, thinking she was just a little too cocky from one-upping him last night. "I don't know." He let loose a sensual smile and lowered his eyelids halfway. "Are you willing to make it worth my while?"

"Ha! In your dreams."

"Oh yeah," he sighed suggestively, intrigued by the color that flooded her cheeks. "I definitely had a few of those last night. How about you?"

"Dreams?" She cocked her head, suddenly lost in her own thoughts. "I may have had a few myself."

"Oh? Care to tell me about them?"

She shook her head. "Why don't you tell me who all will be at this meeting?"

"Changing the subject again." He sighed. "You're good at evasive actions."

"The meeting . . ." she prompted.

"Okay, okay." He turned his mind toward business.

"Chance's father, Norman Chancellor, is heading up the Historical Society subcommittee for this project, so he and his volunteers will be there. But that's about it, other than the marine archeologist they're hoping to hire."

She straightened her arms against the steering wheel as if bracing herself. "I can't believe I'm really going through with this."

He looked at her more closely. "You really are nervous, aren't you?"

Terrified, she wanted to say, but just shook her head. For today, she was going to cross her fingers and hope for the best.

They reached the Visitors' Center—located in the historic district amid antique shops and art galleries—and she pulled into a parking lot. Stepping out of the truck, Jackie noticed the tourists milling about the sidewalks. The smell of fresh seafood drifted on the air along with the sound of horse-drawn carriages. The tall masts of the *Elissa* rose above the restaurants and shops along the bayside pier, marking the Texas Seaport Museum.

"Looks like Scott and Alli are already here," Rory called to them as she freed the baby from the car seat. "But then, I guess we're running a little late."

Watching Chance wrestle a stroller and diaper bag from the trunk, Jackie marveled that people with kids managed to go anywhere, much less be on time. Although maybe it just took practice.

When they entered the center, two elderly volunteers greeted them by name. Spying Lauren, the women came forward to coo in admiration. Jackie watched the parents' glowing pride, and felt the same tug of envy she'd felt last night watching Alli and Scott.

"Is my father here?" Chance asked.

"He's in the meeting room," one of the volunteers said.

"Great." Chance extracted them from Lauren's admirers and led the way past bookshelves, brochures, and cases of souvenirs, to a door at the back.

Jackie followed them into a small meeting room where Scott and Allison stood with a handful of other people eating pastries and drinking coffee. She felt the excitement like a tangible buzz in the air, and realized how important this project would be, not just to the St. Claires, but to the whole town. The museum exhibit would offer a new attraction to a town that thrived on tourism.

And Jack Kinglsey would finally have the recognition he deserved for his contribution to the South during the war.

Moving toward the table with the coffee service, she let her gaze drift toward two men who stood apart from the others. The taller of the two looked so much like Chance, tall and thin with that sheen of "old money," she knew he had to be Norman Chancellor. The stockier man had his back to her, but held himself with a controlled strength that stirred some distant memory. Then, he turned enough for her to see his profile, and her stomach dropped to her feet. Carl Ryder.

She stopped so abruptly that Adrian plowed into the back of her.

"Oops, sorry." He grabbed her shoulders to keep them both from falling. She whirled around, her heart pounding with panic. Adrian leaned back, studying her face. "Hey, you okay?"

"I—I suddenly don't feel so good." An inner voice screamed for her to run straight for her truck. She could race back to the inn, grab her stuff, and be out of town in minutes.

"Oliver, Aurora," the taller gentleman called. "Come meet Mr. Ryder. Carl, my son Oliver Chancellor and his wife. And this is my grandbaby, Lauren."

Jackie peeked over her shoulder as Chance and Rory joined the two men. Of all the marine archeologists in the world, why did they have to hire Carl Ryder for this project?

"We're so pleased to meet you," Rory said, looking slightly awed. Although why wouldn't she be? Carl might look like an easygoing guy with sun-bleached hair and ruddy complexion, but something about the set of his wide shoulders, the calmness of his blue eyes, made people admire him instantly.

The admiration was well deserved since he had credentials out the yazoo and a rock-solid code of ethics. Blast him, why couldn't he be off working for some museum, retired from active diving?

"Jackie?" Adrian asked, drawing her attention back to him. He searched her eyes. "What's wrong? You look like you're about to throw up."

I might.

"All right, folks," Chance's father said. "Now that we're all here, let's get this meeting under way."

Chairs scraped the floor as people settled around the conference table.

"Come on." Adrian rubbed her upper arms in a gesture of comfort. "Grab a seat and I'll get you a cup of water."

There was nothing she could do at this point but brazen it out and pray that Carl didn't recognize her, which was possible since he hadn't seen her since she was a gangly teenager. With a deep breath, she turned around. Carl had just taken a seat at the head of the table, opposite from where she stood. He looked up, smiled absently at her, and started to look away. Then his gaze snapped back and he froze.

A burst of laughter followed his surprise. "You've got to be kidding me." He gestured toward her, but addressed the others taking their seats. "If this is who's providing the key evidence you promised, I'm afraid you people have been had."

Heads turned up and down the long length of the table as everyone looked from him to her in confusion.

"Excuse me?" Norman Chancellor said.

"Well, Jackie?" Carl cocked a brow. "What do you want to do?"

She flushed hot and cold, not knowing what to say as shame burned a hole in her stomach.

"Tell you what." Carl leaned forward, folding his hands on the table. "If you're willing to give up on whatever you had planned, I'll let you walk out of here without an embarrassing scene. None of these good people need to know a thing."

The impulse to bolt returned, but if she did, he'd believe the worst, that she'd come here to steal.

"Jackie?" Adrian squeezed her shoulders. "What's this about?"

Carl kept watching her, waiting. "Your call."

Her hands started to tighten into fists until she remembered she held the envelope with the letter inside. She forced her fingers to relax. "What happened in the islands years ago has nothing to do with this, Mr. Ryder, so I see little reason to bring it up."

"Gee, I don't know." Carl's chair creaked in protest as he leaned back. "It all sounds ridiculously familiar to me:

Buddy Taylor claiming to have a letter that leads to sunken treasure, talking decent, hardworking people into investing money to go after it. So, where is Buddy? Waiting for you to set up the marks before he comes walking in offering his services?"

"My father's dead."

Surprise flickered in Carl's eyes. What followed might have been sorrow, but he looked away too quickly for her to be sure. "I . . . I didn't know. When?"

The sudden lack of hostility confused her, until she remembered that Buddy and Carl had been friends once, a long time ago. Could it be that by-the-book Carl Ryder was sorry to hear of Buddy's death?

"It happened eight years ago," she told him. "On a dive in the Tobago Cays."

"How?"

"I'd rather not get into that here." She kept her eyes focused on Carl, not able to look at Adrian's family for fear of the shock she'd see in their eyes. "I assure you, Mr. Ryder, this isn't a con. The letter I have is real."

"Pardon me if I remain skeptical," Carl said.

"I'm not stupid," she said through clenched teeth. "This is Texas, not the Caribbean. The laws here concerning shipwreck excavation are some of the strictest on the planet and I know the steps involved in getting a permit. I'm not dumb enough to try and slip a forged document past the Texas Historical Commission."

Carl just stared at her.

"One moment," Adrian said, stepping out from behind her so that he stood between her and Carl. "I don't know what's going on here, but my family and I are the ones who approached Jackie, not the other way around, so I assure you she isn't conning anyone."

"Isn't that how all the best cons start'?" Carl asked. "With the marks thinking it was all their idea?"

"And secondly," Adrian went on, "the letter can be easily authenticated, so this argument is pointless. Besides, it's only part of the evidence we've brought. Unless you want to start casting doubt on all of us, I suggest you at least hear us out. Or we can always look for another archeologist to head this project."

Carl glanced around the table, but Jackie still couldn't bring herself to look at anyone. Finally Carl held out his hand. "Let me see the letter."

Everything in her longed to say "screw you" and walk out. Instead, she forced herself to walk the gauntlet of stares to where he sat and hand the envelope to him.

Carl pulled the protective plastic sleeves out, skimmed the letter, then set it aside and addressed Adrian rather than her. "Okay, here's what I'm willing to do. I'll listen to whatever evidence you have to support your claim, then I'll send Ms. Taylor's letter to a lab to have it tested. If everything checks out, then we'll talk more."

People shifted uncomfortably as questioning glances bounced around the room. Jackie's stomach churned. Would the Historical Society want out of the project now that Carl had raised doubts?

Adrian pulled out a chair and nodded for her to have a seat. The solid faith in his eyes made her throat close. She took the seat, knowing the letter was real, but fearing Carl would still advise the commission to deny the permit simply because of her involvement.

Across from her, Scott opened a file folder. "I, um, brought several photocopies I obtained from various museums of letters and documents that support the historical significance of the powder horn"—he aimed a look at Mr. Ryder—"so there shouldn't be any question about their authenticity."

As Scott went into his report, Adrian took the only remaining chair, far down from her.

I'm sorry, she tried to tell him with her eyes. *I know how much you want this, and now I may have ruined it for all of you.*

He gave her a reassuring smile. Rather than ease her guilt, his trust turned her humiliation to anger directed solely at herself because she should have known better. Things like this always happened when she dared to reach for something good. Like Marguerite, she should have stuck with resignation and simple survival.

Chapter 9

Jackie lit out of the meeting so fast, her truck was gone by the time Adrian reached the parking lot. He caught a ride with Rory and Chance and fumed all the way back to the inn.

"Poor Jackie," Rory said from the back seat where she entertained the baby with a stuffed rabbit. "I can't believe Mr. Ryder spoke to her that way."

Chance nodded. "He definitely could have handled the situation better. Like taken her outside to talk privately so the whole committee didn't hear."

"Do you think they'll change their minds about backing the project?" Rory asked.

"Not unless the letter proves to be a fake."

"It won't," Rory insisted with easy faith. "But I'm still worried about Jackie. She looked so upset. I'd die of embarrassment if something like that happened to me. Adrian, you'll check on her as soon as we get home, won't you?"

"Of course," he answered tightly, wishing Chance would break a law just once in his life and drive faster than the speed limit.

When they reached the inn, Adrian went straight to Jackie's room but stopped at the closed door. Never had he trespassed on a guest's privacy, but then, Jackie wasn't a paying guest of the inn. She was a personal guest of the family. Still, he hesitated before knocking. When she didn't answer, his concern mounted.

"Jackie," he called, and knocked again, hoping she wasn't in there crying. The thought of anyone bringing her to tears made him want to hit something. Or someone. "Come on, Jackie, I know you're in there. I saw your truck out front."

The door was jerked open and there she stood, with fury rather than tears blazing in her eyes. "What!"

His head snapped back. "What do you mean, what? I came to see if you're all right."

"I'm fine," she said between clenched teeth.

"No you're not. You're upset, and I don't blame you. Carl Ryder is a total ass."

"Carl Ryder is a perfectly decent man. All he did was speak the truth."

"He accused you of being a con artist."

"Exactly!"

He shook his head in confusion. "Can I come in?"

"Suit yourself. It's your place." She marched to the bed where she'd thrown her clothes in a pile next to her duffel bag.

"What are you doing?"

"What does it look like I'm doing?" She grabbed a shirt and stuffed it into the bag. "I'm saving you the trouble of asking me to leave."

"What the hell gave you the idea we'd want you to leave?"

"Gee, I don't know." She trailed her hand in the air. "Maybe the fact that most people don't want a crook staying in their house, much less go into business with one.

You heard what Carl said." She grabbed another shirt and wadded it into a ball.

"Yes, but now I want to hear your side." He caught her wrist as she tried to shove the shirt in the bag. "Would you quit packing for just a minute and talk to me?" Pushing the clothes aside, he sat on the bed and tugged her arm until she relented and sat down beside him. "Now, tell me what this is all about."

She leaned forward, bracing her elbows on her knees, and dropped her face in her hands. "Everything Carl said is true. My dad was a crook, among other things."

"What does that have to do with you?"

"Adrian . . ." She lifted her head enough to stare at him. "He was my father. He raised me."

"So?"

"Okay, you clearly aren't getting the picture here, so let me bring it into focus." She stood and paced. "My parents divorced when I was five and I came to live with my grandparents in Corpus Christi. Except, every summer, I'd live with my father on his boat in the Caribbean."

"The *Pirate's Pleasure*?"

"No. The *Pirate's Pleasure* was a wreck back then. We worked together to restore it whenever he came to visit me and his parents. He had a sailboat, though, that was big enough to live on. He rented it and himself out to people who wanted to sail around the islands. That's partly how he made his living. Although he made more money scuba diving."

"How do you make money scuba diving?"

"My father had a real talent for finding sunken treasure, not just Spanish doubloons, although you'd be shocked at how much of that litters the floor of the Gulf, but newly lost items like jewelry. That's how he could afford the *Pirate's Pleasure*."

"Your father made enough money scuba diving to buy and restore a Baltimore schooner?"

"Oh, yeah." She leaned her hips back against the vanity. "You wouldn't believe what you can find diving with a metal detector around beaches, especially in resort areas. Think of all those tourists slicking their bodies down with oil, then jumping in the salt water wearing engagement rings with diamonds and other jewelry. We'd bring up thousands of dollars' worth of gold and gems every summer."

"If it's that easy, why doesn't everyone do it?"

"It's not that easy. It takes patience and skill. You could let ten people comb a beach before my father, and he'd still come up with the lion's share of prizes. Same thing with old wreck sites. And because he was so good, he became something of a legend among treasure hunting enthusiasts. So they'd hire him to take them on dives."

"I fail to see how any of this makes him a crook."

With a sigh of frustration, she combed her hair back with both hands. "For one thing, plundering shipwrecks is illegal, it's just easier to get away with it in the Caribbean than here in the States. And . . ." She took a deep breath. "Diving around real wrecks weren't the only treasure hunts Dad led."

"Oh?"

"Yeah." She rubbed her stomach to ease the burning. "While he had people out on the sailboat, he'd spin stories about Jean Lafitte, supposedly handed down through our family, then he'd 'let it slip' that he had a letter with clues to the location of Lafitte's missing treasure, claiming the treasure wasn't in Texas at all, like most people think, but that Lafitte took a large amount of gold with him when he headed for South America. Dad would say the gold went down somewhere in the southern end of the West Indies, where Lafitte practiced piracy during his later days. 'If only I had more money to search for the ship,' Dad would say. And sometimes people would . . . take the bait." She looked away. "They'd return home but send Dad large chunks of money to fund a phony search."

He studied her profile, noting the color that stained her cheeks. "All right, so your father was a con artist. What does that have to do with you?"

"Jesus." She pushed off the vanity and resumed pacing. "I told you, I lived with him while all this was going on."

"Are you saying you helped him?"

"Well, duh." Pulling a roll of antacids from her jeans pocket, she thumbed one into her mouth. "At first, I was too young to really understand that we were doing something wrong. As I got older, though, I knew we were milking money from people with a pack of lies. People who were living on board with us. I'd spend days getting to know them, hearing about their families and their plans for how they'd spend the money when we found the sunken chest of gold. Some of them were jerks, but some of them were good people."

She crossed to the sitting area and stood with her back to him. "Do you know what it's like to look someone in the face day after day knowing you're about to steal their life savings? I got so sick over it at times, I couldn't look at myself in the mirror."

"How old were you?" He rose as well to face her.

"When it started?" She glanced at him over her shoulder. "I don't know. Old enough to walk without falling overboard."

"No, when you stopped helping your father."

"Older than I should have been." She moved to the windows and pushed one of the gauzy curtains aside to stare out at the cove. "The minute I was old enough to understand, I should have stopped going with him every summer. It's just that . . ."

"What?" He crossed to the archway but stayed there, giving her the distance she seemed to need.

"I got along with my grandfather okay, but my grandmother resented having to raise me and made no attempt to hide the fact. My leaving for a few months every year gave both of us a break. Plus . . . Dad wasn't very good at taking care of himself. I worried constantly about what would happen if I wasn't there to make sure he didn't drink too much, that he paid whatever loan sharks were on his tail, and that he didn't spend *all* his money on drugs."

"Drugs?"

"Yeah." She sighed. "That was my biggest fear. That if I wasn't around, he'd go back to smuggling cocaine like we did when I was really little. He always put half of it up his own nose, which was why he was always in debt."

He stared back at her in disbelief. "He smuggled cocaine while he had a child with him?"

"I can remember hiding in the cockpit of the stealth speedboat he used to own, having to be really quiet. He told me we were playing hide-and-seek, and if the Coast Guard caught us, we'd be 'it.' "

"Jesus Christ! Your father should be shot."

"He was."

"What?"

She looked at him. "That's how he died. He was murdered."

"Oh God, Jackie, I'm sorry." He started toward her, but stopped when she stiffened. "How did it happen?"

"The last con he ran, I'd finally had enough." She sank to the old-fashioned divan and rubbed her forehead. "I can't believe I'm telling you all this."

He hesitated a moment, then took a seat beside her. "Maybe you need to talk about it."

"Maybe I do." She looked so exhausted, his heart ached. "I loved my father, I worried about him, and I wanted to watch out for him, but I couldn't take it anymore. The mark's name was Roger Gates, a schoolteacher from Chicago who was so gullible and eager to believe, he gave my father everything: the money he'd inherited from his parents, his retirement fund. He even took out a mortgage loan on his house. The problem was, he kept wanting to go with my dad, not just send money and wait for reports. Dad asked Ti and me to go along and help keep the illusion of a real search going, but we told him he was insane. No way could he pull that off for long."

"You already knew Ti?"

She nodded. "He used to crew for my father and was pretty wild in the early days. He grew a conscience, though, and Dad never did. So Ti and I got jobs crewing for a cruise line on a really beautiful clipper ship." She actually smiled. "The work was hard, but I loved it, and I learned a lot about running a legitimate business. That was when I started dreaming about doing something with the *Pirate's Pleasure,* other than keep it in a slip as a very expensive toy for my dad."

"How long did you work for the cruise line?"

"Two years." Her smile vanished. "Ti and I were out in the middle of the Caribbean Sea when my dad was killed. I didn't even hear about it until . . . he'd been gone a week."

He watched as tears welled in her eyes, but she blinked them away. "How did it happen?"

"According to the testimony at the trial, Roger realized he was being had. He and Dad got into a shouting match out on the boat. Roger pulled a gun and shot Dad point-blank in the chest." She dropped her head into her hands. "The worst part is, I can't stop wondering . . . if I'd been there, maybe I could have done something to defuse the situation. Maybe my father would still be alive."

Or maybe you'd be dead, too. The shock of that thought joined empathy as he remembered the devastating pain of losing his own parents. Unable to withhold some small measure of comfort, he put his hand on her back and rubbed in small circles.

Finally, she straightened, her face stoic. "In the end, Roger went to prison for murder, and I've never figured out how to feel about that. Yes, he killed my dad, but my dad destroyed his life.

"I scattered Dad's ashes in the Caribbean, knowing that's where he'd want to be, then returned to work aboard the *Sea Star*. Unfortunately, the other sailors had heard about my father and either knew or guessed I was a crook, too. They let me know I was no better than a bottom feeder to them. You don't realize how small a ship is until every hand on board shuns you. At the captain's suggestion, I opted out of my contract. I thought about signing on with one of the windjammer ships, but knew the scandal would follow me. The sailing community in that area of the world is too tight to escape something that big.

"So I left the islands and came home to Texas. I was twenty years old and completely alone, since my grandparents had died a few years earlier. They'd named me as their heir, though, so I'd inherited their house as well as the *Pirate's Pleasure*.

"I called Ti to see if he'd consider working for me, then sold the house to start my own business, one that capitalized on people's love of old sailing ships and pirate lore without ripping them off." She shrugged. "I thought as long as I stayed clean, I'd be okay, but every year has been a struggle and I'm running out of savings. Then you came along and offered me this great deal. I knew when I accepted it that I was taking a big risk of resurrecting the past, but . . ." Regret filled her eyes. "I'm really sorry about how it turned out. I honestly thought I had a chance to make it work."

"Who says it won't?"

"Adrian . . ." She stared at him. "All those people heard what Carl said. They're not going to want to raise money for a project that will help me. And they'll have serious doubts about you and your family if we're all working together. I don't want any of you suffering guilt by association."

"Well, I appreciate your concern, and I'm sure the rest of the family will, too, but we're made of sterner stuff than that. If people want to whisper behind our backs, let 'em. It wouldn't be the first time the good people of Galveston have talked about those scandalous descendants of Marguerite Bouchard."

"This is not some little scandal. This could make you a pariah. Do you have a clue what that feels like?"

"Jackie, you're being overly dramatic."

"Am I?" She stood and moved away. "Unless you've been there, you don't know what it's like to have people mistrust you because you're connected to a known thief. And I'm not talking about just people you know personally. During the trial, the story was plastered all over the local news and I had to battle past the cameras to get to the courtroom. After my face appeared on TV, I couldn't walk down the street without people pointing at me.

"For the past eight years I've been looking over my shoulder, knowing someday the past could catch up to me." Her shoulders sagged. "I guess it finally did."

"What happened today doesn't have to change things." He stood as well. "Carl was vague enough that we can gloss over what he said."

"But what if the whole truth comes out? I can pick up and move my business elsewhere if I have to. Not easily, but it can be done. What will you do, though, if being associated with me ruins your reputation? Sell the inn?"

"Not hardly." He snorted. "You forget, our business relies on people coming here from out of town. Since nobody's going to broadcast the details of your past from coast to coast, who cares if a few people in Galveston raise their eyebrows at us? We've lived with scandal for generations. Something like this is not going to scare us off."

She looked at him a long time. "You really mean that."

"I do. And my sisters will feel the same way."

"You'd actually go into business with me . . ." Her control cracked a bit. "Knowing the things I've done?"

His whole chest softened as he watched her struggle for composure. "You mean, knowing you're responsible, hardworking, compassionate, and that you were more of a parent to your father than he was to you? Somehow, I don't have a real problem with that."

To his shock, the tears he'd expected when he'd knocked on the door filled her eyes in a rush and spilled down her cheeks. She wiped at them, looking horrified.

Without hesitation, he stepped forward and gathered her into his arms. She covered her face and let a single sob escape against his chest. Tightening his hold, he made a mental note: *Don't be kind, it makes her cry.*

With a deep breath, she had herself back under control, and pulled away. He let his arms drop, even though he longed to comfort her more. "W-what—" She cleared her throat. "What will your sisters say when they find out?"

"I assure you, they will feel exactly as I do." Seeing the shimmer of more tears, he decided to lighten the moment. "Well, not *exactly*. I doubt my sisters lie awake at night trying to picture you naked."

Surprise flashed in her eyes, followed by a watery laugh. "You never let up, do you?"

"I've always heard persistence pays."

"Are you going to tell them?"

"That I try to picture you naked?"

"No. All that stuff I just told you."

"That depends." He stuffed his hands in his pockets to keep from reaching for her. "Do you want me to?"

Her breath released in a heavy sigh. "I'd rather they know as little as possible. I'm not sure I could look them in the eye, much less work with them, if they knew everything."

"I promise you, it wouldn't be a problem for them, but if it makes you more comfortable, then they don't need to know the details."

She nodded, looking wrung out.

"So—" He turned businesslike. "Since we have to wait for Carl Ryder to authenticate your letter, why don't you make yourself at home, read the diaries, and pretend to be on vacation for the next few days?"

Gratitude softened her face. "That's the best idea I've heard in years."

"All right, then." He nodded and headed for the door. "I'll get out of your hair."

"Adrian," she called. When he turned, she smiled and his chest tightened at the sight of her standing there looking so vulnerable. "Thank you."

"You're welcome."

Chapter 10

When breakfast wound down the next morning, Adrian went into the dining room where Allison and Rory were cleaning up the carnage left by an inn full of guests. "Did Jackie ever come down?"

"Not yet," Alli answered, stacking dirty dishes. "I don't think she's been out of her room since the meeting yesterday. But surely she'll come out for meals."

"She hasn't so far," Rory said as she lifted trays from the warming stands on the sideboard. "Should we send something up to her?"

"I noticed some fruit and granola bars missing from the basket upstairs," Adrian said. "So at least she's eating."

"Still," Allison said, "it can't be good for her to stay in her room so long."

"Maybe she's just really engrossed in reading the diaries," Rory offered.

"Maybe." Alli chewed her lip, looking at the ceiling as if she could see into Jackie's room. "Adrian, you did tell her we don't care about those things Mr. Ryder said, right?"

"Well, I care!" Rory said.

"You do?" Adrian frowned at her.

"Of course I do." Rory banged a metal serving spoon against a tray as she scraped all the leftovers into one pan. "The whole thing makes me furious."

"At Jackie?"

"No. At that archeologist for embarrassing her. And her father, if what Mr. Ryder said is true. And I don't know . . . *life!*" Rory let her breath out in a passionate rush. "I'm sorry, I know I shouldn't get so upset, it's just that we were so lucky, I wish everyone could have a childhood like ours."

"Rory . . ." Alli stared at her. "We lost our parents in a car wreck when you were still a toddler. How is that a wonderful childhood?"

"We had each other," Rory insisted. "No matter what happened when I was growing up, I always knew y'all would be there for me. You're still here for me. Although now I have Chance and Lauren, and you brought Scott into the family, so it's even better. We just need to find someone for Adrian." She winked at him. "Unless he's already done that."

A jolt went through him at her words. "Rory, whoa. Do not get ideas about me and Jackie. I told you yesterday, there is nothing going on between us. And even if there were, she's not at all what I have in mind for long term."

"Why not?"

"I don't know." His nerves jumping, he went to help Allison clear the table. "I guess if I had to describe what I want for a wife—when I'm ready to make that leap—I'd say someone who's a little more of a homebody. Jackie couldn't be more opposite from that."

"That doesn't seem to stop you from giving her that I-want-this-woman look." Rory wiggled her brows.

"Looking and wanting are not the same as signing up for the extended maintenance plan."

"Oh, so you just want to take her for a test-drive?"

"I did not say that." He turned to Allison. "Did I say that?"

"Well, no," Alli said. "But isn't that what dating is?"

"I guess," Rory conceded. "It's just that I like Jackie."

"I like her, too," Adrian said. "But even if she were what I had in mind for a wife, I am a long way from being ready to settle down, so taking a test-drive with someone we're hoping to do business with would be a really stupid idea."

"What do you mean, not ready to settle down?" Rory stared at him. "You just passed the big three-oh, brother. How long do you plan to wait before you start a family?"

"Come on, brat, I just got you two raised. Has it occurred to you I might like a little time on my own before I tie myself down with a second family?"

"Excuse me?" Emotions paraded across her face, going from disbelief to hurt. "Well, gee, I'm sorry. I didn't realize we were such a burden to you."

Oh, hell. He glanced at Alli and saw the same wounded look. "You weren't, and you know it. It's just, I'd like to . . . I don't know, not worry about anyone but me for a little while. And truthfully, I don't think Jackie is any more interested in marriage and kids right now than I am. So, no matchmaking, okay? All it will do is create a really awkward situation for everyone concerned."

"Oh, all right," Rory groused, and he would have breathed a sigh of relief if she hadn't smiled. "Although you're wrong about Jackie not wanting kids. Or haven't you noticed the way she looks at Lauren?"

"What?" He blinked.

"Rory's right," Allison said. "I noticed it, too."

"Give me a break." He laughed nervously. "Alli, you've told me yourself, not all women want to be mommies."

"Maybe not," Alli said. "But Jackie does."

Before he could even think of an appropriate response to that, he heard the sound of someone coming down the stairs. He turned just as Jackie appeared in the doorway wearing a white shirt tucked into worn-out jeans that had a split at one knee. From the swell of her breasts, he knew she'd left off the sports bra in exchange for something more feminine—but what? Plain cotton? Satin and lace?

His libido did a slow spin as he contemplated the possibilities.

She stopped abruptly when she noticed his scrutiny. "What?"

"Nothing." He shook his head to clear his brain.

"Good morning," Rory said brightly, glancing between him and Jackie. "We were wondering when you'd come down."

"Did you sleep well?" Alli asked.

"A little too well, I guess." Jackie sighed. She'd finger-combed her damp hair straight back, accentuating her exotic features. "It looks like I slept through breakfast."

"Not a problem," he assured her. "I can fix whatever you want. Eggs, bacon, French toast?"

"Just a pastry and some coffee will be fine." She rubbed her stomach and he realized she did that a lot.

"Here you go." Rory grabbed a cup and filled it from the silver coffee urn. "Do you take anything in it?"

"No, just black."

Adrian checked the wicker basket of pastries that sat in the middle of the table. "Try one of the bran muffins. It'll soften the blow of that caffeine."

"Thanks." She accepted the coffee cup from Rory and took a sip but made no move toward the table.

Rory nudged Allison and nodded toward the door. "We'll be in the kitchen if you two need anything."

He stifled a groan as they bustled out with their arms full of dishes. So much for Rory not playing matchmaker. Someday his baby sister needed to learn she couldn't order the universe around with the sheer force of her will. Wanting something, even wanting it badly, didn't automatically make it happen.

"So," he said to Jackie as he continued clearing the table, "do you have any plans for today? Other than reading the diaries?"

"Actually"—she stepped closer to him to check out the pastries and he caught the scent of some tropical shampoo that made him wonder how she'd look in a bikini sunning herself on a white sand beach—"I was thinking I should go see the ship before everything goes to hell and I have to leave."

"What?" He shoved aside a fantasy of tumbling naked with Jackie in the surf to concentrate on her words. "First of all, everything's going to work out fine. And second, even if it doesn't, you're free to dive around the ship anytime you want."

"I appreciate that, but I've learned to not count on people's hospitality lasting beyond the moment."

"Not a bad philosophy . . . for a pessimist."

"A realist." Her lips curled up in a sexy smile and his heart rate kicked up a notch.

"Well . . ." He glanced out the window where morning

sunlight streamed through branches of the trees. "If you're planning to dive, looks like you picked a good day for it. Not that the air temperature will make a difference sixty feet underwater."

"True."

"Let me know what time you want to go, and I'll go with you."

"Still trying to get me alone on the beach?"

"That depends. Will you be diving in a bikini or a wet suit?"

"A bikini in November?"

"Hey, I'll be happy to keep you warm."

"That's okay. You don't need to bother."

"Well, you're not going alone."

"Why not?" Her brows came together. "I'm experienced enough to manage a dive this tame by myself."

"Sorry, house rules. No one dives without a buddy."

She rolled her eyes. "If you insist. Can you be ready by ten o'clock?"

"Absolutely. Now, have a bran muffin." He pushed the basket toward her.

She looked over the selection and grabbed a chocolate croissant.

"You know," he said, "chocolate is as bad for your stomach as coffee."

She gave him a cocky look. "Didn't anyone ever tell you: never get between a woman and her chocolate?"

"I think I invented that saying, I just didn't think it applied to you."

"Why's that?" She tipped her head.

"I don't know." He floundered for a reason. "Your whole statement about grabbing whatever's cheap and easy when you're hungry, I guess."

"'That doesn't mean I won't go for rich and decadent if it's offered." She bit into the pastry, and her eyes fluttered. "Oh, this is good. Did you make it?"

"I am the chef."

She took another bite, drawing his gaze to her plush lips. "Oh, mmm, really good. Mind if I take it to my room?"

"Not at all." He tried not to think about covering his body in chocolate and offering himself up as a treat.

"I'll meet you on the dock at ten o'clock." She headed for the stairs, giving him a nice view of her jean-clad backside. Maybe they could cover each other in chocolate. Or wrestle in a big vat of it. Then he remembered why they couldn't do that.

Why did she have to be off limits!

Jackie hurried out the front door of the inn, hardly believing the time. How had the last hour sped by so fast? She saw Adrian already down at the dock, dressed in a wet suit and sitting on a storage bin with his arms crossed over his chest.

She waved, then headed over to her truck and unlocked the metal chest in the bed to get her scuba gear. Once she'd hefted it out, she tugged on the legs of her yellow and black shorty, wishing the wet suit covered more of her legs since the day was clear but crisp.

When she straightened, she saw Adrian heading up the trail. "Sorry I'm late," she called as she grabbed her air tank in one hand and her dive bag in the other. She met him halfway down the hill.

"And here I was starting to think you were the exception that proved all the clichéd rules about women. Now I learn you can't resist chocolate and you delight in keeping a man waiting."

"Oh, I didn't keep you waiting that long."

"Actually, it was worth it." His gaze dropped to the region of her chest. "Forget the bikini. You look absolutely . . . eatable in a wet suit."

"Eatable?" She laughed. "Well, let's hope there're no sharks around."

"None but me."

"You, I can handle," she said with bravado, then nearly choked when he bent over to retrieve her air tank. His traditional black wet suit molded to his muscular back and cupped a pair of buns so firm they should be bronzed. Eatable, indeed.

Determined to keep a cool head, she slung her bag of gear over her shoulder and continued down the path toward the sandy beach. The Gulf breeze became more pronounced as they stepped onto the pier. Overhead, seagulls screeched a hopeful plea for bread crumbs.

"So why are you running late?" he asked as they reached the end of the pier.

"I got caught up in the diaries." She dropped her bag onto one of the storage bins and turned so Adrian could help her with her tank.

"I take it you're enjoying them."

"I am. Very much." She looked down to fasten the inflatable vest that held the tank in place and saw how much cleavage she was showing. Good grief, she thought as she pulled the zipper higher, no wonder Adrian had ogled her. "The early volumes I read yesterday were tedious at times, but for the most part, it's better than reading a novel."

"How far have you gotten?"

"I'm almost back to the part where she meets Jack for the first time."

"Back to?"

"Yeah, I cheated and read that part out of order. I can't wait to get back to it." She sat to pull on her flippers, thinking over all that she'd read so far. The entries had fascinated her right from the beginning, since Marguerite had started by telling how she'd come to be known as a good-luck charm.

The voodoo midwife who'd attended her birth had heard that the mother meant to send the baby to an orphanage. Convinced that such a fate would somehow be worse than being raised in a brothel by a prostitute mother who didn't want her, the midwife blessed the baby, naming her Marguerite, which meant "pearl," and said, "Whoever keeps this pearl shall have good fortune." Then she'd taken a magnificent pearl pendant from around her own neck and draped the chain about the child, telling the mother that the necklace had to stay with the child in order for the blessing to work.

Later, Marguerite learned that the voodoo woman died that very night, and that the necklace she'd passed on to her had once belonged to Jean Lafitte. He'd given it to the woman many years earlier as thanks for her helping his brother, Pierre, escape from jail shortly before the famous Battle of New Orleans.

Surprisingly, Marguerite accepted that her mother only kept her because of that blessing, and seemed amused by the fact rather than bitter. Indeed, her mother's luck had improved when a wealthy patron of the brothel fell in love with her and set her up as his pampered mistress. When his own financial fortune increased, her mother told him the tale of Marguerite's birth, which discouraged him from any thoughts of ending their relationship. He'd also been the one who introduced Marguerite to opera by letting her attend the theater with them, and later, by paying for her music lessons.

Perhaps that was what amused Marguerite so much, the fact that people went out of their way to make her happy once they heard about the blessing. Even the owner of the opera house where she eventually made a name for herself had treated her like a queen—and with good reason. The place had been struggling when she'd first started singing there, but quickly became one of the premier theaters in New Orleans.

As Marguerite's fame as a singer spread, so did the stories of her power to bring good fortune to those around her. Men the world over, including more than one titled aristocrat, went to ridiculous and often hilarious lengths to woo her. She turned them all away, however, clinging to her independence.

Until Henri LeRoche came knocking on her dressing room door. His dark good looks and aura of danger captured her attention from the start. Even so, she'd held him at arm's length, just as she had the others. He wore her down slowly, though, with his seemingly sincere vows of devotion.

Finally, she'd told him the price of her bed was marriage, thinking such a prominent businessman would balk at marrying the daughter of a prostitute. Instead, he'd proposed in such a romantic manner that if Jackie hadn't known how it all would end, she'd have been deeply touched.

He brought Marguerite to Galveston and showed her the island he'd purchased "for her," even though Jackie suspected he really bought it as a perfect base from which to run the illegal aspects of his shipping trade. Then standing on this very beach, he showed her the architect's drawing for the house he would build for her if she married him.

Looking up at the mansion now, at the steadfast façade, Jackie could understand Marguerite's decision to marry Henri in spite of all her doubts. It wasn't the grandeur of the house that swayed her so much as what it represented. Marguerite, like Jackie, had always hungered for a family to love and for true acceptance.

So, she accepted his proposal, and Henri had the house built as her wedding present.

From there on, though, things went from romantic to horrific in a hurry. On their wedding night, Marguerite realized Henri was like all the others, wanting her only for the luck she would bring him. When she confronted him, he didn't even try to deny that he'd lied to her from the beginning. She threatened to have the marriage annulled and he beat her savagely, swearing she'd never leave him or Pearl Island alive. The house that he built as her present became her prison and her fairy-tale marriage a nightmare.

Jackie found it sadly ironic that the necklace that made Marguerite a good-luck charm for others had become an albatross around the woman's neck. If she had been in Marguerite's shoes, she'd have thrown the necklace into the cove. But Marguerite had cherished the pendant as part of who she was, the sheer serendipity of being born at all, and the eternal hope that someday, somehow, she'd find true happiness.

Was that the real lesson to learn from Marguerite? Not to simply survive, but to never give up hope?

"Hey." Adrian waved a hand in front of her face. "You still with me?"

"Oh. Sorry." She shook her head. "I was just thinking."

"About?" He sat beside her to put his flippers on.

"The necklace." She glanced across the water. "Do you think it's really out there?"

"Absolutely. We're convinced that's what Jack was going back for when the gunpowder exploded."

She cocked her head. "Then why didn't you tell the Historical Society about it at the meeting? From what I read in the diaries, I'd say they'd be just as interested in the necklace as the powder horn."

"We have our reasons," he answered evasively.

She studied him a moment, then laughed. "You're hoping to keep it, aren't you?"

He frowned. "Wish to, yes. Plan to, no. We accepted weeks ago that recovering the necklace will mean giving it up. We just don't want to give the Galveston Historical Society free access to the diaries in order to prove its significance."

"Then why do the excavation? I mean, think about it. What if the necklace really does have magic? Not that I believe in such things, but what if you're giving up all that good luck?"

He looked out across the water for a long time before answering. "Jack Kingsley died trying to save that necklace from sinking with the ship."

"So?"

"I've done some reading on the paranormal and what I've learned is that sometimes what keeps a soul from moving to the next plane is an unfinished task. Perhaps Jack's spirit is still trying to rescue the necklace, and won't leave the cove without it."

"So if you recover it for him, you'll free his spirit?"

she asked, studying his eyes. "Do you really believe in, you know . . . ghosts?"

He stood. "Are you ready to go see the ship?"

She laughed. "Let's see, in this case changing the subject would mean yes."

Taking up his dive light, he moved to the end of the dock. "The water will be really murky for the first forty feet. So once we get in, put one hand on this chain." He pointed to a chain that disappeared into the water at an angle. "It'll lead you right to the ship, which sits pretty much smack-dab in the middle of the cove."

"Got it." She slipped her mask in place.

Adrian did the same, inserted his mouthpiece, and stepped off into the water with a big splash. When he reappeared, she jumped in beside him, going under with a whoosh of bubbles.

They swam to the chain, then started down through the brown haze. As Adrian had said, the water remained murky until they reached forty feet, then it cleared drastically. It also dropped in temperature.

Adrian turned to check on her and she signaled for him to lead the way. Just enough sunlight filtered through to illuminate specks of suspended silt and an occasional school of fish that darted through their light beams like flashes of silver. With a pang she realized how much she missed diving in the Caribbean, which was as different from diving off the coast of Texas as the sun from the moon.

For one thing, it was warmer. She'd expected the water to be cold at sixty feet, but not this cold! And the closer they swam to the ship, the colder it got.

The bow of the vessel appeared suddenly in the twin beams of their lights. Her eyes widened in surprise at its remarkable condition. Since it was a wooden ship, any parts not covered in mud should have completely disintegrated within a few short years. Instead, the top portion of the forecastle rose out of the cove's bottom, like a visual echo of how she must have looked while riding the waves.

So this was Jack Kingsley's ship, she thought as they reached it. And wow, wasn't she gorgeous! Jackie had always thought no ship in the world could be more beautiful than her own, but the *Freedom* had a grace and strength she could feel in her heart.

They swam over the main deck, sweeping it with their lights. Gray silt covered everything that wasn't buried completely in mud. She lifted her light and saw that one mast remained, jutting up at an angle with its rigging swaying in the current.

Suspended in the chilly water over the ship, she tried to imagine that night, piecing it together from all she had heard.

When Jack learned that Marguerite had been beaten and locked in her room, he'd raced to Pearl Island, intent on saving her. But to sail right into the cove had been foolhardy, even for a seasoned blockade runner.

Reaching the quarterdeck, Jackie turned to survey the ship from where Jack would have stood. What had gone through his mind in that instant when he saw the flash on the balcony, then heard the boom of the cannon? The impact would have shuddered through the whole ship. Had any of his men died with the first explosion? Had they screamed out in pain?

The night had been stormy, with lightning splitting the black clouds and the wind playing havoc with the sails. A rational man would have ordered his ship to come about and fled the cove. But Jack had been far from rational that night. His refusal to abandon the ship proved that.

Floating toward the wheel, Jackie reached out and took hold of it, sending up a small cloud of silt. Realizing that his hands had held this very wheel sent a shiver racing through her.

Why, Jack? Why risk so much for a necklace? Did you really love Marguerite to the point you couldn't let go of even that small piece of her?

The water temperature dropped again, and a buzzing started inside her head, growing in volume. With the sound came a rush of emotion that tore through her. She clasped her ears, but the buzzing grew louder.

In a frightening flash, she knew what Jack had felt that night: anger, grief, and desperation so profound it cut her heart in two. *Oh God,* she thought as the water pressure squeezed her chest until she couldn't breathe. *Oh God, oh God, oh God.*

A hand grabbed her arm and she remembered Adrian was there, but her mind remained focused inward, fighting the anguish.

Alarmed, Adrian shook her until she finally looked at him. He hand-signaled: *Okay?*

She shook her head: *No.*

He made a fist: *Low on air?*

No. She waggled her hand with fingers spread, then pointed up with her thumb. *Something's wrong. Up.*

He checked his dive watch to see if they were safe for a fast ascent, then signaled back: *Okay.* But when she started up, he didn't see any bubbles escaping her mouth. He grabbed her weight belt and pulled her back down. To make a straight ascent from sixty feet, she'd have to exhale the whole way up or her lungs would burst.

She looked at him with frantic eyes and signaled again: *Something's wrong. Up. Up!*

Okay. But slow!

She nodded and clutched the regulator to her mouth, breathing in short bursts, alarming him further.

Do you need to buddy-breathe?

No. Up! Up! Up!

Okay. When she squeezed her eyes shut, he jostled her, then pointed at his eyes. *Look at me,* he commanded, hoping to give her something to focus on as much as needing to monitor her through eye contact.

Nodding, she kept her eyes fixed on his as he wrapped an arm around her and swam toward the chain that led back to the pier. His heart raced as he wondered what was wrong. He could tell she was getting air, but she wasn't exhaling properly, and the look in her eyes spoke of pain.

Or panic.

He thought of his sister Rory, who suffered from panic attacks. When one hit her, she doubled over and couldn't breathe. Could Jackie be suffering from something like that? If so, they could be in serious trouble. Underwater was no place to lose control of one's breathing.

Although, thank God, she was an experienced enough diver to shut down the natural instinct to struggle against him and swim straight up.

As they moved away from the ship, he felt her body start to relax but only a little.

He stopped at forty feet, just below the level where the water turned murky, not daring to go any higher. With one arm wrapped around both her and the chain, he grabbed her hand and pressed it to his stomach. With his eyes locked on hers, he breathed deeply in and out, willing her to do the same.

Slowly, the tension left her body and her breathing steadied. *Okay?* he signaled.

She nodded weakly. *Up.*

He checked his watch, then held up two fingers, asking if she could handle two more minutes. She closed her eyes in dread, but nodded. Aching for her, he cradled her close, letting the water rock their bodies. Slowly, she went limp, her legs brushing his, her head tucked against his chest.

When the time was up, he deflated both their vests to keep them from ascending too quickly, then nodded. She exhaled and disappeared into the murky level above. He made his own ascent, and surfaced with her near the dock.

The instant she broke free of the water, she tore the regulator from her mouth and took a gulp of air. She'd had enough presence of mind to reinflate her vest so it kept her head above water. He took a moment to inflate his own vest, then pulled his mask off and swam toward her. "What happened?"

"Nothing," she gasped. "I'm fine!"

"What the hell do you mean you're fine?" he yelled, his heart still pounding.

"I just wanted to come up."

"So I noticed." He stared in disbelief as she swam for the ladder with long, fluid strokes, then removed her flippers and climbed to the pier.

Okay, Adrian thought in total confusion. *Nothing's wrong. She's fine. And pigs fly.*

He took off his own flippers and followed her up. When he sat beside her with their legs dangling off the side of the pier, their tanks beside them, he watched her struggle to catch her breath.

"Care to try again?" he asked.

"Try what again?" she said, panting.

"To tell me what happened down there."

"Nothing happened, I just . . . I don't know, felt claustrophobic or something."

"Has that ever happened to you before?"

"No." She managed a breathy laugh, her teeth chattering. "I can safely say nothing like that has ever happened to me before."

"So, what set it off?"

"I, um . . ." She wrapped her arms around herself, her body visibly shivering. "I have no idea. Christ, it was cold down there."

"It wasn't *that* cold." He pulled her against him and rubbed her arms as he looked out across the water, thinking it through. "Unless you bumped into Jack."

"What?" She gaped at him.

"You know, ghosts? Cold spots?"

"Then you admit it was cold."

"Only cold to you. Which makes sense if Jack was reaching out to you and not me."

"Give me a break." She shivered. "You think just because he's my ancestor, I'm connected to him somehow?"

"Not at all. You don't have to be related. Allison told me Scott had a similar experience the first time he dove around the ship."

Her expression turned incredulous as she searched his eyes. "I'm supposed to believe a person who's been dead since the mid-1800s can reach out to people at will?"

"It's possible." He wiped beads of water from her face. "Remember when I told you that sometimes when I'm standing on the balcony, I can imagine Marguerite standing there, too? Well, it's more than that. I can feel her."

"F-feel her?" Another shiver went through her and he rubbed her back to warm her.

"No, that's not quite right. It's . . ." He searched for a way to explain it. "It's as if I can feel what she's feeling, her emotions. And not just faintly. I'm talking actually *feeling* an overwhelming sense of grief and fear and longing. Maybe what you felt down there wasn't claustrophobia but Jack Kingsley's emotions from the night he died."

For a heartbeat, her face remained blank, then she snorted. "Yeah, right. I told you, I don't believe in ghosts."

"Of course not," he agreed, straight-faced.

"I will say this, though." She pinched her nose to clear away the salt water. "Are you sure you want to mess with whatever *is* out there?"

"Ah, so you're admitting there is something out there."

Rather than answer, she burrowed against his chest for warmth. He wrapped both arms around her.

"Truthfully"—he sighed—"we're not sure of anything, but we think this is the right thing to do. Hope so, anyway."

"Hope so?" She tipped her head to look at him, her face mere inches from his. If he lowered his head a tiny bit, he could close his mouth over hers. "That's not very reassuring."

"Sometimes instinct and hope are all you have to go on." For a moment neither of them moved, and he wondered if she ached for the kiss half as much as he did. Seeing beads of water on her cheek, he raised his hand and brushed them away, then trailed his thumb along her lips. Her mouth opened on a sigh as her eyes became heavy-lidded. His body tightened as her breath warmed his hand.

One kiss, he thought, longing to lean closer.

She pulled back before he could act. Just as well, he thought with a sigh. One kiss would invariably lead to another. "Come on, let's get you warm and dry and I'll make you something hot to eat."

Chapter 11

Jackie spent the rest of the day and most of the next reading the diaries word for word—refusing to skim any of it. Sitting against a pile of pillows in what she'd come to think of as the "Princess Bed," she struggled to focus on the page before her, but her eyes stubbornly drifted shut. She didn't want to stop, though, since the entry in front of her had started with the words "Last night, Captain Kingsley came to my bed, and I confess without an ounce of regret that I welcomed him."

About time, Jackie thought. Sheesh, all her life she'd heard about this great love affair between Captain Kingsley and Marguerite, but in truth their relationship had been completely platonic for five extremely long years. Jackie didn't know how they'd resisted each other that long. Marguerite had been captivated by the man since the night they met, drawn to him physically and emotionally. And the way she described how Jack would look at her, "as if his entire being yearns to be a part of mine, to share a pleasure we both know is forbidden. Neither of us speaks of our desire, but in my mind I have loved him a thousand times."

How did a woman resist someone she wanted that much? Especially since Jack Kingsley had been one hot hunk. But fear of Henri kept Marguerite in a constant state of walking on eggshells. She and Henri had formed a fragile compromise after the birth of their daughter, and Marguerite stopped trying to escape. She even pretended for the sake of appearances that their marriage was a happy one as long as Henri went elsewhere for sex. That didn't stop him from beating her, though, for any imagined transgression. Discovering her with a lover would have been a huge transgression. Marguerite might have chanced a beating, she wanted Jack that badly, but she feared Henri would kill Jack.

She also made sure Jack didn't know the true horror of her marriage for fear of what Jack would do. Not that she had much of a chance to tell him. Whenever he came to the house to do business with Henri, he'd stay for dinner and they'd go for walks along the beach or to the music room where she'd sing for him. Henri would always hover nearby, smirking at her when Jack wasn't looking. The bastard knew perfectly well that Captain Kingsley coveted his wife, and he enjoyed dangling her before him.

But now, finally, they were going to do something about the attraction that had been sizzling between them since they met. Jackie tried again to focus on the page, but the words blurred. Maybe if she closed her eyes for just a few minutes . . .

Slumping down, she tipped her head against the pillows and let the diary drop open on her lap. She had the rest of the afternoon to read, so she didn't have to finish it right this second. But she did need to finish all the diaries quickly since the test results for her letter could come in any second. Once the results were in, they'd be back to meeting with the Historical Society about the excavation.

If Carl Ryder decided to make more trouble and derail the project, she'd just as soon head back to Corpus Christi as soon as possible.

Adrian may have assured her his sisters wouldn't care about her past, but if that past ruined their chance to recover the necklace, she didn't think she could handle doing business with them.

With a yawn, she slid down farther as her mind drifted back to thoughts of Marguerite. The woman's struggle to get through every day without giving in to despair touched a chord inside her. Marguerite had managed by concentrating on the good things in her life: her beautiful daughter and her friendship with Jack.

Jackie made the drowsy decision to follow that example and focus on her own blessings as she sank into sleep.

On the edge of her consciousness, she heard a window in the sitting room rattle. She opened her eyes to find the room shrouded in darkness. When had night fallen? The noise came again, like knocking. With her mind sluggish from sleep, she pushed the heavy bedspread aside. Except she hadn't been beneath the covers, she thought as she stood and looked around. The room wavered before her, as if she were drunk. On a chair beside the bed, she saw a forest-green robe trimmed in cascading lace. She reached for it, mindlessly pulling it on over a creamy satin nightgown she didn't even recognize, much less remember donning.

The glass pane rattled again, and she turned with a start. Past the heavy swagged curtains framing the windows, silver clouds moved across the ink-black sky. Then the clouds parted and she saw a man standing on the balcony, silhouetted by the faint light of the moon. Her mind whirled dizzily, making her stagger, then it cleared with a snap.

And she knew in that instant who stood outside. He'd sent word to Henri earlier, requesting a meeting. She'd waited breathlessly all day, praying he would come to the house, but Henri had arranged to meet him at a tavern in town.

Joy and fear filled her heart as she hurried for the door to the balcony, opening it silently. He slipped inside with a gust of night breeze, closing the door behind him.

"Jacques . . ." she whispered, her French accent caressing the name. She ached to touch him but feared he'd vanish like a dream upon waking. He looked more shadow than reality, dressed all in black, his dark hair loose about his shoulders. "What are you doing here? Henri—"

"Is still in town," he assured her, his voice as hushed as hers. "Or I would not have come. I had to see you, though. To tell you . . . good-bye."

"Good-bye?" Her heart clenched. "What do you mean?"

"I won't be coming back to Pearl Island. That's why I asked to see Henri, to tell him I'll not carry cargo for him anymore."

"Because of the Yankee blockade? I've been so worried for you. How did you get through it?"

"Quite easily, I assure you." She saw the flash of his smile and remembered the wicked delight he took in danger. "And it's something I plan to do again."

"But you said you'd not carry any more cargo."

"Not for Henri. Come sit, and I'll tell you." He took her hand and led her to the divan. Moonlight fell over them, revealing the excitement in his dark eyes as he sat beside her. "I know you dreaded this war, but it has given me an opportunity I cannot let pass. Every port in the south is blockaded and planters can't get their cotton to the textile mills in England."

"*Oui*, I know. They have been shipping it by rail here to Galveston for months. Henri's warehouses, they are making a fortune while he searches for captains to brave the blockades."

"He is not the only one. All the shipping companies are desperate. Enough so, they are even willing to hire me."

"I do not understand. Are you saying they would not before?"

"Marguerite . . ." He searched her eyes, then dropped his gaze. "There are things you don't know about me, things I'm loath to tell you. Suffice it to say, my reputation among honest businessmen is somewhat tarnished."

"Because you are a smuggler."

His gaze shot back to her in surprise.

"I have been married to Henri all these years. Do you think I do not know he ships illegal goods?" Resentment burned inside her. "He might have the people of Galveston convinced he is a paragon of moral virtue, but I know the truth of what goes on in his office when he closes the door."

"You've known all along I was a smuggler? Yet you have welcomed my friendship?"

Her anger softened at the look he gave her. Beneath the arrogance and swagger was a man who deeply needed the absolution of true acceptance. "*Oui*, I have known."

"I assure you, it has not been by choice. I was raised into it." Bitterness hardened his face. "When I was old enough to captain my own ship, I vowed I would do so legally. Unfortunately, honest tradesmen refused to trust me, since they had been cheated too many times by my father. And by me when I sailed with him. So I work for Henri and others like him. But now I have a chance to gain people's trust." He took both her hands in his. "This means more to me than I can say. I have few things in this life I am proud of, but I can change that for myself and for Andrew."

"Your son?"

He nodded. "I want him to be proud to be a Kingsley, not secretly ashamed as I have been. If I can do this, if I can help the South win this war, then stay honest when it's over, everything will be different from this point on."

"Which means not working for Henri." Despair tore through her at the thought of not seeing him. "Could you not carry legal goods for him?"

"Perhaps. Although . . . there is another reason I can no longer work for him."

"What is it?"

He hesitated, searching her eyes. "Marguerite, I . . . I simply cannot. For reasons that are best not spoken out loud."

"You come to say you are leaving, that I shall never see you again, but you will not tell me why? How can you do this? You know how unhappy I have been since coming here, how no one in Galveston accepts me. You are, in truth, the only friend I have, and now you would leave me?"

"I tell you, I must!"

"But why?"

He stood abruptly and moved away, stopping before one of the windows to stare out at the night. Her hands felt cold without him holding them. "Sweet God, I swore I wouldn't tell you this, but . . ." He pressed a hand to his forehead, hiding his face. "I cannot keep working for a man when I'm in love with his wife."

Her heart stopped, then resumed with such strength, she felt every beat. "You love me?"

He let out a dry laugh, turning back to her. "More than life, apparently, for I die a little every time I am with you, knowing I cannot have you. I value our friendship, but I also hate it, for I know that is all I will ever have from you. All you can give me."

She sat very still, afraid of what was happening. Words such as these would change things between them forever, if she managed to see him again. But she had kept her love for him trapped in silence too long. She stood and faced him, her body trembling. "You are wrong. I may belong to another by law, but my heart is mine alone to give. And I have given it to you so many times . . ." Her throat closed as tears filled her eyes. "Every time I see your face or think your name, I give my heart to you."

He stood staring at her. Then both of them moved at once and she was in his arms, their bodies crushed together. Their mouths met hungrily. She hardly dared to believe it was real, for she had dreamed it so many times, but the hard press of his body against her, the feel of his hands on her back, the taste of his mouth, were too real to deny.

She clung to him, kissing him with five years of pent-up passion. He swept her into his arms and strode toward the bed—

Someone knocked at the door. "Hey, Jackie!"

She plunged straight down into darkness and woke with a jolt. Jerking upright, she found herself sitting on the bed. Afternoon sunlight stabbed at her eyes. *What the hell?* She glanced down and saw she wore her cutoff shorts and baggy sweatshirt, not a green robe over sleek satin. Apparently, she'd fallen asleep and had had one doozy of a dream. Although the arousal coursing through her body was certainly real.

"Jackie, you decent?" Adrian called through the door.

"Hang on," she groused. Could he not have waited ten more minutes to wake her so the dream could have run its course? She marched to the door and jerked it open. "What is it?"

He blinked at her surly tone, then laughed, his usual chipper self. "Did I interrupt something?"

"I was taking a nap."

"Are you always this grouchy when you wake up?"

"I am when someone wakes me up in the middle of a really great dream."

"Oh, yeah?" His eyes lit with interest. "Was I in it?"

"No, that would be in your dreams." She rubbed her forehead, trying to think. The dream man had looked a little like him: same height, broad shoulders, long black hair, but there the similarity stopped. The features had been stronger, more chiseled, less perfect. Where had all those details come from? If she were going to have an erotic dream—which it would have been if he hadn't woken her—it made more sense for Adrian to star as the lover.

Especially dressed like that! she thought when she dropped her hand and saw his buccaneer costume. Or maybe she was still dreaming and things were about to get really kinky. "Why are you wearing that?"

"I was down on the Strand handing out fliers about the Haunted House Lunch Run. The outfit helps sell tickets." He stepped into the room, holding his arms out to show off the red captain's jacket, loose white shirt, and black pants that hugged his thighs before disappearing into tall black jackboots. She'd seen the outfit before, the night of the Buccaneer's Ball, but wow, memory did not do it justice. "You like it?" he asked with a grin.

"Doesn't do a thing for me."

"Liar."

"Is there a reason you woke me?"

"There is." His grin got even broader. "I ran into Carl Ryder as he came out of the Visitors' Center."

Her stomach dropped to her feet. "And . . ."

"He got the results back on the letter."

She braced a hand against the vanity as her knees started to buckle.

"Everything checked out!" Adrian announced. "He's going to apply for all the permits, which means we're one step closer to an actual excavation."

The air left her lungs in a rush. "Just like that? He doesn't want another meeting? He's taking the job?"

"He's taking the job!" He scooped her up against him and twirled her about three times before dropping her back on her feet. When she teetered, he steadied her by grabbing her shoulders. "Celebration. Tonight. We'll talk more then. I need to start dinner. Chill some champagne." His hands moved up to cup her face and he fit his mouth over hers for one heart-stopping moment filled with tastes and textures. Heat shot through her, landing low in her belly.

And then he stepped away. "Come down whenever you want. You can keep me company while I cook."

She stood there, stunned, as he strode back into the hall and closed the door. Part of her wanted to slug him for arousing her whole body with nothing more than a quick kiss. Another part of her wanted to call him back and demand he finish what he'd started. As if she hadn't been stirred up enough by that dream.

The dream! Her mind zipped back to Jack and Marguerite. She turned, looking about, and spotted the diary lying on the floor. Thoughts of the excavation and cruises and everything else could wait. She needed to know what had really happened that night in the past. Scooping up the diary, she climbed back on the bed and flipped through the pages to find the right one.

Adrian stopped halfway down the stairs as realization hit him. He'd just kissed Jackie! What had he been thinking? Clearly he hadn't been thinking at all, which was why the kiss had ended so quickly. Talk about a missed opportunity! If he were going to do something that stupid, he should have at least been paying attention enough to enjoy it.

He glanced over his shoulder, wondering what her reaction had been. She hadn't punched him, which boded well. In fact, she hadn't reacted at all. Maybe she'd taken the kiss as he'd intended: platonic enthusiasm.

Platonic? *Yeah, right,* he snorted. He didn't have a platonic thought in his head when it came to Jackie. Although that's how he *should* think about her. And since it looked like they really were going to do the cruises, he needed to get a lot more serious about behaving himself.

With that admonishment firmly in mind, he headed downstairs to change clothes and start dinner—after he took a cold shower.

An hour later, Jackie closed the diary with shaky hands and set it far away from her. What she'd read matched her dream too closely for comfort. Her mind searched for a logical explanation. Maybe she'd read more than she remembered before falling asleep, then dreamed about what she'd read. That had to be it.

Although the diary entry didn't stop with Jack swooping Marguerite into his arms. He'd carried her to the bed and they'd made love with a passion that left them both breathless. Afterward, as they lay in each other's arms, he'd asked her to come away with him. Telling him no had nearly killed her. When he pushed her for a reason, she couldn't tell him the whole truth, that she knew Henri would hunt them down and drag her home to beat her. Instead, she'd reminded him of everything he'd just said, about wanting to clear his name. Her running away with him would tarnish his reputation further when word spread that Captain Kingsley had stolen a man's wife. And when people learned whose wife, the scandal would be even worse.

As a respected and powerful icon in the shipping world, Henri would use his power to destroy Jack Kingsley. She loved Jack too deeply to ask him to sacrifice so much for her.

Added to that was a tiny seed of doubt. Henri had been very convincing about his devotion before they had married. What if Jack were no different and was wooing her for his own gain? After all the times she'd been used, she couldn't bear it if someone she cared for so desperately used her as well. She'd rather live in her current misery with the possibility that he did truly love her as he claimed, than risk everything and learn it was a lie. Such a devastation would destroy her.

So she held firm to her refusal to leave Henri, begging Jack to please not waste the night fighting with her.

He'd been angry at first, but she'd drawn him back into her arms, kissing him until they once again were making love.

Afterward, he'd asked her about the necklace she always wore. She told him the story of her birth and how the necklace had once belonged to Jean Lafitte. Then she asked him if the rumors about him were true, that he'd inherited Lafitte's missing treasure from his grandfather.

He'd laughed and told her yes, he had the treasure and he kept it in his cabin to remind him of all the things he didn't want to be. His words confirmed in her mind that she'd made the right choice. Clearing his name meant too much for him to throw his opportunity away.

She had taken off the necklace she'd worn every day of her life and given it to him. For luck, she'd told him, and to keep him safe. He'd nearly wept at her words, and clutching the necklace, he had vowed that he'd keep it with Lafitte's treasure as a further reminder to be a better man. Perhaps then, when he'd proved himself worthy, she'd leave Henri to be with him.

Just thinking of that nearly had Jackie crying, because Marguerite didn't seem to realize the depth of Jack's insecurity. He thought her rejection came from her not thinking he was good enough. Nothing could have been further from the truth. All things considered, though, Jackie supposed their relationship had been doomed from the beginning.

She thought about picking the diary back up and reading further, but then noticed the time. Her mood lifted abruptly as she remembered Adrian's news. The excavation was actually going to happen! Which meant she didn't have to leave Pearl Island with her tail between her legs. She could do the cruises, keep seeing the St. Claires, even be part of the wonderful, almost magical energy that seemed to surround them. Cause for celebration indeed.

Scrambling out of bed, she washed her face and dressed for dinner. She was already at the bottom of the stairs to the apartment before she remembered the kiss. The second Adrian looked up and his gaze collided with hers over the bar, it all came flooding back.

"Hi." She fidgeted.

"Hi." He looked equally uncertain.

Before she could make a fool of herself by saying "About that kiss, can we hit rewind, then forward in slow motion?" she noticed Rory sitting at a computer desk in the corner of the living area.

"Jackie, great, you're here." Rory waved for her to come closer. "I've been working up ideas for cruise packages and want to run them by you before the others get here."

"Hang on," Adrian said, drawing her attention back to him. "Care for some wine?"

His gaze was so steady, she knew this was about more than wine. "I, uh . . ."

"Let me get you a glass."

Wary, she moved around the bar into the kitchen, not knowing what to expect. Surely he wouldn't try to kiss her again with his sister sitting right there. Although a quick glance told her Rory's full attention was on the computer screen.

"About upstairs . . ." he said in a hushed voice.

A shiver went through her as she looked up into his eyes and she realized how close he stood. If he wanted to kiss her again, he wouldn't have to lean forward very far. Just the thought sent a delicious shiver through her.

"You know, the um . . ." He visibly struggled for the right words.

Just act normal, she told herself, fighting the memory of how tasty his lips had been. "Are you by chance referring to that brotherly peck?"

He relaxed. "Exactly. Brotherly peck. I just wanted to be sure you didn't think . . ."

"What, that you want my body?" She cocked a brow, fighting the desire to grab his head and pull his mouth down to hers. "We already know that you do. But we also know you ain't gettin' it, so the kiss didn't mean a thing. Right?" She nearly kicked herself for the tiny note of hope that had crept into her voice at the end.

"Right." He nodded. Then a frown line formed between his brows, as if he didn't know whether to be mad or relieved. "I was just checking."

"Well, it's not a problem." She smiled. "Although if you try it again, be prepared for a knee to the groin."

"I'll keep that in mind." He handed her a glass of wine. "Friends? For real this time. I mean it."

"Friends." She toasted him, wondering how long he'd last this time.

Chapter 12

To Jackie's amazement, Adrian behaved himself completely for the next two days. Even as she met with him and the others to make plans for the cruises, he didn't let one suggestive phrase slip—not even when he walked her out to her truck the morning she left. He just reminded her to save him a cabin on the first half of the first cruise.

What a rip, she thought as she drove down the coast to Corpus Christi. She knew she should be relieved, but at some point, she'd started to enjoy matching wits with him. Wasn't that just like a man, to change the rules right when she was learning how to play the game?

In the weeks that followed, she alternated between disappointment and frustration every time she talked to him on the phone, which she did quite a bit since their plans were going full speed ahead.

They'd settled on the week of Valentine's Day for the first cruise, which would give them time to promote it. The package would include a romantic dinner at the inn followed by live music and dancing in the ballroom on the third floor. For March they'd do a Mardi Gras cruise, then a luau on the beach in April.

The extravagance of the ideas left Jackie a bit dazed, but excited. She started to let herself believe, albeit cautiously, that teaming up with the Pearl Island Inn would lead her to that ever-elusive dream of financial stability.

Throughout the holiday season, she worked closely with Rory and Chance as they put together promotional packets for travel agents and prepared for an advertising campaign, all of which was going to cost a small fortune. Every time Rory blithely tossed out expense figures, Jackie struggled not to gasp and sputter.

Did the woman even know the word "caution"?

Fortunately, halfway through January, in the midst of sanding and varnishing the woodwork in the passenger cabins, surrounded by her hardworking, sweaty crew, Jackie's mobile phone rang with their first booking for the Valentine's cruise. She exchanged a high five with Ti, then headed for the officers' lounge in the stern of the ship for enough privacy and quiet to call the inn.

Rory answered, but passed her on to Adrian so she could share the good news. Pots and pans banged in the background and she pictured him moving around the kitchen with the phone between his shoulder and ear. After she told him about the booking, he brought her up to date on the plans for the excavation. The permits had been approved and a tentative starting date of mid-February had been set.

"So, with luck," he said, "you'll be here for the big event."

And so would Carl Ryder. "Oh. That will be . . . great."

"Okay," he sighed. "Now what are you worrying about?"

"Who says I'm worrying?" She circled between the battered wooden trunk strewn with sailing magazines and the L-shaped, padded benches that served as a sofa.

"I can hear it in your voice. Besides, you worry about everything."

"A habit formed by past experience."

"You forget," Adrian said. "We have Marguerite's good luck on our side. Everything is going to be fine. So, stop it, okay?"

"I'll try." Her stomach relaxed a bit at his admonishment. "And Adrian . . . thanks. You're a good friend."

"Yeah, that's what all the women say."

Laughing, she turned off the phone. Maybe this platonic thing would work after all. And why not? She was used to being friends with men. Lord knew she spent enough time around them. And Adrian struck her as one of those men who had lots of female friends.

Yes, the man was amazingly sexy, but during the last two months, with only his voice on the phone and no visuals to distract her, she'd realized his most attractive qualities were his intelligence, humor, and generosity. He had a way of making a woman feel good about herself and life in general. What woman wouldn't forgo the temporary thrill of sex for a chance to have a long-term friend like that? Especially since her choices seemed to be one or the other. Adrian had given her no indication that he wanted to try for a permanent romantic relationship, so giving in to temptation would be foolhardy. Right?

Absolutely, she told herself.

Although, another part of her sighed, *I bet Adrian does temporary lust really well.*

Finally, the day of the Valentine's cruise arrived. Jackie's stomach fluttered as she mounted the stairs to the quarterdeck. She assured herself her nervousness was due to the cruise. The rapid beat of her heart had nothing to do with the fact that Adrian would show up any minute.

She checked with Ti on the readiness of the ship and crew, then turned to watch passengers board. A jittery stomach was perfectly normal, considering all she had riding on this venture. She'd sunk what little savings she had left into finishing the cabins and hiring the extra hands needed to sail the ship for a four-day cruise.

Thumbing an antacid into her mouth, she surveyed the main deck where the bartender and galley hands were passing out mimosas to excited couples. The February sun played peekaboo behind the clouds, but the tropical music coming over the loudspeakers went a long way toward setting a festive mood.

The St. Claires' idea had been to provide a taste of fantasy and a trip back through time, its theme being a pirate ship sailing the Caribbean Sea. To that end, Jackie had ordered traditional sailor's garb for the galley crew: pullover tops with broad, horizontal stripes and three-quarter-length pants. Her own outfit was a big-sleeved shirt with black leggings tucked into boots. She'd cinched her waist with a bright red sash but left off the jacket due to the blessedly warm weather. For added effect, she'd thrust an antique dagger in the sash and wore two gold hoop earrings.

As for the professional sailors on board, she'd given them free rein to put together whatever old-world attire they wanted, which was the only way she could get most of them to dress up. Although hard-core sailors frequently saw themselves as throwbacks to an age when seafaring men endured months of grueling labor, then blew off steam by indulging in liquor, prostitutes, and knife fights, they didn't necessarily want to dress that way. Despite their condescending attitude, she noticed that once they donned their costumes, they took to their roles with relish. A smile tugged at her lips as she watched the antics of two crewmen as they swung from the rigging like Errol Flynn, delighting the passengers.

The rumble of a Harley cut through the music and laughter on deck. She strode to the rail and saw Adrian half riding, half walking the motorcycle down the pier, drawing the eyes of fishermen and day sailors along the crowded wharf. He wore his hair back in its customary ponytail and his leather jacket hung open to reveal a torso-hugging turtleneck. His faded jeans stretched tautly over his thighs.

Oh man, she nearly groaned aloud at the sight of him. How could she have forgotten just how unbearably gorgeous he was? And she couldn't even gawk openly, like the women in the sailboat across the pier.

When he reached her ship, he looked first at the men in the rigging, then lowered his gaze to her. "Were you about to set sail without me?"

As if, she thought. "Actually, we have one more van-load of passengers coming from the airport, so you're just in time to join the pre-cruise party."

"Party? I'll be right there." He grabbed the saddlebags off the back of his bike and headed up the ramp. She asked Ti to be sure the motorcycle was loaded into the hold, then went to meet Adrian at the top of the gangway. He stepped onto the crowded deck and looked around, taking in the festivities. "Boy, you weren't kidding."

Though noon had yet to arrive, several of the passengers had clearly had more than one mimosa and were dancing to the music or waving to people on the dock. A tarp provided shelter from the weather for the bar area near the foredeck. The crew had also set up a buffet of fruit and finger sandwiches.

"Great job," Adrian said. "This is perfect."

"Actually, this is the easy part. We're used to having parties on board. Things will get more interesting once we set sail."

"What do you mean? You leave port all the time."

"Not for four days at a stretch." Jackie snagged a glass from a passing tray and handed it to him. "Oh well, for better or worse, welcome aboard."

Laughing, he took the glass. "Maybe you should have one of these, to settle your nerves."

"Don't tempt me." She pressed a hand to her stomach.

Speaking of tempting . . . Adrian let his gaze drift over her as he took a sip of mimosa. During the past months, he'd managed to convince himself that he could be around Jackie without wanting her naked. Wrong. Talking on the phone with a couple hundred miles between them did not compare to having her right before him looking like a vision from one of his kinkier fantasies: the one that involved her tying him to her bed in the captain's cabin. Thank God her chest was squished flat under that big-sleeved shirt, or he'd have a hard time not jumping her on the spot.

"So." She clasped her hands and looked around. "You want me to show you to your cabin?"

I'd rather see yours. He shook off the thought and he ordered himself to keep it friendly. "That would be great. The day's warmed up since I left the inn, and I'd like to get out of this turtleneck."

"Okay, then, follow me."

Handing his drink to a waiter, he hitched the saddlebags over his shoulder. "You have no idea how much I've looked forward to this, especially after the winter we've had."

"Oh?" she asked, looking back at him over her shoulder. "I got the impression you were having a good winter."

"Good, but busy." They wove their way through the clutter of coiled lines, then around a mast toward the housing over the main hatch. "Between Galveston's annual Dickens on the Strand, Christmas, then New Year's, we've been booked solid. Things slowed down in January, but with Allison gone on her honeymoon, I've had to pitch in cleaning rooms and doing an endless amount of laundry. Do you have any idea how many sheets and towels we go through in a day?"

"I have a feeling I'm about to find out." She started down the wooden steps, bending forward slightly. The tail of her shirt rose up, giving him a perfect view of her firm, round backside. "Mind your head," she said.

He smacked into the top of the hatch. "Ouch!"

She turned and laughed up at him, the sunlight sparkling in her hazel eyes. "Now you know why men who took to the sailing life back in the old days were usually on the short side."

"Either that or hunchbacked." Rubbing his head, he ducked enough to make it down the steps.

"This is the galley, where you'll take your meals with the crew and other passengers. Just be forewarned, we do our best but the food isn't as good as what you serve at the inn."

"As long as I don't have to cook, it'll be great."

"Officers' quarters are aft." She pointed to a passageway across from them. "The crew sleeps on the level below us, and passengers' cabins are this way." She started down the passageway that led toward the bow.

"I'm afraid your cabin isn't our best, but the trip sold so well, it's the biggest one I could spare."

"I'm hardly going to complain about the response being so good."

"Me, either. It's just . . ." Her hands moved in a restless gesture, as she stopped at the first door on the right. "After you gave me your best room, I know I should have done the same, but . . . truth be told, my expenses are through the roof, and I flat-out couldn't afford to give my nicest cabin to a nonpaying passenger."

"Jackie"—he grinned at her—"it's not a problem."

"Yes, well, here we are." She opened the door and stepped back so he could enter.

He had to turn his shoulders to get through the opening, but the room itself wasn't that bad. He dropped his bags on the narrow bunk and noted the storage drawers underneath, a miniature desk and mirror along one wall, a small closet. Everywhere he looked, varnished wood and brass gleamed.

"The head's through here." She closed the cabin door, then maneuvered past him, filling his nostrils with the tropical scent of her shampoo as she opened a door that was even narrower than the first.

Fighting a rush of arousal, he came up behind her to peek at the sink, flush toilet, and a shower that was basically a drain in the floor with a curtain to pull around it.

"It's small, I know." She turned to give him room, but bumped into him. Their chests and thighs connected for one electrifying instant before she jumped back and came up against the doorjamb. "S-sorry," she said, her voice breathy. "It's kind of tight in here."

He looked down at her flushed face. "It'll be fine."

She stared up at him, her eyes dilated, their bodies

almost touching. "I'll, um . . . find a way to make it up to you."

His gaze dropped to her full mouth, the lips that had fascinated him from the first. *Step away,* his common sense shouted, but the scent of her was filling his head.

One taste, he thought. *Just one small nibble to make up for not paying attention the last time.*

Propping a hand on the wall above her head, he leaned close, breathing her in as he gave her a chance to decide. Her eyes widened, but no knee came toward his groin. He lowered his mouth to hers. Their lips touched, and he stopped for a heartbeat. Then the plush feel of her mouth registered, and he closed his eyes to savor.

A moan rumbled in her throat, vibrating through his body. She surged against him, catching him off guard. He adjusted quickly, deciding a big bite was even better than a nibble. And God, she tasted good. Her arms went around his neck, her fingers in his hair. Heat flooded him with startling speed.

Pulling her close, he moved his hands over her torso, marveling at the feel of her firm, slender body. If only she weren't wearing a blasted sports bra.

Her hands moved to his back, clutching at his leather jacket as if trying to feel him through it, and he cursed his own clothing as well, especially when her pelvis rubbed his arousal through his jeans. Hunger turned to need. He moved a thigh between hers. She gasped at the contact, and he hardened even more.

Cupping her bottom through the leggings, he hoisted her against the cabin wall. Her legs went around his waist as he pinned her there with his body.

"Oh yes!" Her head fell back as he pressed into her core, and the pleasure on her face nearly shot him over the edge. He buried his mouth against her exposed neck and her pulse pounded against his lips. The one brain cell he had still working registered that the bunk was barely two steps away. He could have her on the bunk, her body naked, and be thrusting inside her in a minute and a half. Two minutes, tops.

"Cap'n Taylor?" a deep voice called out in the passageway.

They both froze.

"Cap'n? Are you down here? Mr. Ti needs you on the bridge."

"Shit!" she whispered, then knocked her head back against the wall a couple of times as if to engage her brain. "I'm coming!"

"No, but close," Adrian murmured near her ear.

"Aye, sir! Er, ma'am." Footsteps receded.

Adrian rested his forehead on the wall and laughed in frustration as he let her legs slide back down.

"This is not funny, you . . . jerk!" She shoved hard against his chest.

He stumbled back, only to have his calves collide with the bunk. He let himself fall, deciding it was easier than standing in his current condition.

"I can't believe this," she ranted. "What the hell has gotten into you—kissing me like that?"

Propping himself up on his elbows, he stared down at the obvious bulge in his blue jeans. "Gee, I can't imagine."

"Jerk!" She threw something at him and it landed on his chest. He glanced down and saw the rubber band that had been holding his hair.

"This was not supposed to happen." She managed to pace in the small cabin. "What about us being *friends*? I thought you really meant it. You haven't even flirted with me in forever!"

"Yeah, well, that's easier to do when I'm not looking at you."

"Then don't look at me!" She pressed shaking hands to her forehead, shielding her eyes. "And fix your hair, would ya?"

So she liked how he looked with his hair down, eh? Sitting up, he finger-combed his hair back from his face and fastened it at the nape. "Okay, it's safe. You can look now."

He nearly laughed when she peeked through her fingers before dropping her hands.

She stood before him, looking every inch the lady pirate in her billowing white shirt. "Okay, here's the deal, and the rules. I realize that in some warped way, you enjoy getting me flustered, which, okay, I can handle away from here, but I will not have you treating me with disrespect *on my ship*!"

"Disrespect?" His amusement vanished. "I have never treated you with disrespect."

"What do you call . . . *that*!" She gestured toward the wall where their bodies had been pressed.

He stood and towered over her. "Spontaneous combustion."

"Well, I won't have it!" she raged up at him. "Not on board my ship. I may not be twenty years old and struggling to start my own business anymore, but I am still a woman trying to make a living in a world dominated by men. Do you know how hard I've had to work to win the respect of my crew? Every time I hire a new sailor, I have to prove myself all over again. Well, half the men on board this trip are new, and I will not let you come along and undermine my authority by treating me like—like—"

"A desirable woman?"

"An easy lay."

"Okay, whoa, stop right there!" He raised his hands. "I have never treated you, or any woman, like that in my life, and I resent the accusation."

"Resent it all you want, but watch how you treat me in front of my crew."

He glared back at her, wanting to point out that the kiss hadn't exactly been one-sided, but the fury blazing in her eyes told him she needed to cool off before she'd listen to reason. "Okay. Fair enough. In front of your crew, I won't even *think* of you as a woman."

"Fine." Her cheeks flushed as if he'd insulted her in some new way. "Then if you'll excuse me, I have work to do." She stormed from the cabin.

He dropped back down on the bunk as the full impact of what he'd done hit him. So much for keeping everything friendly to avoid any awkward situations. "Way to go, St. Claire. Way to go."

Chapter 13

By the time Adrian changed into a sleeveless T-shirt and swapped his motorcycle boots for running shoes, he had his physical frustration under control. His mental frustration, however, still simmered as he returned to the party on the deck. The sun had finally beaten off the clouds, driving most of the passengers to the shade of the awning. He headed that way and found an empty stool at the bar. One question, though, kept nagging at him. Did Jackie really think he didn't respect her? Or had that been her temper talking?

He looked across the crowded main deck toward the bridge and saw her talking to Ti. Her stiff posture broadcast her mood loud and clear: uptight and ready to tangle. That didn't, however, mean she was still angry at him. He knew she tended to bottle her emotions up, especially when berating herself, which she was probably doing now that her initial fury was spent.

A part of him wanted to go right up there and goad her into another blowup so she could yell it out of her system and then they could talk like rational adults. If only he knew what he wanted to say once she did cool down.

"What can I get you?" the bartender asked.

He ordered a draft beer, then drew patterns in the

condensation on the side of the glass as he tried to sort out what to do. First he needed to explain that he more than respected her; he found her amazing. After everything she'd been through growing up, she'd started her own business at age twenty. She was strong, determined, feisty. And he wished like hell they'd had a chance to date before that chance had been taken from them.

But it had been taken away.

If he were interested in settling down in the immediate future, maybe he'd risk dating her despite the business complications. After all, things had worked out for Rory and Chance, and their situation hadn't been much different. Except that his sister had known from the start that she loved Chance and had chosen to risk everything in hopes of winning him.

He didn't have that certainty with Jackie. She fascinated him, yes. He enjoyed talking to her, and he damn sure wanted to sleep with her. But he didn't know if he wanted to *marry* her. Even if she had surprised him with nuances to her personality that he hadn't suspected, having to make a decision that huge up front really irritated him.

Most men and women had the luxury of trying each other on for size and letting their relationship develop at a comfortable pace. But no, he had to decide to either go for Jackie all out, or pull back and keep his hands off. If that didn't stink, he didn't know what did. Brooding about it, however, solved nothing. This was the day he'd been looking forward to for months, and while he could kick himself for his earlier blunder, he didn't have to let it ruin his whole trip.

Taking up his beer, he swiveled on the stool to rest his back against the bar and take in the party going on around him. Couples mingled around the buffet table, introducing themselves, while others watched the sailors climb into the rigging.

When the crew started taking up positions at various points, a tangible excitement moved through the crowd. The muffled purr of modern engines rumbled somewhere deep in the belly of the ship. Jackie had told him they used engine power to navigate Corpus Christi Bay, then raised the sails as soon as they slipped past the barrier islands.

He watched as she stepped to the rail with Ti behind her at the ship's wheel. She raised a walkie-talkie to her mouth, apparently communicating with the dockhands on the pier. When the mooring lines were cast off, the ship began to move. A cheer went up among the passengers as people on board and on the docks waved.

"Look, sweetheart," a woman said, pointing upward. "Can you believe they actually climb up there?"

Adrian moved out from under the awning to see four sailors halfway up the mast stepping off the platform onto nothing more than a rope with their bellies draped over the yardarm. They spread out, preparing to unfurl the first of several square sails.

"Man," the woman's husband breathed in awe, "you couldn't pay me enough to do that."

Adrian looked at him in surprise. Personally, he'd love the chance to climb all the way to the top just to see what the world looked like from up there.

As the ship passed Padre Island, the music over the speakers clicked off. Jackie called out to one of the sailors on deck, "Stand by the main topmast stays'l!"

A stocky man with white hair repeated the order back to her in a thick British accent, then gestured to the passengers. "All right, laddies, if you've ever wanted to try your hand at being a sailor, I need some strong arms to heave the halyard."

Adrian set his beer aside without a moment's hesitation and stepped forward with two other men. They took hold of a line as thick as his forearm.

"Keep your eyes on me, and pull in time," the man told them. They gave a few tugs that accomplished little. More passengers joined in and they fell into an awkward rhythm. An enormous triangular sail began a ponderous journey up the mainmast, metal rings clanking while the wrench squeaked. The British crewman at the head of the line began to sing "The Drunken Sailor" in a rousing voice.

Adrian quickly realized the song was meant to help them keep in time. He and the other men joined in singing, "Way, hey, up she rises. Way, hey, up she rises. Way, hey, up she rises early in the morning."

From the quarterdeck, Jackie called out more orders that were echoed back to her. The first of the square sails unfurled and filled with wind.

"That's away!" the man leading them shouted. Taking that to mean they were done, he and the others released the line to the cheers of the watching passengers. The husbands who had helped raised their arms in a gesture of victory, the conquering heroes.

Chest heaving from the exertion, Adrian looked up as the next square sail unfurled. The age-yellowed canvas billowed out with a multitude of patches but still a beautiful sight against the vivid blue sky. He could feel the vibration of the ship through his feet as they picked up speed, slicing through the open waters of the Gulf.

God, what a moment! he thought, feeling alive in a

way he'd never experienced. No wonder Jackie loved her ship and this life, challenges and all.

He glanced to the quarterdeck and saw her standing there, her feet braced slightly apart as she watched her men in the rigging. As if sensing his attention, she lowered her eyes. Their gazes met and held. He smiled at her as pleasure swelled inside his chest.

She returned his smile cautiously, and he knew she shared the same joy in being under way, but the scene in the cabin still lay between them. Exhilaration and awkwardness warred in the air between them . . . along with tingling excitement.

Behind her, Ti asked a question, breaking the moment.

Jackie pulled her gaze away from Adrian, still battling guilt over how she'd acted earlier. Ten minutes after leaving his cabin, she'd realized what a bitch she'd been, lighting into him that way, as if the kiss had been all his fault, as if she hadn't wanted him to kiss her, or hadn't enjoyed it to the point of nearly climaxing right there against the wall. Good heavens, the man could kiss!

Even now, the memory brought the heat of arousal back to her cheeks along with the added flush of embarrassment. She needed to apologize, obviously, but how? She'd never been good at things that required humility.

Well, she told herself, sometimes a person had to do the right thing, no matter how uncomfortable it became. And she definitely needed to do something to smooth over this debacle: for the sake of her business, but for personal reasons, too. She'd come to enjoy Adrian's friendship, dammit, and didn't want to ruin it because of her stupid temper. So she'd apologize, then do a better job from this moment on controlling her temper, and her lust.

• • •

Just before sunset, the *Pirate's Pleasure* slipped into a cove and anchored. They'd stay there for supper, then continue up the coast, getting as much distance as they could behind them during the night in order to reach Pearl Island by afternoon the next day.

After making her rounds, Jackie descended through the main hatch, but stopped for a moment on the steps to survey the galley. The buzz of voices and clatter of dishes filled the air as passengers chatted and laughed together. The servers moved in a steady stream, setting down plates of seafood. She'd had dinners on board before, but somehow this was different. This was what she'd dreamed of doing since she was eighteen and working aboard the *Sea Star.*

A burst of laughter drew attention to a table in the corner where she found Adrian entertaining his dinner companions with some anecdote. Like the other passengers, he'd cleaned up for the evening meal, and now wore a white dress shirt and jeans. Throughout the day, she'd noticed how easily he won people over. He'd worked side by side with her crew far more than any of the other passengers, even helping take the sails down when they'd reached the cove.

She should have expected that of him, she supposed, after how much interest in sailing he'd shown during their phone conversations. Still, it surprised her that he'd been so instantly good at it.

In mid-laugh, he looked over, and saw her. His smile subsided some, but not completely. After a brief hesitation, he nodded to an empty chair at his table. Her heart lifted at the gesture. Was he willing to forgive her so easily? She wished she could join him and pretend nothing had happened. Unfortunately, she still had duties to perform.

She gave him a look of apology and tipped her head toward the main table, hoping he'd remember that some of the passengers had paid extra for reserved seats at the captain's table.

He nodded, letting her know he understood, then turned his attention back to his new friends.

With a sigh, she headed for her table, resigned to an hour of listening to sailing enthusiasts tell her about their yachts and how many America's Cups they'd attended. Normally, she enjoyed such conversations. Tonight, however, she spent the whole time mentally wrestling with what she'd say to Adrian when and if she managed to have ten minutes alone with him aboard a crowded ship.

After dinner, Adrian grabbed his leather jacket from his cabin and wandered topside. He stepped onto the deck and into the midst of another party. In the bar area, strings of white Christmas-tree lights had been strung beneath the tarp, adding a touch of whimsy. For entertainment, three of the crewmembers played old sailing songs on a hand accordion, fiddle, and harmonica. Passengers clapped in time or even danced.

He saw the three couples he'd eaten with: Bob and Sandy, James and Mary, Peter and Georgia. They'd all been strangers when they'd sat down together, but had hit it off instantly. They waved for him to join them, but he shook his head. His body ached from a full day of pulling on lines and learning the rigging. What he really wanted was a little peace and quiet.

Since most of the noise and lights were toward the

bow, he headed for the quarterdeck, where a single sailor stood by the wheel. At his surge of disappointment, he realized he'd actually come looking for Jackie. Although he still wasn't sure what he'd say once they had enough privacy to talk.

"Evening," the sailor greeted him.

Adrian nodded and headed for the rail at the very back of the ship. With the music in the distance, he could hear the pinging sound of the rigging and the lapping of the waves against the hull. Glancing up, he marveled at the number of stars. The Milky Way arched so close overhead, he felt as if he could reach up and touch it.

He envied Jackie this, the sense of freedom and exhilaration he'd felt all day. He loved his life, his family and friends, but a part of him had been feeling hemmed in lately as if life were passing him by.

Voices came from behind him, one of them definitely Jackie. He turned, but didn't see her. Then he noticed the golden light spilling from the hatch to the pilot house, which sat between the two sets of stairs to the quarterdeck. Jackie and the white-haired Brit moved into view. Though he couldn't see more than their heads, they seemed to be bending over something. A sea chart, he presumed. A sonar, ship-to-shore radio, and other instruments filled the cramped space.

"Very well," he heard her say. "It's your watch, Mr. Jamison. I'll be in my cabin. Wake me if you need me."

She turned and mounted the ladder-steep steps to the quarterdeck and he saw she'd donned a navy peacoat over her costume. Not exactly in keeping with her lady-pirate character, but close enough to not ruin the effect completely.

The moment she saw him, she hesitated. He leaned

against the rail, trying to look casual, hoping she'd join him. Thrusting her hands in the pockets of the coat, she headed toward him, then stopped with her feet braced as if for battle. He waited for her opening volley.

"Evening," she said, with no inflection.

"Evening," he returned cautiously. When she didn't say anything more, he looked up at the sky. "Nice night."

"Hm?" She looked up, as well. "Oh. Yes, it is."

He kept his face turned upward, but rolled his eyes sideways to read her expression. A frown flirted across her face as she pretended, like him, to gaze at the stars. Finally, she sighed and stepped to the rail, holding it with both hands and glaring at the dark water.

"Look, about earlier. In your cabin." She cleared her throat. "I'm sorry for the things I said—"

"It's okay. I realize—"

"Do not interrupt me." She sent him an irritated look. "I stink at apologizing, and will do better if I can get it all out in one go."

He hid a smile at the determined set of her jaw, which contrasted with the uncertainty in her eyes. He wanted to hug her and tell her to forget the apology, but motioned for her to continue.

"Okay." She turned toward him and scowled at his chest. "Where was I? Oh yeah . . ." She took a breath and launched into an obviously rehearsed speech. "Ti says when I'm upset, I tend to speak before I think. He's right. The things I said to you earlier today weren't fair. Well, not entirely. You haven't treated me with disrespect, per se, *but* you do enjoy getting me flustered. You can't deny that." Her voice built up steam. "As for kissing me, you have to admit, that went way too far—"

"Is this an apology or an admonishment?"

"I'm working up to it," she growled, then sighed in defeat. "I told you I stink at this."

"So you did." He slumped lower against the rail for a better view of her face. Starlight shone on her cheeks and made her eyelashes look thicker. "Take your time."

She frowned. "I lost my place again."

"How about if I help out?"

She gave him a wary look.

" 'I'm sorry, Adrian,' " he said, " 'for anything I may have done to make your stupid blunder even worse, like drive you half-insane by kissing you back. The truth is, I think you're a really hot stud, and I'd love to jump your bones, but I think we'd both be better off in the long run if we stay friends.' "

She choked. " 'Really hot stud'?"

"Wait, you're not finished."

"I'm not? Oh, I can't wait to hear what I have left to say after that." Her laugh helped his chest relax.

" 'I think you are one of the sexiest men who has ever lived—' "

"Your ego is showing."

" '—and I dream about you night and day—' "

"No, those are your dreams, remember?"

" '—but I value the other things we have.' " He looked straight into her eyes. "Because, you see, I do respect you, as much as I hope you respect me."

Her shoulders sagged. "I do."

" 'I've enjoyed getting to know you as a friend these last weeks as much as I've enjoyed the prospect that we'll both profit financially from our acquaintance.' "

"Exactly."

" 'So I'm sorry for anything I may have done to jeopardize our friendship.' "

She looked at him, her eyes thankful. "Yes. That's what I wanted to say."

"Okay, then." He straightened and held out his hand. "Apology accepted, both ways, I hope."

"Thank you." She took his hand in a firm handshake.

He winced as pain snaked up from his palm.

"What?" She looked down, taking his hand in both of hers and tipping it toward the light from the chart house.

"It's nothing," he said, too late. She'd already noticed the strip of raw flesh on his palm. "Okay, so I have a slight rope burn."

"Slight?" Her eyes widened with disbelief. "Men! I swear, you're all alike the world over. Too stubborn to admit it when you hurt yourself."

"Unlike some women I know who aren't stubborn at all."

"Come on. I'll doctor you up."

"Will you kiss it and make it better?"

She frowned at him. "I thought you weren't going to flirt with me anymore."

"If you'll notice, I wasn't flirting with you this afternoon and we saw how well that worked. I've decided this is safer."

"You are so warped. As for my kissing your boo-boo, forget it. I will, however, be happy to drop an anchor on your foot to take your mind off it."

"God, I love it when you talk rough."

"Will you love it when I pour antiseptic on your rope burn?"

"Be still, my heart."

Chapter 14

"Make yourself at home," Jackie said as she entered her cabin ahead of Adrian. Shedding her jacket, she hung it on a peg and flipped a light switch. Brass wall fixtures came to life, bathing the cabin in soft, golden light. "I'll get the first-aid kit."

Adrian froze when he saw the room. He'd been in the cabin before, the night of the Buccaneer's Ball when Rory had had one of her panic attacks. Jackie had noticed something was wrong and offered them the use of her quarters. That night, however, the room had been dark and he'd been more concerned with Rory than his surroundings.

He must have taken in more than he realized, though, because the cabin exactly matched the setting of his fantasy with Jackie in her pirate boots and him tied to her bed: swagged draperies, gold tassels, wood paneling.

His eyes shifted sideways to the bed, which was set into the wall by the door. A brocade spread tangled with snow-white sheets and a haphazard pile of pillows.

His body hardened in a rush and he turned away.

Okay, you can handle this, he told himself. Uncomfortably warm, he whipped off his jacket and hung it beside Jackie's. To gain some distance from the bed, he circled around a heavy table that dominated the space before a bank of windows and a French rococo fireplace. A thronelike chair sat with its back to the windows and the table appeared to double as a desk. He paused to glance outside and admire the starlit waters of the cove.

Through the partially closed door to the bathroom— or "head" as Jackie called it—he could hear her rummaging around. "Great place," he called.

"Thanks." Her laughter tumbled out, as if she doubted his sincerity. "My father had somewhat, um, lavish taste."

Continuing his path, he stopped before a wall of bookshelves and cabinets, all in a gleaming wood that brought to mind an English manor library. He noted a multitude of volumes on ships, sailing, and history, but most of the shelves were crammed full of paperback novels. He tipped his head to read the titles, hoping for a distraction from the dangerous thoughts running through his brain.

What he found didn't help at all. The titles all contained such words as "ravished," "lover," "passionate," "embrace." He picked up one, opened the discreet flowery cover and stared at the image beneath of a nude couple making out on satin sheets with only a few vital areas hidden from view. His own body stirred in response.

"Sorry to keep you waiting," Jackie said, stepping out of the bathroom.

He slapped the cover closed as he turned and got a further jolt to his system. She'd taken off her bra. Her shirt hung loose enough with the red sash removed that she probably thought he couldn't tell, but . . . heaven help him, he could definitely tell. Her breasts swung enticingly as she walked toward him.

He jerked his gaze back to the book. "You read romance novels?"

She chuckled as she set a first-aid kit on the table and came even closer. "No need to look so shocked. Lots of women do."

"I know." His throat tightened with desire and he had to clear it. "I just find it interesting that you're one of them. My sister Alli, the woman most likely to go for gooey love stories, prefers suspense thrillers. And here you are, the woman I'd peg to read action adventure, with a whole bookcase of romance novels."

"Some of them have plenty of action and adventure."

"True. But they spend more time describing what everyone is *feeling*." He shuddered playfully.

"How would you know?"

"I dated the owner of a bookstore for a while. She talked me into trying a few."

"Oh? What'd you think?"

"Damn good stories for the most part." *With some really hot sex.* He cleared his throat again. "Just, um, not my first pick for reading material."

"I suppose you like hair-raising suspense, like your brother-in-law writes." She went to a stack of straight-backed chairs secured in one corner and carried one to the table.

"When I read fiction, he's one of my favorite authors. Mostly, though, I read nonfiction. Philosophy, mythology, ancient religions, books on the martial arts—"

"No wonder you dated a bookseller. You needed the friend-of-the-owner discount." Crossing back to him, she opened one of the cabinets, revealing a treasure trove of junk food. "So, you like dark rum?"

"As long as it's not mixed with a bunch of stuff that

makes it taste like a kid's drink." He watched as she bent over to open a lower cabinet that turned out to be a mini refrigerator/freezer. As she filled two highball glasses with ice, his gaze wandered to her firm behind and slender legs, perfectly showcased in tight leggings. He tried to not think about running his hands up the inside of her thighs. "Worst hangover I ever had was from drinking trash-can punch made with rum."

"That's what you get for drinking the cheap stuff mixed with too much sugar." She kicked the fridge closed and moved to the table. Hooking the thronelike chair with the tip of her boot, she pulled it out, plopped down, and poured two shots into the cut-glass tumblers. She held one out to him. "To kill the pain."

"What are you going to do, amputate my hand?" He took the other chair and accepted the drink.

"Nothing that drastic." Her laugh sounded slightly diabolical as she opened the first-aid kit. "But I've never received a compliment for my nursing abilities."

"Thanks for the warning."

She took a healthy swallow, exposing her throat briefly, before setting the glass aside. "Okay, let me see your hand."

He sipped cautiously from his own glass. The rum slid down his throat with a blend of smoky, buttery flavors. "Mmm, good stuff."

"It should be. Fifteen-year-old Martinique rum, aged in oak barrels." She made a come-here gesture with her fingers. "Now quit stalling."

Bracing himself, he held his hand out, then hissed when she swabbed it with an antiseptic wipe. "Je-sus!"

Her grip tightened when he tried to pull away. "Oh, it doesn't hurt that bad."

"Well, excuse me, but I'd like to keep what skin I have left on that hand." He tugged harder, then nearly groaned when the tug-of-war made her breasts jiggle.

"Here"—she held on to him with one hand and reached for the bottle with the other—"have another drink and quit being such a baby." After filling his glass, she jerked his hand toward her and bent over it.

His gaze slipped to the deep vee of her shirt, which wasn't laced as tightly as it had been earlier. Sweat broke out on his forehead as he noticed how close his fingers were to the opening. He wondered how her breasts would feel nestled in his palm and moaned as his body hardened.

"Lord, you are a wimp." She laughed, massaging ointment into the palm of his hand.

The sensation traveled straight to his groin, and he imagined her touching him there. He rested the elbow of his free arm on the table and hid his face in his hand. "Talk to me."

"About what?" She blew on his palm.

"Anything! Take my mind off . . . the pain. Tell me about Martinique."

"What about it?"

"Have you been there?"

"I've been to nearly all the islands."

"Which one's your favorite?"

"Bequia. But for personal reasons, not because it's any more or less beautiful than the others."

"Oh?"

"My Grandma Merry lives there along with most of my aunts, uncles, and cousins."

"Your mother's Caribbean?" That would explain her exotic features. "I never hear you talk about her."

"My mother's half Caribbean. Her father was a rich white tourist who apparently didn't want to take home a souvenir quite that big." Releasing his hand, she snapped the lid closed on the first-aid kit.

"Tell me about her." He leaned back, shifting subtly inside his jeans.

"There's not much to tell. She dumped my dad when I was five, and I've hardly seen her since."

"Do you see the rest of your Caribbean relatives?"

"Not as often as I'd like." She leaned back as well and plopped her boots on the table with her ankles crossed. Sitting in the captain's cabin, dressed like a pirate, she looked every inch his fantasy.

He tossed back a big gulp of rum and prayed for strength.

"It's weird," she said, "I really enjoyed the few times my dad took me to see them, but it made me sad, too."

"Why sad?"

"I don't know. I guess because I never really fit in. For one thing, my cousins all grew up together, so I was always the outsider. For another, none of my mother's half siblings like her very much." She wrinkled her nose. "They think she's snooty."

"Is she?"

"Oh yeah." She laughed. When he reached for the bottle, she held her glass out for a refill. "But I love Grandma Merry and she always seemed happy to see me. At first." She frowned as if at some memory. "Until my father would do something to tick someone off, then she or one of my uncles would ask us to leave."

"Do you ever hear from your mother?"

"Occasionally." She ran a fingertip around the rim of the glass. "Mostly I just hear about her through my grandmother. Right now she's living in a mansion on St. Lucia with a businessman who divides his time between her and his wife and kids back in the States." She sipped her rum thoughtfully. "You know, this is really depressing me. Why don't we talk about you?"

"What do you want to know?"

"What was your childhood like? I bet it was great."

"It had its moments."

"Like what?" She smiled and waggled her boots in encouragement. He imagined grabbing her ankles and jerking her over to straddle his lap so he could lose himself in that mouth of hers. "Tell me something happy," she said. "What did you enjoy most when you were a kid?"

"A little kid?" He tried to think, but either rum or lust was fogging his brain. "Traveling. I miss seeing new places, meeting people, and life backstage."

"Your parents were actors?"

He nodded, and took another drink. "Not as successful as Aunt Viv, but yes."

"Did you ever think about going into showbiz?"

"Actually . . ." He leaned forward and lowered his voice. "I'll tell you something, but you can't tell my sisters."

"Oh, goodie, secrets." She dropped her feet and leaned toward him, crossing her forearms on the table.

"I'm serious, you have to keep this to yourself." He let his gaze wander over her face, noticing how soft her skin looked. "They'd feel guilty if they knew, and I don't want that."

"Your secret's safe with me."

"In high school, I was in every production the drama club put on. I really took to acting, and my aunt was a great coach. My senior year, I was one of the leads in

Guys and Dolls. My aunt's agent happened to be in town, so he came with her to opening night."

"Let me guess." She tipped her head. "He saw you act and offered to make you a star."

"Bingo." He took another drink, hoping the numbness in his brain would spread south.

"You're kidding." Her eyes brightened. "Really? So what happened?"

"I told him no."

"You told him no?" She stared in disbelief. "Why?"

"Because he'd come to Galveston to talk my aunt into returning to Broadway." He studied the melting ice in his glass. "The only way she could leave Galveston was if I stuck around after graduation to finish raising my sisters."

"Jesus. You gave up something that big for your *sisters*? Do you regret it?"

"Yes and no. I've had a great life. Really," he insisted. "Although . . ."

"What?"

"A part of me can't stop wondering . . . what if?" His eyes held hers. "You know?"

"Yeah." Jackie's voice became husky as she looked at him, so close, she could easily reach out and touch him. He had the most perfectly shaped mouth she'd ever seen. The memory of its taste made her ache for another long, deep, wet kiss like they'd shared that afternoon. "What if."

"So what's your big 'what if'?"

She shook her head, and laughed in embarrassment at the thoughts running through her brain.

"Come on." He topped her drink off, his voice a teasing rumble. "I told you one of my secrets. Now you have to tell me one of yours."

"You already know all my worst secrets." *Except how badly I want you.*

"There must be something," he said as moonlight from the window caught his blue eyes. "Something about you no one knows."

"No way, St. Claire." She tossed back a swallow and when she lowered her glass, she found him watching her with hooded eyes. The room grew warmer.

"What if I tell you another one of mine?"

Her head swam pleasantly. "God, you're an easy drunk."

"This isn't the rum. It's just something I have to say."

Her heartbeat turned slow and heavy at his sudden intensity. "What?"

"I really wish you'd told us no about the cruises."

"Gee, thanks." She laughed, uncomfortably aware of the hard chair against her sensitive skin. "I look forward to working with you, too."

"I wish you'd said no"—he placed the tip of his finger against her chin—"because then I could have propositioned you for something a lot more personal. My secret is, I have never wanted any woman as much as I want you."

She went still, her skin tingling at his touch. "You only want me because you can't have me."

"Can't?" He stroked his finger along her jaw, making her yearn. "I wouldn't be too sure. I've never seriously tried."

Danger, danger, her mind screamed, but she couldn't seem to pull away. "Yet I'm supposed to believe you want me more than any other woman?"

"You have no idea. You fascinate me." He trailed his finger down her neck, making her pulse pound. "From the moment I met you. At first it was just physical, which is easy enough to ignore. But the more I'm around you, the more I want to get to know you . . . in every way possible."

She ached to lean forward and take his mouth with hers, to feel his whole hand stroking her skin, not just his fingertip.

He pulled back unexpectedly and she nearly toppled into his lap. "Now come on. Tell me one of your deep dark secrets."

Her mind whirled at the abrupt shift in mood. She shook her head to clear it, then looked at him. Was this some new game he was playing? Grabbing her glass, she tossed back what was left of her drink. "Okay, one confession." She looked straight at him. "Now that I've gotten to know you well enough to realize you aren't the shallow playboy I thought you were, I might have gone out with you. Maybe. But that was before. Now there's no way, because this venture means too much to me. I can't afford to blow it over sex. I really can't, Adrian. I mean that."

"Are you trying to convince me or you?" His smile was pure seduction.

"Both of us, I guess."

"Is it working?"

"Right now, I don't know." Lord, she couldn't think with him sitting there, looking so scrumptious she wanted to rip off his shirt and lick him all over. "I want you. But I'm not going to give in to that."

"Just as well." His grin turned wicked. "Knowing you, we'd probably have to arm-wrestle to see who gets to be on top."

She snorted with laughter, even as his words stirred images of his body hard and naked beneath her. "Are you afraid I'd win and damage that big ego of yours?"

"Maybe I'd let you win." Sensual challenge gleamed in his eyes.

"You think I can't take you on my own? Come on, get it up here." She braced her elbow on the table.

He hesitated, but did the same. She put her hand in his, felt his warm fingers close about her. His gaze met hers over their clasped hands. "What are you going to do if you lose?"

"I won't. On three," she said, her tone dead serious. "One, two, three!" She stood and plowed her whole body against his arm, nailing his hand to the table. "I win! I win!" She danced in a circle, laughing.

"You cheat!"

"So? I still win." She laughed harder, falling against the table.

"The hell you do." He grabbed her wrist and jerked her toward him. "I ought to spank you."

She shrieked and struggled. His laughter joined hers as he tried to pull her over his lap. Squirming to get free, she wound up straddling his thighs, her hands flat against his chest, their faces mere inches apart. They both went still. She stared into his eyes, her heart pounding. The hungry look he gave her made her breath catch.

Push away! her brain screamed.

Oh, shut up. She lowered her mouth to his. His hands dove into her hair, tilting her head as he kissed her back, devouring her mouth. Heat crashed through her in waves as their tongues tangled. She pressed closer, wanting to crawl inside his skin. Squirming up his thigh, she found his hardened length straining against his jeans. Had he been aroused the whole time they'd talked? The thought made her moan as she rubbed against him.

His hands slipped down her sides, then up under her

shirt. She arched back, breaking the contact of their mouths when he cupped her hypersensitive breasts.

"Careful," she gasped. He gave her a quizzical look. Embarrassment joined the flush of desire. "I'm really . . . sensitive. There."

"Oh yeah?" His eyes lit. "How sensitive?"

"Very." She tried to lean away.

He wrapped his hands around her rib cage, holding her in place. His voice sounded thick when he spoke. "Take your shirt off."

"I will not."

He looked steadily at her, all playfulness gone. "Cheater's forfeit. Take your shirt off."

She started to argue, but the determination in his eyes sent a thrill racing through her. Crossing her arms, she grabbed the hem of the shirt and lifted it over her head. Cool air caressed her hot skin.

She looked down at herself, sitting naked from the waist up in his lap, his arousal pressing into her, bold and demanding. When his gaze dropped to her full, aching breasts, the dark nipples puckered.

He leaned forward, slowly. She stiffened, ready to jump back if he went straight for the nipples. He didn't. He cupped her gently in both hands and kissed the inside curve of each breast, back and forth, a coaxing whisper of lips. She relaxed with a sigh and closed her eyes. Enjoyment built slowly, a fluttering, melting sensation deep inside that grew and grew, until her hips moved of their own accord, rubbing her aching center against his hardness.

Rather than bracing for his lips on her nipples, she started longing for it, and arched her back in invitation. He avoided them, though, swirling his tongue around each puckered areole.

She buried her fingers in his thick, silky hair, freeing it from the band so it fell about his shoulders. Looking down, she watched his mouth as he licked her lightly. The wet caress made her shiver with need and moan in frustration.

He glanced up, his eyes dark as he opened his mouth and closed it over one nipple, sucking hard.

A climax slammed into her and she threw her head back in surprise. For an instant, she feared she'd pass out. The world spun as she struggled to catch her breath. Then she realized the world wasn't moving, he was.

He stood with her clasped to him and her legs clamped tight about his waist as he strode toward the bed.

"Whoa! Wait!" She gasped for air. "I thought we weren't going to do this."

"Change of plan." He dropped her to the mattress, and braced himself over her, kissing her neck. "One time. To get it out of our systems."

She planted a hand to his chest and pushed him back enough to see his face. The words she meant to say died when she saw the desire in his eyes. "Works for me."

Straightening, slowly, he grabbed one of her boots and pulled it off. His gaze burned into her as he removed the second boot, then he reached for the waistband of her leggings. He ripped them and her panties off in one fluid motion.

"Wait," she said as he started to climb on the bed. When he raised a brow, she grinned. "Strip."

He unbuttoned his shirt with tantalizing slowness. Her breathing went shallow as he revealed, inch by inch, his well-defined chest and stomach. Pulling the shirt free of the jeans, he tossed it aside in a move that made muscles ripple.

Toeing off his shoes, he removed the socks. When he

straightened, he pulled his wallet out of his back pocket, removed a condom and casually set it on the shelf over the head of the bed. Then he popped the snap on his jeans and her gaze dropped toward the sound. She nearly swallowed her tongue when he unzipped the pants and peeled them off.

Oh, my God.

She stared as he straightened, fully nude and impressively aroused. She should have expected it, she supposed. The rest of him was magnificent, so why wouldn't he be magnificent there, too? Still, he was the most enticingly virile creature she'd ever seen.

She lifted her eyes to his. "I want you."

"I'm all yours." He crawled onto the bed, closing his mouth over hers.

The need to caress every gorgeous inch of his bare skin turned her greedy. With her mouth against his, she rolled until he lay on his back, propped halfway up on the mountain of pillows. She straddled his legs and explored him with her hands and mouth. His taste and scent filled her head, making her dizzy.

When she grazed her teeth over his nipple, he sucked in a breath and cupped her head in one hand, but he didn't take over. He lay still, muscles tense, somehow knowing his acquiescence would drive her excitement higher. Thrilled by the freedom, she moved to kneel between his legs.

His abs bunched beneath her lips as she trailed her mouth downward. Sitting back, she feasted her eyes on all of him. Good heavens, he was beautiful, his dark hair loose about his shoulders, his eyes smoldering, his body bathed in soft light. And for this small space of time, he was hers to do with as she pleased.

Her gaze dropped back to his arousal, so bold and

unapologetic. Reaching out a hand, she closed it about him, delighted by the feel of satiny skin over hard flesh. Needing to taste him, she took him into her mouth.

His breath hissed through his teeth and his hand tightened in her hair. She felt him straining for control and knew it had slipped when his hips began to move, his thigh muscles flexing. Soaring with a sense of feminine power, she glanced up the length of his body and found his eyes closed, his head pressed back against the pillows.

"Okay, stop," he gasped and opened his eyes. Reaching over his head, he grabbed the condom. "You're about to end things way too soon."

She laughed, feeling sexier than she ever had as he rapidly covered himself. He reached for her then, cupping her head with both hands as he pulled her to him for a kiss that was wild with need. Straddling his lap, she sank over him slowly, moaning as his hard sex pressed into her, stretching her. He dropped his hands to her hips, urging her down harder until he was fully inside her. Then he let her go, allowing her to set the pace.

Arching back, she reveled in the feel of him beneath her, inside her; the sight of him lying against the pillows. A sheen of sweat covered his taut body and his breath came as fast as hers. In the midst of that heated passion, he smiled up at her. She laughed with pure joy at the feeling of connection, then gasped as he tipped her forward and took her breast in his mouth. Pleasure stabbed through her as he suckled hard, sending her over the edge. An explosion of pleasure and light.

The next instant, she was flat on her back beneath him. She blinked up at him, startled at the sudden reversal. "What—"

"My turn," he said, his voice rough. His eyes intent

on hers, he hooked his arms under her knees. She started to protest the loss of control, but groaned instead as he moved into her with long, hard strokes. Her own hips flexed into him, thrilling to his need, his hunger, until she was lost in it.

He tensed above her as his own orgasm hit, making his body flinch. Then, with a massive shudder of satisfaction, he settled over her, her arms closing about him. She stared at the ceiling, her head still spinning as she felt his heart pounding as hard as her own.

Chapter 15

Adrian trembled from the force of his release for several long seconds before he managed to roll onto his back. "Holy shit!"

"No kidding," Jackie said between gulps of air.

He turned his head and when their eyes met, they both laughed. Gathering her into his arms, he smiled as he caressed her face. "That was, without a doubt, the best mistake I ever made."

Her laughter stilled and the haze of passion slowly faded from her eyes. Realization followed, then a growing look of horror. He found each shift fascinating to watch, considering the flush of pleasure still glowed in her cheeks.

"Ohmygod." She pulled out of his arms to press a hand to her forehead. "Oh, my God!"

He propped himself up on one elbow, his other arm draped over a raised knee. "I take it this means no snuggling through the afterglow."

She stared at him, her gaze traveling up and down the length of his naked body. "Oh. My. *God!*"

"The way you keep saying that, is that one word or three?"

She covered her face with both hands. "What did we do?"

"Do you want the play-by-play or a brief summary?" When she scrambled from the bed, he frowned. "Where are you going?"

She turned to face him, backing away. "I just need a minute to think." She vanished into the head and closed the door with a firm click.

Okay, he thought, so Jackie liked to get a jump start on morning-after regrets. Not surprising. Less wasted time that way, and she did like efficiency.

The question was, how did he feel about what had just happened, other than incredibly sated? He did a quick mental search for regret or an urge to bolt, and oddly found none. Normally, after sex, a part of his brain went on high alert, looking for signs that his bed partner expected commitment. If she showed none, he could relax a little, but never completely. He liked women too much to ever hurt one with false expectations.

Jackie's reaction, however, went a bit beyond "That was fun, but let's not take this seriously, okay?"

He scowled at the closed door, not sure what to do when she came out. Gently extracting himself when a woman turned clingy had become second nature, but how did a man respond to a horrified "Oh, my God!"?

He heard water running in the sink and decided to clean himself up before she returned. Searching the shelf near the head of the bed, he spotted a box of tissue, a novel, a pair of earrings, and . . . a gun.

Hello! He pulled his hand back, surprised, then realized he shouldn't be. The woman lived alone on the wharf; of course she owned a gun.

Reaching past it, he grabbed some tissues and took care of the condom. He was sitting propped up against the pillows with his lower body beneath the covers when the bathroom door finally opened. She stepped out, tightening the belt of a black silk robe, her hair raked back from a face still flushed with passion. She looked tough, exotic, mysterious . . . and he wanted her all over again.

She raised her head to look at him, remarkably steady after all they'd had to drink. "I think it would be best if we chalk this up to too much rum and forget it ever happened."

Her words hit him like a punch in the gut. Then he saw how tightly she held herself and knew this was just Jackie trying to regain control. He smiled at her in empathy. "I have a better idea."

"What?" She turned cautious, and he smiled.

"Let's do it again." To his surprise, panic sparked in her eyes. *Take it slow,* he warned himself and patted the mattress by his hip. "Come here."

"I don't think that's a good idea."

"Just come here," he sighed, then watched the battle on her face before she crossed to the bed. Taking her hand, he pulled her down so she sat facing him. "See, I was thinking." The words came out with barely a slur. "This doesn't have to be a big deal since neither of us is interested in anything serious at this point in our lives. From what I've seen, you're married to your ship, and all I want is some playtime now that my sisters are grown-up and on their own. So, if you're worried I'll try to invade your life in any way, I promise you I won't. We can just be friends."

"Who have sex."

"Exactly."

"Absolutely not."

"How come?" Fascinated by the pulse beating in her neck, he caressed it with the tip of his finger.

"I'm not going to have an affair with you right in front of my crew," she whispered, then glanced at the wall, as if wondering if they'd been overheard. "Or your sisters, for that matter."

"We can be discreet." He ran his finger downward, following the vee of black silk between her breasts.

"Adrian." She grabbed his hand to get his attention. "Your sisters aren't stupid. If we start sleeping together, they'll know."

"You're right," he sighed, thinking close families could be a pain at times. "I can already hear what Allison will say after the hard time I gave her about Scott. Although"—he wiggled his brows—"a little squabble will be worth it."

"For you it will be a little sisterly ribbing, but how do you think they'll treat me six months from now if you and I have a big blowup?" Her eyes pleaded for understanding. "Adrian, I meant what I said earlier. I need this venture to pay off. Which means I need to be able to work with Aurora and Allison, as well as have the respect of my crew. So no, I'm not interested in repeating what just happened. It was great. *You* were great, but it's not worth it."

"I see." She didn't think he was worth it?

"My business has to come first," she insisted, then rubbed her head as if a hangover had already set in. "Which is why I really think you should leave."

He stared at her, absorbing the fact that she was kicking him out of her bed. They'd just shared the best sex of his entire life, which was saying a lot, and she was kicking him out?

"Okay . . ." he said slowly. "Fine." She wanted him to leave, he'd leave. He rose and retrieved his blue jeans, jerking them on with such force, he nearly lost his balance.

"Well, you don't have to go away mad," she said.

"No, just go away, right?" Scooping up his shoes, he sat and pulled them on.

"I didn't say it like that."

"Didn't you?" He looked for his shirt, but didn't see it, so he retrieved his leather jacket from the peg by the door.

"Oh, so now you're going to go somewhere and pout?" She flopped back against the pillows, crossing her arms.

"No, I'm going to go sleep in my cabin so your crew doesn't get any ideas, like you're a flesh-and-blood woman who might prefer a man over a boat and a bank account." He came back to the bed, planted his hands to either side of her hips, and leaned in close to her face. "There's more to life than work, Jackie. Maybe you should lighten up and enjoy it a little."

Her gaze flicked over his loose hair, the gaping leather jacket, his bare chest. Swallowing hard, she brought her eyes back to his and he saw a shimmer of banked desire. "There's also more to life than fun and games."

"Yeah, but without the fun, what's the point?" Shoving himself upright, he looked at her for a long moment, wanting to crawl back in bed, hold her in his arms, and tell her to stop being so scared all the time. Her expression warned him not to even try. With a silent curse, he strode from the cabin, barely resisting the urge to slam the door behind him. Damned stubborn woman!

Jackie punched the pillow the minute he left. Impossible, arrogant man!

"Let's be friends who have sex." As if that would work long-term. And when it stopped working, she'd be

the loser all the way around, while his life would continue with hardly a bleep.

How could he be so selfish and insensitive?

Wrapping her arms around the pillow, she caught his scent on the sheets and regret filled her. She longed to call him back, to tell him she wanted to be with him again and again, for as long as he wanted it to last. But if she gave in to that impulse, how long before her liking him as a friend turned to something deeper? And when it ended, as all good things did, how would she stand seeing him at all? The Pearl Island cruises would have to end.

Aching inside, she glared toward heaven and railed silently at God. *Why can't you play fair just once with my life?*

As usual, no answer came.

Sliding under the covers, she hugged the pillow, yearning for things she knew she couldn't have.

Exhausted and grouchy from lack of sleep, Jackie climbed the steps to the bridge just as dawn brushed the horizon with the first hint of color. The wind whipped beneath her foul-weather jacket, sending a chill across her skin. Joining Ti at the wheel, she held out one of the cups of coffee she'd brought from the galley.

"Thanks." He eyed her over the rim as he took a sip. "You up early."

"Couldn't sleep." Her watch wouldn't start for another hour, but she'd needed the reassurance of standing on deck, seeing for herself how the ship was handling. "How'd we do last night?"

"Da wind light until oh four hundred, but steady off port since."

Sipping coffee, she glanced through the open hatch of the pilot house at the instruments, her ears alert to the sounds of the sails. She'd forgotten how much she'd loved the early morning watch aboard the *Sea Star,* when the world was quiet enough for her to hear every creak and flutter. If the passengers followed form, they'd be drifting up soon to sit quietly and watch the sunrise.

The faint sound of canvas rippling drew her gaze upward. "The main tops'l's luffing."

"Adjust course?"

She glanced back at the instruments showing their position, wind direction, and speed. "No, hold steady but trim the sails."

Ti turned and relayed the order, his voice hushed in the morning stillness.

As Jackie watched the sailor on deck adjust the sheets, Adrian appeared through the main hatch. Her stomach tightened at the sight of him. He looked as relaxed and confident as ever in a pair of chef's pants and a dark turtleneck. When he glanced toward the bridge, she knew the moment he spotted her. He went still, but no expression showed on his face.

Was he still angry?

The question made her chest hurt as he continued looking at her. This was exactly what she hadn't wanted: to have remembered intimacy and harsh words sitting between them like a living creature, a beast that could stay quiet or rise up and snarl right in her face. Or worse, attack and destroy her plans for the future.

His words echoed back to her from the night before. *There's more to life than work.*

I know that, she wanted to tell him. Unfortunately, work was all she'd had for so long, she'd forgotten how to relax and enjoy herself—if she'd ever known.

Finally, he turned away and headed toward the bow. The minute his back was to her, she pulled a roll of antacids from her pocket.

"Dose not candy, ya know," Ti said, frowning at her.

She grinned to cover up her nervousness. "Caffeine and Rolaids, the breakfast of champions."

Shaking his head, Ti nodded toward Adrian. "Looks like you not da only one with trouble sleeping."

Her cheeks heated. Had Ti been in his berth just outside her door when Adrian had stormed from her cabin? "Maybe the motion of the ship's bothering him."

Ti made a humming sound that told her he knew something was going on.

Pretending to look at the jib sails, she watched Adrian climb the steps to the forecastle and move to the bowsprit, as far as he could get from her and still be on the same ship. He stood for a long time facing into the wind, not holding the rail as most landlubbers did, just standing there with his feet braced, gazing straight ahead. Then he kicked off his running shoes and started to move, first rolling his head as if to loosen a kink in his neck. He raised his arms, palms together, and bent forward at the hips, until his ·hands were flat against the deck. Lord, he was limber!

Her brows snapped together as he continued through a series of graceful moves that mesmerized her.

"Is he doing yoga?" she asked rhetorically, amazed that any man, even one as self-assured as Adrian St. Claire, would do yoga in public; most of the men she knew would consider it too sissy. But the moves were intriguingly masculine when he did them. They also required tremendous strength and balance, yet he made them look effortless.

"I don't think da motion of da ship bother him," Ti said.

"Guess not," she said absently, agonizing over what she should do. She needed to make peace with him, but how? Normally, if she made a man mad, she left him alone to stew. She had too much at stake in this case, though. And not just her ship. This tension between them made her feel ill. She wanted back the friendship they'd enjoyed the last few months. Dammit, though, why did she have to be the one to make the first move?

Because, her common sense pointed out, *you have the most to lose.*

Yeah, but two apologies in two days?

Oh, just gut it up and do it!

With a sigh of resignation, she asked Ti to excuse her and headed down the steps. She crossed the main deck slowly, checking lines as much out of habit as a delaying tactic. By the time she reached the foredeck, Adrian was sitting cross-legged, his hands resting on his knees, his eyes closed. She waited for him to open his eyes, but several very long seconds passed without him moving at all.

The coward in her whispered to her to make a tactical retreat. She glanced toward the stairs.

"Did you want something?" he asked, making her jump.

She looked back at him and found his eyes still closed. "Not if I'm interrupting."

"You're not." He opened his eyes but his voice was cool.

"Actually, we can talk later, when you're in a better mood."

His expression filled with offense. "There's nothing wrong with my mood."

"Pardon me for pointing this out, but you're obviously still pouting."

"I'm not pouting. I'm meditating. Or at least I was trying to."

"Well then, I should definitely leave. We can talk later." She started for the steps.

"Jackie," he sighed. "Have a seat."

"No, really, I—"

"Sit! Geez, you're stubborn."

"I am not!"

He gave her a pointed look over his shoulder.

She stomped back and sat cross-legged with her arms wrapped around her knees. "You don't have to insult me, considering I came up here to apologize."

"Actually"—he wiped a hand over his face, looking as tired as she felt—"I think it's my turn."

"Oh?" Her resentment vanished in the face of surprise. In her experience men almost never apologized, and certainly not without a great deal of prompting.

"I won't apologize for what we did together, because that would imply I took advantage of you, which I didn't, or that I regret it, which I don't."

Her face flamed as memories flashed through her mind and still-tender parts of her body pulsed in response.

"I am sorry, though, for how I reacted afterward. It's just that . . ." He lowered his voice. "I've never had that happen before, and I'm afraid I handled it badly."

"Had what happen?"

"Had a woman kick me out of her bed." He blushed. "I don't mean that to sound egotistical, and I swear, I'm not bragging, it's just . . . women usually try to talk me into staying."

She stared at him, not knowing what to say.

He shook his head, laughing in embarrassment. "I've pretty much memorized the 'let's be friends' speech, I've said it so many times, but I've never been on the receiving end of it. Yet, since I've known you, you've given it to me at least three times. I have to say, it feels different hearing it instead of saying it."

"So you're saying I hurt your feelings?"

He frowned at her choice of words. "Let's just say you threw me."

"I didn't mean to," she assured him. "I really do want to be friends. And not just because of the cruises. The thing is, other than Ti, I don't really have any. I used to, when I crewed on the *Sea Star,* but—"

"They all dumped you when they heard about your father."

She shrugged, pretending it didn't still hurt.

"You know," he said, "I've been thinking about that, and I hope you told them all to go to hell before you left the ship."

"Why would I do that? I was hardly innocent."

"Jackie, let me clue you in to something. If you act like a whipped dog, people are going to kick you. It's human nature. If you look them in the eyes and say 'Yeah, I've made some mistakes in life, what's your point?' they'll not only back off, they'll treat you with respect."

"I don't want simple respect. I get that from my crew."

"I imagine that's pretty lonely."

She dropped her gaze. "Which is why I'm really hoping we can get past what happened last night. If you think that's possible."

"It is, but on one condition." He ducked his head to

see her eyes. "That you learn to lighten up a bit. You really are way too serious about everything."

"I know," she admitted. "It's just that I've had to be."

"You've never had anyone you can count on, have you?"

"I'm more comfortable counting on myself."

"Understandable, considering the life you've led."

"I would like to learn, though."

"What? To count on others?"

She let out a dry laugh. "I don't think I'll ever be ready to do that, but I would like to, you know, lighten up, learn to have fun and enjoy myself more. Do you think . . . what I mean is . . . do you think you could teach me?"

Adrian felt his chest melt as he studied her. If ever in his life he'd met someone who needed some playtime it was Jackie. "I don't know . . ." He kept his expression grave.

"I'm not hopeless. I can learn anything I set my mind to."

"Let's see about that. Come here." He patted the deck beside him. "Sit closer."

"Why?"

"Suspicious thing, aren't you? Just sit beside me. Like this." He rested his hands on his knees, his back straight.

She glanced around, looking horrified. "I'm not going to meditate right here on deck."

"What, are you afraid of what your crew might think?"

"And the passengers."

He sighed heavily. "Why don't you just once say, 'Screw what people think'? I dare you."

She started to speak, but snapped her mouth shut.

"If it helps, no, we're not going to meditate, because quite frankly, you are light-years away from letting go enough to do that."

"You don't have to insult me. Just tell me what we're going to do."

"Learn to be still and let go just a little, rather than having to be in charge all the time."

"I can sit still."

"I said be still, inside as well as out. Now, sit like this." He waited as she moved beside him and copied his posture. "Close your eyes," he said in a soothing voice. "Relax. Listen to the world around you." He watched for any signs of the tension leaving her shoulders. "Relax."

"I'm trying!" she said through clenched teeth.

"Well, stop 'trying.' That's the point. Stop doing and just be."

If anything, she became more stiff, focusing all her energy on following his instructions.

He scooted behind her and sat with his legs to either side of her. "Here, let's get rid of this." He helped her off with her coat, then placed his hands on her shoulders, massaging. "Now, relax . . . listen to the water . . . feel the wind . . . breathe deep . . ." Just as her muscles started to loosen, he felt her tense and she started to turn. "What are you doing?"

"I need to check that."

"Check what?" he asked in exasperation.

"Can't you hear it?"

"What?"

"That fluttering sound. One of the sails is luffing."

"So?"

"So, I want to see which one and what needs to be done about it."

"Isn't Ti capable of doing that?"

"Of course he is. But when I'm on deck, he always defers to me."

"Not this time." He took her head in his hands and turned her face forward. "Leave the man alone and let him do his job."

"Okay." She glanced back at him. "But I'm on watch in a few minutes, so let's get this relaxing stuff over with so I can get to work."

He burst out laughing. "You are hopeless."

Her face lined with worry. "Maybe so. Can we be friends anyway?"

"We can try."

"Don't give up on me, okay? I really want you to teach me how to have fun."

"Hmm . . ." He shook his head with mock graveness. "That's a pretty big challenge."

"You're a big guy." She flashed him a cocky grin.

"You would know."

"Adrian!" She laughed, and he drank in the sound. He did love that throaty, earthy laugh of hers.

"Hey, just because we can't have sex doesn't mean we can't joke about it. In fact, maybe that should be one of your lessons: Joking Around 101."

"I have a better idea." She turned serious again.

"Oh?"

"Cooking. I've always wanted to learn and you make it look fun."

A vivid image popped in his mind of Jackie and him in the kitchen together. "Can we do it naked?"

She shoved his chest and he fell back onto his forearms. "You're the one who's hopeless!"

"Okay, okay, I'll teach you how to cook in exchange for more sailing lessons."

"Deal." She started to hold out her hand, thought better of it and pulled it back.

"Chicken."

"Better a wise chicken than a dead duck."

"I dare ya."

She held out her hand. He took it slowly, held it a moment, noticing more closely the unusual combination of calluses and soft skin. Small hands that possessed the strength to command and the skill to excite. He remembered too well how those hands had felt on his body. "Deal."

When he released her hand, she stood and retrieved her coat. "Okay, well, I, um, need to get to work."

"Business before pleasure, eh?"

"That's me." She grinned.

He watched her backside as she walked away, then flopped onto his back, staring up at the sky. What had he gotten himself into now?

Chapter 16

"Dolphins!" someone cried near the bow.

Jackie looked up from the chart she had spread on the roof of the pilothouse to see passengers hurrying to the portside rail. Dolphins? How could that be? They'd entered Galveston Bay already and were winding their way through oil tankers and cargo barges. There hadn't been dolphins in these waters for decades.

Stowing the chart, she turned to the second mate, who stood at the wheel. "Mr. Jamison, she's all yours."

"Aye, Captain." The man kept his attention on their course. Now that they'd left the open waters of the Gulf, they had little room to maneuver and no room for error.

She headed for the steps to the main deck just as Adrian hurried up. "Do you see them?"

"Not yet."

He grabbed her hand and pulled her to the rail of the quarterdeck, as excited as a little boy. "Look! There must be a dozen, at least."

"When did dolphins return to Galveston Bay?" She stared in disbelief at the sleek gray bodies leaping and racing alongside the ship. "I thought the water was too polluted."

"It was! The state's been working to clean it up, though. A few years ago, people started spotting dolphins again, but only one or two. Never this many."

The ship came alongside a slow-moving tug bullying a barge toward the Houston shipping channel, but the finned escort stuck with the *Pirate's Pleasure,* playing among the white-capped wakes that spread outward from the wooden hull.

"Aren't they beautiful?" Jackie laughed, enjoying the salty spray on her face. "No matter how many times I see them, they always thrill me."

"They are quite a sight," Adrian agreed. "I wonder if they'll stick with us all the way to Pearl Island."

"They might." She glanced up to see the private island Adrian called home on the horizon. "I've had them follow me for miles before, but never in a crowded shipping channel."

"Must be your lucky day."

She turned her head and found him smiling at her. *I'm so glad we talked,* she thought. "Must be."

"Then you're starting to believe in luck?"

"Maybe." She smiled. When she looked back toward Pearl Island, some of her happiness dimmed. "Do you think Carl Ryder will be there?"

"Probably. Before I left, Rory said she might have a surprise for us when we arrived. So I bet the archeology crew is there and ready to start."

Tension coiled in her stomach as she went back to watching the dolphins, focusing on good things. Once they docked, there'd be no time for standing quietly with Adrian like this.

"Did you know," he said, "some people believe

dolphins are the guardians of dreams, because they exist half in air, half in water, with air being our conscious thought, and water our subconscious?"

"You really do read a lot of philosophy."

"Actually, that would be folklore, but we all have our weaknesses." He grinned, then glanced out across the water. "Almost home."

She saw the line of palm trees that marked the mouth of the cove. "Well, time for me to get back to work." She tipped her head to check the sails, her attention already diverted.

"Do I need to get out of the way?"

"No." She turned back to him. "Hang out if you want."

"I'd like that." Resting his back on the rail, he leaned his weight on his forearms so he could watch her as she worked. He supposed he should be thinking of work, too, preparing himself mentally for the extravagant Valentine's dinner he would need to prepare in record time. Watching Jackie was much more fun, though. He was glad they'd worked things out this morning, even if they couldn't go with his preferred plan: that they be friends who slept together. As frequently as possible.

Had he really told his sisters last fall that Jackie wasn't his type? Perhaps he'd thought that because he'd never met anyone like her. True, she bore no resemblance to the image of the sweet, domestic wife he'd carried in his head for years, but she challenged him, intrigued him, and kept him on his toes. As an added bonus, she couldn't care less about his looks, which he found extremely refreshing.

His attraction was more than that, though. He simply *liked* her. A lot. The knowledge filled him with frightening speed. He truly, deeply *liked* everything about her.

Good heavens, was this the beginning of falling in

love? With a woman who wanted nothing more from him than friendship? His mind spun at the thought. How had this happened?

Just then, he saw her stiffen. She whirled toward him with such accusation blazing in her eyes, he wondered if she'd read his mind—until she turned away, shading her eyes as she looked toward shore. Straightening off the rail, he followed the direction of her gaze and found they'd already entered the cove. On the dock, news crews had lined up to film their approach.

What in the world? he wondered.

Ti, who stood at the base of the mainmast, called out a question about the rigging to Jackie. She shook her head as if to clear it and relayed an order in a stumbling, unsteady voice, completely at odds with her normal assurance. She looked as unsteady now as she'd been the day they'd run into Carl Ryder.

He remembered what she'd told him about her father's murder and the media frenzy surrounding the trial. As the ship neared the pier, he saw Rory in the Southern belle costume she wore for special occasions at the inn. She waved cheerfully when she spotted him.

Oh hell. This was the surprise his sister had arranged. She must have sent out a press release to every news station in Houston to get this many cameras out. Knowing Rory the way he did, he should have anticipated something like this. If only he'd explained that widespread press could be potentially dangerous, this never would have happened.

But Jackie had asked him not to tell them about her past and he'd honored her request.

Damn.

He looked over to gauge her reaction as all around

the ship sailors scurried to follow orders. Her movements jerky, she pressed a hand to her forehead, as if willing herself to concentrate. He ached to go to her and take her into his arms, but knew he'd only make matters worse. Instead, he stayed out of her way as a tender boat was launched to help tow them to the pier. All the while, cameras rolled and passengers waved.

Good Lord, he thought. *Is that CNN?* His stunned gaze took in a van with *Good Morning America* splashed on the side. His sister hadn't just sent press releases to Houston, she'd sent them to all the major networks! This had to be Jackie's worst nightmare.

The moment the ship was secure, he headed toward her. She had her back to the cameras, and one hand shielding her face. "Jackie, it'll be okay."

"It will not!" she shouted back, then lowered her voice. "What if one of the people I helped con recognizes my face and comes after me? The last thing I need is a lawsuit right now."

"It's your father who conned them, and he's dead."

"I helped."

"You were a minor, and none of that happened in the U.S."

"So?"

He glanced around to be sure no one could hear them over the general noise on deck. "Have you ever been arrested or charged with a crime?"

"No."

"Then stop acting like a whipped dog."

"What would you have me do?" she asked between clenched teeth. "Smile for the camera?"

Ti joined them, clearly agitated. "Ya need to get below," he told Jackie.

Ignoring her first mate, she kept her eyes fixed on Adrian. "How could you do this without warning me?"

"I didn't know, I swear. Rory arranged this on her own." He saw the gangway being lowered into place, and knew the news crews would have access to the ship any second. He didn't think Buddy Taylor's old victims could come after Jackie, but her fear tore at him. "Ti, get Jackie below and stay with her. I'll handle this."

With one last order to Mr. Jamison, Jackie and Ti headed down the steps and disappeared through the aft hatch. Fortunately, the cameras seemed focused on the waving passengers.

Okay, he could handle this. Piece of cake, he told himself as he crossed to the top of the stairs. A few of the passengers were already disembarking, so he waited for the gangway to clear before he started down. Rory was greeting passengers and telling them to go on up to the inn where Alli was ready to serve afternoon tea on the veranda.

As he reached the bottom of the steps, he moved past a female reporter talking into a camera with the ship behind her. Rory turned to him, her face alight with excitement. "Isn't this great! We're going to be on *Good Morning America*!"

"I see that." He didn't know whether to kill her or kiss her.

"Are you the brother?" A harried woman in a rumpled black suit approached him, checking notes on a clipboard. "Adrian St. Claire, the inn's chef, right?"

"That's me."

"I'm pleased to meet you." The woman looked up from her notes and froze with her hand extended halfway toward him. Her pale blue eyes blinked behind trendy glasses, then sharpened. "H-hi. I'm Eva. Phillips. One of the producers with *Good Morning America*. I've heard wonderful things about the food here at the inn."

"I'm glad," he said as he shook her hand and pegged her for a barracuda.

She stepped closer, smiling. "Our segment will focus mostly on the upcoming efforts to excavate the sunken ship, but I'd love to get some shots of you in the kitchen for background color. Would that be all right?"

Standing behind the woman, Rory wiggled her brows, bursting with pride over her accomplishment: a mention of their inn and the quality of the food on *Good Morning America,* for crying out loud! Under other circumstances, he'd share her enthusiasm, but all he could think about was getting the cameras and reporters as far away from Jackie as possible.

When he didn't answer right away, Eva Phillips frowned. "You're not camera shy, are you?"

He laughed at that. "Not in the least. I need to get started fairly soon, though, so why don't we head on up that way now?" He turned to the reporters and raised his voice. "Everyone's welcome for a cooking demonstration in the kitchen. Samples of tonight's dinner included."

As he led the way up the hill, he cast one last look at the ship, picturing Jackie in her cabin. He longed to tell her everything would be all right, but knew she wouldn't believe him.

Jackie thought about what Adrian had said as she paced her cabin, and realized he was right. Some of her fears probably were unfounded. As far as her being a whipped dog, though, she assured herself he was dead wrong. And she'd tell him that, too—just as soon as all those camera crews took off.

The last thought jarred her as she realized she was hiding. Good grief, she really was a cringing coward. And worse, she'd lost her temper with Adrian *again*. Some friend she was.

She berated herself as the evening wore on, knowing she'd never sleep until she thanked him for his understanding and support even in the face of her bitchiness. Unfortunately, she couldn't go to the inn to do that, because the *Good Morning America* crew was still there. She tried calling, but got the inn's answering machine. Then she remembered the little house behind the inn where Rory and Chance lived. If she couldn't thank Adrian in person, maybe she could ask his sister to relay a message.

Leaving the ship, she headed across the beach for the trail that circled the island. A tangle of trees obscured the moonlight, but she found her way up the hill to the quaint little house. She'd discovered it only by accident during her last stay since a stand of trees shielded it from the inn. The natural wood siding and green tin roof further camouflaged it even in bright daylight. In the dark, she never would have found it if not for the single light shining by the front door. All the windows, though, were pitch-black.

Disappointed, she stepped onto the porch debating what to do. She'd hoped to find Rory or Chance at home by now since the Valentine's dinner had ended an hour ago. Surely they weren't already in bed. It wasn't *that* late. Glancing back the way she'd come, she listened to the light rock music drifting through the balcony doors on the third floor of the inn. The party would go on until two in the morning, but hopefully Rory and Chance would return home well before that. They had a baby to think about, after all.

Deciding to wait, she ventured around the corner of the L-shaped porch to a dark area that faced the cove. In the shadows, she made out rocking chairs and a porch swing. She passed up the chairs and sat on a porch rail with her back to a post as she gazed through the trees at the cove. The white lights strung about her ship made it look like something out of Never-Never Land. The music from the inn turned soft and dreamy as a cool breeze kissed her cheek.

Just then, she heard someone step onto the porch near the front door. She moved in that direction, rounding the corner, then stopped when she saw Adrian. He stood at the door in a dark T-shirt and jeans, a white chef's jacket slung over one shoulder.

At the sound of her footsteps, he looked up and squinted into the darkness. "Is someone there?"

"It's me." She stepped forward, into the light. "I was waiting for your sister. I wanted to give her a message for you. What are you doing here?"

"I live here. We traded quarters back in January."

"Oh." She looked around. "It's nice here. I like it."

"Me, too." He smiled, a good sign that he wasn't too put out with her for how she'd acted. "So, what were you going to have Rory tell me?"

She moved closer. "Among other things, I wanted her to tell you thanks for what you did today, you know, leading the press away. Although I hadn't quite worked out how to give her the message without explaining everything. But now I can tell you in person. Thank you."

"You're welcome." He nodded solemnly. "As for telling Rory and the others the whole story, I promise you they'll understand. You should tell them and be done with it. Or let me."

"Sorry, I know better than you how people react when they find out." He started to object and she held up her hand. "I'll think about it, though. Okay?"

"It's a start."

"Are the cameras gone?"

"They are."

"Finally." She sighed. "I didn't think they'd ever leave."

"Me, either." He chuckled. "Although it's my own fault. I got a little carried away by diverting their attention away from the ship, and put on quite a show." He flashed a playful grin that brought out his dimples. "I'm talking juggling fruit, twirling knives, flaming sauces. They ate it up."

An emotion that went beyond gratitude filled her with a warm, glowing softness. *I love you,* she thought, then jolted. Good God, had she really just thought that? Her heart pounded with the terrifying knowledge that the words might actually be true. "Yes, well . . ." She glanced around for her fastest escape route. "You're probably exhausted, so I'll go. I just wanted to say thanks."

"Not a problem. I enjoyed it. But hey, look, I'm a little keyed up and couldn't possibly go straight to bed. You want to come inside and have a nightcap?"

"I . . ." *Don't you dare say yes.*

"I have some Mexican Kahlúa. Perfect for a night like this."

"I suppose I could stay for one drink." *What are you doing? Do you want to get your heart broken?*

"Great," he said, opening the door. She followed him inside, her nerves jumping. Moving ahead of her into the darkness, he clicked on a floor lamp, revealing a casual and inviting living room with a small eating area tucked in the far corner.

"You want cream with yours?" he asked as he headed around a breakfast bar into the kitchen.

"Yes, please." She looked around while he fixed the drinks. Books filled shelves along every wall and sat in haphazard stacks on the floor, making her think of a wizard's cottage in the woods. The leather-covered sofa and overstuffed chair invited a person to settle in and read, or take an afternoon nap. The end table, coffee table, and other accent pieces were all antiques; none of them matched, yet all of them added to the room's welcoming feel.

She could easily see why Adrian had wanted to swap with Rory and Chance. This place was smaller, but cozy and private, while the apartment at the inn was a constant hub of activity. She'd always felt a bit uncomfortable there, but could almost picture herself living in a place like this.

The thought sent another wave of panic along her nerves.

"Here you go."

"Oh!" She whirled to find Adrian right behind her. "You snuck up on me."

"Sorry." He held out a glass.

"Thanks."

"You want to sit in here, or outside?"

"Outside," she said quickly, hoping to rein in her emotions. She followed him out on the porch and took a seat in one of the rocking chairs. A light breeze rustled through the trees.

He lit a candle on the table between the chairs, then

sat with his feet propped on the rail, his ankles crossed. Candlelight played across his face.

"Are you trying to get romantic on me?" she asked, hoping to keep things light.

"Well, it is Valentine's Day," he teased back.

"That it is." She frowned, since she'd actually forgotten. "You should be spending it with one of those women who try to talk you into staying all night."

"You'll do." He smiled into his glass, but looked so exhausted, she wondered if he'd lied about the need to unwind. If so, she should finish her drink and go.

She glanced toward the cove. "I saw the work platform has arrived, but I haven't seen any sign of Carl. I take it he's here, though."

"He is. Allison checked him into one of the larger bungalows, which will serve as his team's headquarters as well as a place for him to live for the next few months. Apparently, he's not too keen on large crowds watching him work. He put up with the camera crews for a while, then disappeared into his bungalow and hasn't been seen since."

"Did they start today, then?"

"Just some preliminary dives to 'establish a grid' or some other technical-sounding term. I think he plans to start in earnest tomorrow." He studied his drink. "Speaking of Carl, I've been wondering about something."

"Oh?" Something in his voice put her on mild alert.

"If I'm being too nosy, you can tell me to butt out."

She steeled herself for anything. "What's your question?"

"That day at the Visitors' Center, Carl's animosity toward your father seemed to go beyond an archeologist's natural dislike for treasure hunters. I was wondering if there's some personal issue involved."

She wasn't sure whether to tell him, but reminded herself they were friends, and friends shared things. "He and my father used to be close. In fact, they both worked as scuba instructors at the resort where my parents met. I don't know exactly what happened, though. Dad never talked about Carl other than to cuss about what an uptight prig he was."

"Definitely sounds like there's a story there."

"Probably." She sipped her drink. "I guess I'll never know now. Dad's gone, and Carl doesn't seem inclined to become buddies with me."

"I noticed." He looked at her with such empathy, her chest grew tight. "I wish we could hire someone else, but he was the Historical Society's first choice, and since they hold the money strings, they call the shots. I'm sorry, though."

"Don't be. He's good at his job. One of the best, I'm told. The project is more important than my personal comfort level."

"This is going to be hard for you, though, isn't it?"

"Only because I worry about how having me involved will affect you and your family."

"Jackie . . ." he said in a warning tone.

"No, let me finish." Her hand tightened around the cold glass. "You've all been very kind to me. I appreciate it, and I hope you never have cause to regret including me."

"We won't." He sighed heavily. "For one thing, we couldn't have done it at all without you."

"I doubt that. Scott's research was pretty tight. You could have managed, and been better off in the long run."

He studied her. "You really believe that, don't you?"

"I know it."

He shook his head. "I take it back. You aren't a whipped dog, you're one of those brave, stoic martyr types."

"Excuse me?" She frowned at him.

"Jackie." His voice gentled as he let his feet drop to the floor and shifted toward her. "You don't have to be tough all the time. In fact, if you ever need a shoulder to cry on, I have two guaranteed not to melt."

A strained laugh escaped her. "I appreciate the offer, but I learned a long time ago that crying to others accomplishes nothing."

"So, you do your crying alone?"

"I didn't say I cried at all. It's a stupid waste of energy." When he gave her a knowing look, she relented. "Well, maybe sometimes in private."

"Like I said, you don't have to be strong all the time." He reached over and took her free hand. "Even though I do admire you for your strength at times."

"Adrian, don't." Her throat closed, making her voice thin. "I've had a really tough day, and it wouldn't take much to make me lose it, so back off, okay?"

"No, it's not okay. I know you're uncomfortable with kindness, because you don't know how to deal with it, but when I think of all you've been through, I wish I could turn back the clock and be there for you all the times you felt frightened and alone."

"Stop. Please." Her shoulder jerked and she set her drink down to cover her face with her hand.

"I'm here for you now, though. I want you to know that."

A sob slipped past her control, and then another.

"Come here." He tugged on her hand, pulling her from her chair onto his lap. She went more willingly than she should have, and curled into a ball with her face buried in the crook of his neck. He wrapped his arms around her, making her feel safe as he rocked back and forth.

"I'm sorry." The words barely made it past her tight throat. "I'm just tired."

"It's okay." He kissed her forehead, which made her cry harder. "Tell me why you're tired."

Lord, what a question! "I'm tired of living in a minefield. Every time I do anything, I hold my breath waiting to see if my world will explode. And I'm angry at my father for putting me in the middle of this." Bitterness rose up, scalding her throat. "God forgive me, I'm so angry at him!"

"You have a right to be."

"No I don't." She lifted her head to stare at him. "He did the best he could. I loved him in spite of his being a big, irresponsible kid, and I miss him so much. But sometimes, sometimes"—her hand tightened into a fist—"way down inside me there's a tiny bit of me that hates him and is almost glad he's gone. Oh God!" Another sob escaped as she hid her face against his chest.

"It's okay," he murmured, rubbing her back.

"I didn't mean that the way it sounded. I never wished him dead."

"I know how you meant it, and it's all right to be angry. He put you in some awful situations, and you're still suffering because of him. But listen to me." Taking her by the shoulders, he straightened her so he could see her face. "You don't have to be afraid anymore. Everything is going to be okay."

"How can you say that? My whole world could blow up and splatter all over you and your family."

"It'll never happen." He used his thumbs to dry her cheeks. "See, we have Marguerite's magic on our side, so we're guaranteed to succeed at whatever we do."

"Well, she may be a good-luck charm, but I'm a curse, so we cancel each other out."

"You are not a curse. And now that you're doing business with us, Marguerite will help you, too."

"Except I don't believe in ghosts."

"Then believe in me." He cupped her face and stared into her eyes. "Because no matter what happens, I'll be here for you."

"I'm sorry," she whispered with tears glistening in her eyes. "I don't believe in you, either. You're too good to be true."

He laughed. "Be sure and tell that to Allison the next time she gets mad at me for being a nosy, overprotective big brother."

"She's an idiot if she thinks that. I wish I'd had a brother like you."

"Well, now you have a friend like me, which is even better since it lets us do the things we did last night."

She let out a laugh as she wiped her nose with the back of her hand. "I need a tissue."

"Well, this proves I'm not too good to be true. If I were, I'd whip a handkerchief from my back pocket and hand it to you."

"You're right. You're not perfect."

"So you'll trust me to stick by you and help you get through whatever happens?"

"Only if you get me a tissue."

"I think I can manage that." Standing with her in his arms, he turned and settled her on the chair. "Will you be all right until I get back?"

She looked up at him and the candlelight shimmered in her damp eyes. "I've done without you my whole life. I think I can manage a few more minutes."

He went inside to get a box of tissues. When he came back out, she was standing by the steps. "Leaving?" he asked with a jolt.

"Yeah." She took a tissue and blew her nose. "I hate to cry and run, but I . . ." She peeked at him through damp lashes, then looked away. "I should go."

The friendly concern shifted to something far more urgent and possessive. He longed to take her in his arms again, only to kiss her this time, not comfort her. "Here, take the box with you."

She shook her head. "I'm okay now." Another quick glance, and the moment grew uneasy. "Thanks, you know, for the shoulder."

"Anytime," he assured her, and tamped down the need to ask her to stay, to take her back into his arms and confess all his own mixed-up confusing emotions.

As she disappeared down the footpath that led to the cove, he finally understood how Marguerite and Jack could love each other for years and never say the words out loud. Once words that powerful were spoken, the pretense of mere friendship would have vanished. Love, once acknowledged, had to be acted on, and neither of them had been ready to deal with the consequences.

But was this really love he felt for Jackie? And if so, what should he do about it? If he told her how he felt, would she run like hell, or give him a chance?

Chapter 17

"Believe in me," Adrian had said. *"No matter what happens, I'll be here for you."*

The words haunted Jackie throughout the night, making her battle the covers, until finally she gave up on sleep. Rising before daybreak, she dressed in shorts and slipped quietly from her cabin. A predawn hush lay over the island as she headed down the beach toward the jogging trail.

Even then, Adrian's words hounded her at every step. *"Trust me. Trust me. Trust me."* His voice matched the rhythm of her feet, sounding more like her father each time. *"Trust me, kid, everything's going to be all right."*

Ironically, he'd always said that just before they had to scramble to escape arrest by some port authority. Sometimes they managed to sail away in the nick of time, but twice they'd forfeited their boat and everything on it. The shock of loss never quite left her, to have all her personal belongings snatched away without warning.

And here was Adrian asking her to trust that some disaster wasn't waiting just ahead. Or that if disaster did strike, he wouldn't bail out on her as other friends had.

Oddly, though, she wanted to believe him with a depth of yearning that frightened her.

She picked up her pace, trying to outrun memories of

the past and current temptation. She pushed herself harder as she finished her first lap around the island and started a second. She ran until her legs ached and her lungs burned.

"No matter what happens, I'll be here for you."

You will not, she silently railed, her heart pounding louder than the crunch of gravel beneath her shoes. *Don't believe him, don't believe him, don't believe him.*

Her own words finally drowned his out just as a stitch started in her side. She stumbled to a stop and bent forward with her hands braced on her knees as she struggled to catch her breath. Her head felt ready to explode, but at least the urge to trust Adrian's good intentions had vanished. Which proved she could outrun anything if she ran far enough and long enough.

Pressing a hand to her side, she straightened so she could walk and cool down.

"I was wondering how long you'd last at that pace," a voice said from the woods.

With a shriek, she turned to find she'd stopped before one of the bungalows. Carl Ryder sat on the porch steps wearing a black wet suit and drinking a cup of coffee. So much for outrunning the things that chased her.

"How long . . . have you . . . been out here?" she panted.

"About three laps. Are you training for a marathon?"

"No, just . . . running." She motioned toward his body. "You planning to dive in the dark?"

"If I thought it would keep the press away, I might do exactly that." He glanced skyward. "Although it's not exactly dark anymore."

She looked up as well and found the eastern sky had lightened to a clear azure with a blaze of orange. "So it isn't. Which means it's time I got back to my ship."

"I'll walk you." He set the coffee mug aside and grabbed the dive bag at his feet.

"That's okay," she assured him quickly. "No need to trouble yourself."

"I'm headed that way anyway."

Great, she thought as he joined her on the trail, leaving her no polite choice but to fall in step beside him. Just what she wanted—to go for a walk with Carl Ryder. They went several yards in awkward silence.

"I've, um, been thinking," he finally said. "You and I will be seeing each other a lot over the next few months. Perhaps it would be easier if we settle a few things up front."

"Oh?" she said cautiously, wondering if he meant to list all her past sins so she understood exactly how little respect he had for her—as if she didn't know that already.

"Yeah," he sighed. "So I'll start by saying I'm sorry."

"W-what?" She nearly stumbled.

"For the way I embarrassed you in front of the Historical Society back in the fall. I had no right to take my anger at your mother out on you."

"At my mother?" She gaped at him. "I thought you hated my father."

"I do. Or did." His big shoulders sagged. "I've been pissed at him so long, it feels weird knowing he's gone."

"Yeah. I, um, I know what you mean."

He gave her a startled look but said nothing for a while. She was on the verge of making an excuse to break into a jog and leave him behind when he spoke again. "So. How'd Serena take Buddy's death?"

She flashed him a wary look, wondering where this was headed. "She sent her condolences."

"She didn't attend the funeral?"

"Mr. Ryder." She stopped and turned to him. "Not that it's any of your business, but my parents have been divorced since I was five."

He stared at her, and then laughed without humor. "Well, I guess that explains why you were always with him, but she wasn't. Funny, though, how Buddy never mentioned it whenever our paths crossed." He didn't say it aloud, but Jackie swore she heard him add: *The sorry son of a bitch.* Carl raked a hand through his rumpled blond hair. "The one time I was enough of a sap to ask how she was, he just flashed that smug smile of his and said, 'Happy as a clam.' "

"I'm not sure my mother's capable of being happy." They both resumed walking. "Unless someone granted her independent wealth, and even then, she'd find something to complain about."

"You look like her, you know. Not exactly, but enough. Especially the eyes. I think that's what caught me so off guard that day. I looked up, and for one split second, I thought it was Serena standing there. 'Bout gave me heart failure."

"I didn't realize you knew her that well."

"Your father never told you? Why does that not surprise me? Jackie"—he stopped just before the wooded trail gave way to sandy beach—"your mother and I were engaged when I introduced her to Buddy."

She stared at him, trying to picture her exotically beautiful and selfish mother with someone who reminded her of a big loyal golden retriever.

"She and I were working at a resort on Bequia. Back then, I was dumb enough to believe everything she told me, but looking back I realize she wanted me to be her ticket off the island and out of poverty."

Jackie thought about telling him that's all Buddy had been, and that Serena had gone through a string of men since, each one progressively richer.

"The resort was looking for another scuba instructor," Carl said. "So I called my good friend Buddy Taylor and said, 'Hey, come on out to the islands. I'll get you a job.' He came and I introduced him to my fiancée, even let him room with me all that summer."

She looked out over the cove, where her ship waited, a solid black shape against the bright sunrise. Carl's team had gathered on the beach, getting ready for the day. She struggled with the twin needs of wanting to be safely on board and staying to hear Carl out.

"I assume you know why Buddy left Bequia?" he asked.

"Not exactly, but I can guess."

"A few months after he arrived, the management caught him dealing drugs. Since they didn't want any bad publicity, they settled for ordering him off the island. When he took off in the shiny new sailboat he'd just bought, Serena went with him, and left me standing on the beach with a dumbfounded look on my face." Carl dropped his head forward, shaking it. "Fool that I was, that was the first clue I had that my fiancée was sleeping with my best friend."

"I'm sorry." She ached for him, realizing he was one more victim that her parents had left in their wake. "I didn't know."

"And I wouldn't be telling you any of this except . . . it's going to be hard for me, seeing you over the next few months. Seeing your mother's eyes every time I look at you. So I just wanted you to understand that if I'm less than friendly, it's not personal. Well, it is, but not aimed at you."

"I truly am sorry. If I could make it up to you, I would."

He cocked his head. "I don't expect you to."

"I know, but—" She stopped as Adrian's advice echoed back to her: *Don't be a whipped dog.* "Never mind."

"I know I should be over her by now." Carl sighed, stepping onto the long expanse of beach leading to the pier. "But Serena's a hard woman to get over. Especially since she destroyed any chance I had of a decent relationship with anyone else."

"You still love her?"

He snorted. "Not hardly. After she and Buddy blindsided me, though, I'm told I have 'trust issues.' Lack of trust has a way of screwing up a relationship."

"Personally, I find trust overrated."

He gave her a startled look, then laughed. "Good Lord, someone more cynical than me. I'm astounded."

She glanced up the hill toward the inn, knowing Adrian would be in the kitchen by now.

"Trust me."

I can't.

A flash of morning sunlight reflected off one of the windows in Marguerite's tower, piercing her eyes. As she raised a hand against the brightness, a passage from the diaries came back to her. The last time Marguerite saw Jack, he'd begged her again to run away with him. She'd refused because of her lack of faith. She wanted to believe he loved her, but couldn't bring herself to trust him completely. She let fear of getting hurt and the memory of past mistakes hold her back.

A chill went down Jackie's back as she realized that lack of faith hadn't only ruined Marguerite's life; it had ended it—even though a part of Marguerite had never stopped yearning for happiness and believing love did exist. She'd been an odd mix of hope and fear, with fear often winning but hope refusing to die.

"Do you know," Carl said as they reached the pier, "I still remember the first time I saw you."

"Hmm?" Jackie pulled her mind away from thoughts of Marguerite and Jack. "I'm sorry, what did you say?"

"I was remembering the first time I saw you. You were barely old enough to walk." They stopped near the johnboat that ferried divers out to the work platform. "When I realized Buddy and Serena had a child, I looked at you and thought, 'She could have been mine.'"

She stared at him in disbelief. "I . . ." Lord, what did she say to that? "I'm sorry."

"Me, too." He looked at her sheepishly. "You seemed like a great kid."

"I . . ." She didn't dare tell him that she'd wished more than once her dad could be more like him. "Thank you."

"Well." Carl started to turn away. "To work, I suppose."

"Mr. Ryder?"

"Yes?"

"I, um, I want you to know, I've always admired your work. It's a small world we live in—treasure-hunting and archeology—and I've heard people talk about you, and well, I know what my father was, and I know I helped him, but there was a part of me that always wished . . ."

"What?"

"That I could be a marine archeologist like you."

Surprise showed on his face. "Have you ever thought about pursuing it now?"

"Yes, and I've accepted that I don't have the time or money to get a degree. But, well, I admire what you do. And"—she took a deep breath and plunged ahead—"I realize I'm only going to be around a few days a month, but if you happen to need an experienced diver on a volunteer basis—" She saw him frown and pulled back. "Never mind. Dumb idea. Forget I said anything."

"Actually"—he nodded, slowly—"I'll think about it."

"You will?" Her heart skipped a beat.

"I'm not promising anything. I have rules I need to follow."

"Yes. Absolutely. I understand."

"But I'll keep it in mind."

"Really?" She wanted to jump for joy. "You're not just messing with me, are you?"

"I'm not messing with you." He smiled.

"Well, then . . ." Trying not to make a fool of herself, she started backing away. "I guess we both have work to do."

"Jackie?" he called as she turned toward the gangway.

"Yes?"

"I hope you won't take this wrong but . . ."

"What?"

"You have your mother's eyes, but the similarity stops there."

She started to say thanks but didn't want to be disloyal to her mother. "Let me know if you need a diver."

"I will."

Chapter 18

"Guess what?"

Adrian turned at the sound of Jackie's voice and found her standing in the kitchen doorway, smiling broadly. "I was beginning to wonder if I'd see you today."

"What, you thought I'd slip away without stopping by?" She sauntered forward wearing a crop-waisted sweatshirt and a pair of extremely frayed cutoffs that showed off her tanned legs nicely.

His gaze dropped to the sexy silver chain around one ankle before he forced his attention back to the sticks of butter he'd been checking for softness. "When you didn't show for breakfast, I started to worry."

"Ah." She leaned a hip against the center island and crossed her legs at the ankle. "You thought I was hiding out in my cabin, too embarrassed to face you after blubbering on your shoulder last night."

"Something like that." Trying not to stare at her legs, he carried the butter to the island where he'd set up his baking station.

"Ha! I'm made of sterner stuff than that."

He looked down into her face, thinking how good

happiness looked on her. "I'm glad to hear you're not embarrassed."

"I didn't say that." She tipped her head. "I'm just not a wimp who lets a little embarrassment send me into hiding. Truth is, I skipped breakfast because I was busy down on the pier."

"How are things going down there?" He added the butter to the sugar and eggs already in the mixing bowl. "Alli's been watching from the window in the gift shop and says there's lots of activity on the beach. I, on the other hand, have been stuck here in the kitchen all day, filling bakery orders."

"Actually, you're not missing much. It's pretty boring when all you can see is what's happening on the surface and the real action is underwater. However . . ." Excitement twinkled in her eyes. "There's a chance that might change for me, which is what I came to tell you."

"Oh?"

"I talked to Carl Ryder this morning."

He studied her. "You're smiling, so I'll guess this is good news."

"It is. Since I'll be around once a month, I asked him if he'd consider letting me help."

"And . . ."

"He said maybe." Her whole face lit. "It's not a yes, but it's a lot more than I ever hoped for. Before our talk this morning, I half expected him to ban me from the area for fear I'd swipe some artifacts to sell on the black market."

"That must have been some talk." He flipped on the mixer to blend the ingredients.

"It was. What are you making?"

"Brownies."

"The gooey, rich kind you made the last time I was here? I *love* those things!"

"You really are a chocoholic." He chuckled.

"You bet. Want some help?" She checked her watch. "I have a few minutes I can spare, and you did promise to give me cooking lessons."

"Well . . ." He made a stern face. "I suppose I could let you help, but then I'd have to kill ya, since you'd know my most closely guarded secret."

She snorted. "I'll take my chances, tough guy."

"I don't know . . ."

"If you let me help, I'll tell you what Carl and I talked about this morning."

"Oh yeah?"

"You were right about there being a personal issue between him and my father."

"Is it juicy?"

She cocked a brow. "Do I get to help?"

"Can you operate a mixer?"

She eyed the machine doubtfully, then shoved up the sleeves of her sweatshirt. "I've never met a motorized piece of equipment I couldn't conquer."

"You do understand we're baking brownies, not changing motor oil, right?"

"You mean that isn't old oil you drizzle over the top to make 'em so gooey?"

"Just get over here." He took her by the hips and slid her between him and the counter. Big mistake, he realized instantly as he looked down at her rounded bottom now inches away from his groin. "So, um"—he cleared his throat—"tell me the big secret. What caused the animosity?"

She looked at him over her shoulder with her hazel cat's eyes. "Carl Ryder was engaged to my mother until he introduced her to his best friend."

"Your father?"

"Yep."

Adrian let out a low whistle. "That would do it. Now keep an eye on the bowl while you add the cocoa."

"How much cocoa?"

"Until it looks right."

She turned her head again. "Do you think you could be a bit more specific? Like add *X* amount?"

"You mean get out the measuring cups so you have that much more stuff to wash when you're done? No, just go by what feels right."

"Oui, Monsieur le Chef," she teased back. "But we beginners prefer exact instructions."

"Ah, but mademoiselle, ze cooking it is only half science. The other half is pure art. You must go by what is here." He tapped at his chest. "Not up here in ze head."

"Ah." She nodded, turning serious again. "Sort of like sailing? Okay, I can handle that."

When she lifted the can of powdered cocoa and started to dump it in, he grabbed her wrists. "Careful. You have to take it slow."

She slumped, which brought her back against his chest. His whole body tightened at the contact. He looked down, and saw her wide-necked sweatshirt had slipped off one shoulder, exposing the strap to her sports bra.

Keep it friendly.

"You know," she said looking up at him, "maybe on this first batch, I should observe, so I know what I'm shooting for."

"Good idea," he agreed, needing some space between

them. "Tell you what. I'll teach you the way my grand-mother taught me." Clearing a spot on the counter next to the mixer, he wrapped his hands about her waist. "Up you go."

She shrieked as he lifted her up and set her on the counter. "What are you doing?"

"When I was little, my grandmother always made me sit on the counter while she worked."

"Probably because you were too short to see what she was doing otherwise."

"No, I think it was to keep me from tripping her as I raced around the kitchen trying to help. Now, watch as I add the ingredients. If you're a really good girl, I'll let you lick the mixer blades when I'm done."

"Oh, will you, Granny? Will you?"

"Only if you're a very good girl." He gave her a wolfish grin.

"My, Granny, what big teeth you have."

"That's not all I have that's big."

She gave him a look. "Just get on with the brownies."

He concentrated on adding the cocoa and flour, telling himself he could handle having her sitting right beside him, her smooth, tanned legs within easy touching range, her trim ankles crossed, and that ankle bracelet driving him crazy with thoughts of running his tongue along it. Turning off the mixer, he tasted the batter. "Mmm, good. Needs a tad more cocoa, though. What do you think?" He dipped his finger in the batter and held it out to her.

She closed her lips around his finger and the warm, wet heat of her tongue licked the treat away. He felt the contact all the way to his groin. Her eyes met his, and he knew she felt it, too, the sizzle of shared excitement.

"How's that?" he asked in a thick voice.

"You're right." She broke eye contact, pretending nothing had happened. "More chocolate."

He added more, deciding she had the right idea; pretend ignorance, as if his body weren't alive with the memory of her mouth closing over him that night in her bed. When he turned the mixer off, she dipped her finger in the batter, then sucked it between her pouty lips. "Mmm, perfect."

He stifled a groan as he removed the blades and handed them to her. "Now, for the best part of baking."

"All for me?" Her hand brushed his as she took the blades and tipped her head. Her pink tongue darted out, licking up chocolate.

"No, you have to share."

"If you insist." She held it out to him. His gaze locked on her eyes as he wrapped his hand around her wrist and licked a second blade clean. Her lips parted and her eyelids turned heavy. Oh yes, she definitely felt the sizzle. Her hand trembled when she took her turn, smearing chocolate next to her mouth.

"You missed some."

"Where?" she asked breathlessly.

"Here." Even as he told himself not to, he leaned forward and licked the corner of her mouth. Her breath caught and sparks ignited. Taking her head in his hands, he covered her mouth with his, molding and playing with her lush lips, sucking the lower one into his mouth. "God, you taste good."

"It's . . . the chocolate," she managed between nibbles.

"Let's see." Without leaving her mouth, he reached sideways and dipped his finger in the batter, then drew it down her neck. His mouth followed the trail, lapping up the enticing blend of chocolate and skin. Her pulse beat wildly against his lips, making him want to devour all of her. "No, I think it's you. Not sure, though." He smeared batter on her collarbone. "Let me try again."

"Adrian . . ." She pressed a hand against his chest. When he lifted his head, he saw a hunger that matched his own blazing in her eyes. "You're getting chocolate on my shirt."

"Well, we can't have that." He pulled the shirt over her head and dropped it to the floor. Then he drew a chocolate *X* over her chest just above her sports bra.

"We shouldn't be doing this." She buried her fingers in his hair, pulling it free of the band. "What if someone comes in?"

"Rory and Chance are in town, and Alli's busy in the gift shop." He pressed her back until she rested on her elbows with him standing between her legs. "We're safe." Looking into her eyes, he smeared chocolate on her stomach. When he bent to lick it off, her head fell back and she moaned in pleasure as her thighs tightened on his hips. Dipping his tongue into her navel, he eyed the bra, longing to remove it so he could paint her nipples with chocolate and lick them clean, but he didn't feel quite *that* safe in the kitchen. "We definitely need to have your next cooking lesson at my house."

"Hmm?"

"When you come back. For next month's cruise." He nibbled his way back up to her neck and drew her earlobe into his mouth. She gave a throaty moan as he drew back slowly, releasing her earlobe from his lips. "Yeah, cooking lesson. My house. In private."

"The cruise?" She lifted her head, her eyes dazed as she frowned at him.

He raked his gaze down her body, spread out like a

banquet before him. "Actually, forget next month. Let's go there now."

She blinked, and he could see her brain kicking in, overriding passion. "Whoa," she said with a breathy laugh. Straightening up, she glanced around. "What just happened here?"

He cocked a brow, even as he wanted to whimper. Why did she have to come to her senses now? And why were there no locks on the kitchen doors?

"I don't believe this." She shook her head to clear it. "What is wrong with us? Can't we behave in a room alone for five minutes?"

"I'm beginning to wonder why we keep trying."

She pushed him back to arm's length. "We agreed we'd be friends, remember?"

"Well, I don't know about you, but I'm feeling very friendly at the moment." He took her hand off his chest and licked the center of her palm. "I want you. Now."

Her eyes blazed with passion for an instant before she snatched her hand free. "But what about later? What happens when you stop wanting me—"

"I'm not sure that'll ever happen."

"—or I stop wanting you?"

Placing both hands on the counter, he met her nose to nose. "Are you at least willing to admit you want me now?"

"Well, duh!" She stared at him. "But what about—"

"Stop." He placed a finger over her lips. "I've been thinking about this for the past two days, and it's suddenly occurred to me that maybe we're both worrying too much about the future. Maybe we should stop running worst-case scenarios and go with the flow. You know, see where this thing takes us."

He watched the struggle in her eyes as longing battled

fear, and knew the instant that longing lost. "I'm sorry, I can't. I have too much at stake. It's not worth the risk."

Hurt struck in the center of his chest. "Let me guess. Your business, your ship, your future. Is that really all you care about? Well, pardon me for thinking this thing between us might be worth a little risk."

"Adrian . . ."

"No, just forget it, Jackie." He grabbed the mixer blades and took them to the sink.

"Oh, so now you're back to pouting because I won't sleep with you?" She jumped down from the counter and retrieved her sweatshirt from the floor, jerking at the sleeves in an effort to get it right side out. "There are more important things in life than sex."

"Yes, there certainly are. Unfortunately, you don't know half of them. You only know the tangible things, the things you can see with your eyes and touch with your hands. You know nothing about the things you have to feel with your heart."

"That's not true."

"Isn't it?" He stepped back to her. "You're so scared of getting hurt, you've trained yourself never to hope or dream or feel. Well, that's a sorry way to live your life. You can have your business, and your ship, and the respect of your crew, but what good does it do you when you have no one to share it with? No family or even friends you let past the surface? You're so sure people will judge you harshly, you never give anyone a chance."

"Yet aren't you judging me now?"

"Only for your lack of courage."

"Fine." She pulled her shirt over her head and jerked it into place. "It's easy to be brave with your heart when you've never had it broken. How dare you judge me, though, while you stand in your successful inn surrounded by family you know you can count on? You haven't walked in my shoes, Adrian St. Claire. So don't you preach to me about courage. Have you ever *once* gone after something, and not gotten it? Ever suffered bone-crushing disappointment?"

"Yes, I have. The day my parents died."

"All right, I'll give you that. But you were surrounded by people to help you get through it. Try having your life shattered over and over again. Then you can talk to me about courage of the heart. But I'll tell you this, I am not going to be one of your victims."

"What are you talking about?"

"Give me a break." She snorted. "How many times have you broken a heart and walked away unscathed?"

"Never." His head snapped back. "I'm always straight with women, and go out of my way to be sure they don't get hurt."

"And I'm sure they tell you they're perfectly happy to be your short-term lover. 'Of course, Adrian,'" she said in a falsely sweet voice. "'I don't expect anything from you but mild affection and hot sex. I don't hope deep inside that you'll fall in love with me and I promise I won't cry when we part. I'll smile and tell you I'm perfectly fine and of course we can still be friends.'" Her voice dropped to normal. "Is that how it goes?"

He didn't answer, but his face hardened.

"I won't be your temporary plaything. I can't afford it."

His voice became hushed. "Who says it would be temporary?"

Her heart lurched at his words. For a single moment, the whole world went still. "Are you saying it wouldn't be?"

"I don't know," he said slowly. "But that alone is different for me. With other women, I've always known going in that it would be short-term. With you, though . . . I don't know anything."

Her chest grew so tight, she could hardly breathe. He was offering her the one thing she wanted more than anything in the world. A chance for family, belonging, love. Not a promise, but a possibility. Only . . . what if she reached out and it vanished? "I'm sorry, it's too risky. I have more to lose than you."

"Do you? I didn't realize broken hearts came in different sizes."

"Like I could ever break your heart." She tried to laugh, but couldn't. Needing air, she turned away. "I have to go." Panic sent her hurrying toward the door.

"Jackie," he called.

She glanced over her shoulder. He stood in the middle of the kitchen, looking strangely alone. But it was an illusion. Adrian wasn't alone. Was he?

"I'm serious about wanting to give this a try even with the complications. This isn't just fun and games for me anymore."

Her throat closed and she had to swallow. Everything in her cried out to stay, to run into his arms and hold on tight.

Nothing good ever lasts.

"I'm sorry." She turned back to the door, and stood for a while, her body shaking. "I need to go." She rushed out the door.

Adrian forced himself to stay in the kitchen as long as he could stand it, then he headed for the front of the inn, needing one last glimpse of Jackie before she sailed away. He stopped short of the front door, though, realizing she'd see him if he stood on the veranda, which would only make him feel like more of a lovesick loser—an experience he could happily have lived without.

Veering to his right, he strolled casually into the gift shop. Knickknacks, books, tea sets, and dolls filled the shelves and table displays.

"Hey, Adrian," Allison called from her perch behind the antique cash register where she was embroidering a pillowcase. "Are you done with your baking already?"

"No, I just thought I'd take a little break. You know, see what's going on down at the beach."

"Well, if you can figure it out, let me know. It all looks pretty boring from here."

"So I hear," he mumbled, moving one of the lace curtains aside. He could see Jackie on the quarterdeck. She'd changed back into her pirate getup and was striding about, barking out orders. She looked so tough, but he knew the vulnerability she hid beneath the surface. Why wouldn't she let him in? He would never intentionally hurt anyone, especially not her.

"Scott talked to Carl earlier," Allison said behind him. "He thinks they may start dredging as early as tomorrow."

"That's nice," he said absently.

"Are you all right?"

"Hmm?" He pulled his attention away from the window long enough to glance over his shoulder. "What was that?"

She frowned at him. "Is everything all right? You've seemed so distracted all day."

"I'm fine." He turned back to the window in time to see the ship move away from the pier. A sense of loss tore at his chest. He wanted to reach out and pull her back. Realizing he couldn't, that he had no control over the situation, filled him with a level of frustration he'd never felt before. "I was just wondering, though, hypothetically, what do people do if they fall for someone who doesn't, you know . . . fall back?"

"Well, now, that's an odd question."

"I'm just curious, is all."

"All right, let me think." She studied her embroidery, then resumed stitching. "If you're a woman, you eat copious amounts of chocolate, watch movies that make you cry, and talk on the phone to your girlfriends for hours and hours about what a jerk the man is, what a blind fool, how unworthy, and they tell you there's someone out there who is much better and far more deserving."

"And if you're a man?"

She scrunched her face in thought. "Contact sports and beer?"

He turned back to the window as the *Pirate's Pleasure* cleared the line of palm trees and disappeared toward the Gulf. Desperation and helplessness nearly choked him. Dear God, was this what unrequited love felt like? Was this the pain Jackie feared awaited her if she gave him a chance?

"Alli?" he asked.

"Yes?"

"Do you think I've ever . . . hurt a woman? Without meaning to?"

"The truth?" She laughed. "Adrian, I don't think you've been with a woman who didn't fall madly in love with you and sob into her pillow when you walked away."

The thought of his past girlfriends, each wonderful in her own way, feeling even a portion of this pain crushed him. Could his sister be right? "Well, you're wrong on one score, at least."

"Oh?" Alli asked.

"There is one woman who didn't fall for me."

Alli went still, then looked up from her stitching. "Oh no . . . Adrian, you said you weren't interested in Jackie. Please tell me you didn't sleep with her anyway."

He didn't answer.

"How could you?"

He rested his back against the wall. "Fairly easily, actually."

"Well, don't hurt her, okay?" Alli jammed her needle in the cloth, securing it. "I have a feeling she's been hurt enough."

"*Me* hurt *her*?" He came off the wall. "What about *her* hurting *me*?"

His sister laughed. "If I thought you were serious, I'd say you're overdue in the rejection department."

"Well, I like that," he grumbled, pacing the gift shop.

"Oh dear," she said after a while. "You are serious."

He laughed, since the only other option was breaking something, and he really didn't think Allison would appreciate that.

"Oh, Adrian." She leapt off the stool and held her arms open. "In that case, you let the little sister you've helped through so much hold you for a change." He let her take him into her arms, her gentle hands patting his back. "If it helps, I assure you rejection isn't lethal."

He wasn't entirely sure about that. What hurt the most, though, was wondering who Jackie had to hug her when her heart ached. If only he knew for sure that things could work out between them, he'd push harder. But what if he hurt her more in the end, exactly as she feared?

Chapter 19

In the days that followed, Jackie didn't talk to Adrian at all. Whether by chance or design, he never answered the phone when she called the inn. She nearly asked for him a few times, but always lost her nerve.

Two weeks of silence drove home just how much she'd enjoyed their phone conversations. He understood her and accepted her in a way no one ever had before, except maybe for Ti. But that was different. Ti didn't make her laugh as freely as Adrian did, or make her feel more alive with just the sound of his voice.

The ache of longing reached its peak the morning the special segment was scheduled to play on *Good Morning America*. She sat in the officers' lounge outside her cabin, sipping coffee as she kept one eye on the TV.

She still couldn't believe Adrian had suggested they date with the hope that it might not be temporary. Good Lord, date Adrian St. Claire? The sexiest man she'd ever met? But he wasn't just sexy. He was funny and generous and kind. Having a man that wonderful want a relationship with her was like having someone stand before her holding out a beautifully wrapped gift box they claimed was filled with joy, and saying: "Here, you want it?"

Of course her instinct was to snatch her hands back

and ask: "What's the catch?" What had he expected? That she'd shrug and say, "Okay"?

She rubbed her forehead to relieve a tension headache that had hounded her for days. If she could just figure out the catch, then maybe she'd have the courage to reach for what he offered. Otherwise, she was half convinced she'd unwrap that pretty box and find it filled with snakes.

Unfortunately, her rejection had hurt Adrian's feelings, and Lord, the man was sensitive! So now she'd ruined their friendship and she had no idea how to fix that.

Footsteps sounded on the deck, letting her know Ti had arrived to watch the show with her. She smoothed the worry lines from her brow a second before he clambered down through the aft hatch. "Did I make it in time?"

"Just barely. I think we're up next." She glanced at the TV. "They just cut to commercial, so you should have time to grab some coffee if you hurry."

"Great." He ducked into the galley and came back with a steaming cup in hand. He'd barely taken a seat beside her when an image of the *Pirate's Pleasure* appeared on the screen.

"Dat us! Turn it up!" Ti said.

She grabbed the remote and turned up the volume as she stared in awe at the screen. Even though she'd worried about the special, the sight of her ship coming into the cove at Pearl Island under sail power sent a thrill racing through her.

The voice of a female reporter invited the audience to join them for a trip to a magical island in search of buried treasure. Jackie sat forward, both hands wrapped around her coffee cup, waiting for any mention of her name. Fortunately, they focused on the history of the powder horn.

The reporter interviewed Carl Ryder on the beach, asking about the excavation and what they hoped to find. He looked ruggedly handsome in his black wet suit with the cove behind him and the wind ruffling his sun-bleached hair. Unfortunately, his manner before a camera could cure insomnia.

They cut quickly to the inn, saying buried treasure wasn't all guests might find while staying on the island, since a ghost supposedly haunted the old mansion. Allison, dressed in a Southern belle costume, welcomed them on the veranda and led them inside for a tour.

"The St. Claires got to love dis," Ti said.

"No kidding," Jackie agreed, knowing they probably had a TV going in the kitchen even in the midst of serving breakfast. "You can't buy advertising this good."

"Not bad for us, either, since dey start with a shot of da ship."

"True."

As Allison led the camera toward the back of the house, the voice-over cut back in, claiming that if old sailing ships, buried treasure, and magic ghosts weren't enough to entice guests to this special getaway, there was the food, sumptuously prepared by Chef Adrian St. Claire.

Sumptuously prepared? Jackie raised a brow. The woman made it sound as if the chef were sumptuous, not the food. Although when Adrian appeared on the screen, Jackie had to admit the word fit.

He smiled into the camera, dimples set to stun as he explained what he was preparing. Jackie's heart ached watching him, knowing he'd hammed it up to shift attention away from her. And he certainly hadn't exaggerated about the show he'd put on. When she compared it to Carl's interview, she could see why they'd decided to show more than just a few brief seconds of him cooking. In fact, they spent half the segment in the kitchen with him showing off.

She remembered him saying he'd wanted to be an actor. Too bad he hadn't pursued it. He'd have been a heartthrob, no doubt about it.

But then she never would have met him.

The thought brought back her earlier tug-of-war, but with a new layer. How could she even think of dating a man with that much natural charisma on top of his incredible good looks? She'd never considered herself lacking in confidence when it came to men, but Adrian was in a whole different league than the average Joe on the street. Did she really want to deal with the constant competition? And what about faithfulness? She'd always thought men had a hard enough time with monogamy; how much harder would commitment be for a man who had women throwing themselves at his feet?

She'd be crazy to get involved with him.

So why couldn't she stop thinking about him and wanting to say yes?

The show cut back to the main set where the anchors thanked the reporter in the field for the piece on Pearl Island, then moved on to the next topic. Jackie clicked off the TV, completely depressed.

Ti turned to her with a beaming smile. "If dat don't sell cruise tickets, I don't know what will."

"Yes, it was very good," she agreed gloomily.

"Okay." He looked at her. "Why da worries on your face?"

"What are you talking about? I'm not worried." She straightened the sailing magazines scattered across the old trunk. "In fact, I'm ecstatic. They showed our ship and mentioned the name but left us out of it. It was perfect."

"I don't mean da show. You mopin' for da past two weeks." He looked at the TV then back at her. "I take it things not go well between you and Adrian?"

"I don't know what you mean." Snatching up her empty mug, she headed for the galley. "There's nothing going on between us."

"Jackie, dis is me." Ti followed her to the coffee machine. "I see da two of you. Dat mon want you, and you want him."

"Okay, so we've got a healthy dose of lust. So what?"

"Dat what he call it? Lust?"

"I don't know!" She rubbed both hands over her face, remembering the look on Adrian's face when he'd said it wasn't fun and games for him anymore. "I'm so confused."

"Den talk to me." He leaned against the counter. "Tell me what confuse you."

She sagged in defeat. "Adrian wants us to start seeing each other."

"And you don't want dat?"

"I don't know what I want. I only know what I don't want. For this venture to fail. To lose my ship. To have to move away and start over."

"You think of dis now, after we commit to doin' dese cruises?"

She snatched up the pot to fill her cup. The last thing she needed was a repeat of the argument they'd had back in the fall. Her hand shook, sloshing hot brew on the counter, and she cursed as she replaced the pot. "All right, if you must know the truth, I didn't have a choice."

"Ah," he said. "Den I right in my suspicions. Even

dough you promise to always be straight with me, things worse dan you let on."

"Were worse." She cast him a sheepish look. "They're turning around now, I swear. Which is why I don't want to mess this up. Although I may have already done just that."

"What you mean?"

She lowered her gaze to her cup. "Adrian is really mad at me right now."

"Because you tell him you don' want him."

"I *do* want him. But I don't want to deal with the fall-out when he gets bored and moves on."

"Who say he will?"

"Give me a break, Ti. When has anything ever worked out for me?"

"You got a point, but a lot of dat ya own fault."

"What?" She looked at him sharply.

"You always put ya faith in da wrong people. Like da men you date. Dey all as irresponsible as ya father or wimps who let you walk all over dem. So of course dey let you down, girl. Adrian St. Claire da first decent mon you know, and if you don' give him a chance, you a fool."

She stood still, absorbing his words. "You're saying I should get involved with Adrian, even though it could ruin things businesswise?"

"You say yourself he already mad. So what you have to lose? Jus' don' keep him danglin' too long. How da old sayin' go? 'All lost to he who hesitates'? Or in dis case, she."

Just like with Marguerite, who lost everything rather than take a blind leap of faith and trust that life wouldn't let her fall one more time into a heartbreaking abyss.

"Yes, but . . ." She swallowed hard. "What if it doesn't work out?"

"What if it don'?" He shrugged one massive shoulder. "What da worst dat happen?" With that bit of wisdom, he filled his coffee cup and headed for the main hatch.

Jackie remained where she was, stunned by his matter-of-fact question. Okay, she asked herself, what if it didn't work out? What was the worst that could happen? Would she die?

No.

Would her business be on any shakier ground than it had been before?

No.

Would anything so horrible happen that she couldn't battle her way through to the other side?

She was still pondering that question, when her mobile phone rang and she went to retrieve it. "Pirate's Pleasure Cruises."

"Is this the ship that was on TV this morning?" a woman asked.

"Yes, it is."

The caller gushed for a bit about how beautiful the ship was, then asked for a brochure. She turned out to be the first of many callers throughout the day who wanted more information on how to book a cruise. Mid-afternoon, an excited Rory called to say the inn was getting swamped, as well.

"Isn't this great!" Rory exclaimed. "I knew it would pay off, but I never imagined the response would be this big. Or this fast!"

"Me, either," Jackie said, feeling overwhelmed.

"I'll bet you sell out for the April cruise by the end of the week."

"I don't know. I'm just glad the first cruise and the one next week sold so well. I'm not willing to bet on a complete sellout yet."

"Well, I am," Rory insisted. "So name your price."

"Pass." Jackie laughed. "I'm not dumb enough to bet with a woman who never seems to lose at anything."

"Except on this you can't lose, either. If you don't sell out, you win the bet. If you do sell out, you win anyway."

"Too bad everything in life isn't like that."

"It is if you dream big and back it up with hard work."

I love you, Rory, Jackie thought, both envious of Rory's faith in life and grateful for her friendship. "Okay, I'll bet you . . . five dollars I don't sell out."

"Not good enough. Let's make it a bottle of champagne. We'll have a celebration lunch when you get here."

"Do y'all celebrate everything with champagne?"

"Of course. And considering how well the show went, we have a lot of toasts to make."

With the mention of the show, Jackie considered asking what Adrian had thought of it, which would be a perfect intro for asking to talk to him. She opened her mouth, but the words stuck.

"Oops, gotta go," Rory said. "The other line is ringing. See ya next week. Champagne on you."

Jackie stared at the phone after Rory disconnected. Damn! Another opportunity lost to hesitation. She hated it when Ti was right, which he usually was. But was he right in encouraging her to give a relationship with Adrian a chance? One way or the other, she needed to make up her mind before next week.

She exhaled in a rush as the thought of seeing him again filled her with equal amounts of eagerness and dread.

The day the Mardi Gras cruise was due to arrive, Adrian volunteered to help Allison set up the tables on the veranda. As with the first cruise, the package included afternoon tea for the arriving passengers, then a more lavish meal inside that evening. They'd also decided to offer free shuttle service into Galveston so guests could join the New Orleans–style Mardi Gras celebration going on in the historic district.

He had a million things to do inside, but needed to at least see Jackie . . . even if from a distance. The need was strong enough to leave him edgy and self-conscious. She'd asked him before leaving if he'd ever once gone after something and not gotten it. He had a feeling he was about to find out how that felt.

The faint sound of calypso music caught his ear and he looked up to see the *Pirate's Pleasure* approaching the cove. The sails billowed with wind as the vessel rode across the water.

"Here they come," Allison said, stepping to the rail and shading her eyes. Down on the beach, guests from the inn sat up on their beach towels. Even Carl's team of divers paused in their work. Joining Alli at the rail, he watched sailors scurry up into the rigging. Other sailors launched one of the tender boats to help bring the ship in and secure her to the pier.

He spotted Jackie on the quarterdeck and fought the urge to go down to the dock to greet her. But he'd decided to give her however much time and space she needed to think things over. If she really didn't want anything more than friendship, he needed to respect that.

But dammit, he wanted to go to her and reassure her, persuade her, seduce her, whatever it took to get her to give them a chance. Why did everything have to be such a big decision, involving their whole future? Why couldn't it be about now, and let the rest just happen?

When the ship was secure, he saw her look toward the house. He couldn't read her expression from such a distance, but he knew she'd spotted him. Longing coiled in his stomach.

"Come on." Allison patted his arm in empathy. "Let's get to work."

He felt his cheeks heat and wished he'd never told his sister about Jackie rejecting him. It was all too horribly embarrassing.

Night had long since fallen by the time Adrian left the inn and headed down the wooded path for home. In the spirit of Mardi Gras, a party was in full swing down on the deck of the ship and the sound of music and laughter drifted to him. He glanced through the trees as he walked, catching glimpses of the brightly lit ship. Was Jackie on deck overseeing her galley crew, or had she retreated to her cabin?

Throughout the evening, he'd looked up every time the kitchen door opened, hoping to see her. She hadn't come, though, making him wonder just how badly he'd screwed things up between them. Self-doubt was a new experience for him, and he'd decided days ago he didn't care for it at all. He much preferred being the one to decide whether or not to be with a woman—not waiting for her to make up her mind. How did other men put up with this uncertainty?

Stepping onto the porch, he caught a movement out of the corner of his eye. With a sense of déjà vu, he turned as Jackie stepped to the edge of the shadows where he could barely make her out. His mood brightened instantly.

"Hi," she said, twisting her fingers together.

"Hi." He cautioned himself not to get too hopeful. After all, she could have come to deliver another let's-be-friends speech.

She took another step forward, into the light, and his heart skipped when he saw what she wore: a short tank dress in a tropical print with a scarf tied about her hips. His gaze followed her tanned legs to the sexy ankle bracelet and flat sandals. That she owned a dress at all amazed him; that she'd worn one for him had his hopes soaring. Surely a dress was a good sign.

"I, um . . ." She smoothed the fabric over her thighs. "I hope you don't mind me waiting here."

"No. Not at all." He stopped himself before he blurted out something stupid like: Does this mean you want to sleep with me?

"Can I come in?"

"Of course!" He fumbled with the keys but managed to open the door. Moving ahead of her, he clicked on the floor lamp by the sofa. "Can I get you a drink?"

"Do you have any of that Kahlúa left?"

"Absolutely." When he returned with two glasses, he found her standing in his living room with her arms wrapped about herself. "Are you cold?"

"No, I—" She dropped her arms. "No."

He handed her the drink. "I understand you lost a bet with Rory."

"Yes. Believe it or not, the April cruise sold out completely. I understand we're celebrating tomorrow."

"Usual place. Usual suspects."

"I'm looking forward to it. I enjoy your family get-togethers."

"So." He glanced at the sofa and his heart started to race with thoughts of heavy petting. "You want to sit?"

"No, I . . ." Her brows drew together as she stared at her glass. "I have something to say, and I want to get it out and get your reaction while I'm standing. That way, if I need to leave—"

"You'll have a faster escape."

"Exactly."

"All right." He braced himself for more rejection. "What did you come to say?"

"First"—her voice turned weak—"are you still mad at me?"

"Jackie . . ." He struggled with what to say. "Truth be told, it's myself I've been mad at. I shouldn't have pressured you. I understand your reservations. I don't agree with them, but I understand them."

"Then—" Her fingers tightened on the glass. "You're still interested in . . ."

"Being more than friends?"

She managed a jerky nod.

"Good God, yes." Setting his drink on the end table, he stepped closer to her. When he saw her body shaking, he rubbed his hands on her bare arms. "Are you sure you're not cold?"

"I'm f-fine."

"You're trembling."

"I'm not cold," she whispered. "I'm scared."

"Oh, Jackie." His heart melted. Afraid she'd drop the

glass, he took it from her and set it beside his. Then he carefully gathered her to him, trapping her clutched hands between them. She felt small and vulnerable, her head barely reaching his shoulder. He took her fists and brought them to his mouth, kissing her knuckles. "You don't have to be scared. I'll never do anything to hurt you."

"I know you won't mean to." She looked up at him, her eyes wide. "People always mean promises when they give them. But keeping them is hard. It's okay, though." Her fingers relaxed enough to caress his face. Even that light touch stirred his senses. "I'm tough enough to take whatever happens."

"You're very tough." He kissed each of her palms, wanting to pull her body snugly against his so he could soak up the feel of her in his arms. They'd rushed things the last time, though, by giving lust free rein. Cupping her face, he decided this time, he wanted to savor every moment, every sensation. "Just don't complain if I treat you gently."

Her face softened as he lowered his mouth to hers and her arms went about his neck. He sank slowly into the kiss, molding her to him, feeling her breasts against his chest, her thighs brushing his as she rose up on her toes. Cupping her bottom, he hardened against her soft belly as he realized this was what he'd yearned for all his life without even knowing it: this tender, tough woman who excited him and challenged him, who both needed and completed him.

Without breaking the kiss, he scooped her into his arms and strode past the sofa to the bedroom. Bracing one knee on the bed, he lowered her to the mattress. His mouth returned to hers again and again as he undressed her, then himself.

She welcomed him into her arms when he lay down beside her, their bodies finally skin to skin. He splayed a hand over her stomach, feeling the heat and softness of her skin. She arched enticingly, drawing his attention to her firm breasts, the dip of her waist, the flair of her hips.

He dragged his gaze to her eyes and smiled. "Every night," he said, drawing her against him, "for the past month, I've imagined having you here with me. Imagined how I'd touch you." His hand glided over her hip, down her leg. "Pleasure you." He swept his hand to the inside of her thigh and up, slowly. "Make you moan."

"I've imagined you, too." She sighed, her eyes heavy as she shifted her legs, beckoning his touch. For this one night, Jackie decided, she wouldn't question; she'd simply enjoy.

His fingertips moved upward, barely brushing her dark curls. "Is that what you imagine?"

"Yes." She flexed her hips as heat built inside her, but he only turned his hand over, brushing her curls with the backs of his fingers. "Touch me."

"I plan to." He smiled as he moved down her body to trail kisses over her stomach. Her trembling started again, but this time from desire as he licked his way back up, teasing her breasts as his fingers continued teasing below with feather-light touches. She arched her back, wanting the frenzied oblivion he'd given her before. Instead he seemed bent on going slow.

Needing more, she ran her hands over his back, then drew her fingernails upward along his skin in a silent demand for heat and speed—the flash of physical fulfillment.

Chuckling, he settled his body over hers, his weight pressing her into the mattress. She smiled in anticipation, thinking he'd take her now, quickly, and end weeks of longing. But he surprised her by taking her wrists and pinning them to either side of her head. He loomed over her, his eyes smoldering. "Are you rushing me?"

"I want you." She squeezed his waist with her thighs, trying to relieve the hot restlessness inside her.

"So demanding," he scolded and brushed his lips over hers. She lifted her head to deepen the kiss but he pulled back an equal amount. When she dropped her head back down, he chuckled, then nipped her bottom lip with his teeth. "This time we do it my way. I want to pleasure you. And . . . I want you to let me."

She frowned at the ominous note in his voice as he released her wrists and slid down her body, stopping at her breasts to torment her with light licks. Her nipples tightened to hard peaks, making her moan.

"Mmm, you are sensitive," he said.

"Yes." She arched into him, wanting his whole mouth. "More."

"You're demanding again." He scowled up at her. "Am I going to have to tie you down?"

She shivered at the thought, but shook her head.

"Then relax and let me play. It's more fun when it's not fast."

It's also more frightening, she wanted to tell him. *When it's fast, there's no time to feel beyond the physical.*

"Trust me," he said as if reading her eyes. "Let go."

Determined to have his way, he lowered his head and resumed teasing her breasts with light brushes of his lips and tongue. Both of them knew he could make her climax with nothing more than sucking on her nipples—but he never even took one into his mouth. She was whimpering in frustration when he finally shifted enough to trail one hand down her stomach toward her aching center. She squirmed eagerly beneath him, lifting her hips.

"Hold still," he admonished, and took one of her nipples between his teeth in a clear warning.

Her breath caught and froze as he slipped one of his exquisitely long fingers slowly inside her. Then she melted with a moan into a puddle beneath him, her legs dropping to the side, her head falling back against the pillow.

Too many sensations came after that to separate one from the other. The suckling pull of his mouth at her breasts, his hand stroking her hot need. He focused all his attention and skill on her, wringing control bit by bit until she stopped caring and gave herself over to him completely.

The tight fist deep inside her that kept her emotions in check relaxed, and feelings rushed through her in a blinding flash that was passion and pain all at once. It lifted her back off the bed as pleasure followed, pushing all else aside. She hung suspended for a moment, then drifted down, her eyes wide.

He settled over her, smiling down at her. She stared back, shaken by all he made her feel. This was what he meant by letting go. Barriers inside her had crumbled, exposing all the needs and desires and yearnings of a lifetime.

He braced himself above her and joined his mouth to hers as he joined their bodies. She wrapped her arms about him, and held tight as he kissed her endlessly, as their bodies moved together, climbing toward a common goal. This time, when the pleasure came, he was right there with her, riding the crest. They clung together as the aftershocks rippled through them.

Slowly, his body relaxed into hers. She kept her arms

about him, staggered by the newness of emotional intimacy coupled with physical pleasure.

Lifting his head, he smiled at her, but the smile vanished when he saw that tears filled her eyes.

I'm sorry, she longed to tell him. *I'm not used to this.*

Understanding softened his face just before he flashed a cocky grin. "See, I told you it can be more fun that way. You don't always have to be in control."

"More fun?" She nearly told him it wasn't fun at all, it was frightening, but it was also thrilling. And tender. And sweet.

"As fun?" he asked, his eyes laughing.

She smiled in gratitude, wondering how he always knew what to say to lighten the mood. "Maybe."

"Well, all right, if you still prefer being in charge"— he sighed heavily and rolled to his back—"I'll happily lie here while you ravage me now."

"Perhaps in a bit."

Chuckling, he pulled her against him. "See, you're not so tough after all."

She settled her head on his shoulder, fearing he was right. Underneath it all, she wasn't tough at all.

Chapter 20

Adrian dressed in the dark as quietly as possible, so he wouldn't wake Jackie. He thought of leaving her a note telling her good morning and to make herself at home. In the end, though, he couldn't leave without one last kiss. He returned to the bed, where she lay in a nest of rumpled sheets, her face soft with sleep.

Bracing his hands on either side of her head, he bent down and brushed his lips along her cheek. She mumbled in protest and snuggled deeper into the pillow. "Wake up, sleepyhead," he whispered, nibbling his way along her jaw. "I need to tell you bye."

Another mumble followed a limp swat of her hand.

"Jack-ie," he coaxed softly and kissed her other cheek. When she still didn't wake, he pulled back to study her face. Maybe a note would be better. Definitely more considerate. Just then she let out a sigh of utter contentment, and the smile that curved her lips was too much to resist.

He lowered his mouth to hers, enjoying the feel of her plush lips, tasting and shaping them until they started to respond. With a moan, she wrapped her arms around his neck. Her body arched toward him, reminding him she was naked and warm beneath the covers.

His body hardened with thoughts of climbing back beneath those covers and running his hands over her smooth skin, exploring every dip and curve. When her tongue licked sweetly into his mouth, he tilted his head enough to see the clock on the nightstand. He had about ten minutes before Rory and Alli arrived in the kitchen to help him with breakfast.

Breaking the kiss, he trailed his lips along her cheek. "I gotta go, sweetheart. I just wanted to say bye. Sleep as long as you want. I'll see you after breakfast."

"Mmm, no," she mumbled, tightening her arms. The covers slipped down, exposing her breasts. "Stay."

"Can't. Time for work." Even as he said the words, his hand cupped one of her delightfully sensitive breasts, stroking the nipple with his thumb. A moan rumbled deep in her throat, flooding his body with hot memories. He indulged in one last kiss that lengthened and deepened as their mouths played.

Her hands slipped down his back and she tugged at his T-shirt. He lifted his head. "Really, I have to go."

"Clothes," she grumbled with apparent displeasure and managed to get one hand beneath the shirt to caress his rapidly heating skin. He glanced at the clock again, thinking of the bread he needed to get in the oven.

Jackie nibbled his neck, making his pulse jump. "Stay."

"I can't. I'll be late," he tried to explain. Although it only took five minutes to walk to the inn. Three if he walked fast.

"Late," she echoed drowsily as her hands drifted around to his stomach. The snap on his jeans made a soft popping noise in the quiet room, followed by the sound of his zipper.

For the first time since the inn opened, Adrian was late to work. When he entered the kitchen, whistling, Allison turned and raised a brow.

"I take it your moping days are at an end?" she asked.

"You might say that," he laughed. At least he hoped so!

Jackie woke to find sunlight streaming into the bedroom. Bolting upright, she looked at the clock on the nightstand and relaxed. It was only eight o'clock, not nearly as bad as she'd feared. Still, she needed to get dressed and down to the ship. Ti would know she hadn't returned last night, but with luck, the rest of the crew would assume she was returning from having breakfast at the inn.

Retrieving her sundress brought a blush to her cheeks as she remembered how attentive Adrian had been the night before. The man did love to cuddle. Even when they weren't making love, he'd wrap his arms around her and hold her close as they talked or dozed. The few men she'd been with in the past hadn't been like that at all. They either left the bed as soon as they could, or moved to their own side so they could sleep undisturbed. Not Adrian. He was most definitely into snuggling. And being playful. And making her laugh one minute, then gasp in ecstasy the next.

The warm memories made her smile. Being held was new for her, but she liked it. It made her feel cherished.

Into that contentment came the disturbing image of him with other women. Was he that snuggly with all his lovers? Affection came easily to him, so probably he was. That didn't diminish the care with which he treated her, though, did it?

She pushed the thought away as she headed for the

bathroom to clean up. Undoubtedly there had been many women in his life. Thinking about them would only depress her. Better to simply live in the present and enjoy being with him for however long it lasted.

Dressed, she stepped into the hall with the intention of heading straight for her ship. The open door across from her caught her eye, though, and she peeked in to see what he kept in his spare bedroom. She found free weights lining one wall, floor-to-ceiling mirrors on another, and a workout bench in the middle of the room. Apparently yoga wasn't solely responsible for that gorgeous body of his, and here at least was something besides reading they had in common. She enjoyed working out when time permitted. Perhaps on her next trip, they could work out together.

Letting herself out of the house, she headed down the path to the beach, her mind filled with images of Adrian lifting weights, muscles flexing and sweat glistening on his skin. Those thoughts segued to fantasies of a different type of workout on the floor in front of all those mirrors.

Her smile broadened until she rounded a bend in the trail and spotted Carl's bungalow. A group of divers emerged onto the porch, chatting and laughing as they descended the steps. Some of them wore dive suits while others were dressed for a day of cleaning and cataloging artifacts. Their voices held excitement as they turned away from her and headed toward the beach.

Envy spurted through her, both for their involvement in the project and their camaraderie. She hung back in the shadows to avoid the awkwardness of walking with them when she wasn't a part of their group.

Just then, Carl stepped onto the porch. "Danny! Can you hold up a bit? I'd like a word with you."

The whole group stopped, glancing back, then exchanging uneasy looks. Most of them were young and she guessed them to be students working toward their degrees in marine archeology. There was one, though, who was older and looked slightly familiar: a short, scrawny man with a fringe of black hair around a bald top and a cheesy grin that seemed too wide for his narrow face. "Sure thing, chief. What's up?"

"The rest of you go on," Carl said, his voice flat. The group complied with obvious eagerness. When they'd disappeared around the next turn in the path Carl addressed the man who was mounting the steps to the porch. "Any particular reason you were late for this morning's meeting?"

"I had a bit of trouble with my truck. No big deal."

"Actually, it is a big deal, since this is the fifth meeting you've almost missed."

"Hey, can I help it if my truck breaks down?"

"You know, you always have some reason why nothing is ever your fault. When I hired you for this project, I hoped you'd be a professional who could help guide the younger divers. Instead, you seem to be the one in need of guidance."

"That's nonsense," the man insisted, his jovial expression turning belligerent. Jackie recognized him then as someone she'd seen drinking in dockside bars with her father a few times. "I'm one of the best divers out there. You can ask anyone."

"Actually, I have been making some inquiries. What I've learned is that, yes, you're a good diver when you bother to show up, but you have no concept of time or how greatly you inconvenience others."

"That's a lie!"

"Then this morning, while we were waiting for you

to get here, I heard a disturbing report from some of the students. They said when you were working the dredge, the screen blew off and you didn't even notice until one of them pointed it out."

"Is it my fault if those wet-behind-the-ears kids don't know how to fasten the screen right?"

"It is if you don't bother to check the equipment before using it." Carl shook his head in grave disappointment. "You're supposed to be one of the team leaders, yet you make an idiot mistake like that?"

"I'm telling you, that wasn't my fault."

"Danny"—Carl rubbed his face—"I have cut you too much slack as it is, but I can't let something like this slide. The dredge you were using yesterday was big enough that, without the screen on the exhaust, you could have sucked up any number of artifacts and blown them halfway across the cove where they may never be found."

"I didn't suck up anything. I know what I'm doing."

"Apparently you don't. I'm going to have to let you go."

"You can't do that!" Danny's skinny face turned dangerously red. "I have a contract."

"And I'm canceling it on the grounds of incompetence."

"We'll see about that when I sue your ass." Danny turned to stomp down the steps, but froze when he saw Jackie standing in the shadows. He flushed with embarrassment until recognition lit in his eyes and he sneered. "What are you doing here? Spying?"

"No. I . . ." She glanced at Carl, catching his startled look. "I'm just walking."

Danny turned back to Carl. "Don't tell me you're going to hire *her*."

Carl's expression turned neutral. "Miss Taylor's presence here is not your concern. I think it best if you gather your gear and leave without making trouble."

Danny tossed one last contemptuous look at Jackie and stomped off down the trail. Apparently the man had less-than-fond memories of her father, but then, Buddy had left a trail of friends-turned-enemies in his wake. Carl turned to her with the calm patience she'd sensed in him before.

"I'm sorry," she said. "I didn't mean to eavesdrop."

He shrugged. "Actually, if someone's going to be that big an ass, they deserve a little embarrassment. Although now I'm short a diver."

"Oh." She started to volunteer, but stopped herself.

He studied her a long moment. "So. You still interested in doing some real archeology?"

"Yes!" Her heart thumped hard against her ribs. "I'll only be here a couple days a month, though."

"Are you available today?"

"I can be, but only until thirteen hundred hours."

"The first dive starts in thirty minutes."

"I'll be ready!" She held out both hands. "Just give me enough time to go over today's schedule with my first mate. Then I'll get into my wet suit and meet you on the dock." Feeling like a kid, she ran all the way to the ship. A few guests had already gathered to watch the activity on the pier where the divers were checking their equipment.

She hurried on board and met a startled Ti in the officers' lounge. After running over the duty roster, she slipped into her wet suit, grabbed her dive bag, and arrived breathless on the dock. Carl was waiting for her in the johnboat they used to ferry divers out to the work platform. She tried to act nonchalant, as if being included on such a project wasn't a dream come true, but the grin that flickered over Carl's rugged face told her she wasn't fooling him. She just prayed her excitement didn't make her clumsy.

When they climbed onto the platform, everyone looked at her.

"Danny won't be with us anymore," Carl said matter-of-factly and no one seemed the least surprised. "This is Jackie Taylor, the captain of the *Pirate's Pleasure*. She's agreed to fill in for him today. Jackie, this is Sam. He'll be your dive buddy."

A young man with sandy hair and friendly eyes stepped forward to shake her hand. "We've all been admiring your ship. I don't suppose you'd give us a tour?"

"Certainly." She flushed with pleasure. "Anytime."

"Okay, let's get down to business." Carl leaned over a chart of the dive area. "Jackie, since you weren't at the meeting this morning, let me go over our goals for today. We've uncovered enough of the stern to access the captain's cabin. Unfortunately, the powder horn wasn't in there, as we had hoped."

She looked at him sharply. "Have you told the St. Claires?"

"Only that we're broadening our search area. We're progressing with the theory that the blast from the explosion may have blown the powder horn from the ship." He ran his finger over the chart. "We've been following a trail of debris to determine the ship's course as she sank. Gunter and I will be working the dredge today."

One of the older members of the team, a large Nordic-looking man, nodded.

"Tony and Sandra will be working here on the platform. You and Sam will be working in the captain's cabin. The horn might not be there, but the cabin is a treasure trove from an historian's point of view."

"Oh?" Jackie asked.

"Everything that's been covered with mud is in such pristine condition, it's like finding a time capsule from the Civil War. Paper, leather, wood, cloth, all of it is intact. I want you to concentrate on going through the desk, cataloging the contents of each drawer before bringing the items to the surface."

"Yes, sir." She nodded.

"Besides"—he smiled at her—"I think it's fitting you be the one to go through the desk, considering Captain Kingsley was your ancestor."

"You're related to Jack Kingsley?" Sam asked.

Jackie nodded, and saw awe spark in several pairs of eyes.

"That's really cool," Sam said. "Wait till you see his cabin. Mr. Ryder's right. It's so intact, it's kind of spooky."

"Anyone have any questions?" Carl asked. They all shook their heads. "Okay then. Let's get wet."

Jackie and Sam were the last ones to go in since he had to show her their system for cataloging all the objects they brought up. Finally, they were in the water, swimming nearly straight down, since the platform was anchored so close to the wreck.

When the ship came into view, she stared in amazement at the amount of mud that had been removed. Following Sam, she swam over the main deck, waiting for the temperature to drop as it had the time before. Other than the expected chill at sixty feet, she felt nothing. Turning her head from side to side, she saw remnants of hemp still dangling from belaying pins along the rail. Gun ports lined the edges of the deck but no cannons. She assumed they'd already been raised.

Reaching the hatch that led to the officer's quarters, they swam down through it. Jackie's pulse raced as she realized this was where Jack had died. Surprisingly, the area showed little damage, although the louvered doors to the officers' cabins hung at crazy angles. Swinging her light back and forth, she saw they still had a lot of dredging to do in those rooms.

At the end of the passage, the door to the captain's cabin stood open, surprising her. She'd pictured it closed, as the first mate had described, with Jack's ghost trying to open it, only to have his transparent hand pass through the knob again and again.

Sam swam ahead of her into the cabin. She followed slowly, half afraid that the strange sensations from her last dive would return. All she felt, though, was wonder to be in Jack Kingsley's living quarters.

They'd been thorough in clearing the mud out in search of the powder horn, but a thick film still covered the floor, cabinets, and the framed pictures nailed to the walls. Her spine tingled as she watched the bed curtain sway gently in the current. A muddy lump on the floor beside the bed appeared to be an oil lamp. Had he sat up at night, reading by its light?

She turned toward the bank of windows. Carl and Gunter were working beyond it, and the beam of a light moved over the jagged panes of glass.

Are you really here, Jack? she wondered, but felt no lingering emotion as she had before.

Again the light moved over the broken glass. She

floated closer and looked beyond the ship into the dark waters of the cove. Had the excavation freed Jack's spirit from the ship? Was he out there, somewhere, searching for the horn?

A dolphin appeared suddenly before her, peeking through the windows. She jerked back, startled, then amused when it tilted its head as if smiling at her. Then it turned and darted off.

Laughing underwater was not an option, but she turned her head enough to share her wonder with Sam. He rolled his eyes as if to say the dolphin was an amusing pest, then motioned for them to get to work.

Chapter 21

At the end of her shift, Jackie headed back to the dock in the johnboat with Sam, grateful for the warm sunshine after an hour underwater. Going through Jack Kingsley's desk had left her feeling torn. Each discovery had thrilled her, but she hated turning everything over to the public. Didn't dead people have a right to privacy? Not that anything had been embarrassingly personal, but still, they'd been his private things.

The most significant finds from a historical standpoint were the manifests and ship's log, but she'd also found a beautifully detailed scrimshaw knife, an ink bottle and quill nibs, a brass button that must have come off one of his coats, and in the bottom locked drawer, stacks and stacks of money in several different currencies.

Running blockades may have been dangerous, but it apparently paid well.

"Jackie!" a female voice called, pulling her from her thoughts. She looked up to find Rory on the pier, waving madly.

"It's about time you came up!" Rory called. "I've been waiting forever."

Alarm skittered through her as the johnboat bumped

against the dock opposite her ship. "Is something wrong?"

"No, but I have news!" A beaming smile lit Rory's face as Jackie climbed the ladder. "I hope you brought that champagne, because we have a whole new reason to celebrate. A huge reason!"

"What?" Jackie turned to accept the air tank that Sam lifted up to her.

"Last night, our aunt, Vivian, went to a premiere party for some new play on Broadway and the producer of the *Good Morning America* segment was there. Although she's not with them anymore. She works for one of the food channels now. They got to talking, Aunt Viv mentioned Adrian was her nephew, and the woman started raving about how wonderful he was in front of a camera. One thing led to another, and—get this—the woman wants to know if Adrian would be interested in having his own cooking show!"

"You're kidding." Jackie let her tank drop to the pier.

"He's been on the phone off and on with Aunt Viv all morning," Rory said. "She's already hooked him up with her agent."

"The one who saw him in the school play back in high school?"

"What?" Rory wrinkled her nose.

"Never mind," Jackie said, remembering that he'd never told his sisters about that.

"Nothing's settled, but Aunt Viv's agent thinks he can work a deal. Can you imagine? Adrian with his own cooking show? Isn't that great!"

"Great," she echoed numbly, wondering where that left their relationship, then instantly hating herself for even thinking that. She should be happy for him—no matter how this affected her. Life had just handed him a second shot at his dream.

"Anyway," Rory said, "change clothes, grab that champagne, and come join the party. Everyone's waiting for you."

Sitting in the big armchair in the living room, Adrian pressed the phone to one ear and his finger to the other, trying to hear the woman on the other end. Even so, Sadie's bark rang through as the sheltie begged for treats. Allison shushed her dog as Lauren squealed for her dad to set her on the floor. Just the sort of background noise he needed to sound professional.

"I'll need to talk that over with my family," he said, dazed by how quickly things were moving. "Three weeks is a long time for me to be gone from the inn."

"Hi, Jackie!" he heard Allison say and looked up to see Jackie standing on the bottom step.

Warmth spread through him, relaxing his insides. He hadn't even realized he was tense until then. He waved for her to come closer as Eva Phillips continued talking about concepts for the show.

"Yes, I like the idea of focusing on brunch menus," he agreed. "It's a perfect tie-in to our B and B."

Jackie handed the bottle of champagne she'd brought to Rory and headed his way. When she tried to scoot past him and sit on the sofa, he caught her hand and pulled her back. Off balance, she fell in his lap.

"Adrian . . ." she whispered, glancing toward his family. He saw his sisters exchange smiles as they continued preparing lunch.

Jackie tried to struggle up, but he anchored her with one arm. "Actually, I haven't decided about moving to L.A. I need to think about that."

Jackie's eyes bugged a bit at hearing that and she finally went still.

"Yes, I understand," he told the producer. "I just don't see why the show can't be shot here at the inn. You seemed to think the setting worked fine before."

The woman argued vehemently, and he pulled his attention away from Jackie long enough to finish his conversation. "I'll talk it over with my agent and have him give you a call." Hanging up, he framed Jackie's face with both hands and brought her mouth to his for a smacking kiss that was just long enough to get his blood pumping. "I've been needing to do that all morning. Where have you been?"

"Diving with Carl's team."

"Oh, really?" He raised his brows. "I'd like to hear about that."

"First, tell me your news. I understand congratulations are in order."

"Mmm, they certainly are." He smiled, thinking about the night before.

"Come on, you two," Rory called from the bar area as she took a wiggling Lauren from Chance. "You can play kissy-face later. We want to hear what the TV people said."

Adrian gave Jackie a long-suffering look. "Little sisters are such a pain at times."

"Well, I want to hear the news, too," she said.

"Okay." He stood and set Jackie on her feet but kept an arm about her waist as they joined the others. "What do y'all think of *Breakfast with Adrian*?"

Rory scrunched her nose, considering it. "Not exciting, but not bad."

"I like it," Alli said. "It's kind of sexy. You know, the whole implication of breakfast after a night in bed."

Laughing, Scott pulled her to him. "You have such a naughty mind."

"Just don't tell anyone." Alli gave him a quick kiss on the cheek. "You'll ruin my reputation as a prude."

"Chance?" Adrian asked. "What do you think?"

"The breakfast part is a good plug for the inn," Chance said.

They all turned to Scott for his reaction.

"Don't look at me." Scott held up a hand. "I stink at titles. Give me a four-hundred-page novel to write any day."

"What about you?" Adrian turned to Jackie.

She glanced around, clearly startled to even be asked. "I, um, I agree with Allison. It has a certain implication women viewers are bound to like. Although"—she frowned at him—"what's this about moving to L.A.?"

He exhaled in a rush, as excitement and doubt battled it out in his stomach. "Eva says it wouldn't have to be year-round, but they want to shoot the show on a sound stage before a live audience."

"Nooo," Rory protested. "They should film it here."

"I agree." He looked at the faces around him and tried to imagine not seeing his family every day. And what about Jackie? That was the big question. How would he continue seeing her if he moved to California? "I'm pushing for here, but she sounds pretty set on L.A."

"But what about the inn?" Rory asked. "The whole reason we started it was so we could stay together."

"Rory . . ." Allison frowned at her. "We can manage without Adrian if we have to. We'd miss him, yes, but we'd manage."

"I know, but L.A.? That's so far." Rory turned to him with that sad, blue-eyed look that always went straight to his heart. "Unless you want to go."

"I don't know what I want. I've never thought about moving away." Well, not consciously since high school. He had been feeling restless for months, though, so maybe subconsciously he'd been searching for something just like this. He tried to catch Jackie's eye for some reassurance that this wouldn't end things between them before they'd even begun, but she'd found a new obsession with picking crumbs off the bar. "One way or the other, I need to go out there for a while. They want me to appear as a guest chef on a few other cooking shows to build name recognition."

"When will that be?" Alli asked, carrying food to the table.

"As soon as they can arrange it." He caught another distressed look from Rory and hid his excitement. "I'll try to keep the trip as short as possible."

As everyone headed for their seats around the table, Jackie started toward her usual chair opposite Adrian, but he grabbed her hand and steered her to the chair next to his. With a start, she realized Rory had already moved the high chair down, which shifted Chance to the foot of the table. Had they discussed this while she was diving, or had Rory just done it automatically?

Feeling conspicuous, she took her new seat. The conversation continued around her but she could barely concentrate. Was Adrian really thinking about moving?

Yes, she realized, listening to the subtle tension in his

voice, the slight strain to his laugh. He wanted to go, but he felt guilty about it.

She wanted to encourage him, even as she wondered: Why now? Why did this have to happen right when she thought she had a chance at a real relationship with the most wonderful man she'd ever met? That alone had frightened her, but now this?

When the meal ended, Rory fetched the bottle of champagne from the refrigerator and Alli set a chocolate cake adorned with fresh strawberries in the middle of the table.

"Here, Chance." Rory handed him the bottle. "You always do this so well."

Seconds later, the cork popped toward the ceiling. Lauren clapped as her daddy started filling champagne flutes. "Sorry, peanut," he said. "None for you. Who wants to make the toast?"

"Actually, I'd like to," Scott said. "If y'all don't mind."

"Of course we don't," Rory assured him.

"Okay." Scott rose and frowned at the bubbles rising in his glass as he collected his thoughts. "I want to say I'm happy for Adrian's news and for how well things are going for the inn. With success comes change, though, and new challenges. Whatever the future brings, I hope the three of you will remember the things in life that matter most, and that's what you have in this room: each other." He reached down and took Allison's hand. "So I'd like to propose a toast to prosperity, happiness, but most of all to family. And to say thank you for letting me be part of this one."

"Hear, hear!" Chance touched his glass to Scott's. "I couldn't have said it better."

"Oh, Scott." Alli stood to hug him. "You've gone and made me all teary."

"Well, there's a mean feat," he teased her.

Jackie turned to Adrian in time to see guilt flash in his eyes before his gaze dropped to the table. Scott couldn't have hit the target better if Adrian had drawn a bull's-eye over his heart.

"To family," Rory said, raising her glass.

"To family," Adrian echoed.

Jackie drank with the others out of politeness, then glanced at her watch. If she didn't get out of there quickly, she'd say something she'd regret, like telling all of them to give the man a break. Did he have to live his entire life for them? "I hate to dash off like this, but I have a ship to sail."

"Hold up, I'll walk you." His expression told her he needed to get out of there as badly as she did. "The rest of you carry on," he said over his shoulder. "I'll be back in a minute."

"Take your time," Rory called.

Jackie debated what to say as they ascended the stairs. Neither of them spoke until they reached the veranda. For once, the area was free of guests.

"Finally, a moment alone." Adrian pulled her to a stop. "I wish you weren't leaving. I hate the thought of not seeing you for another month."

"Sounds like you'll be too busy to notice I'm gone."

"I'll notice." He tugged her closer to him and wrapped his arms around her.

She rested her head against his chest and soaked in the simple pleasure of being held.

"I'll miss you," he said with his chin on top of her head.

Her heart sped up at his words, and a desperate urge filled her to send Ti sailing off without her and ask Adrian not to go to L.A. But such rash behavior held no regard for what was best long term. Closing her eyes, she tried to think of his future, if not her own.

"Adrian, look . . ." She leaned back enough to see his face. "About Scott's toast, don't let that get to you. Yes, family is important, and I envy you your relationship with your sisters more than I can say, but this is one time when I don't think you should put them first. You did that before when you had a chance to follow your dream. You chose to stay home for them. Now life is handing you a second chance. This time, do what's right for you. You deserve this."

His arms loosened. "Are you saying you want me to move to L.A.?"

"The question is, do you want to move?"

"I don't know." He stepped to the railing and leaned back against it. "This is happening so fast, I haven't had time to think."

"Well, you don't have to look so gloomy about it." She thought of how he always teased her into a lighter mood, and decided to try and do the same for him. She summoned a playful smile. "What happened to the guy who thinks life should be fun?"

He lifted a brow. "I like fun."

"I know you do." Her cheeks heated with memories of their night in his bed.

He hooked a finger in the waistband of her jeans. "What did you have in mind?"

"Only that you should go out to California, do the guest shots, have a good time, and see how you like it."

"On one condition." His eyes danced with sexy mischief. "I get to give you another cooking lesson when I get back. At my house this time. With the doors locked."

"Maybe." A thrill went through her at the thought.

"Or better yet . . ." He gave her jeans another tug and she fell against him. "Go with me."

"I can't do that." She laughed in surprise, her hands against his chest. "I have—"

"I know. The ship." He looped his arms about her hips. "Go with me anyway. It's only for three weeks. We'll explore whole new ways of how to have fun."

Meeting his lively blue gaze, she wanted more than anything to say yes, to lean forward and kiss him and agree to follow him anywhere. But how could she jeopardize eight years of hard work that were just beginning to pay off for three weeks of fun? She couldn't afford that much time off! "Adrian," she sighed, cupping his face in one palm. "This is your chance, not mine. Only you can decide what's right for you."

"I know, it's just . . ."

"What?"

"Why did it have to happen now?"

"What's wrong with now?"

"You! Us! Last night!" He rubbed his hands up and down her back. "You finally tell me you're willing to give us a chance, then this comes along."

She moved her thumb over his lips to stop his words. "Do not let me stand in your way. Please."

"Well, I like that," he grumbled.

"Would you rather I beg you to stay?"

"I don't know." Confusion knitted his brow. "I don't know what I want. I just feel . . . trapped all the sudden."

"Well, then." Trying to keep her own confusion out of it, she draped her arms over his shoulders. "I say you have some thinking to do."

He widened his stance and settled her between his

thighs. "If I move, what are the chances you'll come with me?"

Her heart lurched. "Don't you think it's a bit too early in this relationship for us to talk about major moves like this?"

"I'm just asking. They have ports in California, you know."

She leaned away from him, incredulous. "Do you have any idea what a huge deal it would be to move my business to California?"

"I hate this."

"I'm sorry." *I do, too.* She hugged him. "Just think it through, and do what's best for you. Okay?"

"Okay."

"Right now, though, I really have to go."

"Wait." His mouth came down on hers with a swiftness that caught her off guard. All the longing she'd held in check welled up inside her and she tightened her arms around his neck. The kiss turned ravenous as his hands cupped her bottom, squeezing and pulling her hard against him. Feeling his arousal against her belly made her ache with needs that went beyond physical desire. Moaning, she gave herself over, letting him sample and play with her lips and tongue. Heavens, the man could kiss her into oblivion. Her control slipped further, and she wanted to cling to him with all her strength and beg him to stay.

Frightened by the thought, she broke away. "I have to go."

"I'll call you," he said.

Nodding, she hurried down the stairs and headed for the ship without looking back.

Ti met her on the bridge and a few minutes later they

were pulling away from the pier. When she looked back up at the inn, she saw Adrian still standing on the veranda, watching her. The ache inside her increased as she wondered what would become of them.

Chapter 22

Adrian talked to Jackie over the phone every day for the next month, but the day before he would actually see her again in person, his world went from exciting to insane. The scheduled guest of a live cooking show had come down with strep throat. Eva Phillips called Adrian and asked how fast he could get on a plane. As soon as he hung up, he tried to call Jackie, but her ship was already en route and he couldn't reach her on her mobile phone.

When Allison dropped him off at the airport in Houston, he told her that when Jackie arrived, she should tell her he'd call the first chance he got.

The minute his plane touched down, though, a driver picked him up at the airport and took him straight to the studio. Before he could blink, he found himself on the set for *Cooking with Susan,* with a live audience and a brigade of TV cameras pointed at him. The host was petite, blond, personable, and a seasoned vet of live TV. Standing beneath the glaring lights talking to her about hollandaise sauce had a slightly surreal aspect at first, but he quickly warmed to being on stage.

Oddly enough, she seemed far more flustered and fumbled her way through the first few minutes until she dropped an egg on his foot and froze. He stared at the egg, then her scarlet face, and had one split second to decide if he should ignore it, or tease her about it.

"Well," he said, deciding on teasing, "it's better than having egg on my face." The comment had her fumbling and blushing even more. Within minutes, both she and the audience were laughing uproariously.

His turn to blush came when viewers started calling in.

"Yes, I have a question for Adrian," the first caller said. "Are you married?"

"Uh, no." He chuckled, slightly taken aback.

"Involved?" the next caller asked.

"Actually, yes." He flashed Susan a look of confusion.

She laughed, enjoying his moment in the hot seat. "I believe we have another caller on the line. Did you have a question?"

"Yes." The disembodied voice came from somewhere overhead. "When you say 'involved,' do you mean *seriously* involved?"

He smiled into the camera. "I'm afraid you'll have to ask her. In the meantime, I don't suppose you have a question about cooking, do you?"

"I do!" said the final caller in a thick Southern accent. "Will you come cook in my kitchen?"

"Not a chance, I'm keeping him!" Susan said unexpectedly, then looked ready to die of embarrassment at her own words.

When the show ended, the producer came out to shake his hand and tell him they'd had more callers than any other episode in the show's history and several e-mails asking when he'd be back.

By the time Adrian reached his hotel, exhausted but flushed with victory, he had a message to call his agent.

Brian informed him that offers were already coming in from other cooking shows, a publisher wanted first rights to a cookbook, a company that made chef's apparel wanted him to model for their catalog, and a canned-soup company wanted him for a TV commercial.

"You're kidding," Adrian said, stunned as he sat on the hotel bed. "But the show only ended an hour ago."

"Babe, in this business, you move fast or miss the boat. It's like that college football player who was standing on the sidelines. His face flashed across the screen on national television and he had a modeling-contract offer before the game ended. Your face was up there for half an hour, and you were doing a lot more than just standing on the sidelines."

"Still . . ." He shook his head.

"There's one more offer I need to pass on. How do you feel about posing nude?"

"Excuse me!"

"*Playgirl* wants you for a centerfold spread."

"Now I know you're putting me on."

"Not at all. One of the editors is a cooking show junkie."

"You've got to be kidding."

"Babe, I'll be stunned if you don't get similar offers from the gay skin magazines and at least one offer for a porno movie. So tell me now if I pass on those or issue an automatic no."

"No! Good Lord." He laughed in nervous disbelief. "This is unreal."

"Actually, no, this is the real world, so welcome to it. You're a hot commodity. Speaking of, you have a meeting in the hotel bar with Eva Phillips and the network big-wigs. They liked what they saw and are eager to get moving on *Breakfast with Adrian*. It would also be a good idea for you to keep a high profile while you're there. Meet people, socialize. Attend a few parties. I've asked Eva to assign you an escort."

"An escort? As in a professional date?"

The agent sighed heavily. "As in a driver and all-round personal assistant. Call me tomorrow when some of this has had a chance to sink in and we'll go over the offers in more detail. For now, just enjoy. You're the new 'hottest game in town.' "

His head spinning, he hung up from his agent and called Jackie's number. Her ship would be docked at Pearl Island by now, so her phone would be within range of a tower. All he got was her voice mail, so he called the inn next and Rory picked up.

"Did you see the show?" he asked.

"Yes! God, you were fabulous. Alli, it's Adrian. Alli says you were great, too."

"Is Jackie there?"

"She was, but she's diving with Carl right now. She seemed pretty disappointed that you weren't here when she arrived."

"Did she see the show?"

"She watched it with us and looked suitably impressed with how good you were. Although I don't think she cared for those women callers hitting on you."

"Personally, I thought it was hilarious."

"You would."

He started to tell her about all the offers, but everything was too up in the air. He didn't need Rory to get all excited, or worse, start worrying he'd run off chasing fame and fortune and she'd never see him again. If only Jackie were there so he could think things through aloud.

He needed a levelheaded sounding board. "Listen, will you give Jackie this number and ask her to call me?"

"Will do. Also, guess what?"

"At this point, I'm almost afraid to." He chuckled.

"Aunt Viv is coming back to Galveston for a while. Sort of an extended vacation."

"Really? Is she still thinking about retiring?"

"Yep. She sounds pretty tired of life on Broadway. Chance and I told her she could stay with us, since Alli and Scott are living in her house and we have more room."

"You know, I just don't get her being tired of Broadway. Acting has always been everything for her."

"Alli thinks she's lonely."

"I guess." He glanced at his watch. "Look, I have to go. I'm having a meeting with some 'people from the studio' in a few minutes, but I shouldn't be gone long. Be sure and tell Jackie to call me this evening if I don't get hold of her first."

"Will do. And congratulations. You really looked wonderful on TV. I'm very proud of you."

"Thanks." Hanging up, he went to the floor-to-ceiling window and discovered his room overlooked a swimming pool surrounded by lush tropical gardens. On the lounge chairs around the sparkling water were at least a dozen female bodies in some of the skimpiest bikinis he'd ever seen.

Welcome to California, he thought, wanting to laugh. He raised his gaze to the tall buildings shimmering in the bright sun and had the overwhelming urge to tell someone, "I can't believe I'm here. This is so cool!"

The only thing that would make it better would be having Jackie with him. She'd probably make some wisecrack that would help put everything into perspective. Then he'd talk her into going out and celebrating. Or staying in and celebrating, which could be even more fun, he thought with a glance at the king-sized bed.

Then he remembered her refusal to come to L.A. for even a few weeks. What would he do if he had to move? Give up seeing her? Moving the ship would be hard and he'd never get her to leave it behind. And if he did somehow manage to talk her into leaving the ship, what would she do for a living?

The thought flickered through his mind that if half the offers Brian had mentioned panned out, Jackie wouldn't have to work. He could support both of them. *Yeah, right,* he snorted. Like Jackie would agree to live off him.

What if he married her, though?

His heart jolted in shock and he struggled to breathe without hyperventilating.

Okay, he thought slowly, what if he did marry her? First, he'd have to get her to say yes—not a sure bet when he'd had a hard enough time just getting her to date him. Then there was still the whole issue of her moving to L.A. Try as he might, he couldn't see her in the role of a pampered Hollywood wife spending her days shopping and sunning by a pool.

On top of all that, he was right back to having to decide something that momentous up front. Why did everything in their relationship have to be all or nothing? He remembered Jackie telling him to go to L.A., think things through, decide what he wanted. Lord, she'd certainly said a mouthful!

He headed to the meeting in the bar, telling himself he'd talk to Jackie when he got back: not about anything major that would terrorize her, just one of their talk-about-nothing conversations that always settled the restlessness he'd been battling lately. Except cocktails turned into dinner at Spago, which segued into a party at a mansion in the Hollywood Hills. By the time he got back to his room, it was three in the morning and the message light was blinking. He'd missed Jackie's call.

He tried to call her the next morning, but got her voice mail again. They ended up playing phone tag as often as talking for the next three weeks. But when they did get on the line, they talked for hours.

And every time he hung up the phone, he was more determined to find a way around all the obstacles keeping them apart.

Jackie sat at the table in her cabin, trying to balance the books on her antiquated laptop, but smiling into space instead. Adrian was coming home.

He'd been in L.A. for just over three weeks but they'd gone two months without actually seeing each other. Tomorrow, though, she'd set sail for Pearl Island and he was due to fly home the day she would arrive.

His appearances on TV the past few weeks had brought a flood of interest in the inn and the cruises. Especially since he'd been on the Letterman show.

Unfortunately, the conversation on that show had strayed from cooking and the instant popularity of Chef Adrian to the search for Lafitte's treasure and questions about why it was taking so long to find. While he had handled the topic smoothly, it had sent up a red flag to the local media, making people wonder, "Why is the search taking so long?"

From Jackie's last conversation with Rory, she had an image of a disgruntled Carl holding impromptu news conferences on the beach, explaining to nondivers how tricky marine archeology could be.

All in all, the last two months had been an emotional roller coaster. At least she'd had her conversations with Adrian to look forward to. The sheer number of calls lent weight to his claims of missing her.

For the first time since agreeing to a relationship with him, she started to believe that maybe it would last long term, even with the possibility of him moving away—a fact she tried not to think about. He seemed so sincere when he told her she was special to him, and he needed her to add sanity and balance to his life.

That made her smile. He thought she was special. A man who could have any woman he wanted had singled her out to be his special one and only . . . for a while at least. Maybe even for a long while.

A knock came at her door. She looked up to see Ti standing in the open doorway. "Hey, Ti. What's up?"

"You see da paper?" he asked, looking cautious.

"What paper?"

He came forward with a newspaper in hand. "I know dese things full of lies," he said. "So it probably mean nothing, but I know you want to see."

"What is it? More speculation about the missing treasure being a hoax?"

"Not exactly." Ti dropped a copy of the *National Enquirer* on the desk in front of her.

She looked down and froze at the sight of Adrian with his head clasped to the voluptuous breast of Shawna Simmons, Hollywood's newest box office draw. Both he and the impossibly beautiful actress were laughing. The headline read: "Could Things Be Heating Up for America's Sexiest Chef?"

She flipped to the page number printed on the front and found more photos of Adrian having a grand old time at some nightclub with Shawna Simmons hanging all over him.

In her mind she could hear his voice:

"Things are going great, but I miss you.

"I wish you were here.

"I'm so tired, though, all I want is one night at home in my own bed, preferably with you."

Tired? Ha! No wonder he was tired. The snake! Just how many beds had he been crawling into to miss his own so badly? Her mind started off on a tangent, but she stopped it. Dancing at a nightclub did not mean he was sleeping around. Even if he was dancing with one of the most blatantly beautiful women in the world, who had her hands all over him, and was giving him an eyeful of cleavage down the front of her halter dress.

"It probably don' mean a thing," Ti said. "Dat paper make everything sound like more dan it is."

He was right, of course, but she still felt as if a knife had been plunged straight through her heart. She'd actually started to trust the man, to believe him when he said he cared for her deeply. She'd dared to reach for that pretty box of joy he'd offered—and found a snake inside after all. A lying, cheating snake!

Her pulse pounded in her temples until she thought her head would explode. Even so, she forced her face to relax as she leaned back in her chair. "Of course it doesn't mean anything. And even if it did, I don't own Adrian. If he wants to go out partying with some movie star with fake boobs, that's his business."

Ti eyed her. "One word of advice."

"Yes?" She managed a smile.

"Let da mon speak before you cut off his balls."

"I don't know what you're talking about."

When Allison picked Adrian up from the airport, he collapsed in the front seat of their aunt's luxury sedan. The car had been at their disposal for the past several years, since Aunt Viv rarely returned home.

"Hey, nice shades," Allison said, eyeing his wraparound sunglasses before pulling back into traffic.

"They're my disguise, to keep crazed women and rabid photographers from recognizing me."

"That actually works?"

"Not too well, no. Which has me convinced movie stars wear them for the same reason everyone else does—to shade their eyes from the sun." He settled lower in the seat, resigned to the hour-long drive ahead. For the hundredth time that day, he wished he could beam himself straight to Pearl Island, take Jackie into his arms, and say the words that had been burning inside him for weeks now: *I miss you, I need you, I love you.*

He wasn't sure when that truth had formed fully in his brain, but for the past few days, he'd had to struggle not to tell her. Words that big shouldn't be said for the first time over the phone. He wanted to say them in person so he could see her face, witness her reaction. Then kiss her senseless and make love to her for hours.

Tamping down his impatience, he let his head loll back against the seat. "So, fill me in on everything I've missed while I was gone. God, it feels like forever."

"Well, let's see. We've invited Carl to your welcome-home lunch tomorrow."

"That's nice." He yawned.

"Actually, Aunt Viv invited him," she said with a smile in her voice.

"Oh?" He cracked an eye open for that.

"Uh-huh." Alli grinned impishly. "They're both trying to hide it, but Rory and I think they have a crush on each other."

"A 'crush,'" he echoed. "I thought crushes were for kids, not people in their fifties."

"Wait till you see them together. Aunt Viv's playing it cool, the regal queen all the way, but poor Carl's a goner."

"Do I need to have a talk with him?"

"Don't you dare!" She pinched his side. "I swear, you think no one but you should have a sex life."

"That's not true." He rubbed his abused ribs. "I just know what men are like when they have sex on the brain."

"Speaking of, how did Jackie react to those pictures of you in the *National Enquirer*?"

"I don't know. I haven't talked to her since they came out." He frowned over that fact, since, three days ago, she stopped answering her phone or calling him back. Of course, she'd been out in the Gulf the last two of those three days. "I'm guessing she hasn't seen them, or she'd have called to demand an explanation. Had she docked before you left?"

"Just barely. I wasn't able to talk to her, though." Allison looked over at him, smiling. "Patience, big brother. We'll be there shortly."

Chapter 23

Adrian walked straight through the inn, stopping only to hug Rory and kiss Lauren, before stepping out on the veranda. His spirits lifted at the sight of the *Pirate's Pleasure* tied to the pier. The usual scattering of people milled about the beach. He scanned the area for Jackie, but didn't see her. Then he looked toward the trail that led to Carl's bungalow just as she emerged from the trees with one of the other divers, both of them wearing wet suits.

The sight of her made all the longing and love and just plain missing her well up inside him. He wondered how many eyebrows he'd raise if he walked out onto the beach, scooped her into his arms, and carried her off into the woods toward his house. Although did he care?

Allison stepped up beside him and shaded her eyes. "Are they back again?"

"Who?" He followed the line of her sight to a boat trolling just past the mouth of the cove.

"That boat," she said. "It started showing up a few days ago. Right after you were on the Letterman show talking about the treasure. Carl thinks it's treasure hunters. He's been out in the johnboat a few times to explain that if he catches them diving in the cove he'll have them charged with attempted theft of state property. They insist they're just fishing."

"Well, it's possible," he said absently, much more interested in seeing Jackie. "If you'll excuse me." He headed down the hill to the beach. He heard Jackie laugh at something the other diver said. They were halfway to the pier when she looked up and saw him coming toward her.

The smile on her face vanished as she stopped and waited for him to close the gap between them. He barely spared the other diver a nod, his eyes soaking up the sight of her in her yellow and black shorty. Her hair had grown a bit and it framed her face with spiky curls.

"Jackie," he breathed, wanting to take her mouth in a kiss that would last at least a decade.

Her hazel eyes narrowed with anger. "Bastard."

The word caught him off guard for half a second. Then he sighed in resignation. "You saw the pictures."

"I did," she said calmly. "And all I have to say is . . . you're very photogenic."

"So I've been told." He frowned at the lack of heat behind the words. "In fact, I'm a little sick of hearing it."

"How nice for you." She started to step around him.

"Wait a second." Panic made him slip a hand around her arm. He searched her face for volatile emotions but she only glanced down at his hand, then lifted a brow in mild irritation. "That's it? You see pictures of me with another woman and all you do is toss out one wimpy 'Bastard,' then walk away?"

"Adrian," she said, with such icy reserve he wondered where the real Jackie was. "Perhaps you haven't noticed, but I'm not in the mood to talk to you right now."

"Okay, I'll talk. You can listen."

"I don't want to listen, either. I already know the two

standard lines men use when they get caught cheating. You're either going to tell me I'm all wrong and nothing happened or you'll say it didn't mean anything, as if that makes it all okay. Well, do me a favor and spare us both the indignity."

He looked at the other man. "Will you excuse us?"

"No!" She jerked her arm free. "Sam, I'm coming with you."

"The hell you are," Adrian said. "Jackie, if you want to yell at me for what you think I did, fine, but I'd rather do it in private."

"I don't want to yell at you," she said through clenched teeth.

"Oh, yes you do. You've had, what, three days to stew over those stupid pictures?" He relaxed a bit, seeing the flash of anger in her eyes. Some real reaction, finally. "At this point, I imagine you want to do a lot more than yell. So, go ahead. Get it out of your system. Call me every name in the book. Then, when you've calmed down, I'll tell you all about my relationship with Shawna."

"So you admit it? Just like that?" Her face crumpled with devastation. "You have a relationship with her?"

Sam looked from her to Adrian and back again. "Uh, look, I'll just be going."

Jackie's body began to shake while she waited for Sam to get out of hearing range. Then she turned to Adrian, clinging to dignity by a thread. If he brought her to tears, she'd hate him forever.

"Are you ready to listen?" he asked.

"No! I don't want to listen. I don't want to talk. I'm so angry, I don't even want to look at you!"

"You're not angry, you're hurt."

"Hurt? You wish, bucko. I am mad at you for being a sorry liar, and at myself for being foolish enough to believe you when you said . . ." Her breath hitched. "When you said I was special to you. But apparently not special enough to keep you from . . . to keep you . . ." Her lungs locked up. "Look, just back off and give me time to get over this, and maybe we can salvage some shred of friendship—"

"I don't want to be friends." He stepped in front of her and tried to rest his hands on her arms, only to have her knock them away.

"Well, we're sure as hell not going to continue as lovers." She got in his face and lowered her voice. "Because I'll tell you something, Adrian St. Claire, I do not share. You want to sleep with every starlet in Hollywood, go ahead, but do me the courtesy of breaking up with me first." She poked his chest to emphasize her words. "Because if I ever again catch you with another woman, I swear to God, I'll cut your balls off!"

"Ever again?" To her surprise, he flashed that devious grin of his. "So we are going to continue as lovers."

"No we're not." She pulled away. "Because I'm never speaking to you again, much less sleeping with you."

"Of course you are. As soon as you finish yelling at me, we'll talk all you want, then make love, because you look really hot in that wet suit."

"Are you *trying* to provoke me?"

"Beats waiting for you to cool off on your own. How about we continue this at my place? Preferably naked and in bed."

"Grrr!" She stomped her foot. "I don't want to talk to you! *I want to hit you!*"

"Okay. If it gets your anger out of the way faster, go ahead, take a couple of swings at me."

"You're not listening, you jerk!" She shoved him back a step.

"Well, you're not listening to me, either, so we're even. Now come on, take a swing."

"Don't tempt me!"

"I'm serious, Jackie. Take your best shot."

Throwing her hands up, she tried to stalk away.

He quick-stepped beside her like a boxer, taunting her with his fingers. "Com'on. Try to hit me. I dare you."

"Stop it!"

"No. Com'on. Give it a try."

She turned away, then whirled back, her fist flying toward his face. He blocked the punch with his forearm and her temper exploded. She swung again and again, with him blocking every blow. In frustration, she tried a twisting kick toward his rib cage, only to find herself taking a face dive into the sand. Rolling, she sprang into a crouch, and charged like a mad bull. He sidestepped with ease.

Her breath heaving, she turned back, and found him laughing. "This is not funny! I hate you!"

"No you don't." He smiled. "You love me. Or you wouldn't be this mad."

With a cry of fury, she swung again. He caught her wrist and used her own momentum to flip her over his back into the sand, where she landed flat on her back, staring up at a perfect blue sky with her breath coming like a steam engine.

Tears prickled along her lashes. She squeezed her eyes shut as he dropped beside her, pinning her wrists with his hands and trapping her legs with one of his.

"Had enough?"

She waited until she had her tear ducts under control, then opened her eyes to glare at him. "What the hell was that?"

"Tae kwon do."

"I thought you did yoga?"

"I do a lot of things." He released one wrist to brush sand from her cheeks. "Now, are you calm enough to talk?"

"I just have one question." Her eyes started stinging again and her voice went weak. "And if you lie to me, I'll never speak to you again. I can take the truth, whatever it is, just don't lie to me."

"I won't lie to you."

"Did you sleep with her?"

He looked her straight in the eye. "No. For two reasons. One, I'm not her type."

"Give me a break, Adrian. You're every woman's type."

"She's gay."

"What?" She blinked at him.

"You are not allowed to repeat that, by the way, but that's why I went out with her. With Shawna, I don't have to worry about getting mauled—well, not usually. We met at a party my first night there and became instant allies, sort of Us against Them."

"Them?"

"The people who treat you like a slab of meat to be packaged and sold."

"But if she's gay, why was she hanging all over you?"

"She'd just had a huge fight with her lover about coming out of the closet. Shawna wants to, but the lover keeps arguing it will hurt her career. So she called me up, crying her eyes out, and asked me to go dancing so she could blow off steam. I didn't realize she'd use the evening as a chance to get back at her lover by playing up to the paparazzi. Sort of like saying, 'You want people to think I'm straight, how's this?' "

"You didn't look like you were objecting."

"No, I wasn't." He sighed. "Because I understood why she was doing it. She's a nice person, Jackie, who needed a friend."

"That is so like you." She didn't know whether to cry or try to hit him again. "Why do you have to be such a nice guy?"

"Because, at the time, I thought all I had to do was call you and explain. I thought you knew me well enough to realize that I don't lie to women. When I said you were special to me, I meant it. And it really hurts knowing you automatically believed the worst without even talking to me."

She blushed at the accusation, knowing he was right. "What's your second reason?"

"You." He cupped her face, and just that simple touch was enough to make her yearn for him. "I don't want anyone but you. If nothing else, the past weeks have made that clear. Every time I turned around, people were offering me everything you can imagine, some things beyond imagining, but all I wanted the whole time I was out there was to have you with me."

"You mean that?" Those damned tears came back, and this time she couldn't blink them away.

"I do." He smiled gently as a tear rolled toward her temple and he brushed it away.

"I still don't want to move to L.A."

"I know." His face hovered above her, blocking out the sun as his thumb strummed along her jaw. "We'll talk about that later. Right now, I only need this." He lowered his head and kissed her.

At the familiar taste of his mouth, she wrapped her arms around his neck, holding tight, needing him so much it hurt. He tilted his head to deepen the kiss. Heat rushed through her as she molded her body to his, desire building with frightening speed.

He trailed kisses over her face. "God, I want you," he rasped, stroking the curve of her waist and hip. "Two months is way too long to do without you."

"Agreed." She freed one leg to wrap it around his thigh, pressing into him and finding him hard. He kissed her deep and hard until her body quivered.

With a groan, he lifted his head and glanced toward the crowded pier. "I really think it's past time we go someplace private."

Nodding, she let him pull her to her feet. She started to brush the sand from her body, but he grabbed her hand and took off at a fast walk. They headed for the jogging trail, their steps quickening as they turned onto the smaller trail that led up the hill to his house. By the time they reached the porch, they were running.

He pulled her to him, kissing her as he opened the door, skillfully playing her mouth. With one arm about her waist, he lifted her as he stepped inside, then turned and pressed her against the door, closing it. He stared at her, his eyes intense. "I have some things I need to tell you, but first—" He unzipped the wet suit. "I want you naked."

"Adrian!" She laughed at his eagerness.

"Right here. Right now." Taking hold of the wet suit, he started working it down her arms.

"Wait." She dropped back against the door to see his face. "What happened to patience and anticipation?"

His heated gaze fell to her breasts as they sprang free. "Sometimes fast is fun, too."

The suit trapped her arms, giving him free rein to cup her breasts. Her nipples hardened against his palms and a moan escaped as her head arched back. "Oh yes, fast definitely . . . works for me."

His mouth closed over one nipple as he peeled the wet suit away. She wiggled, helping him as she pulled his shirt free and over his head. He kicked out of his shoes and stripped off his pants.

"Bedroom," she gasped.

"Too far." He pinned her back against the door, his hands running over her body. Thankfully, he didn't need to stop for a condom, since they'd covered that issue over the phone. The thought of having him naked inside her for the first time made her tremble even more.

She wrapped her arms around his neck as he hoisted her up and her legs went around his hips. He pressed his hard, bare length against her heat, rubbing back and forth.

"Oh yes. Please," she gasped.

"Mmm, one of my favorite words." He kissed her neck as he teased her with his body, rubbing against her, driving her mad. "First, say you want me."

"Of course I want you. Now, please, now." Her eyes squeezed shut as she lifted herself, trying to take him inside.

"Say you love me."

"I love you," she echoed mindlessly, willing to say anything. He plunged, driving deep, and hit some magical spot that made stars explode. With a gasp, her eyes flew open. "Oh, God, yes. Right there."

He drew back and plunged again and again, with dead-on accuracy, until she shattered apart with only his arms holding her together. He thrust once more and held, his big, muscular body shuddering with the force of his own climax.

His grip loosened, and she instantly tightened her arms and legs, afraid she'd drop to the floor. But then he had her again, cradled against his chest as he carried her. Before the stars had cleared from her head, he'd pulled the covers back and lowered her to his bed. He settled beside her, gathering her in his arms.

Oh yes, she remembered as he nuzzled her neck, *the cuddling part.* A smile curved her lips as she tried to decide which she liked better, explosive orgasms or snuggling afterward.

One of his hands smoothed down her side, cherishing her with tender affection.

A tie, she decided. *A definite tie.*

He lifted his head, his gaze caressing her face as if memorizing every detail. She blushed, imagining how she must look, like a cat who'd just finished a whole bowl of cream.

He smiled back, looking equally content, and mumbled something in a lazy voice.

"What did you say?" she asked, drifting.

"Marry me."

Chapter 24

His heart in his throat, Adrian watched for Jackie's reaction. This, he realized, was far worse than all the other uncertainties combined. For several long seconds, she just kept smiling as if floating in a dream. Then her eyes went wide.

"What!"

"Marry me."

She scrambled out from under him and pressed her back against the headboard. "Ohmygod! I can't believe you said that. What do you mean, marry you?"

Okay, maybe he could have timed this better, but he was committed now. "You know, exchange rings, take vows, grow old together. Marriage. It's not a new concept."

"I know what it is, but you don't spring something like that on a person without warning."

"Jackie," he said slowly, since she looked ready to crawl up the wall to get away from him. "This can't be that big a surprise. I've been chasing after you for eight months."

"I thought you wanted sex."

"Of course I wanted sex. But that's not all I want. Come on, didn't the fact that I call you ten times a day clue you in to something? Do you have any idea what my phone bill has been like since I met you?"

"You want to marry me to save money on your phone bill?"

He gave her a don't-be-stupid look. "That and the fact that I love you."

The air left her lungs in a rush. "Whoa." She looked around, swallowing hard. "I think . . . I'm going to be sick."

She sprang from the bed and raced for the bathroom.

Alarmed, he went after her, but she slammed the door in his face. He stared at the panel, taken aback. Of all the reactions he'd imagined, having her throw up wasn't even on the list. Instinct told him to ignore the closed door and go help her, but he knew she wouldn't want him to see her bent over a toilet.

A minute later, he heard the commode flush and cracked the door to peek inside. He found her sitting on the floor, her head back against the wall, her eyes closed. Getting a washcloth, he wet it and took it to her.

"You know," he said, sitting on the edge of the tub, "you do wonders for my ego."

"Your ego is just fine." She hiccuped, and pressed the washcloth to her mouth. A rush of tears filled her eyes. "No one's ever said that to me before."

"What, 'Marry me'?"

"No. 'I love you.'"

He stared at her. "No one?"

"Not that I remember. Maybe when I was little. I always wanted . . . that. Not just to hear the words, although, that's . . ." She swallowed again. "That's . . . yeah."

"You're not going to be sick again, are you?"

Tears tumbled down her cheeks. "I didn't know it felt like that to hear someone say it."

"It's kind of a shock to the system on this end, too."

"But you've probably said it and heard it all your life."

"With my family, yeah." He watched her dry her eyes. "But never like this. I've never been in love like this before. And I have to say, I'm starting to get a little queasy myself since you haven't given me an answer. So, what do you think?" He managed to smile past his panic. "Wanna marry me?"

"I can't answer that! I haven't had time to think about it." She rose and went to the sink to splash water on her face and rinse her mouth. Squirting toothpaste on her finger, she scrubbed her teeth. "Where are my clothes? I need to get dressed."

"All you have is your wet suit."

She headed back into the bedroom and toward the door to the hall.

"Hang on."

"What?" She turned with a dazed look. This really wasn't going well at all.

"I'll get you something to wear, then we can sit and talk." Off balance and more scared than he could ever remember being, he grabbed a T-shirt and pair of jogging shorts for her. While she dressed, he slipped on a pair of chef's pants. When he straightened to look at her, she still looked so lost his heart twisted. "Come with me."

She let herself be towed into the living room, where he pointed to the sofa.

"Sit. I'll get you some water." When she nodded, he headed for the kitchen and returned with a glass of ice water. Handing it to her, he sat beside her and waited until she took a few sips and some color returned to her cheeks. "Okay. Now tell me what you have to think about."

"A lot of things. Geez!" She pressed a hand to her forehead. "The logistics. The timing. Good grief, there's all kinds of things to consider here."

"Right." He wanted to kick himself. "I guess I got this out of order."

"Got what out of order?" She set the glass aside as if afraid she'd drop it.

"Remember I said I had some things to tell you?"

"When did you say that?" She frowned at him.

"Right before I stripped you naked and we both got distracted. Sorry. Really. I actually had this planned out better. I was going to cook you dinner, talk to you over candlelight, and propose over dessert."

"You mean you *planned* to ask me?" The thought clearly mystified her. "It didn't just pop out on the spur of the moment?"

"Actually"—he took her hand, still icy from the glass—"I've been thinking about it for quite a while, and pretty much nonstop for the last week."

She just sat there, her eyes wide.

"Here's the deal." He rubbed her fingers to warm them. "I don't want to live in L.A., either. Three weeks was enough, believe me. At first it was great. In fact, if I'd taken the agent up on his offer back when I was a teenager, I probably would have eaten it up—and become a completely different person. A very vain, shallow, obnoxious person. So, thank God I chose family then, just as I'm going to choose family now."

"You're going to give all that up for your sisters?"

"Not just them."

"Oh . . . no." She shook her head, looking ready to bolt again. "Don't you dare say me. I already told you not to let me stand in your way. This is your big chance. I don't want you to give it up because of me."

"But that's the thing. After thinking it through, I've realized I'm not giving anything up. At least, nothing I care about. I've talked to Brian, my agent, and asked him to tell the producers I'll only do the show if they film it here."

"But what about the modeling, and the TV commercials, and the cookbook?"

"I've decided to say no to the modeling, since it doesn't interest me, maybe to the commercials, because I do like to act and it won't require moving to L.A., and yes to the cookbook, but somewhere down the line."

"And what if the network says no to filming the show here?"

"Then I won't do it." Staring into her eyes, he trailed his fingertips from her temple to the curve of her cheek. "I finally figured out that what I want is to live and work here at the inn, surrounded by people I happen to enjoy. I only felt restless because you weren't in the picture yet." His fingertips moved to her chin. "I'm tired of only seeing you once a month, though, so I want you to move your business here, and I want to sail with you whenever possible. Now, what do you think?"

"I . . ." She swayed into his touch, wanting to give in, then pulled herself back. "I don't know."

"What do you mean, you don't know?" His hand fell away.

"Adrian, this is huge!" *It's everything I've ever wanted and I'm scared to death to reach for it and have it blow up in my face. I don't know where the bombs are in this minefield.* "I need some time to think this through."

"I see."

She saw the hurt in his eyes and rushed to soothe his feelings. "Oh, please don't take that the wrong way. Please. I just need to think."

"All right," he agreed, visibly struggling to understand. "I'll wait for your answer, since I don't really have a choice, but I want to know one thing. Did you mean it when you said it? Or did you just blurt it out when you were too excited to think straight?"

"Blurt what out?" She frowned.

"You said you love me."

"I did?" Her lungs constricted. "When?"

He stared at her.

She thought about it, then blushed. "Oh. Then."

"Well?"

"I . . ." The words stuck in her throat. "Oh God, this really is hard."

"Tell me about it." He squeezed her hand in encouragement. "If it helps, I promise not to throw up when you say it."

She took a deep breath. "I love you." With the words, the reality of it swelled up inside her. "I really do love you. More than I can say. I love you so much, it scares me."

"It scares me, too." He took her into his arms and held her tight.

She pulled back to see his face, and the love shining in his eyes. Of all the things she'd expected out of life, loving a man like Adrian and having him love her was the most miraculous surprise of all. "Wow."

"Exactly." He kissed her lips, lingering over them tenderly. The nerves jumping inside her settled, and she relaxed against him, kissing him back. He lifted his head to smile down at her. "So. If I have to wait for your answer, what do you suggest we do for the rest of the day?"

"Hmm?" She frowned.

"You know . . ." He trailed a finger down her neck. "You, me, total privacy, and the rest of the afternoon. Whatever will we do?"

She sighed, infected by his lighter mood. "Can it be something that doesn't involve major life decisions?"

"Absolutely." He grinned. "As I remember, I promised you a cooking lesson before I left."

She nodded. "That's right, you did."

"And I don't know about you, but I'm starving. Do you think you could eat?"

"I don't know." She pressed a hand to her stomach, but it seemed to have settled. "Depends on what you have in mind."

"Well, let's see what we have to work with." He took her hand and led her to the kitchen. "I asked Rory to clean out all the perishables while I was gone, so we're going to be limited."

Leaning against the counter, she watched him rummage through the pantry. At least he provided a nice distraction, wearing nothing but his chef's pants, his hair loose about his bare shoulders.

"Let's see, I have rice, white wine, some dehydrated mushrooms, and Parmesan cheese." He turned to her with a bottle of wine and a wicked gleam in his eye. "I'll teach you to make risotto."

"Risotto?" She frowned at the unfamiliar word.

"An Italian rice dish. You'll love it." He opened the wine and poured them each a glass. "The secret to great risotto is to keep everything very wet while you're cooking."

"Wet?" she echoed, suddenly suspicious of his smile. "Does that include keeping the cook wet, too?"

"Oh yeah." He wiggled his brows as he handed her a glass. "This lesson definitely involves keeping the cook wet."

The suggestive tone of his voice made her belly flutter. "Why do I get the feeling that keeping me wet doesn't mean giving me lots of wine while you teach me to cook?"

"Perceptive woman." Grinning, he pulled her to him for a kiss that ended all too quickly. As he straightened, he patted her bottom. "Let's get started, shall we?"

Jackie was still blushing the next day when they headed to the inn for lunch with the family. As she'd suspected, Adrian's idea of keeping her wet had been to stand behind her with his hands up under her T-shirt while she attempted to cook a very complicated rice dish. When she'd complained that she couldn't concentrate with him caressing her breasts, he'd dipped his hands downward, beneath the elastic waistband of the shorts. Laughing and squirming, she'd tried to fend him off, but he'd been determined to be playful.

Not surprisingly, the risotto had been a disaster, but everything else about the evening had been . . . fun. She'd never laughed so hard in her life, or enjoyed such open, lighthearted sensuality.

Since the rice had burned, they'd done some more rummaging and come up with a bucket of ice cream.

They'd fed each other with her straddling his lap,

facing him. Since they'd both been naked by then, they'd
done a lot more with their mouths than eat ice cream,
and she'd wound up on the table as Adrian's very sticky
and giggly dinner. A delayed shiver of delight went
through her at the memory of cold ice cream followed by
Adrian's hot tongue on various parts of her body.

"You're grinning," he said, as they headed down the
stairs to the apartment.

"Am I?" She felt her eyes twinkle. "I can't imagine
why. Besides, so are you."

"Hmm." He squeezed her hand. "I was just wondering what Rory and Alli have planned for dessert."

She laughed. "God, if it's ice cream, I'll never make
it through lunch with a straight face."

"Oh, but there are whole worlds of sweet things we
can try." He gave her flaming cheeks a quick kiss before
they reached the bottom of the stairs and stepped into
the usual noise and chaos of his family.

The sisters stood in the kitchen working while Chance
chased Lauren across the toy-strewn living room. Sadie
raced about begging for attention as everyone talked at
once. For the first time, Jackie didn't feel like an intruder
as she entered the madness.

To her surprise, she saw Carl sitting alone at the bar,
looking overwhelmed. She nearly laughed, since she
remembered the feeling well. The St. Claires could be a
bit much to take at first.

"Aunt Viv," Adrian said.

Turning, Jackie noticed an older, more elegant version of Rory setting the table. She wore a yellow pantsuit
that belonged on a fashion runway and her red-gold hair
had been swept into a stylish French twist with a streak of
sliver adding dramatic flare.

"Adrian." The woman opened her arms and let Adrian wrap her in a bear hug that lifted her off her feet. "About time you got home from La-La Land."

He laughed. "An apt name for it. Have you met Jackie?"

"Not yet, since she just got here yesterday and you've been selfishly monopolizing her." The woman extended her hand, smiling. "Hi, I'm Vivian. Aurora and Allison have been telling me all about you."

"I'm very pleased to meet you." Jackie's stomach tightened as she wondered what had been said.

Vivian turned back to her nephew. "Well, tell me about your trip. I hear you're getting all kinds of offers."

As Adrian talked with his aunt, Jackie went to sit by Carl. "How'd the last shift do yesterday?"

Carl scowled as he dragged a chip through some dip. "Still no sign of the powder horn."

"It's so frustrating," she said.

"But common." He sighed. "I can't tell you how many times I've gone after something and found lots of valuable artifacts, but not the one I was hoping for. You'd think I'd be used to it by now."

"Do we ever get used to having what we want slip through our fingers?" she asked.

"Probably not. Giving up on this one, though, is going to be harder than I expected."

"What do you mean, give up?" She stared at him. "I thought we'd keep searching until we found it."

"We're running out of funding."

"What's that?" Rory asked from the other side of the bar.

Carl hesitated, and she saw in his eyes he wished he hadn't spoken. "We're, um, running out of money for this project. If we don't find the powder horn in the next few weeks, I'm going to call it quits."

Silence descended on the room. "Nooo," Rory said. "You can't do that. We'll raise more money. Won't we, Chance?"

"It's not just that," Carl said. "There's not that much left to bring up besides the horn. We have a good collection of artifacts now, enough to create an impressive exhibit for the museum. When the cost of searching becomes greater than the value of what you're searching for, it's time to stop."

"But you *have* to find the powder horn," Rory insisted, making Jackie's heart ache. She looked about and saw the same distress in everyone's eyes.

"If it helps," Carl offered, "I haven't given up yet. There's still a chance we could find it in the next few weeks. Hell, we could find it today."

"Of course you could," Vivian said, coming up to Carl with a smile. She slipped her arms around one of his. "So let's stop all this talk of giving up, and eat. This is supposed to be a welcome-home party. Not a funeral."

"Since we're all together," Adrian said as everyone settled around the table, "I have some news to share."

Jackie flashed him a look, half afraid he meant to tell them he'd proposed to her. Instead, he told them about his decisions regarding the show. In their usual fashion, they debated it while passing bowls and bringing up other topics until they were discussing three subjects at once.

Jackie glanced at Carl, who sat catty-corner from her, listening to Vivian, clearly enthralled.

When the meal ended, Allison stood. "Who wants dessert? I made cheesecake."

"With cherry topping?" Adrian asked as he looked at Jackie. "Sounds delicious."

"And whipped cream," Allison added, making Jackie's cheeks go up in flames. Whipped cream and cherry topping? A whole barrage of erotic images came to mind.

"I'd love some." Vivian patted her stomach, which emphasized her stunning figure. "Since I don't have to squeeze into any costumes for the next few months, I can afford it. Carl? Do you want anything?"

His gaze drifted over her body, his cheeks turning nearly as red as Jackie's. "I, um . . ." He cleared his throat and looked at his watch. "I can't. Work to do. I should go."

He rose and Vivian walked him to the base of the stairs, wishing him luck finding the powder horn. When he disappeared, she struck a pose with one hand on the banister, the other over her heart. "Is he not the yummiest man ever?"

"Aunt Viv!" Alli scolded with a laugh. "You're scaring that poor man to death. He can barely put a sentence together around you."

"I know." She glided back to the table. "Although I can't decide which side of him turns me on more. He's such an intriguing blend of shy intellectual and rough adventurer."

"A bit of advice." Scott waved his fork at her. "Watch out for the shy ones. They can sneak up on you when you least expect it."

"Oh, but they're so much fun to corrupt," Vivian said.

"Or to let them corrupt you." Scott winked at Alli, who blushed.

The phone rang. "I'll get it!" Rory jumped up and

grabbed the phone in the living area. "Adrian, it's for you. It's your agent."

Adrian gave Jackie's cheek a quick kiss before taking the call. "So, have you heard from the network?"

"I did," Brian said. "Congratulations, it's a go."

"That's great." Adrian glanced over to the table where everyone was waiting for news. He gave them a thumbs-up signal, and they quietly cheered.

"We talked some about what they have in mind for the show's image and publicity. They definitely want to go with the sexy single chef to capitalize on your popularity with the message boards."

"What message boards?"

"You're joking, right? There are message boards all over the Internet where women discuss just about anything you can think of. You're a hot topic on several of them. My assistant—who spends way too much time cruising those sites—tells me the boards are all blazing over the photos that went up this morning at NationalEnquirer. com."

"What, the Shawna pictures again?"

"No. The ones of you having a fistfight with a mystery woman on the beach, then reenacting *From Here to Eternity*."

"What!"

"The consensus is split over whether you two were just horsing around or you're dating a real man-basher. With your permission, I think we need to have my assistant play the woman-in-the-know and assure everyone you were horsing around. Anything else makes you look like a wimp, which is not the image we're going for."

"Chance," Adrian called. "Pull up NationalEnquirer. com."

Chance crossed to the computer desk in the corner of the living room and keyed in the address.

"There's also a poll for *Enquirer* readers to vote on who they think you should go with, Shawna Simmons, or the jealous girlfriend on the beach."

Adrian stood behind Chance, watching the page materialize with a picture of Jackie taking a swing at him. The rest of the family gathered around him.

"Oh. My. God," Jackie whispered as Chance clicked on the link, and more photos appeared beneath the headline: "Sexy Chef Goes from Frying Pan to Fire . . . Girlfriend Finds Out about Shawna."

He glanced at Jackie's stunned face and wrapped an arm around her as he talked to Brian. "I don't believe this. How did they get those pictures? That only happened yesterday." Then it dawned on him. The boat trolling by the mouth of the cove. "Geez, those weren't fishermen. They were goddamned paparazzi! What is with people? I'm a chef, for Christ's sake. Not a movie star."

"You're a celebrity, whether you like it or not. And the people at the network are eating it up. They're hoping to pull in a whole new audience with this show."

"Look, Brian, this is getting way out of hand. I'm flattered women find me attractive, really, but this playboy image the public has of me is very uncomfortable. I happen to be involved with someone, and I'm hoping to get married."

The moment the words left his mouth, Jackie stiffened and his family turned wide eyes his way. Damn! He hadn't meant to tell them like this.

"You're hoping to do what?" Brian half shouted.

Adrian looked at Jackie's pale face. "Married. If she'll say yes."

She stared back at him, conflicting emotions filling her eyes. He saw his sisters exchange a look of excitement and wished he shared their confidence.

"I see." His agent let out a heavy sigh. "So how do you feel about long engagements? Very long, very secret engagements?"

"What do you mean? If I get engaged, I'm not keeping it a secret."

"You will if you're wise. Look, Adrian, here's how it works. The network makes money off advertisements. What they can charge for those ads is based on the number of viewers the show pulls in. Right now they see you as a double-hitter. Not only are you a good cook, which will bring in the viewers who actually care about that, you're a hot-looking single straight male who cooks. The network is not going to be thrilled if you get married between now and when the first show airs. In fact, they're going to be royally pissed off."

"What am I supposed to do, not get married because my show might lose a few viewers?"

"Just keep it quiet until we have the contract signed. Then, when the time is right, we'll talk to the publicity people about the right way to announce it. Maybe we can get some mileage out of it."

"Whatever." He rolled his eyes. When he hung up, he turned to find everyone but Jackie watching the computer screen in an obvious ploy to give them privacy. Jackie stared back at him with wounded eyes.

"I'm sorry," he said quietly. "I didn't mean to do that."

She looked away rather than answer, and his chest muscles contracted. Why was she so set on keeping his proposal a secret? Was she trying to spare him embarrassment when she turned him down?

"You know," Vivian said to the room at large, "when it comes to people who feed off celebrities, I never quite know whether to hate their guts or admire their tenacity."

"Hate their guts," Scott said. "In fact, I think I'll put a slime-ball paparazzo in my next book and crush him to death beneath a mountain of tabloids."

"Oh, to be a writer." Vivian sighed in envy.

"I have to go," Jackie said in a quiet voice. "I need to get my ship ready to sail."

Chapter 25

Jackie heard Adrian follow as she hurried up the stairs, and quickened her pace. "Would you wait!" He caught up with her on the veranda. "You can't just take off like that. Talk to me."

"About what?" She turned to him, her body shaking. "God, this is so typical of my life! Now you know why I never go after anything."

"What? Why?"

"Because it hurts, dammit! It hurts to have everything you reach for snatched away at the last minute."

He stared at her, dumbfounded. "Surely you don't think I'm going to let any of *that* make a difference?" He flung an arm toward the house.

"Adrian . . ." She pressed both hands to her forehead. "You want this show. Not just for yourself, but because it will help the inn, which means a lot to your whole family. You're going to jeopardize that for me?"

"No. For *us*," he shot back. "Two months ago, you stood right here and told me to think about what I wanted, then for once in my life to put myself first. Okay, I've thought about it a lot and I know what I want. You! I want you, and a life for us here on Pearl Island. If that includes a cooking show, fine. If not, so what?"

The air left her lungs as the fight drained out of her. "You mean that?"

"I do." His shoulders sagged in relief when he saw his words were getting through.

"Oh, Adrian!" She flung herself against his chest and wrapped her arms about his neck. "Please be sure, because I don't ever want you to resent me."

"I won't." He rubbed her back. "In fact, just to end all this nonsense about turning a cooking show into some warped version of *The Bachelor,* I think we should go ahead and announce our engagement."

"Ho, no!" She dropped her heels back to the ground. "I told you, I need time to think."

"What's the matter?" He grinned. "Chicken?"

"No, it's just—"

"You're scared. I know." He took both her hands in his, then kissed them one at a time. "We're talking about the rest of our lives. It's very scary business. But every time I think of the big picture and start freaking out, I bring it back down to basics." He squeezed her fingers. "Do I love this woman? Yes. Do I want to spend my days with her, not just my nights? Yes. Can I see myself growing old with her? Yes."

She stared at him, remembering last evening and seeing it too, them being together for years to come.

"So, how about you?" he asked, looking uncertain. "Do you love me?"

"Yes," she said in a small voice.

"Do you want to spend your days with me?"

"Yes."

"Can you see yourself growing old with me?"

Her eyes prickled. "Yes."

He took a deep breath. "Will you marry me?"

"Yes."

"Thank God." He hugged her to him as relief flooded his senses. "See, that wasn't so hard."

"Yes it was." She gave his arm a weak punch.

"But you didn't throw up this time." He pulled back to smile at her, and thought she'd never looked more beautiful than she looked at that moment with watery eyes and a red nose. "Pretty soon, we'll be able to say 'I love you' every day and you won't even get queasy. You just need practice."

She laughed and hugged him again. "I love you."

"See? Easier, right?" He held her tight, absorbing the feel of her body against his.

"I don't want to make a public announcement, though."

"Why not?" He pulled back to frown at her.

"Because . . ." She struggled. "For one thing, you are way too popular with the press right now, and I don't want my name and face splashed all over the place. Thank God the pictures on that Web site were so grainy."

"Jackie." He released a heavy sigh. "I think you worry about that entirely too much."

"Please?"

He narrowed his eyes, contemplating his options. "How about this? If anyone asks, I'll tell them I'm engaged, but if they ask who I'm marrying, I'll say it's none of their business."

"I don't know . . ."

"People are going to find out sooner or later. You can't live your whole life hiding from the past."

"I know. But just downplay the engagement, okay?"

"I guess that means I can't climb up on a tall building and shout, 'Jackie Taylor agreed to marry me!'"

"Good God, no!" She laughed.

"Darn." He grinned. "But you *are* going to marry me."

"I guess I am." She smiled at him with love and happiness shining in her eyes. "Right now, though, I really do need to go."

"Okay." He loosened his arms. "When you get back to Corpus, we can run up my phone bill tossing around dates for the wedding and making plans to move you up here. How's that?"

"All right." She kissed him.

"And remember." He held her face in both hands. "If you start freaking out over everything, bring it down to basics. Okay?"

"Okay." She nodded and kissed him one last time. "I'll talk to you in a couple of days."

He watched her go, hating the thought of not seeing her for four more weeks. How had Marguerite stood it all those years watching Jack sail away? At least he knew when Jackie would be back, and that soon he wouldn't have to watch her go at all. The thought of her moving to Pearl Island as his wife filled him to near bursting.

He headed inside and jogged down the stairs to the apartment, jumping past the last step to land on both feet.

Everyone turned, waiting.

"Well?" Rory asked.

"We're getting married!"

Rory shrieked and bounded over to throw herself against him. Allison came next, more sedate but equally happy. Chance gave him a high five but Scott snorted in disgust. "This is so not fair."

"Why do you say that?" Adrian asked.

"After what you put me through the day I proposed to Allison, you should have to suffer at least a little."

"Well, if it helps, I'm not married yet." Even as he said it, Adrian crossed to the phone to call his agent back. He wanted the network at least to know the single-chef angle was not an option.

Two weeks later, Jackie wanted to shoot herself for agreeing to marry Adrian. Or shoot every member of the press; not just those who wrote for the tabloids, but members of the legitimate media. The feeding frenzy had started when someone at the network leaked the news of Adrian's engagement.

Adrian had refused to take calls from reporters who wanted the name of the bride-to-be, but that had only stirred up more interest. So NationalEnquirer.com posted a reward for any information about the mystery woman on the beach. Twenty-four hours later, they had Jackie's name and her entire past.

The headline for the story they ran read: "Chef Adrian Getting Conned?"

The story had included enough details to set off an explosion of accusations in Galveston when members of the Historical Society realized Carl Ryder had been letting Jackie dive with his team. Those accusations triggered local news stations to start asking questions, which led to a special report on Houston's evening news.

Pacing the officers' lounge on her ship, Jackie held the phone to one ear as she watched the report via satellite dish.

"Can you believe this?" Adrian demanded on the other end, watching the same station. He'd warned her earlier in the day that reporters had come around with TV cameras wanting to do interviews. He'd refused, but they'd cornered Carl on the beach and asked him about the excavation.

"I knew something like this would happen," she said as the reporter asked Carl if it was true that a suspected con artist and artifact forger had been allowed to participate in the search for Lafitte's treasure.

Standing on the beach with the wind buffeting him, Carl gave the reporter an impatient look. "To my knowledge, Jackie Taylor has no record of ever being charged with any crime."

"But isn't it commonly accepted that she and her father were suspected of conning people into going after artifacts that didn't even exist by creating phony documents?" the reporter persisted.

"Ms. Taylor was a minor living with her father during the time of that alleged activity."

"Is it true she's the one who provided the document that prompted the state to spend taxpayer money on this search?"

"Yes." A muscle flexed in Carl's jaw. "And that document was tested for authenticity."

"Is it possible for a forgery to pass those tests?"

"It's extremely unlikely."

"But it is possible."

"I'm completely satisfied that the document was real."

"And yet you haven't found the artifact you're looking for after an extensive, and very costly, search."

"Look," Carl said. "I know exactly what you're getting at, so let me state right here that a large part of the search was funded by private donations, and Jackie Taylor has not received one dime of that money."

"And yet," the reporter countered, "according to

sources, she runs a charter business that has enjoyed a substantial increase in business since the search began, so she has profited indirectly."

"I'm not privy to Ms. Taylor's business records, so I can't answer that. I will tell you that the work she's done for the state on this project has been voluntary, so she hasn't made any profit off that."

"Thank you, Mr. Ryder." The reporter turned toward the camera. "Earlier today, KTEX spoke with a former friend of Ms. Taylor's late father."

Jackie's stomach nearly heaved when Danny's cheesy grin appeared on the screen.

"Oh, my God," she whispered, sinking to the sofa.

After a few initial questions, Danny looked straight into the camera and said, "Jackie Taylor's father was nothing but a thief and a liar, and he taught that girl every trick he knew. Why, if there ever was a powder horn in that cove, it wouldn't surprise me if she stoled it right from under Carl Ryder's nose to sell on the black market."

The reporter turned to the camera. "Neither Ms. Taylor nor her business partners, the owners of the Pearl Island Inn, were available for comment."

"That bastard!" Adrian shouted. "Who the hell was he, anyway?"

"A diver Carl fired." Heartsick, she grabbed the remote and turned the set off.

"I notice they don't mention that!"

"Adrian." She rubbed her head. "This can't be that big a shock to you. We knew all along the truth might come out."

"This isn't the truth. It's a bunch of ridiculous accusations."

"Some of it's true."

"Not the part about your conning the state of Texas and stealing the powder horn."

"We have nothing on our side to prove that."

"Unless Carl finds the powder horn," he said. "That will shut the media up."

A hard lump of dread formed just below her heart. "What if they don't find it?"

He didn't answer right away. "I don't know."

"I do." She dropped her head in her hands. "If Carl doesn't find the powder horn, it'll only get worse. Before long, people will start accusing you, too. I know what it's like to be shunned, even by people you thought were your friends."

"Don't you dare say we should break up to spare me from this scandal."

"I'm afraid it may take more than that at this point." Regret enveloped her as she thought of her dreams for a brighter future. "We'll need to sever things completely. I'll cancel the cruises as discreetly as possible."

"How, when they're selling better than ever?"

"I don't know, but I think it's best for y'all."

There was silence on the other end.

"Adrian? Are you still there?"

"You're serious, aren't you?"

"I don't see any choice. I'm not going to take you and your family down with me. I love all of you too much."

"And if you cancel the cruises, what are you going to do for a living, since you weren't exactly making it before that?"

"I don't know." She sighed. "Move back to the Caribbean. Rename my ship. Try again."

"Just like that. You'd run away."

"Do I have a choice?"

"Hell yes, you have a choice. Quit being a whipped dog and fight back!"

"How?" she demanded. "Call up the press and say 'I'm innocent. I'm innocent'? I'm sure that would go over real well."

His voice turned steely. "I'm not going to let you dump me over this."

"Adrian," she sighed. "Please don't make this harder than it is already. Please. We need to do what's best for everyone."

He fell silent again.

"Adrian?"

"Look, I think we need to end this conversation right now, because if we don't, I'm going to say things I know I'll regret."

"Like what?"

"Like *You're a goddamned coward without enough backbone to stand up for yourself!*"

"Excuse me!" she sputtered, ready to argue, until she realized the line was dead. She stared at the phone in shock. "He hung up on me!"

Chapter 26

Shaking with fury, Adrian paced his living room. He couldn't believe Jackie would break up with him over this. And yet he could. She had to be the most stubborn, self-reliant . . . self-*sacrificing* person he'd ever met! And she'd lectured *him* about the need to put his own needs first? Well, he wasn't going to give in without a fight.

Pulling on his running shoes, he headed down the trail for Carl's bungalow. At least she didn't know the network people were pushing him to break off the engagement due to all the crap in the news. First the tabloids had decided to paint him as a wimp in an abusive relationship, now they were accusing Jackie of ripping off the state of Texas.

Carl's bungalow came into view, and he jogged up the steps, intending to demand they step up efforts to find the powder horn. Angry voices came from inside. He pounded on the screen door anyway, making it rattle. Carl opened the main door, looking flustered.

"Did you see the news?" Adrian asked through the screen.

"I did." Carl sighed. "I'm sorry."

"What are you sorry for? You're not the one accusing Jackie of all this horseshit."

"I just wish I could have done more to defend her. Getting to know her these last months, I realize how much she's been through, and how little she deserves the hand life dealt her."

"That's why you have to find the powder horn. No matter what it takes."

"That's what I've been telling him," a feminine voice said from the cool, shadowy interior.

"Aunt Viv?" Adrian looked past Carl and found his aunt standing in the middle of the front room. "What are you doing here?"

"Telling this idiot that he can forget about ever seeing me again if he goes through with his plans."

Sighing in defeat, Carl opened the screen door.

"Plans?" Adrian stepped inside, looking from his aunt to Carl and back again. "What plans?"

"He's calling off the search." Vivian crossed her arms.

"What?" Adrian turned to Carl. "You can't do that."

"I told all of you weeks ago this was coming. The powder horn wasn't in the defined search area, which was the aft portion of the ship and the path she traveled while sinking. To continue searching would mean establishing another search area, but in which direction do we go? And what if the horn isn't there? Do we define another section, and another? Continuing the search at this point is completely impractical."

"But the horn is out there," Adrian insisted. "I know it. I can feel it."

"But out there where?" Carl gestured in frustration. "We can't search the whole cove. If the item were metal, we might have a shot at stumbling over it with metal detectors. But Scott's research indicates it was made completely of horn and leather. The only way to find it is through systematic dredging. I'm sorry. Truly. But the funds we have left for this project need to go toward preserving the items we've already brought up and creating the museum exhibit."

"What if we continue searching on our own?" Adrian asked.

"If you want to waste your time and money, be my guest. Just remember that if you find it, it belongs to the state."

"This isn't about possession of the powder horn." Adrian wanted to shake the man. "It's about saving Jackie's reputation."

"I realize that," Carl said with genuine remorse. "And I'm sorry."

"God!" Adrian turned away, feeling the rage of helplessness. He looked at Vivian over his shoulder. "Talk to him, will you?"

"I'll try. Unfortunately, the man is as movable as a granite boulder."

"Not in all things, apparently." Carl blushed as the two of them looked at each other.

"True," Vivian said, a secret smile curving her lips.

"Jesus." Adrian shook his head. The last thing he wanted to watch was two lovers making eyes at each other while his world was crumbling. "I need to go."

He slammed out the door and headed down the path toward the beach, needing time and space to think. This late in the day, the area was completely empty. He walked to the end of the pier and stared out at the cove. The sun hung low in the sky, casting shimmering light across the water.

Well, Jack, we failed. We failed you and Marguerite. And we failed Jackie.

A gust of wind blew up off the water, sending a chill through him. Suddenly exhausted, he sat on one of the storage bins and braced his elbows on his knees with his head in his hands. There had to be an answer. Beneath the pier, the waves rushed in and out, but nothing came to him.

As dusk gathered, footsteps sounded on the wooden planks. He looked up to find Scott heading toward him.

"What are you doing here?" he asked sourly, remembering Scott's wish for him to suffer.

"Allison and I have been up at the house waiting for you to join the celebration."

"Celebration?" He frowned when Scott held one of two champagne flutes out to him. "What in the world could you possibly find to be happy about on a day like this?"

"Oooh, I don't know." Scott sat beside him, stretching his legs out and crossing his ankles. "Life in general. And me being the luckiest son of a bitch who ever lived."

Adrian looked at him.

Scott grinned from ear to ear. "Allison's pregnant."

"What?" Adrian's heart lifted.

"We've known for a while, but she wanted to get past the first trimester before she told anyone. Today, though, we went in for the sonogram and . . ."

"And . . ."

Scott's smile got even broader. "Twins."

"You're kidding?" Adrian wanted to laugh. "Twins? God, that's . . . perfect. Really perfect. Alli must be beside herself."

"She's so happy, she's been laughing and crying since we found out."

"How are you holding up?"

Scott chuckled. "I'll let you know as soon as the shock wears off, but for now, I feel pretty damn good. Twins. Yeah." He shook his head, looking dazed. "So, what's up with you? Are you out here fuming over that news report?"

Adrian's good mood evaporated. "That, and Jackie wants to call off the engagement. She's convinced she's going down and taking all of us with her."

"I have to say, I don't envy her at all. Having people hang your whole life out for public inspection is enough to get my stomach going."

"Really?" Adrian said straight-faced, since he knew how Scott felt on the subject. "And here I thought you liked being interviewed."

"Nearly as much as having a root canal. It occurs to me, though, that you and Jackie are going about this all wrong."

"What do you mean?"

"Rather than avoiding the press, why not do the opposite?"

"Actually, I've been trying to tell Jackie exactly that. She won't listen, though. She wants to keep her name out of the news."

"Too late for that," Scott said. "At this point, what does she have to lose? All her secrets are out. Why not go on the offensive? Hire a press agent. Face the world as the happily engaged couple to balance the negative reports. One thing about public opinion, you can turn it in an instant with the right illusion."

"Telling the world I'm in love with Jackie Taylor, and that she's a decent, honest person, would hardly be an illusion."

"All the more reason to do it."

"A press agent, huh?" He mulled it over, then shook his head. "She'll never go for it."

"Maybe you're just not trying hard enough to convince her." Scott arched a brow. "Now, come up to the house and congratulate your sister."

"I'll be there in a minute." When Scott left, Adrian turned back to stare over the water. The sun had finally dropped below the horizon and the first stars had come out. He remembered the night he and Jackie had stood on the balcony, gazing at the sky. The memory was so clear, he swore he could feel her presence there beside him. Was she looking up at the same stars? Making a wish? Did she even know how?

If he could make one wish, it would be to have her with him now. If only he could talk to her in person and convince her to believe in all the possibilities and promise their future held.

Jackie stood on the quarterdeck, staring up at the sky and aching as if a part of her were dying. She knew she was doing the right thing, but she missed Adrian desperately, yearned for him with everything inside her.

Don't, she warned herself. *Don't want. Don't hope. Don't dream. You'll only get hurt in the end.*

And yet, these last months, she'd let herself hope for so much, she didn't know how to stop. A part of her heart she'd held in check all her life yearned with a vastness that felt as wide and deep as the Gulf. She focused on the brightest star in the sky and pictured Adrian in her mind.

I wish you were here.

The only answer was the whispering of the breeze and the lapping of the water. Turning away, she headed for her cabin, then lay awake for hours, before finally drifting to sleep.

Sometime in the night, she heard a noise, like the scuffling of boots out on the main deck. Since no one was on board but her, the sound jolted her to full wakefulness. She forced herself to lie still, listening. The footsteps moved to the lounge, heading straight toward her door. In one fluid move, she grabbed the gun off the shelf above her head, sat up in the middle of the bed, and bracing the pistol in both hands, pointed at the door.

The door opened, revealing the silhouette of a man backlit by the moonlight coming through the aft hatch.

"Freeze! Or I'll blow a hole through your chest the size of Barbados!"

"Shit!" The intruder stepped back so fast, he hit the door and moonlight fell on his face.

"Adrian!" She lowered the gun, her heart in her throat. "What are you doing here?"

"I came to talk to you."

"It's the middle of the night. How'd you get on board?"

"I climbed over the gate."

"Couldn't you have called?"

"Oh yeah, talking on the phone has been so effective the past few days, why didn't I think of that? Now, do you think you could put that cannon away?"

She turned and put the gun back on the shelf. "What time is it?"

"Around two A.M., I think." He came forward and climbed onto the bed on all fours. "Scoot over."

"What are you doing?" She moved back against the wall to give him room.

"Lying down." He flopped onto his back and draped an arm over his eyes. "I've had a bitch of a day, then spent five hours on a motorcycle getting here, and now I have the headache from hell. You got any aspirin?"

She stared at his big body stretched out on her bed, stunned by his presence, then climbed over him and went to the medicine cabinet in the head. Still reeling from the thought that he'd cared enough to come after her, she returned with the aspirin and a glass of water. "Here you go."

"Thanks." He sat up and took them from her, then frowned at what she was wearing. "Is that my shirt?"

She tugged at the tail of the white dress shirt that she'd started sleeping in as a way to be close to him. "You, um, left it here that first night."

"Oh yeah. I forgot." He swallowed the aspirin, then set the glass on the shelf. "Okay, here's the deal. You are not breaking up with me."

"Says who?" Her amazement vanished as she planted her hands on her hips.

"Says me. I'm the guy who doesn't take no for an answer, remember?"

"Well, this time you'll have to."

"Like hell I do. First we're going to find the powder horn."

"You mean pray Carl finds it. I'm not diving any-more. Not with the media accusing me of stealing it."

"Carl's calling off the search."

"Oh great." She sank to the bed beside him. "I'm totally screwed now."

"No you're not. We're going to find the powder horn together, then we're going to shove all those accusations down everyone's throats."

"If Carl and his team of archeologists can't find it, what makes you think we can?"

"Because you told me yourself your father was one of the best treasure hunters in the world, that using a metal detector isn't just skill, it's a talent. I'm willing to bet you inherited some of that talent."

"Maybe I did, but the powder horn isn't made of metal."

"No . . ." He smiled. "But the pearl pendant inside it is on a gold chain."

Hope stirred, but she held it back. "What if the necklace isn't there?"

"It is."

"How can you state that like it's fact!" Exasperation drove her off the bed and she went to stand before the windows.

"It's there," he insisted. She heard him come up behind her. "I've been thinking about this all the way down here. Captain Kingsley doesn't want some team of strangers to find it. It's too personal. He wants us to find it, because we're family. We're part of him and Marguerite. It was meant to play out this way."

She turned to search his eyes, hope and resolve battling within her. "I don't believe in ghosts."

"Yes you do." He smiled down at her. "That day when we went diving together, you felt Jack. Admit it."

She looked away. "I felt something. But . . ."

"What?"

Beyond the windows, moonlight danced hypnotically on the dark water. "I haven't felt anything since. Whatever was trapped on the ship left once the excavation started."

"Or escaped to go after the powder horn."

She looked at him sharply since she'd thought the same thing. "What are you saying?"

"We might not know where the horn is, but I'll bet you anything Jack does. All we have to do is reach out to him. Let him guide us. But you have to have faith."

"Faith in what? Ghosts?"

"Faith in . . . *everything*." He took her hands and squeezed them. "Faith that the love Jack and Marguerite shared is so strong, they won't go on to whatever awaits us after life unless they can go together. Faith that I love you enough, that I won't go on in this world without you. Faith that we can find the horn and clear your name."

"If Carl is gone, and I suddenly 'find' the horn, everyone will think I stole it and that I'm only turning it over to save my neck."

"They won't, I assure you. If it were just you and me and my sisters, maybe, but no one in their right mind is going to accuse Oliver Chancellor, of the Galveston banking Chancellors, or Scott Lawrence, world-renowned author, of helping you cover up attempted theft."

She stared at him in surprise. "You'd risk their reputations for a necklace? Does it mean so much to you?"

"Jesus, Jackie, don't you get it? This isn't just about the necklace. It's about you, too. You're part of me now, and part of my family, so of course we'll do whatever it takes to help you. I know your own family let you down at every turn, but I'm asking you to believe that we won't do that. If you can't believe in all of us, at least believe in me. You and I are meant to be together." He cupped her head and stared into her eyes. "At some point in your life, you have to believe in something. I'm asking you to start by believing in me."

"But that's just it, Adrian, I do believe in you. That's easy. It's life I don't trust." She freed one hand to touch his face. "I love you so very much. I can't stand the thought of hurting you just by being around you."

"You hurt me by not being around me." He took her into his arms, making her heart clench. "I'm not letting you go or giving up. Especially since I have a plan for how we can fight back." He loosened his arms. "As soon as we find the powder horn, we're going to hire a publicist, and give the media a story that will put everything they've printed so far in the shade. By the time we're done, people will know the whole truth, not just the ugly parts. That's going to take guts on your part, though." He caressed her face. "I'm asking you to have the courage to fight for us. And to marry me no matter what people think."

"Courage, I can handle. Because you're wrong. I'm not a gutless coward."

"Then you'll try?"

If only she could be sure she wouldn't hurt Adrian and the others. "I'll make you a deal. I'll go back to Pearl Island and we'll look for the powder horn. If we find it— *if*—I'll face the media and . . ." She took a deep breath. "Yes, I'll marry you." He started to speak and she placed a finger over his lips. "But if we don't . . . you'll let me go."

"Deal," he said without hesitation, and kissed her palm. "Because we will find it."

"I wish I had your faith." She wrapped her arms about his waist and held on tight.

"Well, we'll have the rest of our lives to work on that." He kissed the top of her head. "For now, though, let's get some sleep. We'll head back for Pearl Island as soon as it's light."

Chapter 27

When they arrived at Pearl Island, Adrian had Jackie pull her truck around to his house rather than stop at the inn. He carried her gear inside and called Rory to find out where Carl was. "Even though he said we're welcome to search, I'd prefer to do it without him looking over our shoulders."

"Actually, Carl's gone," Rory said. "He left this morning."

"Well, he certainly cleared out fast."

"Faster than he expected, apparently, since his gear is still here. He and Aunt Viv had a big spat," Rory explained. "She headed back for New York first thing this morning. The minute he heard, he took off after her."

"What about his team of divers?"

"When they heard Carl was gone, they went back to their hotel in town."

"Perfect," Adrian said. "We'll have the cove to ourselves."

"What are you going to do?"

"Jackie and I are going after the powder horn."

"You brought her back with you?" Rory's voice rose with excitement.

"I did." He smiled at his sister's enthusiasm.

"Great! But do you really think you can find it?"

"What's this?" He laughed. "Doubt from the Sunshine Girl?"

"Not at all," she countered with a sniff. "When are you going down?"

He looked up as Jackie came out of the bedroom in her wet suit. "Just as soon as I change." Hanging up, he gave Jackie a quick kiss. "Give me two seconds."

She nodded and waited as he changed into his suit, her stomach rolling as she thought about how much rested on finding the horn—not just her future, but the hopes and dreams of Adrian's whole family. Taking a calming breath, she prayed she wouldn't let them down.

When they arrived at the beach, she saw Rory standing on the dock with Lauren perched on her hip and Chance shading them with a golf umbrella. Allison and Scott were also there, fanning themselves with brochures from the inn. They brightened when they saw her and waved.

"What are they doing out here?" she asked. "Don't they know it's too hot this time of year to stand around in the sun?"

"Hey, gang," Adrian called as they stepped onto the dock, not looking the least surprised to see them. "I take it y'all are the cheering section."

"And help, if you want it," Scott answered. "I've got my scuba gear in my car."

"Jackie?" Adrian turned to her.

"Tomorrow I may take you up on that," she said. "Today I have a theory I want to check out. If it proves true, we'll have a defined search area to start with, so maybe, hopefully, we won't be faced with sweeping the whole cove."

"What's your theory?" Adrian asked.

"The day Carl fired Danny, the jerk they interviewed on the news, I overheard them talking. Danny had been operating the dredge without the screen on. If he was clumsy, he could have sucked up any number of artifacts, including coins and other metal objects, and blown them outside the area Carl had set."

"Could the dredge have picked up something as big as the powder horn?" Scott asked.

"Absolutely," she answered. "And that's really our only hope. I want to sweep in an arch around the area I think Danny was working that day, and see if I can pick up a trail to follow. I'm guessing on a lot of this, but maybe we'll get lucky."

"Sounds like a plan," Adrian said with confidence.

She shook her head at him. "You did hear the words 'theory,' 'guess,' and 'lucky,' right?"

"Faith, Jackie." He winked at her. "Faith."

As Scott and Allison helped them gear up, a dolphin lifted his head out of the water and chattered at Jackie. "Hey, Chico," she greeted him.

"Friend of yours?" Adrian asked as Lauren clapped her hands in delight.

"Sort of," she laughed. "For some reason, he singled me out as his personal playmate, and follows me around every time I dive."

"A man with discerning taste," Adrian said.

"Just don't let him steal anything from you. His favorite game is keep away, and he's really good at it."

Chico flipped water at her.

"Yeah, yeah, I'm coming," she told him, then looked at the sun. "We'll stay down for one hour, come up for two, then go back down. Which means we only have time for two dives today."

"There's always tomorrow," Adrian told her.

Trying to not think of the odds against success, she nodded. "You ready?"

"I am if you are." He pulled his mask into place.

"Wait!" Rory stepped forward and hugged her brother, then startled Jackie by hugging her, too. "Good luck. We'll be waiting up at the inn, where it's cool, but we're all pulling for you, okay?"

Allison hugged Jackie next. "We know you'll do it."

Adrian hid a smile at Jackie's stunned reaction. The woman clearly needed more experience with affection, and he meant to see she got it. "Let's do it," he said, and stepped off into the water.

She jumped in after him and they headed for the wreck site. A murky haze persisted even at the lower depths, due to all the recent activity, but he could still make out the ship in the beam of his light. He followed Jackie as she swam over the main deck. She started to swim past the aft hatch that led to the officers' quarters, but he tapped her shoulder.

When she turned, he signaled that he wanted to see inside the ship. Descending into the passageway was like entering an underwater tunnel. He swung his light back and forth, taking in the louvered doors to the officers' cabins. As they slipped through the door at the end, he stared about in wonder. Carl had shown them some of the pictures they'd taken, but nothing matched seeing it in person, actually being inside Captain Kingsley's cabin, even with it stripped bare.

She motioned toward the windows at the back. The team had removed all the broken glass to make diving in the area safer. Jackie's dolphin friend, Chico, appeared on the other side, swimming in eager circles. When they swam through the opening, the dolphin came right up to Jackie and shook his nose in her face, then turned and flipped off to the right in a burst of speed, as if saying, "Chase me, chase me."

She glanced back at him, rolling her eyes at the animal's antics. He nodded in agreement, the closest they could come to sharing a laugh underwater. Turning back to the task at hand, he saw that the team had excavated a wide trench leading outward from the ship.

Jackie turned on her metal detector, then motioned with her arm, showing the pattern she planned to search, starting to the left of the ship and moving clockwise. He moved into position above her and held both their lights while she began a painfully slow pattern. She'd put her depth setting on shallow for the first sweep. If they didn't find any metal, they'd do it again with a deeper setting. If that didn't work, they'd sweep a wider arch one depth setting at a time.

At the end of their first dive, they'd barely covered any distance. As they headed back to the surface, he understood why Carl and Jackie had resisted trying such a daunting task. They broke the surface near the pier, and climbed up the ladder.

"Any luck?" Allison called from the veranda.

"Not yet," he shouted back. He helped Jackie shed her tank. "That's quite a sight."

"It really is." She pinched her nose and blew to pop her ears. "One dive down, ten jillion to go."

"Or maybe we'll find it on the next one," he countered.

Using the water hose next to the storage bins, they cleaned off their gear and headed for the inn to visit with the others and wait for their two hours to pass. When it had, he looked around and realized Jackie had disappeared. He found her standing on the veranda, staring at the cove.

"You snuck away from me," he said, leaning on the post beside her.

"Just enjoying the quiet." She smiled at him, but he saw lines of strain about her eyes. "It seems weird, though, looking out at the cove and not seeing my ship. Or Carl and his divers."

Adrian glanced that way, then back at her. "I guess I'm more used to it. The guests from the inn tend to spend most of their time in town when the ship isn't here." He studied her. "So what's the real reason you're out here?"

"I don't know. Just thinking, I suppose."

"About . . . ?"

"What you said last night. You know, about Jack wanting us to find the horn. While we were down there I guess I started expecting . . . never mind."

"That he'd guide us right to it?"

"Something like that." She blushed.

He tipped his head to see her face better. "Maybe you should listen harder."

"Maybe I should stick with searching my pattern like I've been trained to do."

"Jackie, sometimes you have to stop listening to your head, and listen to your heart. Like sailing or cooking; half science, half instinct. Follow your instincts. What can it hurt?"

She thought for a moment, then shook her head. "It's going to take long enough doing this the right way. Let's not get sidetracked."

"All right. We'll do it your way."

On the next pass, Chico pestered both of them non-stop, swimming in close like he wanted to be petted, then darting off if they reached for him. Jackie tried to ignore him and concentrate on the metal detector. Like the first dive, though, the hour ended all too quickly.

They surfaced with the sun already low in the sky. "Dammit," she said, after inflating her vest. "I really thought we'd find a coin or button or something. Anything."

"We'll search more tomorrow." Bobbing beside her, Adrian wiped a hand over his mouth to clear away the salt water.

She looked at the sun, which hung low in the sky. "Actually, let's go down one more time today."

"Three dives in one day? That's a lot of time at sixty feet. Besides, we'll be pushing nightfall."

"I know. I just want something to go on tomorrow. If you're willing."

He gave her a look that was part fondness, part impatience. "I told you, woman, I'm with you on this all the way to the end. If you want to go back down, we'll go back down."

She looked at him, smiling as love filled her. "Okay, then." She nodded. "One more dive."

Shortly before dusk, with the family gathered once again on the dock, they slipped back into the water. Chico was waiting for them by the ship, but the minute Jackie turned on her metal detector, he raced off toward the mouth of the cove. She shook her head, amused even though his game had started to annoy her.

He returned a few minutes later, watched her for a

while, then swam in and goosed her with his nose before taking off. Incredulous, she turned and exchanged a look with Adrian. *Did you see that?*

He just shrugged, but his eyes were laughing.

She glared in the direction the dolphin had gone, wondering what the point was to playing keep away when he didn't have anything he was keeping away.

Or did he?

A tingling started along her skin, like a faint echo of what she'd felt all those months ago. She looked at Adrian again, and found him patiently watching her.

Listen to your heart.

He was right about so many things, maybe he was right about this, too. Dredging up some shred of faith, she gazed off toward the mouth of the cove and opened her heart.

Jack, are you out there? As if in answer, the tingling intensified.

She looked back at Adrian and reached for her light. In perfect understanding, he handed it to her and motioned for her to lead the way. She swam slowly through the murky water, quickly losing sight of everything but the brown haze. A part of her scoffed at the stupidity of what she was doing, but the farther she swam, the more compelled she felt to continue.

Without warning, they hit a pocket of cold water and the haze cleared as if they'd entered a dome-shaped chamber that the silt couldn't penetrate. In the center of the pocket, Chico swam in a tight circle. She exchanged a look with Adrian, saw her own excitement reflected in his eyes.

Together, they headed for the spot directly beneath

the dolphin. When they reached it, she waved the detector over the area. It registered a small amount of gold close to the surface. She looked at Adrian, her heart racing. He took her light and nodded for her to dig.

She waved her hand, fanning away surface silt, until she uncovered a mud-caked object. Cleaning it off, she found the powder horn completely intact. She looked at Adrian, stunned. He gestured toward the surface.

They swam in tandem, her heart racing the whole way up. They broke the surface to find full night had fallen. Adrian raised a light and waved it toward the inn. His family came charging down the hill as they swam to the pier.

"You found something?" Rory called.

"The powder horn!" Adrian called back. Hooking one arm about the ladder, he motioned for Jackie to precede him. "Jackie found it!"

She lifted her metal detector for Chance to grab. "I need a bucket of fresh water."

"I got it." Scott grabbed a bucket from the storage bin and filled it from the hose.

When Jackie scrambled up the ladder, everyone gathered around her, trying to see the powder horn in the faint light. She dropped it in the water, though, so it wouldn't dry out and crack.

"Let's get it to the inn," Adrian said. "Where we can see."

"Do you think the necklace is inside?" Allison asked as they moved in a tight group up the path to the inn with Scott carrying the bucket.

"There's something inside it," Jackie said as they reached the veranda. "My metal detector says it's gold."

"Here, have a towel." Allison handed them each one for a quick rubdown before they went inside.

Still chilled from the water, Jackie shivered as the air-conditioned air hit her. "Should we take it to the kitchen, clean it off and open it up?"

"No," Allison said. "I want to open it in the office."

Jackie looked at her in surprise, but noticed Rory and Adrian were nodding.

"The office, definitely," Adrian said. When Jackie sent him a questioning look, he smiled and turned to Allison.

"We've never felt Marguerite in the back of the house," Allison explained. "Only in the areas that face the cove. We thought she might want in on this."

"Okay," Jackie conceded, no longer one to scoff after what had just happened in the cove. She motioned to Scott. "The office it is."

Rory hurried ahead and spread papers over the desk. Scott set the bucket down on the paper as Chance flipped on the floor lamp. Her hands shaking, Jackie started to reach inside.

"Hang on," Adrian said.

She looked up in time to see him hold his hands out to his sisters. They each took one, then turned and reached for their husbands' hands. They stood in a semi-circle around her, joined by so much more than just their hands.

"Okay." Adrian nodded. "We're ready."

She flexed her finger, hope shimmering inside her. Keeping the horn inside the water, she gently cleaned the surface, then lifted it out long enough for them to have a look.

"Well?" Chance asked Scott. "Does it match the horn in the drawings you found?"

"Absolutely." Scott grinned broadly. "See, there's George Washington's initials."

"But is the necklace inside?" Allison asked.

"Let's see." Holding her breath, Jackie gently eased off the leather end. It resisted, then came away, intact, thank goodness. She looked inside and smiled, then glanced at the expectant faces before reaching in to lift out the object inside.

A gold chain dangled from her fingers, sparkling in the light from the lamp. And hanging from the chain was a large pearl in the shape of a teardrop, with a ring of diamonds resting on top like a crown.

For a heartbeat, no one moved.

"I can't believe it," Rory finally whispered.

"I can," Adrian said as Jackie returned the horn to the protection of the water.

"It's so beautiful," Allison breathed. "More so than I imagined."

"Can we hold it?" Rory asked.

Jackie held it out to them, enjoying the look of awe on all their faces. Rory took it, and gasped the moment the pearl nestled into the palm of her hand. "Allison, feel this."

Wonder filled Allison's eyes when she held it. "It tingles like . . . magic."

Adrian held out his hand, accepting it. He studied it a long time. "No. Like hope. I think that was Marguerite's magic. She never stopped hoping and dreaming. Her love for life was infectious. She made people believe in possibilities. Even Henri. But he didn't understand it. He just tried to possess it, control it, keep it to himself. But you can't own hope, any more than you can own someone's heart."

"Yes," Allison agreed softly. "Which was why she gave the necklace, and her heart, to Jack."

"And in doing so, she gave him back hope," Adrian said. "Hope for himself. Hope for their future."

"No wonder he couldn't leave it to sink with the ship," Rory added.

Jackie stared at the necklace resting in Adrian's palm, marveling at how it gleamed in the soft light of the office. "Too bad you have to give it to the state."

Allison smiled at her siblings. "We never told them about the necklace. Only the powder horn."

"That's true." Scott nodded gravely.

"We'll have to tell them," Chance said, earning a scowl from the others.

"I agree." Jackie nodded. "It's the only honorable thing to do."

"But—" Rory looked at all of them. "Why should they get it when we found it?"

"For Jackie's sake," Adrian said firmly. "We're doing this completely aboveboard."

"You're right," Rory sighed.

Jackie stared at them, grateful, but hardly believing they'd give up something that meant so much to them for her.

"Don't look so glum," Chance told Rory, draping an arm over her shoulder. "We might not have to give it up. I've heard of cases where the state has relinquished a find to living descendants. Maybe we can prove the necklace belongs to the three of you."

"Actually," Rory said, looking at her sister, "it doesn't belong to us."

Allison nodded and turned to her brother. "Marguerite gave it to Jack."

"That she did. So . . ." He undid the clasp and moved toward Jackie. "It belongs to Jack's descendant."

"Oh! No!" Jackie tried to back away. "Don't you dare! It belongs to the state."

"Until they claim it, then." He silenced her with a look, then moved his hands behind her neck to fasten the clasp. "For all the hopes and dreams they shared, as well as the love, I give you the pearl, as Marguerite once gave it to Jack."

She looked about and found all of them smiling at her. A lump rose in her throat as she turned back to Adrian. "I—I don't know what to say."

"Say you'll marry me, and be part of my life and part of this family. Be daring enough to grab hold of your chance for happiness."

"Oh, Adrian!" She flung her arms around him as tears filled her eyes. For once she didn't care. If people thought her weak for crying, let them. "Okay. I will. God, I love you so much." Lifting her head, she smiled at the others. "I love all of you so much."

Rory and Allison, both with one arm around their husbands, reached out to her with their free hands, telling her they loved her, too.

Overwhelmed, Jackie covered the pearl with her hand—and felt the tingling warmth fill her body in a rush. Startled, she glanced around, all her senses alert to a sound that wasn't quite heard, a light not quite seen.

She looked at the others, and saw they felt it, too. "What was that?"

"Marguerite," Adrian whispered.

"And Jack," Allison added.

"Do you think . . ." Jackie swallowed. "They're finally together?"

"I do," Adrian said without hesitation, then arched his brow at her. "Do you?"

"Believe in magic and ghosts?" Her hand tightened about the pearl as she searched the room with her senses. Marguerite and Jack were gone, she somehow knew that, but they'd left behind something that had the strength to endure. She turned back to Adrian, smiled into his eyes. "I believe in love. Which is the strongest magic of all."

Epilogue

"Stand by for action."

Jackie heard the producer's words as she and Adrian stood perfectly still in the music room of the inn, each holding a bite of wedding cake to the other's mouth. The gauzy veil that hung down her back from a circlet of white flowers had been fluffed, her cheeks dusted with a hint more blush, the designer gown checked for the slightest blemish, and Marguerite's pearl straightened so it rested above a hint of cleavage. As they waited for their cue, she saw mischief flash in Adrian's eyes, an all too familiar sight.

Don't you dare, she warned him with her eyes, knowing it was useless. Whatever he was planning, he'd do, and she'd be the hapless straight guy to his jokester; all of it caught on tape for their growing number of fans. At least here, surrounded by people, he couldn't get nearly as risqué as he did during their private kitchen encounters.

"Three. Two. One." The producer signaled the cameraman. She and Adrian opened their mouths and took bites of cake as the wedding guests cheered.

"Not bad, Jackie," Adrian said after swallowing his bite. "You actually pulled it off."

"You sound surprised." She gave him an arch look.

He may have baked the cake and done the actual decorating, but she'd made the icing.

"I'm impressed." He nodded. "Really."

She flushed with pleasure. "So I finally mastered one culinary feat?"

"No, I meant I'm impressed you got all the powdered sugar off in time for the wedding."

"Oh, you!" She gave him a playful shove.

Laughing, he pulled her to his side and glanced at the camera. "Now you know the real reason I'm marrying this woman."

"Because I'm turning into such a good cook?" Jackie offered brightly, knowing the comment would earn some laughs. Truth was, she was next to hopeless in the kitchen and becoming famous for her blunders.

"Nooo." Adrian scooped a dollop of icing off the cake. "Because you taste so sweet covered in sugar!"

She shrieked as he smeared the icing down her neck and pretended to eat it off for a second before turning back to the camera. "That's it for this show, and the season. Thanks to all our loyal watchers for your questions and your good wishes. Join *Cooking Lessons* next year when we'll bring you a taste of the Caribbean and highlights from our honeymoon. Well, some of the highlights." He grinned down at her. "Say good-bye, Jackie."

"Good-bye, go away!" She waved sideways at the camera, her eyes eating up Adrian. Having the show crew around on her wedding day had helped her forget for brief snatches what a momentous thing she'd done just an hour ago; out on the lawn beneath a rose-covered arbor, she'd married Adrian St. Claire!

The magnitude of that life-changing event filled her as he took her in his arms and covered her mouth with a deep kiss that was all too brief. When he lifted his head, he looked equally dazed with happiness.

"I love you," he said, with a wealth of feeling.

"I love you, too." Just saying the words still made her heady.

"And we'd love a taste of that cake," Rory said pointedly.

"Oh, sorry." Blushing, Jackie turned to see Rory and Alli waiting at the front of a line of wedding guests. The sisters looked stunning in their burnished-gold bridesmaid dresses and fall flowers in their hair. Well, Rory looked stunning; Alli looked radiant and hugely pregnant with twin girls. Their husbands stood with them, dressed in tuxes since they'd served as groomsmen.

Pulling away from Adrian, Jackie took up the cake cutter and eyed the towering white monster, deciding on a plan of attack.

"Whoa, wait." Adrian wrapped his arms around her from behind, taking her hand in his before she could wreak havoc on his creation. "Think surgery here, not 'Jackie the Ripper.'"

Together, they cut neat slices and laid them on small china plates. Ti came through the line next, tugging at his bow tie. He'd complained royally about donning a monkey suit, but when Jackie had told him he didn't *have* to be in the wedding, he became offended and informed her no one else would be giving the bride away.

"Ya look beautiful," he told her.

"So do you." She winked, laying a piece of cake on the dainty plate he held in his massive hands.

He scowled at her compliment. "Now when we cast off?"

"Just as soon as we can get away." Exhaling a deep

breath, she looked around the crowded room. "Which could take a while."

Nodding, Ti went to join the crew as they waited for her signal to return to the ship and prepare to set sail.

When she'd told Adrian about her lifelong dream to sail the *Pirate's Pleasure* to Bequia to see her family, he'd suggested doing exactly that for their honeymoon. She'd objected at first, saying they couldn't afford to spend that much time away from the inn, and her charter business.

He'd given her a look that said he knew the real reason behind her reluctance. Thanks to the cooking show, they had the time and money to take off sailing for half of each year if they wanted. But after the awkwardness of her past visits, Jackie wasn't sure how welcome they'd be.

Adrian had finally badgered her into at least calling her grandmother to tell her she was getting married. The day she placed the call, a few of her aunts and uncles had been at the house. They'd all insisted on talking to her, and demanded to know why she never came to see them anymore.

When she hung up, feeling dazed, she'd asked Adrian what he thought of their change in attitude. He'd suggested the change was as much with her as them. After the past few months of interacting with his family, she wasn't as defensive and standoffish as she used to be. Plus, her father was out of the picture.

So, as amazing as it seemed to her, they were about to embark on an extensive sailing trip around the Caribbean that would include a stop to see her family.

First, though, they needed to get through the reception.

Vivian and Carl came through the line next, with Vivian holding a resplendent Lauren. "Priddy!" Lauren informed Jackie, touching her own frilly peach dress.

"Yes, peanut," Jackie agreed. "You are very pretty. Want some cake?"

"Cake!"

"Here you go." Jackie placed a slice on the plate Vivian held out, then looked at Adrian's aunt. "Are we eating or dieting today?"

"Eating," the woman announced. "I only have one nephew, and I'm not going to deprive myself on his wedding day. Besides, I've officially retired from Broadway."

"Retirement seems to agree with you," Jackie observed. They hadn't seen Vivian for the past four months, but when Adrian spoke to her on the phone, he insisted his aunt had never sounded happier.

"Retirement and marriage," Vivian said, smiling at her new husband. She and Carl had eloped to Maryland when he'd chased after her to New York. "By the way, Carl's been hired for a dive off the coast of Grenada, so it looks like you two aren't the only ones headed for the islands. If you make it to St. George's, you'll have to come see us."

Adrian gave Jackie a questioning look. "Can we make it that far south?"

"We can try," she answered.

Carl held out a plate, as well. "Just be warned, I may put you to work diving."

"In that case, we'll definitely make it." Jackie sliced a piece of cake for him, realizing that by an odd twist of fate, the man was now her uncle. Before he could move away, she touched the pearl pendant. "I never got to thank you personally for talking to the state on our behalf."

"You're welcome. I'm glad they agreed to let you keep it."

"Me, too," she said, thinking how inadequate the words were to describe how she, Adrian, and his family had felt the day they'd received the news. Although that was only one of many gratifying days that had followed since she had found the powder horn. As the rest of the wedding guests filed by, she thought of all the good turns her life had taken.

Following Scott's advice, they had hired a publicist, and soon the media had done a complete about-face. *Good Morning America* had even returned for a follow-up story. By then, they'd been interviewed enough that she'd learned to relax before the camera—with a lot of coaching and encouragement from Adrian. Their teasing banter had given the network the idea of including her on the cooking show. After two months of filming, the first episodes were just starting to air, but the show had already been heralded as the perfect blend of cooking, comedy, and romance.

Never in her wildest dreams would Jackie have imagined herself as the co-host of a cooking show, being financially secure, and having a warm circle of family and friends. She looked around the crowded room at all the people who had become special to her during the last months: the show crew had abandoned their equipment to descend on the wedding buffet; Scott and Chance chatted with her sailors; and in the far corner, Rory and Alli held court with volunteers from the Historical Society.

In spite of her busy schedule, Jackie had helped out with the new museum exhibit as much as possible. The work had allowed her to become part of a community in a way she'd never experienced before. The highlight was the day the exhibit had opened to the public. She'd stood and watched as people viewed the replica of Captain Kingsley's cabin, learning the truth about his heroism and honor.

"How you holding up?" Adrian asked her an hour later.

"Pretty good, actually," she told him, as he slipped an arm about her waist. "As much as I'm enjoying this, though, I'm counting the minutes until we can get out of these fancy clothes."

"My thoughts exactly." He grinned.

When the time finally came for them to depart, the guests gathered on the lawn, lining the path down to the pier. She and Adrian made a dash for the ship beneath a barrage of birdseed, her gauzy veil flying out behind her. A camera on the dock had been set up to film their departure, although a second cameraman would be traveling with the ship's crew to shoot highlights of the trip for upcoming shows.

She and Adrian went to the stern rail of the quarter-deck so they could wave good-bye as the ship pulled away from the dock.

The setting sun was coloring the sky as the brand-new sails began to unfurl and fill with wind: yards and yards of pristine white canvas, without a single tatter or patch. Looking up, Jackie imagined how it all would look caught on film: like a fairy tale come to life.

Happiness filled her and she threw her arms around Adrian, hugging him tight. "Thank you."

"For what?"

She leaned back enough to see his face. "For teaching me to believe that sometimes dreams do come true."

Don't Tempt Me Brownies

3 large eggs
1 cup sugar
1/2 cup brown sugar
3/4 cup soft butter
1 1/2 teaspoons vanilla extract (or 2 teaspoons dark rum)

Sifted together: 1 cup unsweetened cocoa
1/2 cup flour
1/2 teaspoon baking powder
1/2 teaspoon salt

1 cup chopped pecans

Preheat the oven to 300 degrees F. Butter and flour an 8-inch square pan.

In a mixer, beat the eggs at medium speed until fluffy and light yellow. Add both sugars, butter, and vanilla, and beat until creamy. Add dry ingredients, mix until well blended, then add nuts.

Pour the batter into pan and bake for 45 minutes. Check for doneness with a toothpick. Remove from oven. Use the handle of a wooden spoon to create holes at two-inch intervals and frost while still warm.

Fudge Frosting

1 5-oz can evaporated milk
1 12-oz bag semisweet chocolate chips
1 cup sifted confectioners' sugar (increase to 2 cups for a
less gooey topping)
 chopped nuts

Vanilla ice cream, optional

Just before the brownies are done, empty the evaporated
milk and chocolate chips into a microwave-safe mixing
bowl and heat on high for approximately 2 minutes. Stir
and heat for another 30 seconds to 1 minute, until well-
melted and blended. Stir in sugar and pour over warm
brownies. Sprinkle chopped nuts on top and press gently
into icing. Let brownies sit until completely cool before
cutting into squares. Or scoop ooey-gooey brownies
warm from the pan onto a plate and top with vanilla ice
cream.

NOTE: This recipe provided by **Sandy Tindell of
Orlando, Florida.**